Buckshot Higgins
His Life and Treasures

Buckshot Higgins
His Life and Treasures

Charles Moore Hackley III

Library of Congress Control Number: 2008910615
ISBN: Hardcover 978-1-4363-8732-3
Softcover 978-1-4363-8731-6

This is a work of fiction. Names, characters, places and incidents either are the product of the author's imagination or are used fictitiously, and any resemblance to any actual persons, living or dead, events, or locales is entirely coincidental.

This book was printed in the United States of America.

To order additional copies of this book, contact:
Xlibris Corporation
1-888-795-4274
www.Xlibris.com
Orders@Xlibris.com
54705

Contents

Illustrations

Preface

THESE MANUSCRIPTS WERE placed, per Mr. Higgins's instructions, in the safe at the Buckshot Higgins's ranch in New Mexico by Clarence Blankenship, Mr. Higgins's general manager and confidant of many years. Upon the demise of Mr. Higgins in 1961, Mr. Blankenship retrieved the manuscripts and presented them to the law firm who was to execute the last will and testament of Mr. Higgins. In writing, the legal counsel was instructed by Mr. Higgins to "see that they are printed and copies presented, first to all known family members and/or their descendants, and secondly there are to be an additional 1,000 copies printed and placed on bookshelves in public libraries where the average person can have access to these records."

Mr. Higgins's legal counsel, for unknown reasons, has been party to frivolous judicial filings and proceedings since 1961. The manuscripts were not released and put into publication until September 2007. Even then, only one manuscript up to October 1910 was released. Mr. Blankenship recalls at least two other manuscripts that have not surfaced. Pressure is being put on the law firm to do a further search of Mr. Higgins's papers and to bring to light the other two manuscripts and any and all other documents. It is rumored that there are a number of maps that accompany the manuscripts that have not been seen.

These manuscripts may parallel the example of the great chronicle recorded by Andrew Garcia in the early days in Montana titled *Tough Trip Through Paradise, 1878-1879* until discovered by Mr. Bennett H. Stein and published for the public.

You are invited to read and enjoy this great personal record of the life and events of Mr. Percy "Buckshot" Higgins (1881-1961).

Introduction

IN A RECENT article in *U.S. News & World Report* (November 26-December 3, 2007), excellent coverage is given to the meanings of the many ancient kivas found in the Four Corners area of the southwestern United States where Utah, Colorado, New Mexico, and Arizona join borders. Mr. Jay Tolson, the author, writes the following:

> New Mexico – it is a blindingly bright Southwest autumn morning in Frijoles Canyon, site of a good-sized Ancient Puebloan settlement whose spare but suggestive ruins make up the core of New Mexico's Bandelier National Monument. I am alone, my labored breathing the only sound disturbing the cottony silence in this part of the canyon. Having just climbed 140 feet up three sets of ladders and worn rock steps into a large cleft in the canyon wall called Alcove House, I now descend a ladder to the dirt floor of a covered circular chamber called a Kiva. In the dark cool of the room, I find myself in what is unmistakably a sacred place. Even though it is a recently rebuilt structure, unlike the roofless Big Kiva on the canyon floor only a half mile away, this room inspires the same sense of reverence you feel in or around other ceremonial chambers built by the Ancient Puebloan People (sometimes called the Anasazi) and their modern-day Pueblo descendants . . . . Despite variations in design, most of these sacred chambers have certain common features. Entered from a hole in the ceiling, they typically have a fire pit, a ventilation shaft, and a small indentation or hole in the floor called a *sipapu.* That hole is crucial because it symbolizes the spot from which the original human inhabitants of this world . . . emerged before embarking on their journey to find the ideal home . . . .

Some feel that these kivas were an integrated part of the many communities established by Aztec companies sent north by Montezuma in the early fifteen hundreds. Legend dictates that from seven hundred to two thousand men laden with gold, silver, and precious stones were sent from Mexico City north to the present-day southwestern United Sates. In the expansive Southwest, these men were to design and build hiding places for this fabulous treasure. The treasure was to be the foundation for a new and even bigger Aztec civilization. The August 1880 issue of *Harper's Weekly* explains how an Aztec center was established in Pecos, New Mexico, where an eternal flame was to burn until word would come from Montezuma giving further instructions. These treasure-laden men were to take their families with them. Communities were established to support this intricate, difficult work. Their families planted gardens and orchards and managed flocks of sheep and goats. In order to fulfill the sacred spiritual part of their lives, they designed and constructed the all-important kivas.

In her article "Among the Pueblos" in the August 1880 issue of *Harper's Weekly*, Susan E. Wallace writes the following:

> Our secret cause of the Pueblos' ready adherence to our government is their tradition that, "Far away in the eternal yesterday," Montezuma, the brother and equal of God built the sacred city Pecos, (New Mexico) marked the lines of its fortifications, and with his own royal hand kindled the sacred fire in the estufa (Kiva). Close beside it he planted a tree upside down, with the prophecy that, if his children kept alive the flame till his tree fell, a pale nation, speaking an unknown tongue, should come form the pleasant country where the sun rises, and free them from Spanish rule. He promised that chosen ones that he would return in fullness of time, and then went to the glorious rest prepared for hi in his tabernacle the sun.
>
> I have seen the remains of that forsaken city, once a might fortress, now desolate with the desolation of Zion. Thorns have come up in their palaces, nettles and brambles in the fortresses thereof. It is a habitation for dragons and court for owls. The site, admirably chosen for defense, is on a promontory, somewhat in the shape of a foot, which gave a broad lookout to the sentry. In the valley below the waters of the river Pecos flow softly, and park-like intervals fill the spaces toward foot-hills which skirt the everlasting mountain walls. The adobe houses have crumbled to the dust of which they were made, and heaped among their ruins are large blocks of stone, oblong and square, weighing a ton or more, and showing signs of being once laid in mortar.
>
> The outline of the immense estufa, (Kiva) forty feet in diameter, is plainly visible, sunken in the earth and paved with stone; but all trace of the upper story of the council chamber has vanished. On the mesa there is not a tree, not even the dwarf cedar, which strikes its roots in sand and lives almost without water or dew; but, strange to see, across the centre of the estufa

lies the trunk of a large pine, several feet in circumference – an astonishing growth in that sterile soil. The Indian resting in its fragrant shade, listening to the never-ceasing west wind swaying slender leaves that answered to its touch like harp-strings to the Harper's hand, clothed the stately evergreen with loving superstition, which hovers round it even in death; for this is the Montezuma tree, planted when the world was young.

When Pecos was deserted the people went out as Israel form Egypt, leaving not a hoof behind. They destroyed everything that could be of service to an enemy, and the ground is yet covered with scraps of broken pottery marked with their peculiar tracery.

The Oriental Gheber built his temple over deep subterranean fires, and the steady light shone on after alter and shrine were abandoned and forgotten; but the fire-worshipers on the stony mesa at Pecos had a very different work. The only fuel at hand was cedar from the adjacent hills, and shut in the dark enclosure, filled with pitchy smoke and suffocating gas, it is not strange that death sometimes relived the watch. When the chiefs, who had seen the kingly friend of the red man, grew old, and the hour came for their departure to their home in the sun, the charged the young men to guard the treasure hidden in the silent chamber. Another generation came and went; prophecy and promise were handed down form age to age, and the Pueblo sentinel, true to his unwritten creed, guarded the consecrated place beside the miracle tree, daily climbed the lonely watch tower, looked toward the sun-rising, and listened for the coming of the beautiful feet of them that on the mountain top bring glad tidings. Their days of persecution ended, they no longer ate their bread with tears, and a century of prosperous content went by; then they were shorn of their strength, and their power was broken by inroads o warring nations. The cunning Navajo harried their fields and trampled the ripening maize; the thieving and tame less Comanche carried off their wives and sold their children into slavery, and their numbers were so reduced that the warriors were too feeble to attempt a rescue. Hardly enough survived to minister in the holy place; hope wavered, and the mighty name of Montezuma was but a dim, proud memory.

Yet the devoted watchmen dreamed of a day when he should descent with the sunlight, crowned, plumed, and anointed, to fill the dingy estufa with a glory like that when the divine presence shook the mercy-seat between the cherubim. The eternal fire flickered, smoldered in embers, but endured through all change and chance, like a potent will; it was the visible shadow of the Invisible One, whose name it is death to utter. Sent by his servant and law-giver, his word was sure; they would rest on the promise till sun and earth should die.

At last, at last constant faith and patient vigil had their reward. On the wings of the wild across the snowy Sierras was heard a sound like the rushing of many waters, the loud steps of the promised deliverer. East, toward Santo Domingo, southward from the Rio Grande, there entered Santa Fe an army with faces whiter than the conquered Mexican. Their strange harsh language was heard in the streets; a foreign flag bearing the colors o the morning, white and red, blue and gold, was unrolled above the crumbling palace o the Pueblos. The prophecy was fulfilled, and at noon that day the magic tree at Pecos fell to the ground.

After the American occupation, the remnant of the tribe in Pecos joined that of Jemez, which speaks the same language. It is said that cacique, or governor, carried with him the Montezuma fire, and in a new estufa, sixty miles form the one hallowed by his gracious presence, the faithful are awaiting the second advent of the beloved prophet, priest, and king, who is to come in glory and establish his throne forever and ever.[1]

Figure 1

John Mix Stanley: Abandoned "Catholic Church"
and convent, Pecos, 1846.[2] page 470

1 Susan E. Wallace, "Among the Pueblos," *Harper's Weekly* XLVI, no. 274 (1880): 224-225.

2 William H. Emory, *Notes of a Military Reconnaissance, from Fort Leavenworth, in Missouri, to San Diego, in California, Including Part of Arkansas, Del Norte, and Gila Rivers* (Washington: Wendell and Van Benthuysen, 1848).

Figure 2

"The Watch for Montezuma"[3]

Why else would there be such an extensive propagation of kivas throughout the Southwest if it was not the establishment of communities of workers and their families building secret hiding places for Montezuma's treasure?

There are many well-established places in the great, expansive southwestern United States that have been discovered, investigated, cataloged, and preserved. This lengthy list includes such places as the exquisite kivas at Aztec, New Mexico; Montezuma Creek, Utah; Montezuma's Cave, Arizona; Mule Creek Canyon, Utah; Pecos, New Mexico; Chaco Canyon, New Mexico; Mesa Verde National Park, Colorado; Salmon Ruins and Aztec Ruins, Bloomfield, New Mexico; and Canyon of the Ancients, Colorado, which has over six thousand documented archeological sites, including innumerable kivas. Some of the descendants of the Aztecs living in

---

3 Paul Frenzeny and Jules Tavernier, "The Watch for Montezuma," *Harper's Weekly* XLVI, no. 274 (1880).

their modern-day pueblo villages still perform rituals in their kivas and in many, many more remote sites in the great, expansive southwestern United States.

This intriguing, unique, powerful story of Buckshot Higgins, taken from his own detailed manuscript, provides a fresh insight. The manuscript has been kept from the public since his death in 1961. This personally written story of Mr. Higgins's life and participation in finding some of the treasure is filled with mystery, adventure, and murder. He tells of the signs showing where the sites are and of the gold map plates that pinpoint exact locations. Petroglyph markers that point to the many other sites in the expansive southwestern United States are described. Live with Buckshot on the Navajo Reservation. Go with him into treasure rooms that open with water-balancing stone doorways. View the vast amounts of gold, silver, and precious stones stacked on shelves and along the walls of man-made treasure rooms. Learn about the dangerous sites along with the false ones to discourage treasure hunters who are not seeking to use the treasure for good. And what of the curse on the treasure? Many have perished or met with untimely accidents and death, including unexplained plane crashes, mysterious explosions, and painful run-ins with those still protecting the sites today.

How much of the treasure has been discovered and removed from the many intricate sites? What is still hidden in unique treasure rooms, waiting to be discovered? What does the proliferation of hieroglyphics throughout the Four Corners area announce and point to?

Look for the clues – not only of gold and silver, but about how to live life! Your time will also end. What will be the legacy that you leave behind? Remember, there has never been a statue or monument ever built to a small-thinking, stingy, pessimistic type of person.

Chapter 1

"PEEERRRCCCYYY!" HANABAH SCREECHED.

Oh, how I hated that name! I was named after my mother's father because my mother said it was the right thing to do. She had run away to marry dad and felt guilty that she had not let her father know. She and her father were very close, but not close enough to break the ties of true love that she had for my dad.

Ever since I had been nurtured by Hanabah while I was on my deathbed, she had felt it her duty to scream out my name in that gosh-awful high-pitched voice of hers. It was as though she was so very proud to finally have a son she could call her own and that she felt duty-bound to order me around.

Hanabah was a Navajo woman who was probably in her sixties or seventies when she came across the terrible scene of what was left of my family. She was traveling south along the old Navajo Trail near Shiprock, New Mexico, when she saw our family wagon. My father and mother were both dead over in the shade of a juniper tree. Two families traveling the trail had stopped to supposedly assist us, but in reality, they were pilfering all they could get their hands on.

I remember one of the men saying, "George, you take the animals and put them with Josh to herd along with ours. Take the harnesses and wagon tools and put them in your wagon. This old wreck with the broken rear wheel won't be of any use."

I was lying under the wagon in the shade on one of my mother's handmade quilts with my little sister, Martha. She had fallen asleep from exhaustion. She was dehydrated from the several days we had been stranded there with very little water and only some jackrabbit broth for strength.

Of the two women with the wagons, one had a gentle countenance and seemed honestly concerned about me and my sister's condition. We had come down with some type of ague and were completely laid up. First, my sister had become sick and began throwing up. Then my mother developed a rapid fever and weakness.

To pile on top of our miseries, as my father was turning the wagon around, the left rear wagon wheel struck a large rock. One of the spokes broke, causing the tire to slip from the felloes. This then caused a twist on the left rear hound that supported the back axel, and it snapped. Our wagon was hopelessly broken-down. The fine team of bay mules could not pull the wagon in that condition.

My father made a bed for my mother and Martha under a nearby juniper tree and placed a canteen and a small bucket of water with a cup next to them. The bed was just a couple of blankets laid out on the sandy ground, but it provided some comfort and protection.

"Percy," my father said, "you saddle up your mule and see if you can catch up to the wagon train and tell them of our troubles. I know they are in a hurry to push on to Gallup, but we need help."

By the time I returned on the mule, old Jake, my father had also come down with the ague and was lying next to my mother and sister, gasping for air. At ten years old, I was not prepared for all that was happening.

We had packed up all of our earthly belongings into our well-used covered wagon and set a course for a town south of Gallup, New Mexico, called Ramah. The town was not far from the Zuni villages and would provide a wonderful place to have a farm and perhaps a trading post. For several years, my father's old-time friend Philip Manning had been trying to get my father to leave our homestead in southern Utah and come and join him in a partnership.

My father had been directed by President Brigham Young to take his family and settle in one of the several communities in southern Utah. That was where I was born and spent my first ten years of childhood. They were good years, but there were plenty of hardships. The greatest trial was losing my older brother to sickness. He was a sickly baby and always seemed to have trouble with breathing. When he was seven and out working with my father in the small hay field, he began to choke. By the time my father brought him to the house, he could hardly breathe. A neighbor was nearby, and the two of them gave him a priesthood blessing, but to no avail. He just gasped a last breath and slipped away. I loved him so much.

Other setbacks included flash floods that took our community dam, so our crops were left high and dry. The men and boys would work hard to haul rocks, move dirt, and get logs for a new dam; but it would always take more time than the crops could stand without water. Some of the hay, vegetables, and little patches of cotton would make it; but the harvest was always small – too small to provide for a growing family.

The final blow came when Indians ran off our two milk cows, two beef cattle that Father was working to be a powerful team of oxen, and several sheep. Without these animals, we just could not see any future where we were living.

About that time, the letter came from Brother Manning, and father decided it was time to make a change.

"Now, Percy, you will have to be my right hand as we travel," my father said. "I need you to see to the stock each morning and evening. Make sure they are watered and that there is good feed for them to be put out on. We have to be careful that Indians don't run them off. You will need to keep a good lookout."

My father was a firm believer in the divine origin of the Constitution. He felt that if it was adhered to, our nation could be a very powerful place for good. Having lived through the trying times of the assassination of the Prophet Joseph Smith and his brother Hyrum and being run out of the great city of Nauvoo, my father was determined to fully protect his family from any further such dangers. He was a very good shot with his .50-caliber cap-and-ball rifle. He had also purchased a delightful .41-caliber cap-and-ball rifle for me and taught me to hunt and bring home food. We shared a common shotgun that would later play an important role in the name Buckshot I have been called most of my life.

My father was fond of saying, "Without the Second Amendment in the Bill of Rights allowing us, as citizens, to bear arms, the rest of the amendments would be useless."

My life experiences have shown me that this is true. Tyrants and thieves are fearful of an armed citizenry. I once heard a traveler say that an old Zulu saying supports our Second Amendment in that "an armed society is a polite society."

* * *

Hanabah came around the bend in the trail just in time to see the two families loading up what they wanted of my family's belongings. Not only were they taking all of our survival tools, animals, and bedding, but also our flour, hardtack, jerky, coffee, beans, and corn.

Now Hanabah is no one you want to cross! She stood about five feet six inches and was all muscle and sinew from years of survival. She had contracted smallpox when she was a child as a result of the Navajo Long Walk in 1863 to 1864 to the Bosque Redondo. Her face was extremely pockmarked. This fearful look and her normal unruly hairstyle put fear in most people who did not really know her. She had learned English on that fateful trek.

"You *la' cha i'* thieves!" shouted Hanabah. "You steal from the dead you have not even buried, and you leave these children to die! No, you will not do this without a fight!"

With that, she took a stand between my sister and me on the blanket under the wagon and the pilferers.

I had not been able to reach the retreating wagon train that we had been traveling with. I too had become very feverish and sick. I turned old Jake back toward my family and fell off the mule as I reached them.

My father crawled over to me to try and help me, but he was so sick, he could hardly do anything. He struggled to lay out the quilt from the wagon underneath it so I could lie in the shade. He retrieved Martha from beside our mother and brought her to lie with me.

"Percy, I love you very much, and you have to make it through this," my father said. "Take care of Martha with everything you have. Your mother is gone, and I am afraid that whatever we have will soon take me. Get the broth in the kettle and fill the canteen from the spring. Remember the rifles and the shotgun, and fixings are in the false bottom of the wagon if you need to use them. Rest, save your strength, and pray. Someone will come soon to help you. I love you."

Those were the last words I ever heard my father speak. He was a good man.

The kind woman spoke to Hanabah.

"You cannot take care of this little girl. I can and I will treat her as my own daughter. Her brother there will probably die. You can work to try and save him. My man and our friend will bury the mother and father."

As I listened and tried to make sense of it all, it appeared as a crazy dream. I was not sure what was happening. I only knew that I must fight to stay alive and try in some way to help Martha . . . And then I must have drifted back into a coma.

"Where am I? Where is Martha?"

I struggled to get up off the travois that Hanabah had rigged from wood from our old wagon and the wagon cover to fit behind old Jake. She darted from leading Jake back to where I was. She put her hand on me to steady me and assure me she had everything in control. That was her way.

"Where are we going?" I asked.

"We are going to my home where I will heal you of this sickness," Hanabah answered in her shrill, confirming voice. "You are lucky to be alive. Many who have drunk of the water from that spring have died. The white man has a name for it that I do not remember, but we call it the water of slow death."

I struggled to clear my mind and to figure out what was happening.

"Where is my sister? Why is she not with us? Did she also die?"

"She was taken by the good woman to raise as her daughter," Hanabah said calmly, but still with the high-pitched voice and Navajo accent. "I could not care for her. She will be fine."

"And what of my parents?" I asked her, already knowing that they were dead.

"They were buried where you saw them lie in the shade of the tree," she said. Rocks were placed over their grave to protect it. Someday, I will take you there. But now you must rest and get strong."

"But what of all our things?" I asked. "Did they take all we had?"

"Yes, they took everything from the wagon," Hanabah said, not knowing what we had as a family. "I had to fight them for the cover and your blanket. They thought the blanket was bad and so did not want it. I saw your mule with his saddle on over in the trees and knew they did not see him while he ate."

She had stopped Jake and handed me the canteen. I remembered what she had said about the water.

"Don't worry, I have only good water for you," she said as if reading my mind. "I knew where to find good water."

I drank slow and long. Water had never tasted so good. My mind raced through so many things – my childhood, my loving family, our fun times and some of the trials, my father teaching me to shoot and hunt.

"My name is Percy. What is yours?"

"They call me Hanabah, and I belong to the Bear clan."

Although still in a feverish state of mind, I continued to ask questions to try and make sense of all that had happened in the last two days.

"Did they take everything from the wagon?" I asked. "We had some books that told us of God. Are they gone?"

"Yes, I had a hard time just trying to help you," she said. "There were many of them reaching and searching through all the stuff in the wagon. I did find a good knife and belt before they got to it."

"Guns, guns, did you see any guns?" I asked.

"No, there were no guns," she answered calmly as she adjusted the travois and tried to make me as comfortable as possible.

That was probably good news as they had not discovered where my father had hid them in a false bottom of the wagon. On the other hand, I did not know how far we had come and if she could go back and find them.

How was I to explain to this Indian woman how to open the false-bottom compartment of the wagon and remove the guns, the powder horns, bullet pouch, shot pouch, and the tins of caps? Even if we had not gone very far, could I persuade her to go back and look for them? My head was really spinning from the fever and sickness, and I had a hard time focusing my eyes. I was burning up with fever, and lying on that makeshift drag in the sun was not helping. But I had to try.

"Please, I must ask you to do something for me," I said.

She turned from where she was retying the rope holding the travois legs to the saddle on old Jake and quickly came to my side.

"What is it?" Hanabah asked. "Do you need more water? Here, I have some dried meat. If you chew it long enough, it will help keep you strong."

"No, I do not need any water," I said. "The dried meat would be good."

She went back to Jake and took a small bag from her personal pack that she had tied to the saddle. Her pack was simply a blanket with her belongings wrapped up in it and with a piece of rope or cord tied to each end, making a sling she could put over her shoulder to carry it on her back. She had hung her container of water from the saddle horn. This was a yellow gourd with woven netting surrounding it and a thong attached to the netting so it could be carried.

"Here, do you need to . . . ," she said, pointing between my legs, "while we are stopped?"

"No, but how far are we away from the wagon and the graves?"

"We are about a half day from that place," she said with a funny a look on her face. "It is not good to go back there."

"I know, but there are guns hidden in the wagon," I said. "We must get them. I want them, and they can help us get food and protect us."

"My foolish one, the sickness has made you forget," she said with a very sad look on her face. "I have told you that they took all of the things. They did not even let me have any of the food. We must move forward as fast as we can so we can get to my home to get food."

"No, please listen to me."

Tears were very close to flowing, and I am sure she could sense my strained feelings.

"At the back of the wagon," I said urgently, "if you look for a small wooden plug on each side of the floor and pull them out, the back piece of wood will come out. You will see a hole that this board was covering. Look inside, and you will see three guns. On one side, you will find the bags and a horn. Please bring it all. It is all I have left of my family, and I will use them to help you."

All of the strain of the sickness, the loss of my parents and sister, and lying in the sun must have caused me to pass out. The next thing I remember is that I was lying on the old quilt, now dirty and stained under a tree, and it was getting dark. I staggered as I got up to relieve myself. I saw the travois pieces held together by the wagon cover, and some pieces of rope were together and discarded nearby. My father's canteen was on the blanket as were some pieces of the dried meat old Hanabah had given me earlier.

I was almost beside myself as I tried to make sense of all that had happened in the past couple of days. I had lost everything in life. I was stranded out in the middle of a barren land with no one in sight nor any noises that were familiar. I still felt light-headed and feverish. I knew that my end had to be near. How could a ten-year-old possibly survive?

We had had prayers as a family. I knew and saw the hand of God in many aspects of my life, but it appeared he had abandoned me. Why? What had I done to deserve this treatment? What did he expect of me? I felt that I was about to explode with feelings of loneliness and anguish for the loss of my family.

I made a feeble attempt at prayer, feeling that there was nothing else I could possibly do other than just cry myself into oblivion. I knelt beside that quilt and asked God if he knew of me and my condition. I then asked if he could help me. I couldn't hear or see anything of substance – just the quiet blanket of nightfall being pushed over me by the mysterious scheduled disappearing of the sun in a shrinking red ball.

As the cold of the desert surrounded me, I sought the warmth of the quilt that I had watched my mother make years before. This and the wagon cover were all that I had left of my family. I had no way of making a fire. The stars began to show up in the dark sky, and I heard the lonesome yip and howl of a coyote a long way off. Still with fever and drained of my strength, I soon dozed off in a deep sleep.

* * *

I smelled smoke with a mixture of the aroma of coffee. I heard the cracking of the dry wood as it burned.

"Well, Percy, it looks like you had a good night's sleep," said Hanabah in her squeaky voice.

Startled, I sat up and turned to see her squatting by a very small fire with a small tin cup sitting beside it being warmed up.

"I thought you had left me," I sheepishly said, but with great relief.

"Oh, my little one, I would never do that," Hanabah said. "We are a family now. I have no one else, and you have no one else. We must always be true to each other and do all we can to help each other. In time, we can learn and build a fine life."

With that said, she went back to tending the fire and getting it to burn a little brighter. I went off behind a tree to relieve myself and try to compose my feelings. It was the dawning of another beautiful day; but my day was still one of pain, confusion, and uncertainty.

My mother taught me a lesson that I have always carried with me. And that lesson is that one should never be unthankful. She had read to me several times from modern-day scripture and had me memorize it. This scripture, Doctrine and Covenants 62:7, was further imbedded in my mind when my father gave me old Jake: "I, the Lord, am willing, if any among you desire to ride upon horses, or upon mules, or in chariots, he shall receive this blessing, if he receive it from the hand of the Lord, with a thankful heart in all things."

I went a little further and dropped to my knees to thank the Lord that Hanabah had come back for me and that I had hope. About that time, old Jake came wandering toward me and gave a little grunt like he always did to greet me. Oh, how happy I was to see him! I led Jake over to the fire where Hanabah was sitting.

"Percy, I left you yesterday after you went to sleep from the sickness," she said. "I took Jake and rode him as hard as I could back to the wagon. I searched and searched for the hole with the guns. Finally, I took a rock and opened it. The guns were wrapped in the blanket, and next to them were the other things you told me about. I got lost coming back during the night. I should have let Jake bring us back, but I forced him into a wash when I thought I heard a group of warriors coming toward us. This caused us to get mixed-up in our directions and took us longer to come back."

Mixed with all the grief, relief, fever, and dizziness emerged a wonderful elation as I carefully ran my fingers over the contours of the two rifles and the shotgun my father had prized. They are in my possession even today and bring me a comfort that is very hard to describe.

Hanabah, to say the least, was a great blessing in my life. From appearances, she did not seem to have much to contribute, but she had a determination and resolve not found in many. Her life had been very difficult, and so she could say from experience that no matter what is thrown at you, you will survive if you just keep moving forward.

She would never accept just lying down and giving up. Her brightness each day was like the morning light. She always charged forward with energy as though it might be her last day, and she was going to make the best of it.

I am sure her pockmarked face, arms, and legs dissuaded many a young man to overlook all of her real attributes. Having made the Long Walk from her home near Gallup, New Mexico, to the Bosque Redondo of over four hundred miles, she too had lost her family to sickness. She knew the heart-wrenching pain of such a loss. She knew what it was like to lose everything and to rely on the support of strangers. She did not talk about it much as I believe it caused too much pain; but she did share with me that she had been starved, beaten, abused, and deserted. Hanabah never told me how she got back to her family land that she lived on, but I do know that anyone who even remotely challenged her right to her area to live on faced a formidable foe.

Navajos have not historically lived on deeded land. Instead, each family claims an area in which to have their hogan, corrals, woodpile, outbuildings, and enough land to graze a flock of sheep and perhaps some horses. This was what Hanabah claimed for her inheritance on the high plateau north and a little east of Gallup toward Coyote Canyon. Ironically, the road leading to her place took off from what later on became Route 66 north, passing Kit Carson Cave. Kit Carson was the military leader who directed the roundup of the Navajos and forced them on the Long Walk.

* * *

We traveled for several days in a southern direction following the old Navajo Trail toward Gallup. About opposite Tohatchi, New Mexico, we turned southeast toward the little community of Coyote Canyon. The center of the community was a trading post ran out of the remains of a military fortification.

While crossing the wide plain toward Coyote Canyon, Hanabah pointed out to me the Navajo V-shaped trap used to run antelope to a drop-off into a deep wash. There, those who were not killed from jumping into the wash were soon killed. The group then had a good quantity of meat for the winter. She said that they only made such a drive once a year. This was so the antelope herd could rebuild its numbers, and so they did not get too shy about being run into this trap. She said that it took many men to line the V configuration, lying in wait while others found the antelope herd and pushed them toward the trap. At the right time, those hidden along the narrowing runway would jump up and wave blankets to keep the antelope running toward the narrow spot where they would fall into the draw.

Several times along the way, Hanabah would stop and gather some plants and cook or grind them up. She would put them in her tin cup, add water, and have me drink the mixture. By the time we reached Coyote Canyon, I was off the travois and riding on Jake.

"Percy, I want you to put this mud on your face and arms so you look like one of the *Diné,* so you look like one of us," she said. "I want you to stay on Jake and stay away from the trading post over there next to the hill. The traders will become suspicious if they see you and especially if they think you are a white boy. Until I can get you settled in with me, I do not want them to try and take you away."

Still being sick and thankful for her care and not knowing whom to trust after seeing our belongings stolen, I did as she told me.

The trading post was situated in the center of the mouth of the canyon. The canyon was perhaps three hundred yards wide at this point. Hanabah pointed to the south side of the canyon toward a group of juniper trees and indicated that she wanted me to stay in the trees. Riding on old Jake, I soon had him tucked into the trees where I could see out, but no one could see us. Hanabah's blanket pack and the rolled-up wagon cover with the two rifles and shotgun were rolled up and tied on behind the saddle. It took some skill to work between the trees so as to not lose anything.

The closer we had come to the trading post, the more hogans we had seen. We saw several small flocks of sheep being tended by children but had never really came close to anyone. I watched as Hanabah walked to the front door of the rock and mud building and then disappear inside. She had not really said anything about why she wanted to go into the trading post although I figured she must have need of some supplies to take to her home, wherever that was. I had seen several men and a woman sitting outside the trading post watching us as we separated, and I rode up into the trees. I was still feeling sick and had a hard time focusing my vision, but old Jake knew what to do. We stopped where I could watch the trading post and not really be seen, or so I thought so.

With a snort and quick side step, Jake moved faster than I reacted, and I found myself on the ground with a very mean-looking Navajo man looking down at me. Jake had moved over to one side of the clearing and was wide-eyed and nervous. I suppose part of it was that he had been completely surprised, and that is pretty hard to do to a good mule.

"What do you have in the packs on your mule?" the man asked me.

He spoke in very good English, but with a very stern tone and look. He had a headband holding his long hair in place. A turquoise necklace with a silver bear was around his neck. He had on a red shirt with white checker-type patterns. He wore a very ornamental belt with silver and turquoise inserts that held up his canvas-type blue pants. On his feet, he wore hard-soled moccasins that I would later recognize as standard fare for most Navajos. The formidable part of his dress was the very large knife in a sheath hanging from the belt, or at least the size of the sheath was very wide, and I could imagine the size of the knife.

He had the upper hand as he stood glaring down at me.

"There is my pack and the pack of Hanabah's," I said.

This was the first of many times that I would see a fear or at least a great respect come over someone by just the mention of Hanabah. He immediately stepped back but then leaned forward and offered his hand to me to assist me to stand.

"Do not tell Hanabah that I bothered you," he said in an almost-pleading voice. "Can I help your further?"

He was already backing out of the clearing and turning to leave. I could tell that he did not want to chance facing Hanabah.

Between the fall from old Jake, my sickness, and the scare the stranger put into me, I must have passed out again and fallen to the ground. The next thing I knew, I was looking up into the fierce pockmarked face of Hanabah as she was trying to give me some of one of her potions mixed into some water.

"Why is my boy on the ground, and whose tracks do I see here?" she asked. "Did someone hurt you? Are you okay?"

Her rapid questions did not give me much chance to answer, but she did not seem to want to have my answers. She was very astute at sizing up a situation and making a decision as to what should be done.

"We do not have far to go to my hogan," she said. "We must push on so we can get you the right medicine and sing to the spirit to make you better. Come, let me help you up on the mule again. Are you okay?"

I answered in sort of a low grunt to let her know that I heard her, but I was in no condition to really help myself. Aboard old Jake, I was soon dozing from his "rocking chair" gait. It felt good. I was so grateful that I had Jake and Hanabah to take care of me. What an odd combination of assistance – an old mule and a fierce-looking old Navajo woman, both with a loving spirit that I will never forget.

"There is my home and now your home," she softly said with her penetrating voice.

My blurry vision outlined a very crude structure that would later on prove to be the humblest of all homes – even for all of the Navajo lands. It was nothing more than cedar logs about five to six inches in diameter and about twelve feet long placed in a teepee-type fashion and then covered with mud. She had built it all by herself. Not only were others fearful of her, but they did not even want to help her. She had built a doorway that looked much like what you would see protruding from an Eskimo igloo. The doorway protrusion was a little over five feet tall with a crude door installed to make the home secure. The door hinges were made of leather – probably from some old harness. Inside in the center of the floor area was an old rusty stove with the doors missing and no connection to the opening in the roof for the smoke to escape. Around the inside circular wall were Hanabah's meager belongings. There were some clothes in bundles, some cooking utensils, an old horsehide trunk, and some rolled-up sheepskins. A lot of other clutter took up space around the walls on the floor.

As she would point out later to me, a circular hogan-type home is very efficient whereas a white man builds a home with a fireplace at one end and then must build a big fire to heat the whole room. In a hogan, a very small fire in the center keeps everyone warm and does not take nearly as much wood.

I very willingly slid off old Jake and, with her help, stumbled to the door and into the dark interior. Even though it was full daylight, you could not see much from just the limited light coming from the chimney hole and the open door.

"Here, sit on this bundle, and I will lay out a bed for you," Hanabah said with care in her voice. "You have had a bad trip, and we need to get you well."

I sat, as she directed, with my back to the log wall. What a relief from the rocking of a mule ride!

"Can I have some water?" I asked.

"Of course, Percy," she said. "I will fetch the canteen."

She gave me the canteen, and I drank my fill of that wonderful nectar of life. Water is so common most of the time and taken for granted, but oh, the blessing of it when absent or in short supply.

Hanabah, with all her apparent shortcomings and lack of material things, was a gem. She had more love in her, if given the chance to come out, than most people will ever see. She had been beaten up and bruised from the experiences of life, and this had caused her to put a figurative scab over her exterior. But underneath, she was pure love.

She made a bed for me on the floor of this humble dwelling from a sheepskin she unrolled. Over the next few years, I was to get used to such comfort, and it was with great difficulty that I learned to sleep on a white man's bed. But I am getting ahead of my story.

For the next week or so, Hanabah waited on me virtually hand and foot, first feeding me a broth with some meat in it and supplementing this nourishment with potions that contained native plant materials. My strength gradually came back as my head cleared and the dizziness disappeared. She was a great physician. I would learn later how respected she was in this occupation and how many thought her powers did not come just from potions, but from a higher source.

My mind, of course, did not shut down during this time of physical healing; and I spent a lot of time in anguish as I thought of my little sister and my parents. I could not believe that I had lost them in such a quick and unexpected way. Each one was so special and had so much to give. I loved them so much. The tears would flow at times, even though I was not fully thinking of them. The warm, streaming tears down my face would then trigger my thoughts, and the feelings would be even more intense. I began to believe that this pain and anguish would never end.

"Percy, I can see your tears, and I know your pain," she said. "I too lost my loved ones to sickness. I watched them in pain and misery as they slowly died. Your feelings in your mind will also heal, just like your body is healing from the bad water. It takes time, and there is nothing that you or I can do to shorten the time. I am here to help, but you must be strong and know you have a full life ahead of you."

Those were perhaps the strongest words she ever said to me in a deep teaching way. They seemed to go right to my heart, and I knew what she meant. But as hard as I tried, I could not speed up the process of stopping the tears and keeping the longing for my family from my mind and heart. Of course, through life – as I have lost other loved ones – I do know, as Hanabah told me so long ago, that it does take a preset time; and there is nothing you can do to shorten it. Yes, you can fill your time with activity or sleep or force the feelings back, but they and the tears will take their course.

I knew that Jake was being taken care of by Hanabah and that she was probably using him to make her job easier. Old Jake was a special blessing to me. His unique mule personality was nerve-wracking at times, but every time, I relaxed and did as my father had instructed me.

"To get along with a mule, you just need to remember that a mule is twice as smart as a horse," my father had told me over and over. "They are not stubborn as a lot of folks think, but they are thinking. Show them what you want done and then give them their head, and they will do what is needed. Yes, they, like us, sometimes have to be taught several times. But once they understand, just relax and enjoy their talents."

Hanabah and Jake had a great relationship. I often wondered if it was because they were both so determined to get done what was at hand. She could get him to do or go where I couldn't go, and old Jake even seemed to enjoy it.

My father had said, "Some of the best characteristics of a mule are that you do not have to shoe them because they take on the hard hoof of their father, the jack, and not of their mother, who is a horse. Another benefit is that a mule will pack half again as much as a horse. Where a horse will comfortably carry three hundred pounds, a good mule will pack 450 pounds all day long."

I had learned to tightly pack old Jake, but with my small size, I had to have help lifting the packs and pulling tight the cinch and lash rope. My father was a master at tying the diamond hitch to hold the packs in place. We had used an old sawbuck type of saddle on old Jake. The thieves who stole my family's items took that. Luckily, I had left the riding saddle and bridle on old Jake when I came back from trying to reach the wagon train. This saddle was an old Western saddle with a large set of old army saddlebags. Father had put a number of leather tie strings on the corners of the saddle apron for tying things to the saddle. I had an old Navajo blanket for a saddle blanket.

"Okay, so you have a blanket. But I can make a better one, and it will be more beautiful!" Hanabah would often say. She never did get around to making one.

Another thing that my father had pointed out about mules is that the man credited with having the most wisdom in all of the Old Testament accounts, King Solomon, rode a mule. Not only that, but his father, King David, also rode a mule. *1 Kings 1:33* says, "The king also said unto them, Take with you the servants of your lord, and cause Solomon my son to ride upon mine own mule, and bring him down to Gihon."

I could envision the great King David and his very wise son riding on gallant mules across the countryside. At times, when I was on old Jake, I would pretend that I was Solomon and sit up straight and act like a prince – for indeed I knew that someday, I would become a prince and hold the priesthood as my father had held; but that is for another time to tell.

I regained my health and marveled at the beauty of the setting where Hanabah had located her old-time hogan and living area. Her land claim was integrated with the top of a great plateau, but in a cirque so that the hogan, her garden, sheep pen, and general living area were surrounded by a wall of layered sandstone. This wall was about fifty feet high and made a circle from the south of her land all the way around to the northeast. She or someone had cut steps into the wall directly behind the hogan so you could quickly climb to the top and there, observe miles and miles of country. This wall protected her layout from storms and prying eyes.

You could see the elevation changes by the types of trees growing on the plateau. On the top were giant ponderosa pine standing as sentinels and guardians as though protecting the simple beauties against the storms of life. Interspersed with the orange-barked giants with their five-needle clusters of needles and large heavy cones were piñon pines. They were much shorter, and their cones were prized by the Navajos because of the pine nuts they produced. Pine nuts were not only a rich and delicious food, but also a form of currency. They could trade the nuts for all their basic needs at the trading posts. A special quality of the nuts was that they could be kept for several years if protected from the elements and rodents.

Just below the piñon pine band of trees, at a little lower elevation, are juniper trees, which are sometimes referred to as cedar trees. These stubby trees look much like the piñon pine trees in stature, but instead of needles, they have a strange type of green growth extruding from their branches called fronds. Juniper trees are much valued for their trunks, which are cut for fence posts and firewood. They are a hardwood type of tree that burns long and hot and gives off a wonderful aroma. Another product are it's fruits. They are a very bitter blueberry that is used for medicinal purposes. They have a very powerful ability to stop diarrhea when ground up into a mushy form and taken internally.

* * *

"While you have been sick," Hanabah said, "I have used Jake to help me pull some dead tree branches for firewood and to repair my sheep pen. I used the ropes we took from the wagon. He is a very strong mule. We must make sure we take good care of him."

"Did he do as you told him, or was he stubborn as he sometimes is with me?" I asked, finally feeling my full strength back and trying to inject some levity into our conversation.

"Percy, once I explained to him that he was my special friend and the only one I had to help me take care of you," Hanabah said, "and that I once had mule stew and it tasted very good, he did exactly what I said."

I saw just a trace of a grin as she turned to finish putting food in the pot for our supper.

I was hungry, but I put my thoughts into the wide-open spaces. On Navajo land, you will never be lost as far as knowing what compass directions are since all traditional Navajo homes face east. Hanabah explained to me that the spiritually accepted belief among her people is that a great happening will come from the east. It is thought that there will be a return or an announcement made to the Navajos from the east.

About fifty feet in a northeast direction from the doorway was her woodpile. She and Jake had pulled in a great inventory of dead tree limbs and trunks. An old dull, rusty axe was sunk into a stump, waiting for someone to reduce the woodpile into smaller pieces. It was easy for me to guess what one of my jobs was going to be.

A well-worn trail ran from the doorway for about one hundred yards to the base of the sandstone wall. The trail then paralleled the wall for about fifty feet to a pool of clear pure water. The water trickled from a crack in the rock wall a few feet up a miniature box canyon. From the crack in the rock, the water flowed over a ledge and fell into the pool. I can still hear the delightful sound of that water and taste its cool refreshment. Four giant ponderosa pine sentinels grew in a semicircle around the spring, keeping it cool with their shade in the summer and protecting it from storms.

The water must have been flowing for many years in this manner as a distinct channel had been cut by the years of water flowing from this unique source. Below the pool, where we dipped our canteens and pails to get water for our domestic needs, was another smaller pool just right to bathe in. Just below that pool was a elongated natural troughlike rock configuration where up to fifteen sheep at a time could be watered. The water then flowed into a gulch and then into a tributary canyon that eventually connected to the Rio Puerco that cut its course through Gallup and onto the mighty Colorado River. Small beginnings lead to great power if directed by the right source.

The view to the east was of tree-covered mountains like the plateau we were on. The sunrises were spectacular! I guess this is where I learned to enjoy a new day so much. I have always liked sunrises more than sunsets. Sunsets make me too melancholy.

Chapter 2

THE NEXT FOUR years were blissful and a time to heal from my losses. I worked as directed by Hanabah and learned so much about being self-sufficient. As I have mentioned, she had her own herd of sheep, and we planted and harvested a garden each year. I spent most of my time taking the little band of sheep out of the old corral and letting them feed in the woods and clearings on the plateau. She made periodic trips to the trading post at Coyote Canyon and even to one closer by, but she did not like the trader there. She said that he cheated her and tried to get her to tell him where she got the gold trinkets she sometimes traded. At that time, the gold objects did not excite me very much as I thought they were just a private collection she had somehow acquired.

When herding the sheep, my favorite place was some distance from our hogan – toward the north and east where there were a lot of old ruins. I loved, while supposedly watching our little herd, to dart in and out of the buildings and play warrior. The buildings must have been for short people as the doorways were quite small. The walls were very thick and made of a type of shale. There was not any mortar used. The shale rocks were laid very precisely so they seemed to interlock. Even small pieces were inserted to make them windproof. A few times, I found myself on a cold wintry day building a fire inside the walls to keep warm. The walls completely protected me and my fire from the wind.

Of great interest to me was the large circular buildings built about half in the ground and the other half above ground. In part of the walls where the plaster had not fallen off were some wonderfully colored paintings of gardens of corn and squash. There were men dressed in brilliant costumes with multicolored feathers and cloth.

I loved to imagine I was there and could hear the music as they danced just like the pictures depicted them dancing. Those were memorable days.

Two memorable experiences happened during that time. My most memorable experience was trying to prove to Hanabah that I could do all that a young Navajo man could do. When I was about twelve years old, the challenge came.

"Percy, you are a good son to me, and that is the way I think of you," Hanabah said one day in a reflective mood. "You have learned well what it takes to keep food on the table and to help me build a strong place to live. You are all that I have asked for, but as times are changing, I do not think you would be able to do what Navajo boys do to prove themselves."

"What do you mean by that?" I asked inquisitively. "I can do anything that a Navajo young man can do," I added with pride and bravado.

"My son, for many years, Navajo boys proved their manhood by tracking a deer or antelope until it fell over from exhaustion. And then he would smother it with a bag full of corn pollen," she said. "This was part of a very sacred ceremony. First, he would prepare himself with long runs. Next, he would gather pollen into a small leather bag from the cornstalks as they matured. He prepared himself for the challenge by going to a sacred spot he chose to pray for strength and help in taking an animal. As you know, a deer or antelope must always be feeding to survive. They are not like a horse or mule or cow or sheep that eats and then lies down for a long time. They must eat and always be on alert for danger. If one pushes them for about three days and does not let them eat, they will fall from exhaustion. At this time, the boy would take the bag of corn pollen and put the animal's nose in it and with a prayer of thanksgiving, smoother it. This ritual takes great skill and endurance. You must be a very good tracker and have patience. You want your prey to be so nervous that it does not eat, but not so nervous that it quickly runs away from you and has time to eat while you try to catch up. This is indeed a very complete test of a young man. He must be a master of many skills."

Well, the challenge was on. I had to prove to Hanabah that I could do this wonderful thing. That summer, with her help, I made a small leather bag and collected just the right amount of pollen from our garden to fill the bag. I practiced tracking her sheep as I herded them for her almost every day. There were deer on the plateau, but I did not see them very often. In fact, I had wanted so bad to take my rifle and see if I could shoot one, but Hanabah had told me that I needed to wait a little longer before I used one of the guns. The reality was that she knew nothing about guns, and she did not want me to get hurt.

I spent some time contemplating the challenge, and I practiced trailing and imagining what it would be like to be on my own following a deer across the plateau for three days. I felt I would not get lost, but I wondered how I would keep the deer moving during the night. Hanabah said that the best time was when there was a full moon so I could see better. This would help me stay safe and help me push the deer along.

Well, the day came. The sun had not come up yet, but the cool breeze that proceeds dawn was stirring. Hanabah had a fire going and was waiting in anticipation as I awoke and got ready. Wanting to encourage me and to help, she prepared me a bag of jerky mixed with some dried fruit. She let me take our best canteen, and she let me borrow her treasured hunting knife and sheath. I took a sort of club for protection, a leather sling that I was not too good at using, and, of course, the treasured bag of pollen.

"I know you can do this great thing," Hanabah said. "I will be waiting for you and praying for your safe return."

I nodded a fleeting response and set off on a jog toward the east where I knew deer would be eating in the early-morning hours.

I made my first mistake by choosing a wily mature mule deer buck. He was so stately in his rich summer brown color, and most of the velvet was gone from his antlers. I should have pushed one of the younger bucks, but in my exuberance and determination to be the best, I went after the majestic alert leader of the herd. He sensed that I was up to no good and bounced off into the juniper trees as mule deer do.

He was quickly out of sight among the trees, but with each bounce, he left very easy tracks to follow. I knew that I must not push him too hard. I needed to just keep him off guard so he would not stop to eat or drink much. As you know, mule deer always stop just before they go over a ridge and look back to see if the danger is following them and to sort of size it up. Sure enough, I watched him stop in the little saddle about a half mile away on the main trail out of the basin. I then shifted my speed into a jog and moved right along, not having to watch for tracks. I slowed and crouched down in the saddle so as to not give him too much of a fright.

Below me and to the right was a long clearing where the main trail followed a bit of a wash. I knew that if he was really spooked, he would run along that trail trying to distance himself from me. On the other hand, if he was questioning how much danger I might be to him, he would probably just stand in the shade of one of the trees just short of the clearing where he could watch the saddle. Sure enough, as I looked between the branches of a large sagebrush so he could not see me, I could make out his outline between a bushy juniper tree and a large old snag of a blackened tree that was left from a fire that happened years before. He pawed the ground once and lifted his head, snorting as he tried to catch any scent that might clue him about the danger.

My father had taught me – and Hanabah had confirmed – that any old mule deer worth his salt will always travel uphill rather than downhill if given a choice. If he is really spooked, he will go downhill, but just for a short distance, and then seek higher ground to give him a better view and easier way to head out. If wounded, the fellow will always go downhill unless there is a very substantial barrier to traveling that way.

I put into practice what I had been told by Hanabah and just lay there looking at him from my concealed position. I knew he could not or would not eat while fearful.

I also knew that he would try and sneak uphill from his position rather than shoot down the main trail if I did not fully expose myself. So I retreated back behind the hill and quickly moved to the left and up to a higher point where I could see the several passes above my wily target that he would probably use to leave the little valley. I decided just to sit and wait him out. I knew from watching deer that they are not really grass eaters but instead browse on brush – especially bitterbrush, a plant that was plentiful on the plateau area. I knew that as he snuck along, he would try to eat on these bushes. Usually, these bushes grew in patches on south-facing slopes away from the trees, so he could be easily seen if he chose to eat there.

Sure enough, he relaxed somewhat and chose a trail that led up to one of the small passes that would take him into the next little valley. He slowly moved along the trail, occasionally looking back and always sniffing at the air to see if he could catch a whiff of any danger. I was protected in that the warm valley air rose to the high points so he could not smell me. Even then, Hanabah had smoked my clothes and moccasins and made me stand in the smoke for what seemed like an eternity to give me a fire smell that she said would help me in my tracking should I get downwind from my prey.

There was a small patch of bitterbrush ahead of him that I knew he might wander toward and try to eat. As he wandered along the trail, he saw the bitterbrush and worked his way up into it and took a couple of bites of the stems. I had found a rock of the right size and loaded up the old sling. Staying hidden so he would not see my movement of circling that rock in the sling pouch over my head, I let it build up speed and then let it fly.

Not being very good with a sling, this first shot on my quest to prove myself landed a little short of where I wanted it to go, but it did the job. The buck heard it hit. He stopped browsing and made a dash for the saddle. When he arrived in the saddle, he did as usual and looked back to see if anyone was coming after him. Not seeing anything and not knowing that I was just several hundred yards a little above and to his flank, he trotted over into the next canyon.

This is the way that it went into the dark of night. I finally let him lie down about dusk. I was grateful for this as I knew I would not be able to see him until the moon was fully up. I was anxious to see what the reflective light of the moon would show. But there he was, in all his grandeur, watching his back trail. I knew that he was getting hungry and perhaps thirsty. In this larger canyon, there was a small stream created from a swampy area. I figured he would head for the water as soon as he felt safe. I had to prevent this as I knew that there were no more water sources farther north or east. His only course would be to circle back to territory that he knew. And this was likely.

I really felt good and proud that I had accomplished what I had so far. I knew that there was still a lot of challenging situations to go through as my buck became hungry and thirsty. He also knew the country better than me and knew how to evade his enemies, such as hunters like me and even the dreaded mountain lion. Lion tracks were seen even near Hanabah's sheep corral, but she said that they had not bothered her flock for many years. She said she put a curse on them and a potion around the corral. I had overheard conversations back in the settlement where the men figured that a lion would eat and kill a deer about once a week.

About halfway through the night, I watched as he stood up and stretched, sniffed the air, and rubbed his antlers on a small piñon tree. The itching of the velvet must still be present. He started wandering and looking for food or water. I had to keep him off guard, but I did not want to fully spook him. It would be difficult to track him in the moonlight, and he could just try to circle back to his home ground. I would not be able to catch up to him until way after daylight. I was about two hundred yards from him at about the same elevation, except for a big old rock about fifteen feet high I had climbed up on. It was from here I could watch his actions. I watched as he headed toward the marshy area. I climbed down and, very quietly, headed for a high spot where I could see the water. Just as I figured, he went straight for the water. As he dropped his head to take a drink, I let a rock fly so that it landed about one hundred yards in front of him with a dull thud. He jerked his head up, snorted, and then spun around and headed back along his trail. Was he headed back to his clearing?

This was the cat-and-mouse game that I played through the night and into the next day. I played the same guess-and-move-and-spook role as I did on the first day. But then I made mistake number two. With my limited expertise using a sling and as luck would have it, the rock I slung with the leather-thonged sling with a leather pouch sailed through the air and hit the buck square on the rear end. Away he flew, and my heart about stopped as I thought of not being able to keep up and that he would get to water and food, and I would lose momentum in the chase.

I had no choice but to find his tracks and begin tracking. Luckily, I knew the country where he was headed pretty well. Sure enough, the wily old buck headed right back to where he had probably been born. In fact, by the afternoon of the second day, I saw him watch carefully the movements of a couple of does not too far from the clearing and then meander over toward them and finally start to graze again.

By the morning of the third day, I could tell that he was getting irritable and real jumpy and that he had lost some of his stamina. He would not go as far when spooked and hardly dozed at all when he would lie down. I could see the wisdom in this exercise and how it really taught patience and finite observation. But by now, I was starting to get tired. I had eaten the jerky mixture and drank from the canteen, so physically, I was okay; but my eyes were having a hard time staying open. I knew that keeping him away from water was more important than keeping him away from food, and luckily, the water sources were very limited in this plateau area.

To my surprise and elation, after I startled him again and got him to move, he headed to our little stream not too far downstream from where we watered the sheep every day. I knew the area well and knew where I could intercept him so as to watch for him to try and drink. As I got to my planned vantage point and was sitting in a comfortable place, I saw some movement near the watering spot I had anticipated he would try. I could not fully make out his outline, but something about the coloration in the shadows did not seem right. Then I caught a glimpse of him coming through the trees toward the water. As he came opposite of a fairly large boulder just short of the water, a huge mountain lion jumped down upon him! He pushed his back legs with all the strength he could muster and tried to run off and discharge this fatal enemy. In his weakened condition and with the lion on his back with claws punched deep into his frame and biting through the back of his neck, he was soon to the ground. There were a couple of futile kicks and a muffled throaty sound, and then it was all over.

I was exhausted when I got back and eager to tell Hanabah of my adventure.

"Hanabah, I tried, but a mountain lion got him before I could finish him off with the pollen," I said. "Please come with me, and let me show you where it happened. But let me load up my gun in case he is still around."

"I want you to load up the one with two barrels and that shoots many pieces," she said, being astute and knowing somewhat about guns.

She was, of course, referring to the shotgun. This was a special weapon that my father had had made by Jonathan Browning, who was living in a town north of Salt Lake called Ogden. They had been good friends in Nauvoo before the exodus and traveled part of the way together to Salt Lake. It had a very large bore of about three-quarters of an inch, making it about a 10 gauge. This old gun was a cap and ball with two hammers that each had a hollow nipple to fall on. When loaded, the nipples had a cap placed on them to ignite the charge of powder in the respective barrels. My father had taught me that there are only two charges for the gun. You could put one charge in one barrel and the other-size charge in the other barrel. That way, you had a choice when it came time to shoot.

"Son, we can't afford to have all the choices of shot for the gun," my father said. "We have only two sizes of shot. One is for birds and rabbits, and the other is for large animals and for defense of the family."

That was what I had to work with – the gun that Hanabah had rescued from my family's wagon several years before. The powder and caps had been kept in a dry place in the hogan along with the guns, still wrapped in the thick oilcloth my father had protected them with. I had taken them out from time to time and oiled the parts the best I could with the little oilcan that was in the possibles bag.

"I hope I can remember how to load the barrels with the right amount of powder and shot and then put the right amount of wadding in to keep the shot from rolling out of the barrel," I said to myself as much as to Hanabah.

"Please be careful," Hanabah said. "I saw a man shoot two of his fingers off one time after he got his gun loaded. He was upset, and with one hand over the barrel, he pounded the gun on the floor. The part that fires it snapped open and then closed, and the gun went off. They called him Three-Finger Jack after that."

I respected of black powder very much. My father had let me watch him blow out stumps and rocks from our homestead. The power of just a fairly small amount put down in a hole between the roots or under a rock was impressive. One time, I saw a big old stump split in half and lifted up out of the hole we had dug around it, just as though the hand of God had reached down and plucked it up. It went about three feet in the air and came down beside the hole, just as my father had planned. Another small charge, and out came the other half of that old stump.

"Percy, those little handfuls of powder saved us about a day and a half of digging and sweating," my father said.

You know, black powder is made up of charcoal, saltpeter, and nitrate. The formula is very simple and can be used to make the stuff if you are careful. Many a man has died or been maimed by not paying attention to the great power of this marvelous concoction.

I loaded the barrel on the right with the bird and/or rabbit shot load and the other with what we called a buckshot load – that is, with the measuring tube filled twice and poured down the barrel. I then pushed a cloth wad on top of this powder charge. That is so the powder and shot do not mix. Then I carefully took four of the larger shot from what my father called the buckshot bag and put them down the barrel. On top of these shot, I pushed another tight patch to keep them from rolling out of the end of the barrel. Now all that was left to fire this very powerful load was to cock the hammer back and place a cap on the nipple. Then by pulling the trigger, the hammer would hit the cap, causing it to fire; and the fire would go through the hollow nipple into the barrel and ignite the powder. The powder, in turn, would ignite, expand, and push the shot out of the barrel.

I was trying to show Hanabah my great knowledge and, I am sure, had a bit of an arrogant attitude as I felt like I was becoming a real man. She tolerated all of this and encouraged me to hurry up so we could get to the kill site before it got dark.

To tell the truth, my insides were in a knot. I could remember watching my father shoot this old beast loaded with buckshot. The recoil even rocked him, and he was a good-sized man. I had only shot it once with the double load, and my shoulder hurt for a week or more – let alone my behind as it knocked me on my butt. I was sure hoping that I would not have to pull the hind trigger of those double triggers as that was the one that would set off the left barrel with all of its fire and thunder and kick.

I had Hanabah carry the powder horn and possibles bag with the shot, patches, and caps. The hickory ramrod used to load the shotgun fit in some hollow thimbles between the two barrels on the underside of the gun. The gun was very heavy for my skinny frame, but wanting to be a man, I tolerated the awkwardness of trying to keep the barrels up out of the dirt as we hurriedly walked down the trail to the spot down in the little canyon where the lion had killed my buck.

I wanted to show her the spot where it all happened to vindicate what I had told her I had done for the challenge. One part of me was feeling guilty that I had not finished the ritual by suffocating the deer with the hard-to-come-by corn pollen. The other part of me was relieved that I had not had to take the buck's life in such a way. I had helped my father butcher domestic animals; and of course, Hanabah and I had, from time to time, killed and butchered a sheep for meat. In all cases, my father or

Hanabah made quick work of actually killing the animal so it did not suffer. I was not really sure what the buck would have gone through if I had suffocated him.

There ahead of us was the bend in the trail where we would be able to see where the buck had been ambushed. I slowed and carefully poked the old shotgun and myself slowly around the rock. I had not cocked either of the hammers back as this was too much of a risk of an accidental shooting. I could see blood on the ground and, wanting to show Hanabah the spot, rushed forward with her in tow.

"Look! Look!" I said excitedly. "See, here is the blood and hair from where the lion killed my buck!"

Hanabah, with all her wisdom of the outdoors and just naturally cautious from all the ventures she had witnessed, glanced quickly; but I could see her looking into the stand of trees where the blood trail showed the lion had dragged the big old buck.

"He must me a very big lion to drag your buck like this," she said very nervously.

"You did a great thing, Percy, and I know you would have finished your job if you could have had just a few more hours," she said. "The lion had an easy time attacking your buck because the buck was tired and hungry and thirsty. He was not watching carefully enough and let himself be taken. Yes, you have done what was needed, but the lion stole your prize."

Suddenly, we heard a low growl and a rustling noise in the juniper trees where the lion had dragged the deer. Instinctively, I pointed the shotgun toward the spot and backed up toward Hanabah. Before I could do anything other than cock back the right hammer, the lion came crouching out of the tree line and came toward us. I let go with the light load, and he seemed to be taken aback by the noise and pain. It really did nothing but make him mad.

"Shoot him again, Percy," Hanabah said in a very calm but firm voice. "Do not let him get to us."

I could see her step forward to the side of me with her big old hunting knife in her hand. Though filled with the rush of fear and an excitement I had never felt before, I was comforted at the same time to know that she was ready to fight.

I had reached up with my left hand and cocked the hammer for the left barrel. The lion, having gained his senses after being hit with all that small shot and bloody about his face, gathered his legs under him again to make a leap at us.

Those who have shot at big game – and I suppose at humans in time of war – will tell you that they do not remember the noise of the gun going off. It is a phenomena that is hard to explain.

I sure felt the kick of the double powder load and saw the lion twist in midair and come crashing back to the ground very still. I do not remember sighting down the barrels at him but just pointing in his direction. The buckshot did its job and ended his life of killing.

"Percy, see, this is where one of your pieces went straight to his heart," she said. "Here is where one went into his brain, and here is where one blinded him, and this one broke some of his teeth. You are a great hunter!"

She dug deep and retrieved each one of those shot and put them into a special bag that she later hung around her neck. We fully skinned out the cougar and braintanned his hide. She hung the hide with pride in the entranceway of the hogan for all to see, even though very few ever visited.

From then on, she would brag to everyone that she saw about how I saved her life, and she would show them the buckshot from the bag around her neck. She would point to me and say, "Buckshot." As most Navajos take on an event name such as Running Bear or Swift Eagle or some other name, it just seemed natural that my event-changing name became Buckshot. She would insist that with my shotgun I could "never no not miss." Everyone not ever having occasion to hear my real name therefore called me by that name. I became Buckshot Higgins.

Chapter 3

THE SECOND EVENT of those first years occurred when I turned fourteen. The rumor had circulated for several years that Hanabah had taken a young white boy and was raising him, but she would not talk about it with anyone. Those who occasionally traversed her property reported seeing me herding her sheep, but the fear they all had of her prevented anyone from really asking about the details.

"My son, I want to take you to the trading post with me today," she said. "I have to take some sheepskins and wool to trade for some thiinngs!" she added in her high, shrill voice.

In fact, if she did not want to answer a question or put something off, her favorite answer was, "I cannot do that because I have thiinngs to do!" Or she would say, "Do not bother me. I have thiinngs to do!"

"Go get Jake and saddle him," she said. "We will need to pack the hides and wool on him as they are too heavy for us to take any other way."

We had learned to take my old Western saddle and use it as a packsaddle. We were fortunate that the saddle was a double-rigged saddle, so it gave us more stability. In addition, my father had insisted that a breast collar was attached to the front of the saddle and that a crupper was attached to the back of the saddle. This way, no matter if old Jake was going uphill or downhill, the saddle stayed put right in the middle of his back. Since the withers of a mule are much narrower than those of a horse, it takes this type of configuration to keep the saddle in place.

We went to the old Toahani Trading Post that was operating at that time. It was closer than the one at Coyote Canyon, but with the heavy awkward load, I guess she wanted to go the shorter distance. I had heard her say many times that she did not like the trader and felt he was always trying to trick or cheat her.

Having free run of her hogan over the years, I had noticed a small box she kept hidden under some clothing along the far wall. She had told me early on about it, saying that it was her special property and that I was never to look in it or bother it in any way. I have always had a great respect for people, and I am very loyal to those who have helped me. I never once tried to look in the box or, for that matter, was ever really curious as to what it might contain.

We got ready to go, loading old Jake to the hilt with all we could get on him and still keep the load balanced.

"Go get the box in my clothing and bring it to me," she said.

This was quite a shock or at least an event out of the normal way of our everyday lives. To be trusted to retrieve the box gave me a special feeling, and I hoped that maybe she would show or tell me what was so special about its contents.

"Here is the box," I said. "What do you want me to do with it?"

"Just set it on the chopping stump there while I tie up old Jake," Hanabah said. "I want to show you what is inside, and today, I want you to learn how to trade with the gold."

I knew enough to know that gold was valuable, but I did not understand how it was used to trade or barter with. In fact, my whole education to that point about economics was very, very limited. I had seen very few coins of any kind in my entire life. My parents had been so poor that most of their purchases were accomplished with pure trading.

"Here, look into my box," she said.

Inside the ornate wooden box were several lumps of gold and about a dozen or so pieces of jewelry or gold figures that I supposed were used for ornaments of some type.

"At night, when you go to sleep, I take some of these pieces and melt them down to just lumps," she said. "They are easier to trade this way. The trader weighs them and gives me value for them to spend on his stock of items in the store. I do not know if he is treating me fair, but I do get a lot of things from just one small lump. I tried to trade the figures a couple of times, but the traders just seemed to be confused about their value. In fact, both traders have tried since then to get me to tell them where I got them. That is my secret, and I will not tell anyone except you if you are with me long enough to help me in my old age."

If anyone would know where buried treasure of any kind would be, one would think that the Indians would know. They traverse the country every day and are always poking into the smallest holes, looking for food of some type. A rabbit burrow or a plant root system could yield some wanted food. They knew where all the rock writings were and perhaps even knew of their true meaning.

"With the hides and wool, I will only take one lump of gold," she said. "We should have more than enough to get all the supplies that we need for the coming winter months."

I believe I have failed to mention that on that high plateau, in the wintertime, it got really cold; and the snow was sometimes several feet deep. This made going out to the trading post very dangerous as the trails were icy and steep, and they had drop-offs in places that could get one badly hurt. To take the long way around would take a day or so longer.

About four hours later, we arrived at the Toahani Trading Post (the name means "Near to Water People" in Navajo). It consisted of a building made of adobes about fifty feet square. There was a heavy windowless wood front door hanging on very substantial hand-forged hinges. Two stone steps provided access to the door. There were two hitching posts in front with two Indian ponies tied to the one on the left. There was a window about two feet square on either side of the door. Ends of logs protruded from the front building wall about a foot from the top. These were the roof support logs.

Along one side of the building, I could see some high windows about ten feet up, and they were partially hidden by the overhang of the gently sloping shingle roof. A couple of old cottonwood trees had spread their leaf-laden limbs over the post from the rear of the building, providing some shade and protection from storms. Out back, I could see about an acre of corrals with sheep, ponies, and several cows in the various pens. In addition, there was a type of storage or warehouse building.

Hanabah had begun addressing me as "son" ever since the lion incident. Rarely did she call out my real name. Usually, it was only when she wanted to get after me for something I did or didn't do right or when it was an emergency.

"Son," she said, "you take old Jake to the back by the other building and wait for someone to help you unload and count the hides and weigh the wool."

During my stay with Hanabah, she had always tried to talk to me in English. I suppose it was for two reasons. One was that she wanted to impress me and perhaps practice her skill. I also think it was in deference to me and to not embarrass me by talking Navajo. Needless to say, I did pick up on the Navajo language quite well, being young and inquisitive; so when Junior Beal came out back and started talking to me in Navajo, I knew what to do and did as he said. He didn't seem to expect anything else. My skin had tanned over those last several years, and my clothing was as the other boys of the area. I suppose that I even gave off the same smoky, mutton grease, sweat bath odors as everyone else of that era and time.

Junior was about ten years older than me. He was a good worker and had the full trust of the trader. We unloaded the skins and wool much to Jake's pleasure. He started to nose around for something to eat.

"Here, let me show you where you can put him in a corral, and I will get some hay for him," Junior said.

It is funny how words can conjure up feelings. I had not heard the word "hay" for years – ever since we had left the settlement and headed south. A whole load of memories and emotions briefly came over me.

With Jake taken care of and the skins and wool accounted for, I wandered around to the front of the post; and because the door was open, I went inside. I will never forget the shock it was to me to see all of the goods behind the extensive counter that ran around the room. The practice then, and for many years later, was to have all the canned goods, cloth, clothing, tools, or anything that was for sale to be behind a counter. The trader and his helpers stood behind the counter, took the order from the customer, and then placed the items on the counter in front of the customer. In other words, there were no open shelves that a customer could go and pick out their own goods from. I suspect, and it was alluded to several times in my dealings over the years, that the traders were protecting their supplies from theft.

In my whole life, I had not seen such a supply of goods for sale. I did not even know that some of the items I saw even existed. My mouth must have been a little open, and my eyes were giving me away as a first timer.

Hanabah was standing in front of a large number of canned goods and miscellaneous items, giving orders to the trader as to what she wanted next. Junior had come in and reported to the trader the amount of skins and wool that had been delivered. She and the trader were in a bit of a discussion about paying for the supplies.

About this time, the trader's wife, who I learned later was named Mary, startled me by asking me who I was and what family I belonged to. Being caught off guard, I muttered that I was Hanabah's son. She continued her questions with eyes that held your attention and could see right through you.

"I did not know that Hanabah had a husband or any children," Mary said.

It was a double push for me to be talking to a white person in English and to be in such a rich atmosphere of merchandise. I admit I was vulnerable to her questions from all aspects. Hanabah was so busy that she did not hear any of this as she was on the other side of the store, and there were several other customers talking and bargaining with the trader's assistants.

"Well, she saved my life when my parents died on the trail up near a place called Shiprock," I said. "She has taken care of me for about four years. This is my first time to come down from her home in about four years."

I had blurted all of this out before I even thought of what impact it might have on Hanabah or on my situation.

Mary sent out a feeling from her conduct that she truly could be trusted and that she really cared. I felt at ease talking to her and did not feel I had opened up any possible reasons for concern. I am glad that I had picked up on all of this because she came to be like a second mother to me, in addition to Hanabah. Her background and education gave me the polish that I would need in order to handle the great wealth that Hanabah would introduce me to.

"Have you had any schooling?" Mary asked.

"No, but my mother used to have me read out of the Bible and Book of Mormon," I said.

"Book of Mormon? Are you a member of the Mormon Church?" she asked.

"Yes, I was baptized and confirmed when I was eight years old by my father," I said.

"Frank and I are members of the church although we have not been able to go to any meetings for several years," she said. "We have some of our families living in the Salt Lake area. Do you have any books that you can read from?"

"No, and I am not sure I can remember how to read," I said.

About this time, Hanabah noticed I was in the trading post and talking to Mary. She seemed uncomfortable and motioned for me to join her. She was waiting for Frank to tell her how much the gold lump was worth so she would know how many more supplies she could buy.

I saw Mary move around behind the counter to the little office near the back of the store where Frank was busy doing some calculations. She spoke to him in hushed tones, and then he looked up to get a better look at me. They appeared to come to some type of conclusion or agreement. Frank came back over to us and, with a big smile, held out his hand to shake mine and introduce himself.

"And what is your name?" Frank asked.

"He is called Buckshot," Hanabah blurted out before I could give him an answer.

"And what is your last name?" Frank asked.

"My last name is Higgins," I said proudly, standing up a little straighter.

"So we have Buckshot Higgins living here in our area," Frank said. "I am very happy to make your acquaintance, Buckshot. You make sure and take good care of Hanabah. She is a good customer."

That was how it all started for me to be reintroduced back into civilization. Mary and Frank took an interest in me and offered to help me in any way they could. For several years, I was not really sure of their intentions. It seemed that Mary was honestly interested in my welfare and education, but I kept getting the feeling that Frank was just trying to use me to get at Hanabah's secret of where she had found the gold.

* * *

I made several more trips to the trading post with Hanabah over the next year or so. Mary and Frank were always there to greet me and inquire of my well-being. Several times, Frank even gave me a couple of pieces of horehound candy, which soon became one of my favorite treats in life.

In the spring a couple of years after my first trip, after shearing our little flock of sheep, we made another trip to the trading post. With old Jake loaded with hides and wool and with another melted gold piece, we set out. This time, we took a little different route. We swung to the south around a prominent rock outcrop that had a layer of coal exposed at its base.

"There is more than coal here," Hanabah said. "Look over at the pictures on the rock. Where there are happy goats, there is treasure."

Sure enough, on the rock was a drawing of several goats, and some of them were shown as almost dancing. I noticed another figure that caught my attention. It was of a man represented by an upside-down triangle for his body with normal-type legs. His head was round and had a type of headdress that looked almost like a crown. He was holding the end of a rope that went out from him and coiled into a shape that looked like a target with a bull's-eye. A spear pointed a little upward to his left.

We continued on to the trading post. She never said another word, nor did she elaborate on what she had meant. I had learned over the years to never really push her on any subject she did not seem to want to elaborate on.

On this particular day, there was quite a large group of families around the trading post. There must have been about thirty adults and about twice that many children. As they looked up and saw us coming, the children all tended to run over to their parents and try to hide behind them. Except for one family, the parents themselves were very uncomfortable. It was the legend, if you will, that had been built up around Hanabah with her distorted pockmarked face, fierce look, and unruly hair. She was the representative of evil to them. And I suppose, as her family, I too must have had a bit of a bad reputation.

She did not pay any attention to them but went straight to a family over near the corrals. The man and several women and a whole passel of kids all came toward us. The man, whom I was introduced to, was Jimmy Willeto; and the three women were his wives. All of the children were his also. I learned that since the deaths of so many Navajos on the Long Walk back in '64, as a people, they saw the disproportionate numbers of women to men and that the men should take as many wives as they could afford.

I noticed immediately one of his daughters who was one of the most beautiful creatures I had ever seen. Her skin was so smooth and toned that it reflected the very sun. Her shiny coal black hair hung down her back almost to her waist. A contagious smile was always a part of her appearance. She was blithe and wiry and so full of energy. I closely watched as she flitted in and around the children, teasing, helping, and directing many of their actions. I even caught her looking my way a couple of times, and this conjured up feelings within me that I had never felt before.

I was left holding Jake with his load while Hanabah and Jimmy moved over to a corner of the corrals and began talking in a guarded, but very animated manner. I could catch her voice raise every so often, which meant that she was not pleased with something. Jimmy, who I gathered was about the same age as her, wore his hair in a traditional Navajo cut with a wide-brimmed, domed cowboy-style hat. I could never quite figure out why most Indians would spend so much on a cowboy-type hat and never put any kind of crease in it. Maybe it was pride, and they just did not want to look like a white man cowboy.

Hanabah, regaining her sense of why we were at the trading post, motioned for me to come over to the corral corner and bring Jake.

"I was just telling *Hasteen* Jimmy about how you shot the cougar and saved my life," Hanabah said. "He is very impressed that you have such a 'thunder gun' and know how to use it. He thinks you are a very brave man and that you need to be partners with us. I have wanted to talk to you about our sacred treasure but have wanted to wait until you are a little older. But now we have a problem, and I agree with Jimmy that we need you as a partner to help protect us."

Wow, what is this all about? I wondered.

"First, you must take Jake over to the storage building and have Junior help you unload him and take a proper count," Hanabah said. "Then come back here to talk with us."

"Hey, Junior, *yataheh*," I said. "How have you been doing? I have some more hides and wool."

"I have been doing good," he said, but I could tell that he was not real happy about something.

"Is there anything wrong?" I asked.

"I probably should not be telling you this," Junior said. "But because you live a long way from us, you need to know that some of the young men are very mad at Frank, our trader. They have caught him cheating their families. They say he pays them less for their sheep, and then he takes away from the credits that he records in the books. Some say he charges them for every little service, like moving their animals to market after they have sold them to him. And then the worst thing is that he charges them a very high interest. There is talk that they are going to get even with him. I have tried to warn him and especially his woman, but they say I am just spreading rumors. Be careful, my friend, and do not get caught up in this fight. It is not yours."

Other than the excitement of the lion shooting, my life with Hanabah had been pretty calm. I had enjoyed a warm place to live, plenty of food, work to do, and a beautiful setting from which to learn about what God had created. Most of all, someone had cared enough to show me love, to listen to my questions, and to teach me traditions and history so I might not make some of the major mistakes in life. Of course, the loss of my parents, sister, and brother had been the defining events in my life; but they, as do other such hurts, dim with the passage of time.

Was my life about to take some new turns? Were their events being set up that would further test my soul?

Jimmy and Hanabah were sitting cross-legged on a blanket in the shade of one of the cottonwood trees near the corrals. As I sat on the edge of the old wooden watering trough next to them, I sensed a high tension.

"Jimmy, you must move your family up on the high ground to my land and get away from where they know you live," Hanabah said. "They do not dare come up to my land, for they must know I will curse them, and my son will not let them hurt us. We can build you some hogans and make our place strong. You have sons who are strong, and your girls can herd our sheep as we build."

"No," he said with a very firm tone. "I was given my land by my father, and it is almost as well hidden as your home. As you know, anyone coming to my place must come over a pass if they come on the main trail into my valley. My dogs always let me know when anyone is coming. They cannot even sneak into my area over sheep trails as my dogs will let me know. My three homes are strong, and my women and children can fight."

"But, Jimmy, you have not seen the look of the lion as my son and I have seen," Hanabah said. "These men do not care if they kill any of your family for the treasure. You cannot stop them by yourself. You are a very wise man who has healed many with your great medicine, and you know that the sickness that comes with greed for treasure cannot be stopped. Men will kill for gold and silver. You must listen to me. You have nowhere else to go!"

This last comment was made with her normal almost-scream, high-pitched voice to emphasize the point.

"No matter what the others think, you are a good woman, and you have taught me much over the years about plant medicines that have made me well-known as a healer," Jimmy said. "You have helped me to become a very respected man with many sheep and ponies. You have shared your treasure with me so my families have never had to go without. I know you speak from your heart, but I am a man and can take care of my families. If they get close, I will send one of my sons to get your help. And remember, I will never tell them of the treasure you have shared with me, even if they kill me."

"Oh, Jimmy, you are a proud old man who does not know the harm that can come," Hanabah said. "You know that the white man defeated our whole nation and sent us away to starve and die of sickness. You were there with me and know I speak the truth. You know that if enough of them come to find the treasure, they can defeat you and hurt your family. I will always be your friend, and I will be ready to come and help you with my son and his thunder gun."

The day was pretty well spent. Hanabah gathered up our bundles and had me put them in a place up behind the trading post where we would camp for the night. Jake had been put in the corral by Junior and was munching away on some hay. The night would be cold as it is in a desert-type country, but not near as cold as it was up where we lived on the plateau. I gathered enough firewood for our fire and then drifted down to the trading post to see what Hanabah was trading for. I saw Jimmy and his families load up their trade goods and belongings into two wagons pulled by some small but stout ponies. There were four ponies to pull each wagon. They were needed because the wagons were heavy with so many people and belongings. Even then, some of the children, especially the young men and girls, walked. It was a lot more comfortable to walk if you had to ride in the springless wagon unless you could be on the seat with the driver. This was the only place the ride was comfortable as the seats were mounted on springs.

I had learned from Junior that the name of Jimmy's beautiful daughter was May Fern.

"My friend, there are many other young men and even some of the older ones who have their eye on her," Junior said, laughing as he told me her name. "You will have to beat many to get her hand. Besides, Jimmy watches her very close and is not happy with anyone getting too close."

I was standing in front of the trading post as the families headed north on the wagon road down the draw toward their land. May Fern was following along behind the wagons with several of her brothers and her sister. My heart skipped a beat when I saw her turn and wave at me. I waved back and stood there until they went out of sight around a bend in the draw. What had happened to my heart? I had never before felt such wonderful feelings welling up inside my mind and heart.

"Why, hello, Buckshot," Mary said from behind the counter as I entered the door of the trading post. "I had seen Hanabah come in earlier and wondered if you might also have come along. I have something I need to ask you."

My young mind was about ready to explode with all the information and feelings that was being forced into it, and now Mary wanted to know something from me? Not having much chance to talk to others over the last few years and being naturally shy, I didn't really know how to react to her approach. Before she could pursue her question, I gave a little cough and asked if there was something to drink as I had left our canteen at our camp.

Mary reached over to a shelf full of some bottles. She took one and opened it with an opener that was attached to the shelf.

"Here, try this," she said, handing me the opened bottle of sarsaparilla. "It will solve your thirst, and it tastes really good."

Can you remember the first time that you had a bottle of sarsaparilla? Well, I tell you I have never forgotten that experience. I had never dreamed that anything could taste so good. It was not cold, but the tangy dark drink seemed to not only quench my thirst, but also seemed to invigorate my very being.

"Thank you so very much, ma'am," I said. "This is a great drink!"

"Buckshot, I know that you are a smart young man," Mary said. "I know that your mother taught you to read, but that you have not had the chance in the last few years to keep up on reading. To really get ahead in the changing world, you must be a good reader, and you must know how to cipher. That is, you must know how to keep books. Frank and I would like you to come and live here at the trading post where we will teach you to read better and have you learn how to keep books. I don't expect you to give me an answer right now as you need to talk it over with Hanabah. We have thought that maybe she could move closer to the trading post, and we could even give her some work so it would all work out. Anyway, think about it, and let me know as soon as you can."

I just looked back at her with a stunned look as that was the way I took the request. I finished drinking the sarsaparilla and handed her the empty bottle. I walked across to the other side of the store where Junior was helping Hanabah sack up all of our foodstuffs in grain sacks so we could pack them on old Jake. I had been complaining to her about how dull the axe was and how hard it made chopping the hard wood of the dead juniper trees we pulled into our woodpile with Jake. She had just sort of shrugged it off and really didn't say much. But there in the middle of all our stuff was a brand-new axe and a new file that I could use to keep it sharp. It is always good to like simple things and know when you are being blessed with them.

We slept in camp that night up behind the trading post and then arose early the next morning to pack Jake and head back home. We could not leave the sheep penned up any longer without food. We had placed some water in the old hand-hewn trough, but that would be all gone by now. I was struggling inside with all the news I had to tell Hanabah about the danger to the trading post and trader and the offer they had made to me. I had pretty well forgotten or minimized the "partnership" and the treasure that she and Jimmy had been talking about. Other than the few pieces of jewelry she had let me see in the box and the lumps of gold she had melted down, there did not seem to be a lot of substance to the treasure story.

After traveling for about two hours, we came to a clearing where there was a small spring, grass for Jake, and some good shade provided by some large trees. We turned Jake loose to graze and then went over to a big flat rock to sit on.

"My son," Hanabah started.

"My mother," I began at the same time.

We were stumbling over each other's words. Luckily, we both thought it was funny, and we laughed at the awkward start.

"My son, you speak first as you are the man in our family," she said.

"No, my mother, I respect your wisdom and guidance and want to hear from you first," I said.

"Very well," she said. "I have a heavy burden to tell you about. It concerns what Jimmy and I were talking about back at the trading post. I am very fearful that he is going to be harmed by some terribly bad people who want what he and I have been sharing for many years. I will tell you the story so you will understand. Jimmy and I feel that your heart is in the right place, and you will not do foolishly with the treasure we are to share with you. Remember this one rule: You cannot prosper from these riches if you let greed and dishonesty enter your life. You have to use the treasure to help first your family and then other deserving people."

Hanabah got very quiet for a minute and looked like she was trying to remember something important.

"While Jimmy and I were captives at Bosque Redondo," she said, "we tried to help an old Navajo man who was very sick. He had the sickness of the lungs and struggled to breathe. We stole and cheated in many ways to get healthy broth for him to eat as he was so weakened by his sickness. One day, as he could feel his end was coming, he asked us to sit and listen to a secret he had been hiding for many years.

"'I am not really a full Navajo,' the old man said. 'My mother was one of the descendants of the Aztecs that were sent north from the marvelous city ruled by our great father Montezuma. He sent hundreds of men with their families north to return to where our fathers had originally come from. Each man carried a very heavy weight of gold and silver and valuable stones of rich color. This treasure was to be the foundation for a new start for the Aztecs. At the time, some bearded strangers with huge riding animals and tools of death that spit fire were invading Montezuma's center place. There was fear that these warriors may win and that to disappear back north might be the best course of action. Montezuma gave those he sent north with treasure and their families with instructions to hide the treasure in secret places. They were to wait for messages to come telling these families that those left behind were coming to help start this new kingdom and life.

"'My ancestors were the designers of where the treasure was to be hidden and how the sites were to be constructed and marked,' the old man continued. 'The center point of all this activity was set up at what is now called Pecos, north of the hated Spanish city of Santa Fe. An eternal flame was started soon after my ancestors arrived at that spot. They began building a town and sending out scouts to look for good hiding places. As far as I know, that flame still burns today. My ancestor from which my mother came was sent to a very rich area for hiding treasure because the land had many canyons and was hard to travel in. The great rock walls of the canyons and the great rock statues were easy to put on maps, so no matter how long it took for Montezuma's plans, the maps and markers would be easy to lead to the treasure places. My ancestor not only was in charge of designing the hiding sites, but to help in directing the building of the sites and then to make the marks on the rocks to work with the maps so the treasure caves could be found again.

"'Because it would take a long time to build the hiding places so they would hold all the treasures and be closed up tightly and look natural,' the old man said, 'all the workers and overseers took their families with them and set up villages. In these villages, they set up places of worship that I have heard some call kivas. These are structures that are dug partway into the ground and then lined so the walls can be painted on with pictures of our ways. Walls are extended up so a roof can be put over the big room. Then an opening is created where those who would do the rituals climb down on a ladder to the sacred ceremony. Some of our ancestors even taught others we found in this great expanse of land some of our ceremonies. The Zuni and the Hopi saw the wisdom of what we have, and they too have such religious places. The Navajo were a very stubborn people and, because of their greater numbers and their own traditions, would never really let my ancestors teach them. The Navajos let my ancestors live in the rugged land to the north of their ancestral lands and even tolerated some of our villages on the edge of their lands. These were places the Navajos did not really want as they were too difficult to live in. There were not many places to plant crops, and water was hard to find. Our villages were small due to our small numbers. Our people were experts at making the land give us food. We even made places for water to collect so that even small flows of water would gives us ponds with lots of water for our plantings and drinking and bathing. We did not like the way the Navajos treated their bodies by heating them in small huts so they would sweat and then go out and lay in the sun and let the sweat disappear. We believed our bodies should be washed clean with water and a plant mix that took away the dirt and sweat.

"'My grandparents told me that not many years after our ancestors became settled and had completed a number of hiding places for the treasure,' the old man continued, 'they were surprised by another very large group who arrived from the south carrying more gold and silver and beautiful stones. They were in bad shape and told a terrible story of destruction and slavery by the bearded ones. Some even thought that Montezuma had been killed. Most agreed that he could not be killed and that he was still among our people, trying to organize them to fight back or come north with the rest. These new treasures made it necessary to look for more hiding places. My ancestors and the others who were in charge had determined to divide the treasure up into many sites and that even this area of so many canyons should not have all the sites. Scouts were again sent out in all directions to find good hiding places. Places were found even not far from where these *solados* now have us prisoners. They would not have taken me if I had been younger. I am sorry that I came, but I gave up and let them take me as I felt I could help some of my grandchildren. Now even some of them have died with the pox at this bad place, and I too will die before we can go back home.'"

Hanabah shifted herself and asked me to go get the canteen, some dried meat, and a can of peaches from our supplies.

"Before I go on and tell you the important part," Hanabah said, "we must get something to eat and drink. You will want to see one of the treasure sites. I will take you there today, but it will take some strength to get there and open it, so you will know what I tell you is real."

I was so caught up with what she was telling me that I brought back a can of corn instead of peaches. I stumbled on my way back from where old Jake was grazing and spilled some of the water from the canteen.

"My son," she said, "slow down. There is much yet to tell, and we have plenty of time to do all I will show you and still make it back to our home. But you must listen to the details. The maps are hidden, and only the signs on the rocks can guide you. You will have plenty of wealth for a full life, but as I have told you, you must not ever get greedy or use the treasure for evil. You know that I have healing knowledge and some powers that I have learned to trust from a great god, but some say that the treasure has a very dark curse upon it. They say the curse shows itself with false power the treasure owner thinks he has because he is rich with gold and silver and stones. He then wants more and more, and as it unfolds to him as he finds the maps and secret hiding places, he does evil things to fill his hunger for power and wicked ways. This is why I was going to wait to tell you of this wonderful secret until you were a little older and could maybe better understand between good and evil. I must tell you now because evil men are threatening Jimmy and his family as they too have been looking for the treasure and think he can lead them to it. He too has been melting down some of the pieces of gold and trading with the gold. Because he has a larger family and a greater need, he has been trading many pieces. Now let me finish the story that Navajo Jim Begay told to Jimmy and I those many years ago."

"'The two of you have been so kind to me,' the old man said slowly. 'I know you have done things to get me food and even these extra blankets. Now let me tell you the signs of where the treasure is and even where your first site can be found. All of the treasure places have pictures drawn on rocks to show you where they are. These pictures are sometimes mixed in with the pictures made by the ancient ones who lived in the country before my ancestors came. But if you look close at the mixture of pictures, you will be able to see which ones are about the treasure. The picture to look for is one or more happy mountain goats or mountain sheep. The higher their front feet are off the ground, the closer you are to a treasure site. Next, look for a picture of a hunter. The bigger the covering on his head, the greater the size of the treasure. And next, look for a rope in a circle pattern and then some type of pointer, such as an arrowhead or spearhead or even a bird beak pointing in the direction of the site. The entrances are always made of three rocks. Some are very big, and some are not. The main stone is like an upside-down triangle with two support rocks, one on each side. You must be very careful in opening the site as there are some sites that are fake and will cause harm to those who pry them open. The bad sites are marked on the maps, but you must find a map in one of the sites so you will know the locations. The maps are made from gold. These sheets of gold show the mountains and rivers and canyons and where the treasure sites and false sites are. The gold plates are so designed that they are put in a three-legged stand so that specific plates with holes of various shapes will let the sun shine down through the shapes onto the site map plate. This is how you will know where all the sites are.

"'Our stories tell of the ancient ones writing many instructions on such plates and burying them in the ground or caves to save them,' the old man continued. 'The Zuni south of Gallup have a sacred mountain in which they say is a whole room full of such records that can be made into a book that tells of sacred things. This is why they will not let you climb on the mountain. I have told you much information that you really do not need to know, but I have no one else to tell. And when I am gone, the secret will be gone. I am the last of those who know the whole story. And one more thing. Always remember the power of water. Now listen close and follow my directions so you can you can find one of the little treasure sites where there is treasure and a first-step map that can lead you to the other sites. If you look and study, you will be able to find the three large sites along with the many smaller sites.'

"He then described to Jimmy and I how to find the first site by going to the cave near Gallup named after the hated Kit Carson who was responsible for capturing us and marching us to that terrible place," Hanabah said. "He went on to tell us to go in a northern direction to a red rock at the head of a steep canyon near the coal I showed you. After we returned to our land, Jimmy and I followed his instructions. After much searching, we found the pictures. They were hidden, so it was hard to see them. They were the pictures that I showed you on our trip to the trading post. We followed the direction of the arrow, and there were the three rocks hiding one of the treasure sites. But how were just the two of us open such a place? The main stone was taller than Jimmy, and the stones were so fitted that you could not even get a knife blade between them. And *Hasteen* Begay had not lived long enough to tell us the secrets of opening the sites. Jimmy and I were disappointed, to say the least.

We needed to get back to our own lands and take care of our sheep and such. Others were making sure things were taken care of for Jimmy, but I had not purchased any sheep nor built my hogan. But I knew that not far from this site, I wanted to claim my own land.

"Jimmy treated me like a sister," Hanabah said. "As we are both from the same clan. He has given me support. And I, in turn, have shared a lot of information with him about healing. I seem to have been born with a sense of what should be done, and I have learned so much about plants and how to use them in not only curing our people, but in helping sick animals. One time, I had almost my whole flock of sheep down with a mysterious sickness. It came to me to feed them a fuzzy-leafed plant in a soup mixture and to get them to throw up. I did so with much difficulty as I was alone. But it worked. Jimmy has had occasion to use this same plan on several people with good results. I will show you someday the plant I am talking about, and you will then have the knowledge.

"You know, my son," Hanabah continued, "knowledge is power. The person who has the knowledge is more powerful than the strong ones if he uses the information for good. There is always an answer, but you must be listening for the answer. Sometimes, it comes as a dream or thought. Sometimes, it comes as a still small voice. You must be in tune, and you must ask, and it will be there. This is what Jimmy and I did. We separated and went in two different directions, agreeing to meet back at the treasure door site in a little while. I went up the narrow steep canyon toward the tall rock. I was curious as to the shape of the tall rock. What was it sitting on, and did it have any signs on it? I found nothing special on the rock, and so I carefully went down into the beginning of the canyon where water was coming out from rocks like the spring at our home. I drank. And as I was pushing myself back from the little pool of this wonderful water, I was told – not by a voice I could hear with my ears, but with a voice in my head – to turn and look down the canyon and follow the water with my eyes. At a place where the water disappeared over a rock, I saw a ditch carved into the rock just to the side of this main little stream. The strange part was that there was a rock carved so as to act as a dam in keeping the water from going into this side ditch. This rock was in grooves so it could be pulled straight up and then be placed in the main water channel so the water would then flow into the ditch. I had heard of such ways to make water go to fields of corn and squash so it did not have to be carried in buckets to the thirsty plants, but why would someone make such a system up here in this place? There was no place for fields in this steep rocky mountain."

"My mother, where did the ditch go?" I asked. "Did you follow it to see if there were any gardens?"

"Let me tell you what I had discovered, and I am going to show it to you today," Hanabah said. "So that we have enough time, for it will take time for the water to work, I will stop my story now. And let us move on up the trail to the site. We still have a ways to go. Now what was it you wanted to tell me?"

I had become so interested in her story and so excited that I could be part of some secret treasure site that I had all but forgotten my news and offer. I was jarred back to the present with her question, but I did not feel that it would have been a good time to bring up all that I knew. She was about to share with me a very important part of her life and that of *Hasteen* Willeto and his family. I did not feel my little situation was that important, nor the information about Frank and what was being said about him. In hindsight, perhaps if I had told Hanabah, she could have done something about it; and Frank would have survived, but such are the decisions in life.

I quickly caught Jake, who had been grazing nearby. I checked the cinches on the saddle and double-checked the ropes holding the sacks of goods. Oh, how I wish we had a good packsaddle. I had seen one for sale at the store. It was over $4, and because I did not fully understand money and trade amounts, I was afraid to ask Hanabah about such a purchase. We were soon under way, following the switchback trail up toward the top of the plateau. It was a warm, sunny day with a slight spring breeze. A jay and then a long-tailed magpie chattered at us as we disturbed their feeding. About halfway up the mountain from the location of the trading post to our land was the fork in the trail where we had entered into the main trail from our excursion to the rock art and coal site. We took this trail again and were once again headed toward the steep canyon with the tall rock at the head of it.

"Listen," Hanabah said. "Can you hear the water falling from the rock? That is where we must go so I can show you how it all works. Take the packs and saddle off Jake and turn him loose over there in that clearing. There is enough grass for him for the time we will be here. Put the saddle and supplies under that tree where Jake can see them. I do not think I have ever told you how much of a blessing you and that mule have been to me. Before you came along, I had to pack everything and do all my work all by myself. I even made long treks to other treasure sites just by walking. In fact – and I do not believe I have ever spoken to you about this – I was returning from a place very far north where I had seen treasure sites when I found you. But we will not talk about that now."

I did as I was instructed as fast as I could because I wanted so bad to see this treasure site and what it held. Jake sensed my urgency and probably interpreted it as fear or something else negative. He kept shying away from me as I tried to unpack and unsaddle him.

"Damn you, Jake," I said. "Hold still so I can get this rope untied. It is for your own good. Soon, you can be just eating grass and enjoying the day. Now hold still."

In the meantime, Hanabah had worked her way down into the canyon and was standing by the little waterfall that was echoing its pleasure of falling over the diversion rock. In a few minutes, I was there with her and all wild-eyed, watching her gently move some of the gravel away from the small ditch entrance with its blocking rock set into the grooves.

"Now watch as I change the water from going down the canyon to flowing in the ditch toward that pile of loose rocks over there," Hanabah said.

Indeed, it looked like the ditch just dead-ended into the loose rocks. Where could the water possibly go from there?

"Now watch carefully as I pull this rock from its blocking place and lay it across the stream," she said. "Notice that the water then has to go into the ditch and head to the rock pile."

Sure enough, the water had soon filled the small ditch and, with just the right amount of slope, was flowing to the loose rocks and disappearing. Why was this so important to what we were doing here?

"Come with me now," Hanabah said. "We will follow the canyon downward for a short distance, and I will show you the three rocks that the rock pictures point to."

About one hundred yards downward, we came to a leveled-off part of the canyon. The canyon was about seventy-five yards wide. On the south-facing side were the three triangle-shaped rocks. The larger of the three, which was about ten feet high and shaped like an upside-down triangle, was supported on both sides by smaller triangular-shaped rocks – each about four feet high. All three rocks were tilted back about twenty degrees to match the natural slope of the hillside of the canyon.

"My son," Hanabah said, "remember that the builders of these sites had a lot of time on their hands and used a lot of patience to complete their assignment. They did not have any tools or parts like we see at the trading post with the wagons and plows and shovels and picks. They had to plan and use what was at hand. Sit here on this bench rock and watch carefully."

I wondered how many times the creators of this site had sat as we were doing, watching for what I did not know. The bench rock was about thirty yards from the treasure-site rocks just across the streambed where the natural flow of water would have been flowing if we had not diverted it into the ditch. From where we were sitting, I could guess that the water was flowing into a spot out of view to about where the top of the main rock door was. What was this all about, and why did we have to sit and wait?

"Buckshot!" she said, getting my attention.

Just hearing her say my new name startled me as Navajos seldom, if ever, call you by your new name if they are family. I could only remember her ever calling me by that name one time, and that was when she was so excited because one of our ewes gave birth to triplets. I could tell she was anxiously excited and waiting for something grand to happen.

"Now watch carefully," she said. "The big rock is going to start moving!"

Try as I may, I could not fathom how such a large rock could ever move. I knew that even if I could put a harness on old Jake and hook a large chain – like one I had seen at the trading post – in some way to the rock, it could not be moved. Had my adopted mother lost her mind?

A small grinding sound and then small rocks and some fine dirt rolled down from above the large rock as it seemed to come to life. The apex or bottom point of this large triangle started to move away from its resting place and lift up toward us! I fell over backward from the rock bench as it seemed this slow motion was going to make the rock come after me!

Hanabah laughed at me as she turned and held out her hand to bring me back upright so I could sit beside her and watch this great event.

"Silly one!" she said. "Do you not remember me telling you that Hasteen Begay said to watch for the power of the water? The stream of water we changed has reached the point behind the big stone and in a basin carved into the backside of the stone it is filling up. As soon as the water weighs more than the balance of the stone, it will open so we can go inside the place of treasure. The big stone hinges on the smaller ones. We only have a short time to go in and out because as the basin tilts with the stone, it begins to empty, and the stone closes back. Perhaps it would reopen with more time as the basin refills, but Jimmy and I have never left that to chance and have never wanted to be captured inside and waiting to find out."

This huge main stone tilted back further and further until it came to about a ninety-degree position and stopped. This created an opening that was about three feet wide at the bottom and about six feet high. A full-grown man could easily walk inside. The light that the opening allowed let one fully see a room about fifty feet deep and about forty feet wide. There were several rows of shelves all around the sides of the rooms. Resting on these shelves were beautiful plates, cups, swords, shields, and jewelry items of all types. They were all engraved or carved with very fine sculpturing, and many were inset with stones of either a transparent green or an opaque red. There were several shades of both the green and the red. As we walked into the room, a chill went up my back, and a flash of some sort of memory went through my being as though I had been here before.

"Quickly, you may take one item while I choose the small ones I need for us," Hanabah said. "Ones I can melt down and use to trade with. Do not choose anything too big or too fancy."

There were several woven baskets full of items that had not been finished. They looked like the artisans were still in the process of shaping and engraving them before they had to hide them away. I saw a slender-bladed dagger with a silver-colored blade and a gold-inlaid handle with one green oval stone that seemed to reach out to me to take. I knew I could make a sheath for it and maybe use it for hunting or defense if needed.

I could hear the water pouring from the basin and could see it falling into a hole in the floor of the room about halfway back. As Hanabah had said, the stone began to lower, and I had no desire to be in there when it closed. We both moved quickly toward the door and made it outside before the door once more completely shut.

"I will go and turn the water back to its normal course while you go get Jake and load him up," Hanabah said. "It is time to go home and tend to our sheep and thiiiings."

I was brought back to reality as she played that favorite word of hers on her tongue and had it sing out in a long, elongated high-pitched syllable.

What an experience. An experience of a lifetime. Almost a dream beyond a person's wildest dreams. Or was it a dream? No, for in my hand, I clutched very tightly the double-bladed dagger inlaid with gold designs and the green stone in the handle. What a treasure! I had never thought that I would ever own an item so elegant and precious.

I did not see what type or shape the items were that Hanabah collected. I did see her place them in a piece of cloth and then tie the cloth in a knot to hold them. She returned to the clearing just as I was double-checking the sacks on Jake. She took the cloth with the pieces in them and inserted it into one of the sacks that had the end available and then tied the end shut.

We arrived back home in time to water our little flock and see to their comfort although they had not grazed as usual. Tomorrow, I would let them eat longer than usual – besides, I needed extra time on a hillside looking over them to think of all that had happened in the last two days.

* * *

For a boy of just sixteen, all of these happenings took some time to sink in. It was a full two days later before she and I got around to fully talking again. We had resumed our daily routine of sheepherding that included watering them and taking them out to pasture in the nearby hills. Then we would herd them back to the watering spot, have them drink their fill, and then put them back into the sheep corral not far from our hogan. We had firewood to gather and chop and water to pack in buckets for our own cooking, drinking, and clothes washing. Life was a steady but pleasant routine, and after all, it was a beautiful spring. Summer was coming when I could sleep out at night and watch the vista of stars and try to conjure up the many shapes they offered for my view. With just a little imagination, one could see any form of adventure or items of life in an endless show.

I had taken my dagger and wrapped it in a piece of the oilcloth that my weapons were wrapped in and tucked it away with them. I had put some of the oil I used to clean and keep my rifles and shotgun from rusting. I had begun to think of the design for a sheath for the dagger so it could be used but would not show its beauty or value to anyone as I carried it with me.

"My mother, may I speak with you about my thoughts?" I asked.

"Yes, my son," Hanabah said. "I have been waiting for all that you have seen and been told to sink in and to cause you to wonder and think about them. We have had a good day, and the darkness is starting to come. Sit here by the fire with me and tell me of your thoughts."

"First, let me tell you of my thankfulness for all you have done for me," I said. "I know that I would not have survived had you not come into my life when you did and saved me from that terrible water sickness. The others would have left me to die with my parents. Then let me thank you for teaching me about life and how to survive and grow. Thank you for teaching me to work and show me how to do my part. And thank you for your many talks about being honest and telling the truth and showing me the importance of helping others. Thank you for telling me of a great power who guides our lives and is willing to help us if we live right and ask for help. And thank you for sharing with me the great secret treasure place and all that it holds. I do not fully understand what is to be done with it all, but I await your guidance in showing me what we can do with it."

"I am very happy that you have listened to my talks and learned your lessons well," Hanabah said. "You have brought great comfort to me as I become older. I had sometimes wondered of what value I would ever be for living because I never had a family of my own. But you have brought love into my life, and you have a deep goodness that has rewarded my efforts to teach you the right way. I have much more to teach you now that you have become a man and can accept the load of using what we have to help others and to defend us against those who would take it away. But those lessons and knowledge are yet to come. Now what else have you to talk to me about?"

"My message is one of sadness and a heavy heart," I said. "I must tell you of a plan, and I must ask you about my future that could take me away from our home so I can learn. Please listen to me as I try and explain and then give me the help I need to know what to do."

Even in the dark, I could feel her tense up a bit as she prepared for something that was not pleasant, but she had experienced so much in life that she would know how to shield herself from most of the hurt. The little fire in the middle of the hogan was lazily burning the piñon pine sticks and a piece of a stump. The smoke rose slowly but faithfully upward and escaped into the night through the dome in the center of the roof. The warmth the fire gave off, the popping of the dry wood burning, and the flickering of the light it produced were almost trancelike. This was a setting where we had had many lessons and stories and had learned to listen and exchange ideas. I was so thankful for our lives and where we had come to.

"Junior tells me that the young men are planning to kill Frank, the trader, sometime soon because they have much against him," I said. "They say he is cheating their families and is not honest in his measurements or prices. I feel because I now know this that I have somehow become responsible for this deed, or in some way, I am guilty if it happens. What am I to do? What can I do? I am just a small young man, but I do have the thunder gun. But I cannot fight all of them."

Hanabah sat quietly, staring at me intently with her earnest eyes.

"Before you tell me your thoughts on this matter, let me tell you the second part of my message," I said. "Mary, the trader's wife, has asked me if I would come and live with them, where they would teach me to read books and learn how to do the business of a trader and even help you with what they would pay me. They do not seem to know of your treasure and feel you are very poor and could use more money. She says that you could come and live close to the trading post also. They would find us a place."

The reality of what I was saying was sinking in and even startling to me.

"How could I go and leave you alone here and not be here to herd the sheep and gather the wood and water and protect you from the lions and bad men? How could I leave you and Jake to make the trips alone to the trading post and know that you would be safe? How could this be done?"

Hanabah did not answer for a long time. I began to feel uneasy, like maybe I had hurt her so deep, she had no answer or that she thought I might be just up and leaving her now that I knew about the treasure. Could she not know me enough to know that I would not hurt her for anything or anyone?

"You have come to know the things that a man must know and make choices about," Hanabah said. "Life can seem very difficult at times. Answers come from asking, as I have told you. Most of the time, we can come up with the answers from what we have experienced, but there are times when we have no experience to pull from. Then we need to think and ask for the way to go. These are very important parts of life, and I think we need to think about them for a day or two before we try and answer them. Do you agree with me?"

I must have reached a stage of maturity in my life as this was the first time Hanabah had ever asked my opinion about such important matters. I was pleased that she asked for my opinion about waiting to come up with an answer, but at the same time, I was anxious to have an answer so all of this was not hanging over my head.

"Yes, my mother," I said. "I agree with you that we need to think about what to do and to ask for help in deciding what to do. I feel good about this way to come up with the right answer. These things can make a big difference in our lives. Know that I love you and would not do anything that would hurt you or place you in a situation where you had no help for living as we have. Thank you for listening to me and letting me explain what I have on my mind."

"You are a good son," Hanabah said. "We have experienced much together. You will make good choices. I too love you."

That ended our talk. It was profound in that this was the first time she had ever expressed her love to me as such. She had praised my efforts and work but never come out directly and said she loved me. This was a wonderful thing to hear. I have never forgotten the feeling that comes to the recipient from such a direct expression and have tried in my life to express with a direct approach this expression to those I love. Yes, she taught me much and gave me such a rich legacy of the basics of life.

That is how we set about deciding to change our lifestyle and way and place of living. I talked to Frank and Mary again about my further education from them and the opportunity of working in the trading post, but I was still concerned about leaving Hanabah up on the plateau alone. They suggested she come and live nearby.

There was an abandoned government rock building about a quarter of a mile up a side canyon from the trading post. The walls were about eighteen inches thick of hewn stone. The stone had come from a local quarry and was crafted by a local Navajo, *Hasteen* Moore. The building needed a new wooden floor, a new roof, a couple of windows, and a new door. We would need a stove to make it warm and to cook on. Frank said he would give us all that was necessary at his cost and that my work would pay for it. He estimated that I could pay for it all within six months, and then the money I earned would go to supplies for Hanabah and me. I talked to Junior, and he volunteered to help me repair the building. He could see that with me also working at the post, he would not have to work as hard nor do the menial jobs. He was excited to have a helper. He also expressed his thankfulness to have me nearby should the young men decide to do anything foolish to the post or to Mary and Frank. He said that everyone knew about Buckshot and his deadly accuracy with the thunder gun. He also said everyone feared Hanabah and her rumored temper and spells and what she might do if any harm came to me. We really had a fearful reputation!

At first, Hanabah did not want to change her life.

"I have lived this way for many years," she said. "I do not want to change now. I have never lived outside of a hogan except during those terrible days the army held us, and I did not like that."

I had longed to live in a real house like I had grown up in with my parents. I knew the advantage of a good waterproof building when it rained. I knew that with a real stove, we could be warm, cook easier, and keep things cleaner than with our dirt floor. Yes, this would be better for us, and I could learn to read better and maybe even become a trader someday with my own post.

I pointed out to Hanabah all of these things and the fact that I could be closer to Frank and Mary with my thunder gun and buckshot. Maybe I could help protect them. I secretly hoped I could learn the truth about why the young men hated him so much. I was hoping that he really was not cheating their families. Maybe I could somehow make a difference.

Another benefit was the use of one of the post corrals to put our sheep in at night. I would have to clean out the manure each week, but it was a safer and much larger corral than we had had at our place. With me working at the post, Hanabah would now have to take our little herd out each day by herself. She agreed that it would be good for her to be out in the country with the sheep. It would be good exercise and not a big burden as she had been doing this all her life. A local family had lost their father to sickness, and so their portion of land for herding their sheep was now available for us and our sheep. The family had burned their hogan and left to go stay with the wife's family. It was the custom of the Navajo that if someone should die in the hogan, it had to be burned to the ground because of the evil spirits who would take over the home.

Of interest is the way the medicine man would cleanse the hogan if he was called into hold a sing to help cure the sick. Hogans were constructed so that there were no corners inside. That is, the interior is round with just one door. The medicine man, using a feather or other handheld symbol, would enter the hogan and leave the door open. He would then perform a cleansing by singing a sacred song and walk all the way around the inside, chasing any evil spirits out the door. The door was then shut, and a Navajo rug would be hung over the door to prevent the evil spirits to enter back into the hogan. Then a sing would help for either one, three, or five days to cure the sick person. This was a very sacred event and relied not only on medicines given to the sick person, but also on the calling of spiritual powers for help with the cure. Jimmy Willeto told me many stories of his experiences regarding these ceremonies as he was one of the most respected medicine men in the whole area.

"My son, I have given the things you have told me much thought," Hanabah said. "I know that I am set in my ways as I have spent many years living like I do. I remember when I found you that I said in my heart that if I could have you as family, I would do whatever it would take to make the best life for you. Up to now, that has been to just see that you grow and are fed and learn about all we have around us. You have learned your lessons well. But I cannot teach you the white man's ways. I do not believe that all of their ways are good, but they do have power in their knowledge. You too must learn some of the important things so you can have a good life. I want you to be prepared to have a family and be able to support them. Just raising sheep is no longer the way to go. I can see the wisdom in you learning to read the books and be able to keep the accounts. Do you really think we can make a good place to live out of the old rock building?"

Hanabah finally had seen the light. We began our move and the repairs to the building about midsummer. We had moved in, and I was working at the post by the coming of fall. It was so much better to be in a completely weatherproof building and to be able to cook without fighting the smoke and mess of an open fire on the floor. Frank even found a barrel that Junior filled with water each day or so from a barrel he had in the post wagon each few days. He would fill the wagon barrel from the windmill not far from the post. To have a covered barrel just outside our door was a real treat. We were living a good life.

Chapter 4

FOR THE NEXT few years, things went pretty well as we had planned. We paid off the materials for fixing up our new home, and we even had a sort of savings account at the store from my wages and the selling of wool from our little flock of sheep and from hides from ones we butchered. We even increased the size of our flock of sheep because we had a larger corral, and the land to graze them on was more productive for grass than up on the plateau. Hanabah truly was happier with our better home, prosperity, and the closeness to the trading post where we could purchase all of the new items that became available.

One of the better items that continued to surprise us was the new types of food available in what back then were first referred to as airtights. We now call them tin cans, but in the old days, we knew them as airtights for obvious reasons. To be able to purchase all types of vegetables and soups was a marvel to us and a huge change from having to rely only on what we could grow for ourselves. And because we had no way to preserve any foods except for drying them as jerky or dried vegetables, the airtights were a true blessing. The only confusion I never could understand was why they would can tomato juice, which was not one of my favorites. These marvelous fruits of the garden were not readily grown by us, but the same juice was put in an airtight and called tomato soup. How could they suggest that tomato juice instantly became soup just by heating it up? Soup, to me, had substance with meat and vegetables or noodles.

My days working at the trading post were long and full of hard work. I would help Junior with unloading the supplies for the post when Frank would come back from Gallup with his wagon loaded as full as he could get it. We would have sacks of flour, boxes of airtights, and other such items like baking powder for making fry bread, sarsaparilla, and horehound candy. We also had picks and shovels to unload. Every once in a while, one of the families would purchase a new wagon. The wagon would be in pieces and shipped as freight. Frank would have Junior drive one of the other post wagons to town along with him to bring back this extra freight. Secretly, I was waiting until I could be trusted enough to make the long trip into Gallup and see the railroad tracks, the train, warehouses full of goods, and all the people and stores that Junior told me about.

There were also the chores of cleaning the corrals and feeding the trade animals that Frank took in. When there were enough sheep, cattle, or ponies, a buyer would come by the post and purchase them from Frank and herd them away to market. It took a while before I fully understood how trading, purchases, and goods all fit together.

Mary was very kind to me and insisted that I spend at least two hours each day reading and helping post the books. She and Frank had an extensive library of several hundred books. This was very good for the time we were in, and I was very happy to get this kind of relief from the hard work of helping run the store and yard. There always seemed to be some sort of remodeling or building project going on that Frank had me work at. Junior and I completely rebuilt the corrals and even added pens over that period. We put in a new type of sewer system, and we helped repipe the living quarters for Frank and Mary.

Once, I was exposed to the books of the store. I began looking for any discrepancies that might lead to why some of the people who traded at the store would think they were being cheated. Although the members of the various families were fine with me, they did not tell me what they thought as they did to Junior. I suppose it was because they thought I was on Frank's side because I was white and might not really listen to their complaints. Junior and I, however, became fast friends; and he would tell me from time to time about the complaints he got from people in the community. You have to know that the community was made up of about three hundred families who lived in the hills and countryside in all directions from the trading post. I suppose that there were about one thousand people in all if you counted the children. They all supported themselves by raising a garden of some sort, usually corn, squash, and melons. Each family had a few ponies that they rode or used to pull a wagon, and then there was the family herd of sheep with a few goats mixed in for mohair production and for eating.

After extensive time working in the store and pulling items from the shelves, I began to get a picture of the system. I waited on the family members as they came to trade. I learned how they were given credit for sheep, hides, wool, handmade jewelry, and the beautiful blankets that some of the women wove. Another part of the trading post business was the extensive trade in pawn. That is, a person would bring in something of value and present it to the trader, and he would evaluate it. He would offer the person about 25 percent of the retail value of the item as a credit that they could spend on store items – whether food, tools, or clothing items. The person then had ninety to 120 days to redeem the item by paying the value issued to them, plus an interest rate on the money loaned. If they could not, or did not, claim the item within the specified time, the item was put up for sale. The trader really made out well because his cost into the item was only about 25 percent of its value plus whatever the going rate for interest at the time, which, as I recall, was only about 3 percent to 5 percent for a loan from a bank.

My favorite place in the post was the pawn room. There were always early-model Winchester rifles and Colt Single Action pistols. Most of the pistols and rifles were chambered for the .45-long Colt although I did see one chambered for the hard-hitting .38-.40. This pistol had been pawned by Maurice McCabe. He pawned it several times while I worked at the post and, of course, came and retrieved it before it came up for sale. I always kept my eye on it. This pistol had a silver rattlesnake down the back strap with turquoise eyes! As I would fondle these beautiful weapons and realize how superior they were to my thunder gun, I knew that I must someday own at least one of each. Still though, my thunder gun, when fully loaded and at close range, would be of greater use or do more damage than either one of the rifles or pistols. My thunder gun, with its two 10-gauge loads of buckshot, could clear the whole room!

There were stacks of Navajo rugs. Each stack had been graded as to beauty and texture. The finer the weave – that is, the more threads per inch – usually, the more valuable the rug. Another factor considered for value was what type of dyes were used to color the wool threads. Commercial dyes were coming on strong; but they had not reached a point, as they would later on, where they replaced the natural dyes from plant materials. A good weaver spent many hours not only preparing the wool from her flock by combing it, cleaning it, and spinning it by hand into yarn, but also testing each piece of yarn and choosing which color to give it. She then spent time gathering plant materials such as leaves, plant stalks, and even bark from certain bushes and trees to boil. In these poultices of boiling water and plant materials the graded yarn would go to be colored to the proper tint for the design she had in mind. I have never been able to even begin to comprehend where the weavers come up with so many wonderful designs. They seem to come from an unpublished book of some sort, but I know that is not true. There is a God-given talent each weaver seems to have that enables her to come up with configurations that almost defy description. I have asked many of the weavers where the designs come from; and most just shrug their shoulders and using their chin as a pointer, as almost all Navajos do, point upward to indicate that it is a gift from a power in the sky.

I have been told that the first blankets were really serapes, like the Mexicans use to keep warm. That is, each blanket had a hole in the center where the head goes through, and the blanket is worn with half hanging down in front and the other half hanging down in back. I have seen a few of these and have even worn one on occasion. They are a wonderful piece of clothing, providing warmth and protection from the wind, but at the same time, allowing you to use your arms and hands for the work that needs to be done.

Another feature to always look for to see if the blanket is authentic is the *chi'indi* line. That is, a thread that is purposely woven from the interior of the design out through a corner of the border. At first, one would think this is a flaw in the design; but in reality, it is a thread purposely woven there to let the devil out of the rug.

In the pawn room were also many pieces of beautiful silver jewelry. Most of the jewelry was inlaid with turquoise. Not only were the Navajos able to trade and acquire the regular greenish-blue turquoise stones to inlay, but they had been able to find sources for turquoise stones with a reddish tint. I was told that the sources for these exquisite stones was either Mexico or from the Apaches who had several mines – the largest and best being near Silver City, New Mexico, called Santa Rita. The ornamentation of the inlays were exquisite! Frank had designed a series of parallel sticks that hung from a nail in the wall at the back of the room for putting rings on. Each ring was placed on one of the sticks. Several rows of these beauties made a unique display and always seemed to be full. As I would handle the waist belts with inlaid silver conchos and the intricate squash blossom necklaces, it would bring to mind the treasure room that had jewelry even way beyond these pieces in workmanship, beauty, and value. It was rarely that I saw a Navajo jewelry piece with any type of gold used.

For over two years, as we became involved with our new life, there in the shadow of all the happenings at the Toahani Trading Post, I do not recall us ever talking about the treasure site. I had taken my dagger from its hiding place in a niche I had found in our stone home and played around with it when Hanabah was not at home, but that was all I remember. I do not think that Hanabah even melted down any of the small pieces of Aztec jewelry to use for trading. We got along pretty well with what the flock provided and with my pay.

* * *

I was just starting to doze off after I had day of work cleaning out the corrals when Hanabah pushed open the door of our home.

"Peeerrrcccyyy!" she yelled in her shrill voice. "Come quick and help me get Jimmy inside!"

I jumped up and ran outside without even putting my boots on. I jumped from the top stair of our porch toward her. As soon as my bare feet hit the cold gravel, I was wide awake and trying to make out what was going on in the limited light of the evening. There was Hanabah trying to get Jimmy down off his pony. His hands were gripping the homemade saddle horn in an almost deathlike grip, and since his saddle was handmade from an old Grimsley packsaddle so his body was jammed between the horn and the superhigh cantle, she was not having any success. I could tell from his slumped body and blood on his clothes that Hanabah's concern was real.

"Jimmy, you have to let go. It is okay. We are here to help you," Hanabah pleaded as she pried his fingers loose, and I pulled from the other side to get him to fall into my arms.

Jimmy was a small man, so I could easily carry him into our house and lay him on my bed. I had found an old iron bedstead and concocted a sort of mattress that I placed over the rawhide bedsprings. No matter what I said, Hanabah would not sleep anywhere except on her tanned sheep hide on the floor in "her room" that she had at one end of the building separated with some hanging blankets.

"Oh, Jimmy, Jimmy, what have they done to you?" Hanabah said. "I told you they would keep trying to find where you were getting the gold."

"My son," she continued, "get me the clean towel and fill the basin from the pan of hot water on the stove. We have got to get him cleaned up and get to his wounds. He did not deserve this kind of treatment."

I learned later from Jimmy and from his daughter May Fern that three men, who had apparently been watching for their chance to waylay him, surrounded him as he was walking through the trees not far from his hogans to check on one of his flocks of sheep. They demanded to know where he was getting the gold he was trading for goods at the Standing Rock Trading Post.

After Hanabah and he had talked several years ago about some stranger asking questions at the Coyote Canyon Trading Post, Jimmy had decided to change where he did business, and so he began trading at Standing Rock. But here again, someone at the post in using the gold pieces in Gallup told the story of Jimmy showing up with the gold from time to time. Men's greed does terrible things to those who become infatuated with a determination for riches without any balance of goodness.

As the men pressured Jimmy to tell them his secret, he hollered for help but was soon quieted as they knocked him unconscious and kicked and beat him. They searched him and found a single piece of gold that he had melted down the night before. This so infuriated the leader that he kicked Jimmy one more time very viciously, and that is when he received the broken ribs on his right side. One of his family had heard him yell and alerted others. They ran shouting into the trees.

May Fern was herding one of the flocks not far from where Jimmy was attacked. She too heard the yell and, picking up a good throwing rock, also ran to where she had heard the yell. As she ran up the trail toward Jimmy, the three men ran toward her, trying to get away. Her aim was right on. The first man ducked as he saw the rock coming. The second man was not as lucky. The rock bounced off his head, leaving a nasty gash with blood flowing freely. The trio, seeing their retreat blocked on the main trail, made a quick left turn and scooted on down through a patch of cactus toward the canyon bottom and the road where their horses were tied. Even though they did not get the information they sought and had damaged Jimmy, they too suffered with cactus spines in their legs and behinds, and one had a big bloody knot on his head. This only infuriated them, and they vowed to come back and get what they considered their just due.

The family at his side could tell that Jimmy had been hurt very badly. May Fern demanded that someone go saddle his pony so they could put him on it and get him some help.

"There is only one person that I know who can help our father and make sure he is taken care of," May Fern said. "We must take him as fast as we can to Hanabah. She will take care of him, and she and Buckshot will protect him. We can take care of all of our father's business here and even defend against anyone who comes back. There are enough of us, and we can rely on the dogs to let us know if anyone comes near our homes."

It was May Fern who had lead the pony carrying Jimmy from his homeland to our home at the Toahani Trading Post. This journey for Jimmy was very painful due to his broken ribs and other wounds from the beating. The pain had caused him to grab on to that saddle horn and hold on with all the strength he had to keep his balance and try to endure the pain. That makeshift high-backed saddle was a real blessing in keeping him upright and supporting him so May Fern could concentrate on following the shortcut trails she knew to get him to our home.

Hanabah immediately set about getting some of her medicines made up so she could give them to Jimmy for the pain and to apply them to the wounds.

"The part that I hate the most is the broken ribs," she said, more to herself than to May Fern and me. "We will have to ask for help from above to make sure the ribs are not so damaged as to cut any parts inside of him. It will take many weeks for him to heal."

"May Fern, do you think that you were followed?" Hanabah added quickly. Before she could answer, Hanabah asked, "Does anyone else know that you brought him here?"

"No, Hanabah," May Fern addressed her with great respect, "I was not followed. I checked several times when I would stop to rest on high points along the trail where I could see my back trail. But yes, the whole family knows that I brought him here. But they will not tell. They are prepared to defend our homes and will fight anyone who comes near them."

"Good," Hanabah said. "I know your mother, Winona, and the other two are very strong and will not let anyone know where Jimmy is."

"Buckshot," Hanabah said, addressing me by my Navajo name in front of May Fern, "you go tell Junior and Frank and Mary of our situation and swear them to secrecy about our guest. The word must not get out so those men will not return."

I am surprised that Hanabah used my Navajo name in front of May Fern, but I was happy because I knew it impressed upon her my strength and manly position in our home.

"Now, my daughter and my son," Hanabah said. "I must say something about what has brought all this evil to us. You both have been told of the treasure room and the many other treasure sites. You both have been to the treasure room and have seen the great wealth it holds."

My mind raced as I listened to Hanabah talk. So May Fern, this beautiful, special person who was capturing my heart, was also privy to the whole story of the treasure! And she too had been taken to the treasure room and saw how it opened with the water flow, and perhaps she also had taken a valuable piece.

"I knew that Jimmy was using some of the treasure to feed his family and that he was trading at a new post at Standing Rock," Hanabah said. "Because we did not hear of any more strangers asking questions about the gold, he and I had figured that, whoever they were, they had lost interest."

There was one thing that I have never been able to figure out, and that is how the Navajos can communicate without any apparent contact with one another. I knew that Hanabah had lived with me at the trading post for over two years and had not traveled anywhere. She had been herding our flock of sheep each day, but could she and Jimmy have met somewhere and talked? I knew from traveling with her many times back and forth from our first home that when she starts to walk, she can outwalk even the fastest horse or mule. This is especially true when you get into tough country with lots of rocks, trees, and cacti.

"This is why I have not used the gold here since we moved here," Hanabah said. "I did not want Frank to take any more into Gallup and stir things up. He has asked me several times over our stay here when I was going to bring him more gold. I still do not trust him with our secret. Now with this terrible thing happening, we must be very careful that no one finds out where Jimmy is and that they do not figure out the connection between him and I. We want you two to have this treasure for yourselves as we know that you have the right heart and desires in life. Do not let us down."

Can you even begin to imagine my thoughts? The view of life at that point was a mixture of elation, mystery, wonder, and a sense of responsibility that I was overwhelmed with. I needed to clear my head and ponder on all of this. Was I on a trail that I could not get off of? And then why would I want to go in any other direction?

* * *

"Frank, I know that you believed that Hanabah and I were trustworthy and honest, or you would not have us living and working with you here at the post," I said. "I have something that I must ask of you and Mary and Junior. Please know that this request is of the utmost importance and, in fact, a life-or-death situation."

It was early morning, and customers had not made it to the trading post. Frank was in the little office going over the books. Mary was still involved in the living quarters, and I had seen Junior out back feeding the stock.

"You sound pretty serious, Buckshot," Frank said. "What could be all that important here in this laid-back part of the world?"

I could sense that he was not fully paying attention and probably just thought I was having indigestion or something. I reached over and closed the books. This got his attention really fast.

"Buckshot, that is not the way you should do things!" Frank replied in a very curt way as he arose from his chair to his full six-foot-one-inch height.

He had a temper, and I could feel the tension rising, but he had to understand what was going on, and I had to do it in such a way that would not divulge all of the details. I could not let him know the whole truth about the treasure. What a tricky position to be in – and with Jimmy's life at stake.

"I am sorry, Frank," I said. "But this is the most important thing I have ever had to talk to you about."

"Well, get on with it, and it better be real important!" he said with firmness.

"Frank, Jimmy Willeto came to our home last night all beat up and hurt real bad," I blurted out. "This was from a beating by some strangers way over by his homes. He needs to stay with us so Hanabah can tend to him while he recovers. It is very, very important that these men do not know where he is. They are determined to do him harm. Hanabah and I are asking you and Mary and Junior to not let anyone know he is staying at our place so he will not get beat up again."

His demeanor immediately softened as he heard about Jimmy. He knew Jimmy to be a very kind and respected man in this greater part of Navajo land and that no one would ever have reason to do him harm

"Why did they do this? Who are they?" he asked with a bit of fire in his eyes.

"At this early point, Jimmy has not been able to tell us the whole story," I said. "As it unfolds, we will explain it all, but can you help us in keeping his stay a secret?"

"Yes, of course," Frank said. "Can Hanabah do all that needs to be done? Is there anything I can help with?"

"I believe that she has most of what she needs, but if you have some towels or bandage material, I am sure it would be helpful," I said. "He is pretty bloody from a couple of head wounds."

"Mary! Mary!" he called out so that she could hear him from where she was in the living quarters.

"What is it, Frank?" Mary asked.

"I need some bandage material and some cloth to clean wounds," Frank said.

"My goodness, is it bad? Who is it for?"

"Please, just get me all you have on hand, and I will let Buckshot explain," he replied.

"On second thought," Frank said, turning to me, "let's leave Junior out of this. He has a tendency to tell too many people about too much of the business that goes on around here. Did anyone come with Jimmy? What about his pony and saddle?"

"His daughter May Fern brought him here," I said. "She led his pony. The saddle does have some blood on it."

"Is she staying with you and Hanabah also?" Frank asked.

"We really have not talked about that, but I suppose she will want to be beside him and take care of him," I said. "We still have to take our sheep out and will need the help."

Frank mused for a moment. Mary brought in an armful of white material for bandages and some other cloth for cleaning wounds.

"Buckshot, you take these clothes to your home," Frank said. "Go out the front and around the post. I will call Junior in from the back so he will not see you. As soon as you get home, wash the saddle and anything else that is bloody. Make up a story that May Fern has come to learn from and help Hanabah, and keep Jimmy out of sight."

Well, that is what we did. Junior got curious a couple of times and asked some questions about May Fern staying with us. We had divided the house when we first moved in with a couple of blankets so as to make two rooms; so May Fern stayed in Hanabah's "bedroom" while I slept in my bedstead in what was a multipurpose kitchen, living room, and bedroom.

When I told Mary what I had requested of Frank, she fell right into the spirit of things and even suggested that May Fern come over to the post during our reading time at the end of each day to join us and learn to read. What a blessing that was! This gave me a special time with May Fern where I got to see her real intellect and know her better. Soon, she was outreading me in just about every way. She was such a quick learner.

Mary had us read not only from scriptures in the Bible and Book of Mormon, but she also had copies of other delightful books, such as *The New England Primer of 1777* with all its prose and inspiration and patriotism and the wonderful McGuffey's Readers. I believe there were seven books that made up the set.

Mary had the very latest set of 1879. As I recall, the lessons taught included every aspect of family, friends, and animal relationships. A story I will never forget was titled "The Widow and the Merchant." It told about a merchant with a kind heart who helped a widow, and as she proved her trustworthiness, he rewarded her with a special gift. I just wish the educators of today were still using these well-proven tools to teach the basic values that are so needed in this day and age. The basic education May Fern and I received from Mary put us on a path toward our wonderful life together.

Well, Jimmy was soon on the mend with Hanabah's tender care. I continued to work at the post, and May Fern took the sheep out most days but always had them back in time for our reading lesson.

Besides my regular chores and work at the post, Frank had me become more and more involved with the bookkeeping of the business. We had ledger books with accounts for the families whom he trusted to carry a balance of credit for when they sheared their sheep or would bring in a new woven Navajo blanket or have sheep or cattle to send to market.

I began to see why the young men of the community were talking themselves into a frenzy over being what they thought was cheating on the part of Frank:

First of all, the young men who were making the most fuss had never really worked. They did not have an education although the government presented them with the opportunity to learn at boarding schools. They put up a front of seeming to be hurt so that they could not continue their traditions and still make it in a changing world.

Secondly, the perception these young men had of business was that a trader should just "trade dollars." That is, if he purchased an item for $1 from the wholesale warehouse in Gallup and brought it to the post way out in their community, he should sell it to them for $1. Ludicrous as this thinking may seem to anyone with an understanding of business and all the expenses involved, this nevertheless was their mind-set. Someone at the wholesale warehouses was feeding them the wholesale prices and fanning their discontent without explaining how business really worked.

Thirdly, when the trader purchased blankets, jewelry, animals, wool, or hides from their families, they felt that he should pay them the same amount as if they were selling their items at retail in Gallup. Yet they were not willing, in almost every case, to make the effort to go to Gallup themselves and market their products.

Finally, when they saw that the trader was making a very sizeable profit on merchandise by reselling their products and/or by selling pawn, they were incensed! Admittedly, the profit percent was much higher than "in town," but with the investment and risk that had to be taken with the uncertainties, the traders considered it to be a fair percentage.

As I learned all of this and also about the mind-set of the community, I could see that an explosive situation was brewing unless someone could negotiate some type of compromise. This was very unlikely in that both sides were so ingrained in their thinking and had been so for many, many years.

And then there was the ever-present trigger that would put this powder keg into a regrettable event. For whatever reason, alcohol in just about any form – from beer to wine to hard whiskey – taken by a Navajo or just about any person soon causes all reason to vanish.

* * *

We had a hard time keeping Jimmy inside as his wounds healed. The broken ribs caused him pain with every breath, but there was nothing Hanabah could do except bind them up to lessen their movement and, thus, pain. All of this healing took about six weeks. Members of Jimmy's family drifted to and from his home to see him, but we had to keep the traffic to a minimum so no one would suspect he was staying in our home. Once, when the door was open to let in some fresh air, a woman going after plant material farther up the canyon passed by and looked in. Jimmy was sitting on the edge of my bed, and I do not know how she failed to recognize him or at least be curious as to who he was. Hanabah later saw her while she was gathering her materials, and she made no mention of the event.

May Fern and I seemed to grow closer and closer in our thinking and everyday activities as all of us lived and worked together with Hanabah and Jimmy. You have to know that I was basically very shy, but my heart kept telling me that I should be paying more attention to this special creature. What wonderful turmoil! I had no education about the fairer sex and not even a clue as to how to proceed with any more than a cursory friendship – but my very being was tugging at me to extend my opportunity to become even closer.

One day, while helping her move a tub of water that she had been using to rinse some clothes after scrubbing them, we accidentally touched hands; and I thought I would explode with that happening. We just stood there holding hands with a tub of water between us.

The next day, as we were returning home in the twilight of the evening after our reading session with Mary, our hands seemed to meet; and that was the official start of our courtship. We both were nineteen years of age. That was a proper age for courtship back in those days. The feelings of those days are emblazoned on my heart and in my mind. She was such a beautiful person in every way. When I was with her, I knew what heaven must be all about!

We knew the day was fast approaching when Jimmy would be leaving to go back home. We all sat in our home, and while eating a great meal of mutton stew and fry bread, we discussed a plan. Jimmy's family had been checking from time to time at the Standing Rock Trading Post and discovered that the strangers had not been seen. They also hadn't surfaced at Coyote Canyon. Our assumption was that they had had enough with the altercation where they had hurt Jimmy so bad. Maybe that rock that May Fern had thrown had knocked some sense into the head of at least one of them; but we could not be sure, for when greed takes hold, men will do strange things to get what they want.

Jimmy was the senior of the group and had traveled somewhat. He had been as far away as Albuquerque to the east and Flagstaff to the west. These were significant towns because they represented the approximate eastern and western boundaries of the traditional Navajo Nation. The northern boundary was pretty well recognized as Navajo Mountain, and the southern boundary was accepted as the Zuni lands. Jimmy was finally well enough to speak.

"I feel we have been tested to see what we will do with the great treasure we have been given," he said. "We could have taken it and hired a group to go and kill those men. We could have gathered up the treasure in wagons and gone to one of the great towns and spent it on homes and parties and more wagons and horses. We could buy up land and have a large ranch. And then we could give it away to everyone around us and watch as they become drunk with the evils it would buy them for a short period of time."

"But no," he continued, "we have licked our wounds and stayed the course we have always known of working and learning. I am very proud of my daughter for learning how to read. She has shared with me stories from the book about our maker and the other book that is a history of our people from long ago. All the things she has told me are true, for they teach us to love one another and that evil is wrong. When I first became a healer, I was taught that man has very limited powers compared to our maker. I have learned that we must rely on what May Fern says is God to look with favor down upon us, and if we ask with a pure heart, he will hear us. The great blessings I have had in life of healing, many have always come from this source, and I tell the people about it although there are many who do not believe. I see that

Buckshot is a true man, even though he does not have the pure blood of the Diné running through his veins. His heart is in the right place with love and respect and honesty. He will make a fine son-in-law."

What had just happened? We had not even talked about marriage, but Jimmy could see the change in his daughter and probably watched me as I walked on air when I was around her. It is not much of a challenge to see when young lovers are head over heels with each other.

"I feel we must come up with a better plan to make use of the treasure so we do not have more trouble," Jimmy continued. "I think that we should take pieces of the treasure to faraway places like Albuquerque or even a place I have heard about called Denver. We can go there in disguise so they do not know who we really are or where we really come from. If we are careful and not followed, we can trade pieces of the treasure for money that can be spent anywhere. The second part of the plan is to decide what we are going to do with the money before we had it so we are not tempted to spend it foolishly. I have seen people who come into wealth make bad choices as they think their new wealth is unlimited and that it has all of a sudden made them very wise. Wealth cannot make one wise. True wisdom only comes from hard work and experiences helping others and learning about the good ways of life."

I think back on his great wisdom, and I am so thankful that he was such an important part of my life. I thank the Lord that I had the sense to listen to him. I thank the Lord for Hanabah and all that she brought into my life – especially May Fern.

"Your idea is very wise, Jimmy," Hanabah said, sensing an opening. "Buckshot would be the perfect one to travel and learn how to make the trade. He has learned much about how the trading post works and how money changes hands. I do want to point out that you have taken on a much bigger burden than my son and I. You have chosen to have three families, and therefore, there are many members of your family. I want you to know that my heart tells me that your family should have whatever they need. I want you to know that the treasure is not to be divided up by our two families, but by the needs of those who are good and honest and want to raise families who will be raised in the same way. I have no greed in my heart, and I know my son's heart is pure and also feels the same way."

I nodded in agreement and watched as Jimmy shifted his body enough to know that he too was waiting for such a declaration. Jimmy pondered what was said for a few moments, and then he continued.

"I think that we should decide now what is needed for our family members to allow them to continue to grow and become the best they can without any charity," he said. "I do not want anyone to have a free ride where they do not have to put forth effort to learn the value of work. And I want all my children and grandchildren to learn to read and write and to be able to keep records of all they do. Hanabah, we have been so blessed with children who can make this happen. I wish that both of you will take this load upon you and promise me and Hanabah that you will not fail in this."

May Fern and I took each other by the hand. We looked into each other's eyes and confirmed our commitment and then turned to face both Jimmy and Hanabah.

I spoke for us.

"Jimmy and my mother, we promise we will honor all the things that are said here and that you have taught us. We will work hard to make sure the family is taken care of as you have instructed."

Chapter 5

MAY FERN AND I were married a few months later on October 17, 1900, in a traditional Navajo ceremony held at the Willeto ranch that was attended by people from miles around. Jimmy conducted the ceremony as a shaman has the authority to do so under Navajo tradition. We then traveled into Gallup where the bishop of the local ward solemnized our union.

Mary and Frank had introduced me to Bishop Roundy and his wife, Anne, about a year before our marriage on one of their trips out on to the reservation. They were such friendly people and so concerned for all the members of the little Gallup branch of the church. Bishop Roundy had been a bishop of one of the wards in Utah before moving to Gallup to work as a stationmaster for the railroad. He interviewed me and ordained me an elder some six months before our marriage when Frank sent me on one of the regular freight trips into Gallup. Frank had me make that trip just for such a purpose.

May Fern and I continued to study the Gospel on our own and with Frank and Mary. I had the privilege of baptizing her and confirming her as a member of the church in November of 1901.

I feel I should share with you our discoveries regarding the truthfulness of the Gospel and the fact that it has been restored back here on earth through the prophet Joseph Smith. May Fern and I spent many evenings studying the scriptures to determine for ourselves where the scriptures pointed for a full, purposeful life. Just like the rock pictures point to physical treasure, we felt very strongly that the Bible, Book of Mormon, the Pearl of Great Price, and the Doctrine and Covenants would give us direction for the great and true treasures of a purposeful life.

The foremost truth we found to be answers to our prayers. It is sometimes difficult for people to take the first step of kneeling and asking for guidance. Our exposure to the scriptures with Mary brought us to this great truth from the Book of Mormon in the Book of Moroni:

> Behold, I would exhort you that when ye shall read these things, if it be wisdom in God that ye should read them, that ye would remember how merciful the Lord hath been unto the children of men, from the creation of Adam even down until the time that ye shall receive these things, and ponder it in your hearts. And when ye shall receive these things, I would exhort you that ye would ask God, the Eternal Father, in the name of Christ, if these things are not true; and if ye shall ask with a sincere heart, with real intent, having faith in Christ, he will manifest the truth of it unto you, by the power of the Holy Ghost. (Moroni 10:3-4)

We prayed and did as Moroni admonished. We received answers to our prayers, so we knew we were on the right path. I remember my father teaching me about the priesthood and how someday, I too would hold it as he did. He had been ordained to the Melchizedek Priesthood by President Brigham Young. He emblazoned on my young mind the fact that men, no matter what leaning they claimed, could not act in God's name without the priesthood. He was so proud of the fact that he could trace his priesthood ordination right back to the Savior himself. He told me that Brigham Young had been ordained to the priesthood by the Three Witnesses to the Book of Mormon with Oliver Cowdery as the mouth for the ordination and that he, Oliver Cowdery, had been ordained to the priesthood by Peter, James, and John, apostles of old who appeared to him and Joseph Smith on the banks of the Susquehanna River in 1830. They had been ordained by the Savior himself. I knew the importance of this, and as I shared these facts with May Fern and we studied the scriptures together, we grew in our knowledge of the Gospel and worked every day to do and be as the scriptures taught.

As I stated earlier, I was ordained by the bishop of the Gallup ward, and he gave me his priesthood lineage. He too could trace his sacred ordination back through President Brigham Young and this to the Savior himself. I knew I had the true priesthood to act in God's name. I have seen the power of this many times in my life.

But I get ahead of my story. I love to dwell on the love we had and the great years we spent loving each other. Tragedy came into the picture that dictated some changes in our lives.

I have told about the undercurrent that was going on at the trading post. Well, shortly after May Fern and I got married, a lot of things seemed to fall apart. Frank and Mary gave us a wonderful reception at the post and had it all decorated up for the occasion. We were really treated special by the majority of the community, but there always seem to be disgruntled people in life who want others to be as miserable as they are.

Hanabah insisted that May Fern and I move into the rock building while she had a new hogan built. One of the features about a hogan is that it can be built in a relatively short time since it consists of just one room with one door. Well, we had sort of a house raising and built her new home within a couple of weeks on the other side of the canyon about two hundred yards from us. We all got along well and had things going pretty smoothly. With the wedding, reception, and hogan raising, we did not give the treasure and direction of it all much thought.

* * *

On a Monday morning in the spring of 1901, Mary said she would be going into town instead of Frank to get the week's merchandise and supplies. She wanted me to go along to drive the wagons. I say wagons in that we had the regular big old freight wagon that we could hitch up either two big old workhorses, or if we used the trailer wagon for extra merchandise, we could add an extra team. This day, we figured that a double team was needed as we had some farm implements that needed to be picked up. The tribe had authorized a disk, harrow, and small planter be purchased for the local chapter. This was so any of the families who wanted to plant larger fields would have the implements to do it with. Things were looking up in our community. We had even started building a rock chapter house where we could hold meetings and events.

I asked if May Fern could go as she wanted to do some shopping, and Mary readily agreed.

"We women need to stick together," Mary said. "I can teach her a thing or two about spending your money." She laughed and said, "We need to leave in an hour or so. Frank is preparing the list of supplies."

Junior, who was still our mainstay at the post, said he was glad it was me and not him going into town as he hated that old long ride on the bumpy wagon. I laughed as he sort of jumped up and down, demonstrating how happy he felt. He helped me wrangle the two teams and get them hitched to the main wagon. We then had to attach the bull prick to the main wagon with the chain attached to the front axel. This arrangement allowed for the team to start the main wagon rolling and then for the trailer wagon to come into play. It was like when a train starts up and the cars jerk forward one by one. The bull prick was a straight piece of iron rod with a ring of metal that slid along it to the stop at the end. A short piece of chain held the rod just below the rear axel of the wagon. The short tongue of the trailer wagon was attached with a chain to this loop of steel that slipped along the bull prick.

We had an additional seat we placed on the sideboards of the main wagon right behind the seat for the driver. Both seats were mounted on a set of springs. This made the wagon ride bearable. As you know, freight wagons of that day did not have springs. The wagons were at the mercy of the road with its rocks, chuckholes, and ruts. May Fern and I sat in the front seat. Frank handed Mary the list and gave her a kiss. He then helped her step up on the hub of the front wheel so she could then step into the wagon and take her place in the second seat. He then handed up a lunch she had prepared for us. I rather enjoyed the twenty-mile trip into Gallup. Our teams could step right out, and we could be in town in about four hours. By pushing it, we could load up and be back a little after dark; but for this trip, we were to stay overnight. This was to prove to be fortunate for us.

We had no communication at the trading post other than someone riding horseback. Frank had thought about putting in a telegraph and connecting it into the main line that ran from Gallup up to Shiprock but could never justify the cost.

"You sure know how to get the most out of the teams," Mary said as we moved right along the dirt road.

"Frank bought good animals, and he keeps them well fed. They are young and even then, like to get out and go to town," I said with a laugh. "I will have to slow down for the draws. That last rain made the bottoms a little rough with all the new gravel washing in."

We had a pleasant trip. The weather was cool. Some clouds floated lazily in the sky, giving us a shot at shade every once in a while. The wagons contained folded-up tarps for covering the freight, but we did not have the bows in place to make them true "covered wagons." We did not anticipate any rain, so we just enjoyed the breeze blowing in our faces. You know, there is nothing quite like driving a four-up team and seeing and feeling their power. They even have a smooth smell of sweat that lets you know they are relaxed and pulling their best.

I loved Mary's homemade bread sandwiches. She also made her own jam that gave us variety, along with the sliced roast beef sandwiches. Her cookies, pies, and cakes were to die for. Each trip provided some of these delicacies. I always waited until the lunchbox was open to see what dessert we would have to work on.

We arrived in Gallup and went straight to the warehouse district next to the railroad yards so they could load up our freight. The women only had to walk a short distance to the hotel we always stayed at. I, in turn, took the teams to the stockyard a few blocks away to unharness them and put them in corrals for the night.

A night on the town was to eat at the Cattleman's Café next to the hotel. You could have a juicy T-bone with all the trimmings for $1.75 and then a piece of their famous apple pie for another 10¢. What a treat.

"May Fern, let's go over to the mercantile and see what is new," I said. "They will still be open for about another hour."

"Make sure not to spend any of *my* money," I laughingly said to May Fern.

"What do you mean *your* money?" she asked. "Once you earn it, it becomes *our* money, and you have put me in charge of spending."

She had learned fast, but I knew that she was frugal and would not fritter it away. I went straight to the hotel where I ordered a bath. By the time I had finished cleaning up and went to our room, the ladies were back. We chatted for a few minutes, and then Mary went to her room.

* * *

The excited pounding on our hotel room door jolted me from my sound sleep. Who could possibly want me at this before-dawn hour?

It was Junior.

"Quick, you have got to come back to the post," he blurted out. "They have taken Frank and are going to kill him!"

"Kill him? What are you talking about? Who is trying to kill him?" I asked.

"Some of the young men got real drunk on some stolen whiskey and have raided the trading post," Junior said. "They have set fire to the buildings and turned all the animals loose. There is no one to stop them. Frank tried to fight them, but they wounded him and drug him away. They say they are going to kill him!"

"What about Hanabah? Where is she?" I asked.

Junior was shaking as he tried to answer my questions.

"I do not know where she is," he said. "But everyone in the community knows what is going on. I rode here as fast as I could. I was afraid they would also kill me. I hid for a while until I could catch a horse."

By this time, May Fern was fully awake and packing up our belongings. We only had one valise; and so with my putting on my shirt, pants, hat, and boots, we were ready to go.

"You go talk to Mary and ease the news to her," I said. "I will go straight to the sheriff's office and see if I can gather up a posse and get some weapons. I will also see if I can get a buggy that will carry all of us."

I ran as fast as I could with Junior in tow to the sheriff's office. The county was controlled by the white folks, and the sheriff was not known for his kind feelings toward Navajos. Gallup had been a place for tribal members to go on weekends to trade and, in too many instances, to get drunk. As whiskey was not allowed on the reservation and drunkenness was not openly tolerated in town, those who did get a bottle would rapidly chugalug it down, severely endangering their life. They would then seek a place to tolerate the drunk. Many times, they would end up in the Rio Puerco under one of the bridges. Drunkenness was a major problem and a major cause of death for the Navajos. Many times, the members would get drunk in the wintertime and decide to walk back home. With the warmth and feeling of invincibility the whiskey gave them, they would start the long walk. Each spring, more than several bodies would be found where they had come to a barbed wire fence and just slumped over it and died.

I walked through the open door to the sheriff's office to find two deputies arguing about who would clean up the cells or at least who was to supervise while some of the inmates cleaned up the terrible-smelling mess.

"I need some help," I said. "The Toahani Trading Post has been set on fire, and I am afraid that the trader may be in danger."

I was dressed like a Navajo, so they did not give much credence to my statements.

"How do you know this?" questioned one of the deputies.

"This man right here just rode in from there," said the other deputy.

"Even if it is true, you have to understand that the sheriff is out of town in Santa Fe at a conference," the deputy said. "There is just the two of us, and we sure don't want to go out on the res and try and save anyone. You will have to wait until the sheriff gets back."

"And when will that be?" I asked with complete shock at their attitude.

"Oh, I bet he will be back by the first of the week," said one of the grinning deputies looking at the other.

I have a temper, and back then, it was always very close to the surface. I could plainly see that they were not going to be of any help. I turned before I knew I would say something to get myself in trouble and pushed Junior out of the doorway ahead of me into the street.

The bishop lived just a couple of blocks away, so I yelled at Junior over my shoulder.

"You go to the stable or corrals and get us a buggy with a fast team that will carry all of us. I will get some help and meet you there."

The bishop's wife answered the door.

"Is the bishop in?" I asked. "I have an emergency."

"Why no, he left yesterday on a buying trip for the railroad and will not be back for several days," she said. "What is the emergency?"

"I think they might be doing Frank harm – maybe even kill him out at the trading post," I blurted out. "I need some help. The sheriff's deputies won't help. I need some guns and anyone who will go with me."

"What about Mary and May Fern?" she asked.

"They are here in town with me on a freight trip and are okay," I said.

To make a long story short, I finally found a member of the elders' quorum, and he agreed to go along with me. In addition, he had quite a collection of firearms and was able to loan me a Winchester in .30-.30 caliber and several boxes of shells. The sun was still not up by the time he and I arrived at the stables.

Junior had a surrey all hitched up with a pair of beautiful geldings that looked like they were real travelers. Mary, in tears, with May Fern supporting her, was just getting into the backseat of the three-seater. I got up front with Brother Brimhall. Junior and the baggage, guns, and canteens were in the middle seat.

"Now don't you boys get my buggy or horses all shot up," said the stable hand.

This, of course, put Mary into a fresh set of crying. Couldn't he understand what was going on?

The team was everything they appeared to be. They moved briskly along. In spite of the poor road for such a surrey, we made it to within a mile or so of the post within two and a half hours. We could see the smoke coming from the canyon although we could not see the buildings themselves. About the time we would be able to see down into the canyon bottom, those who had caused the trouble would be able to see us. Brother Brimhall and I decided to leave the buggy with Mary and May Fern and go the rest of the way on foot. Junior said he would also stay and take care of the horses.

"If you hear shooting, you make sure and load the women up in the surrey and head back toward town," I said to Junior off to the side where the women could not hear me.

I was very concerned about Hanabah as I knew she was not the type to back off from a fight or to retreat if she thought she could save someone. Outnumbered though, I was not sure what she might do. *If I had only taught her how to load and fire the thunder gun properly*, I thought. Even then, she might have figured it out and loaded it for her protection.

We made it to the hill overlooking the post in just a few minutes. All seemed to be quiet. There was no movement except for the smoke rolling lazily upward from the corrals, warehouse, and trading post. I was glad to see that Hanabah's hogan was still intact. I could not see our home, but with no smoke coming from that direction, I assumed it also had not been harmed.

We slipped down over the rimrock a little south of where the main road cuts through to the canyon bottom. The road might be watched, and we wanted to surprise anyone who still might want to make a fight of it. Generally, my experience with drunks is that they go from a euphoric high with the whiskey to a stupor low, then to a sleep, and then a very painful hangover. I was betting that our attackers were in the latter stage by now and were not in any condition to put up much of a fight. I could imagine trying to shoot with a gigantic headache and blurry eyes.

"Let's stay fairly close together and circle around to the right," I said. "I want to get to Hanabah's hogan before we reconnoiter the trading post buildings to make sure she is okay."

"All right," he said, "but keep a sharp lookout for any signs of the raiders sleeping it off by the buildings."

Brother Brimhall also had a Winchester lever action in .30-.30 configuration and a Colt Single Action in .45-long Colt caliber. I had been told that he was a very good shot, especially with the rifle.

Once I got past the smoldering corrals and could not see anyone in the way, I began to run toward the hogan and yelled for Hanabah.

"Percy, Percy, they have done a terrible thing," Hanabah said comfortingly as she opened the door. "There was not anything I could do to stop them. They knew better than to harm me but told me to stay away and stay in my hogan, or they would kill me."

"I love you so much and am so happy to find you okay," I said.

I threw my arms around her. I could feel her body snuggle up to me in a thankful moment of love.

"Everything else we can repair or replace," I said.

"I will come with you to find Hasteen Frank," Hanabah said. "I saw them take him away down the canyon."

We first went over to the smoldering ruins of the trading post. The thick adobe walls were still standing. The roof and floor had burned. All the goods and furniture were either burned or scattered around the yard. We could see a few sheep and a couple of cows grazing a little ways down the canyon, but no sign of any other life.

As we were walking down the canyon, I glanced into the wash about one hundred yards below the doorway of what was left of the buildings. There, staked out in a large flat of the wash, was Frank. He had been brutally killed and mutilated. It was one of the saddest days of my life. He had been good to me and taught me much.

"We need to have a plan," I said. "Mary should not see Frank this way. Let's see if we can find some lumber and nails and build a box to put his remains in. Then we can give him a proper burial. Hanabah, will you please go back along the road to town and meet with the women and Junior. Have them come to our house while we take care of Frank."

When drunk, there is no organized plan, even one of destruction. As I looked over the remains of the warehouse, which was also a small repair shop, I found a handsaw, a hammer, and nails. There were enough pieces of lumber for Brother Brimhall and me to make a crude coffin for Frank. We found that one of the wagons had not been fully destroyed. We pulled it out where we could hitch up the surrey team to it when the surrey came up. With the wagon and Junior's help, we retrieved Frank's body, put it into the coffin, and nailed a top on it.

It was a little after noon by this time, and some of the local families started to show up to view the terrible tragedy. The talked among themselves in muffled voices, and then each family went over to our house and expressed their sorrow to Mary. It was a sad day for everyone because of bad judgment fueled with the curse of whiskey!

"Sweetheart," said May Fern as she came to meet me with the wagon bearing the coffin, "Mary was pretty well resigned as to Frank's fate even when you and Brother Brimhall left us to go check out the trading post. She is strong, and we have had a good talk. She would like it if he was buried in the little hill to the south overlooking the trading post. She said that he had laughingly said one time that if anything ever happened to him, he wanted to be buried there where he could watch over his dream. Can you take care of that?"

That was one of the great attributes that May Fern had. She could quickly look over a situation, make a firm, good decision, and then see that the details are taken care of. She had such a pure heart, and it was so full of love for good people.

"Sure, I saw a shovel over near the shop," I said. "I will see if I can find a pick, and we will get a grave dug. It is best if we can have the funeral before sundown."

We had the service on top of the little hill with all of us there, along with several families from the community, to wish Frank goodbye. One of May Fern's brothers rode up about the time we were filling in the grave to tell us that Jimmy's families had learned of the terrible event and were on their way to help in any way they could.

May Fern, Mary, and Hanabah stayed at our home while Brother Brimhall, Junior, and I slept in the hogan. We took turns watching during the night should any of the worthless scoundrels show up for more evil, but as in most cases like this perpetuated by liquor-filled cowards, we heard no more from them for several weeks.

The next morning, after a breakfast of what we could come up with, we helped Mary sift through her living quarters. She was able to find a couple of pieces of dinnerware and a few other keepsakes, but most of her possessions were either destroyed in the fire or stolen by the evil perpetrators. It was easy to see that Mary was drained of spirit, and physically, she was left without her normal exuberance. As her best friend at this great time of need, May Fern was doting over her in every way possible. Mary had been such a support for us and had taught us much.

Jimmy and his families pulled onto the scene of devastation about midafternoon. They arrived with three wagons of food and camping gear. Many of the older children walked as there was not enough room for them in the wagons. They soon set up camp between our home and Hanabah's hogan. They each embraced Mary and let her know of their love as they remembered how she and Frank had protected Jimmy when he was in need.

"Mary, my family will be here until you are completely satisfied with organizing all of the things that we can put back together and rebuild for you," Jimmy said from his stance on a box in front of our house. "We know how to make adobe and corrals and to find your animals and see that they are accounted for."

Mary was sitting in one of our chairs in the shade by our front door. She managed a small smile and nodded her approval to what he said.

With the help of Jimmy's three families and families from the community, we had the fiasco cleaned up and looking as best we could within about a week. New corrals were built for the few animals we could find, and a place was designated over in the wash in the main canyon to bury all of the items that could not be salvaged. After hauling a number of wagons full of such material, we systematically caved the sides of the wash in to completely bury the items out of sight.

We did not pressure Mary for any thoughts she had for the future. We watched as each day, she would walk to the little hill where Frank was buried and kneel by his grave for a while. Grief takes time, and time is a great healer. She needed time to try to accept all that had tragically happened. We were there to help her as she and Frank had given us all so much of themselves.

Jimmy and Winona, May Fern's mother, Hanabah, May Fern, and I had a meeting. We talked about what we could really do to help Mary. We had physically helped as much as we could to clean and straighten things out, but the trading post could not operate in this sorry condition. Should we dip into the treasure and help her purchase what was needed to rebuild? What was her desire for the future? We had been watching and waiting for her decision, and it wasn't long in coming. About ten days after returning and while Jimmy and his families were still camped and working as best they could to rebuild the trading post, Mary asked if we would all come and sit by her in front of our house so she could tell us something.

"All of my precious friends," she said, "I could not have asked for more than what you have given to me at this sad time in my life. You have given your all. I love you and thank you, but I must move on with my life. I have decided what I want to do."

Everyone was quiet as we waited to hear what she had to say. This would be a turning point for all of us. This was our home as well, and we needed to know what she wanted so we could build around her desires.

"I will leave and return to Salt Lake as soon as I can get transportation," Mary said. "I need to settle up my affairs in Gallup with the wagons and merchandise. I have a small savings account in the bank there that Frank and I had put together. We had invested all we could into the trading post in hopes it would provide a very substantial anchor for all the local families. But alas, our dreams and Frank's life were taken from us. I cannot go on without the love of my life. In fact, I do not want to go on here without him. I need to start over, and I have family in the Salt Lake area that will be my support. Please do not think ill of me for quitting and leaving. I just cannot continue on. Therefore, I want to give this post for what it may be worth to Buckshot and May Fern. They are very capable and can build it back if they so choose."

Chapter 6

LIFE IS A complete testing ground to see what you are made of. Each one of us is tested mentally, physically, spiritually, and emotionally in a major way at least once. I felt as though this great turn of events was a test almost beyond what I could endure. Yes, there was opportunity and hope for a great future, but the burden of responsibility was so complex and included so many families. I did not know if I could do it. May Fern and I were both twenty years of age, and we were being handed the reins to an all-encompassing community operation. What a wonderful set of mixed blessings. On top of all of this, May Fern had just informed me that she was carrying our first child.

"Jimmy, I need you and my mother to help us make some very big decisions," I said. "We cannot put this post back together without money to build back the buildings and to stock it with merchandise. In addition, I feel that we should help Mary in some way by perhaps purchasing the wagons and teams that are in town, along with the supplies that have been loaded onto the wagons. What do you feel is the best thing to do with all of this?"

Before he could answer me, I noted some activity over by the charred post buildings. All of the people were gathering on the far side of the burned-out buildings, but I could not see why. As I hurriedly walked to where I could see, I saw three mounted men. Upon closer inspection, I saw that they were wearing badges. I knew it must finally be a visit from the sheriff's office.

Mary was in our house gathering her belongings and saying her goodbyes to May Fern and Hanabah. In all the commotion of the last ten days or so, we had not seen to taking the surrey back to town. We just assumed that it would be the transportation for Mary or whomever in going back into town to settle affairs there.

"We are here to notify you that the owner of the surrey has filed charges of theft of it and the team and harnesses," the deputy said.

I couldn't believe that he was saying such a thing with all the destruction right in front of him.

"We are here to take it back and find out who stole it," he added.

My indignation level went from zero to right over the top in one second flat. Here was a widow who had just lost her husband and all they owned, and these public servants were concerned about a surrey and team of horses. And even then, there were two trading post wagons in town and two teams of horses that represented way more in value. I have never been able to understand bureaucrats and the arrogance that they acquire the minute they think they have some authority.

"Well, you see, sir, we have just had a man murdered and the complete destruction of this trading post," I said. "The matter of the surrey and team are the furthest from our minds, and as you can see, they are right over there in good shape. In fact, the widow is about to take the surrey to return to Gallup to settle her affairs."

The two deputies I had spoken with in Gallup at the sheriff's office must not have ever mentioned our conversation and notification that there had been a raid on the post. To the credit of the deputy doing all the talking, he was fully taken aback with this information and quickly dismounted and took off his hat. The other two followed his lead, and they too dismounted and removed their hats. Someone had taught them a few manners.

"Where is this widow woman?" one of the deputies asked in a softer tone of voice. "I would like to see if we can be of service to her."

I turned to see if I could find out where Mary was. She was just about over to the surrey that Junior had all hitched up. May Fern and Hanabah were helping her carry items she would take with her in the surrey.

"That is her over there in the blue bonnet putting things in the surrey," I said, motioning toward her. "If you look up on that hill, you will see the headstone of her husband's grave. We buried him a week ago Tuesday. He was murdered by the bunch who also burned down the trading post. She was lucky that my wife and I had taken her into town for the weekly merchandise run. She too would have probably been killed."

The deputy, who I later found out was Charlie Dunham, gave some quick instructions to his two assistants about tying up the horses and starting to look around while he went over to talk to Mary. I watched as he walked over by the corrals where she was and struck up a conversation with her.

* * *

Our group had a meeting and decided to purchase all that Mary wanted to sell, including the wagons and teams, and that we would even give her an amount that would make her feel like we were not taking advantage of her. We just might recoup some of the items from the post if any of the men were caught. It was a bit of a gamble, but we wanted to err on the side of being fair with her. She had lost so much with Frank being murdered. Her life needed as big a boost as possible.

She returned to Gallup in the surrey with May Fern and me. We saw to it that she completely settled all her affairs and got on the train to take her to Salt Lake. It would be a circuitous route as there was no direct rail link, but she would be there in a few short days. She sent a telegram ahead so her relatives would know of her situation and would be expecting her.

May Fern and I explained to her that it would take us a little while to come up with the money to pay her, but that we had a source for the funds. We agreed on a total amount and said our goodbyes with tears and heart pangs. We kept our word, and due to the circumstances of life, we never saw her again.

In the meantime, as agreed on before we left with Mary to go to Gallup, Jimmy and Hanabah went to the treasure site, opened it, and took sufficient gold and silver items that we would need to fund the purchase of the trading post reconstruction. We were so blessed.

Then we learned the news at the bank with Mary that the national government had passed the Gold Standard Act. In fact, it had been passed a year before the tragedy, on March 14, 1900. The significance to us was that it established the standard as to the value of gold! The timing could not have been better. We needed to take some of the melted items and present them to a banking institution or to an assayer's office so we could get currency for our purchases and for hiring workers. We would no longer have to sneak around and go through the extensive barter negotiations for the value of our melted gold!

The act states that the law was to be "an Act To define and fix the standard of value, to maintain the panty of all forms of money issued or coined by the United States, to refund the public debt, and for other purposes .... Be it enacted ... that the dollar consisting of twenty-five and eight-tenths grains of gold nine-tenths fine, as established by section thirty-five hundred and eleven of the Revised Statutes of the United States, shall be the standard unit of value, and all forms of money issued or coined by the United States shall be maintained at a parity of value with this standard, and it shall be the duty of the Secretary of the Treasury to maintain such parity."

Mary also worked with us to help us establish credit with the wholesalers at the warehouses in Gallup. In fact, she left a deposit with them of several thousand dollars so we could move forward in getting the trading post back up and going. While at the bank with Mary, I was able to get one of the managers to explain to me what configuration the bank most wanted in buying and selling gold. They wanted ingots that had uniform size and weighed just a certain amount. As I talked with him further, he had several molds of the size the bank preferred, and he let me have one. It was made of cast iron so gold could be melted in it. What a find!

May Fern and I were then able to hitch up the teams to the wagon and trailer wagon, fully loaded with our supplies and the farm implements. After seeing Mary off, we left for our Toahani Trading Post. We promised Mary that we would never change the name.

Our main concern, after all the events seemed to settle out, was what the perpetrators of the murder and destruction would think of our reopening the post. Did they still have their distorted outlook as to what the post was all about? Hanabah knew most of the group as they were young men from local families. Several were from Tohatchi and a couple she recognized from Coyote Canyon. All were of the lazy, ne'er-do-well type. We knew they were cowards and needed liquid courage in order to have the guts to do any damage. We did a lot of talking about how we could prevent such a reoccurrence.

The first order was to set up shop. That is, we needed to get some semblance of a store so we could do business. The only building that remained intact was the warehouse behind the main post building. It had been cleaned up by the extended family and community crew and just needed some counters and shelves. We adjusted our operation to what the building would allow and were open in just two days.

Hanabah had been questioned intensely by Deputy Dunham. She was so incensed about the whole tragedy that she gave them all the information they needed as to who was involved and how it all unfolded. She later told us about what she saw and how she almost became a victim.

"I had just returned from grazing our sheep up the main canyon when I saw a group of about a dozen young men ride toward the trading post from the direction of Coyote Canyon," Hanabah said. "They were talking loud and bold like they were drunk. They were all mounted on ponies. Some were riding bareback. As I was trying to put the sheep in the corral, three of them – Tony, Larry, and Timothy – rode over to the corral before the sheep were all in the corral and scattered them.

"'Hey, old hag, we are not afraid of your spells and curses," they had said. "Today is the day we will show you and your son, the great Buckshot, that we are strong and do not have to fear. Where is he so we can show him our power and have a party with his sexy wife?'

"Inside, I wanted to reach up and yank him off his pony and beat him senseless," Hanabah said. "But there were three of them. And about that time, two more came out of the back door of the post, dragging Frank. I could see from the blood on him that one was holding a bloody axe handle that Frank was out of the fight.

"Knowing that sometimes it is better to retreat into a safer position and regroup," Hanabah continued, "I slipped away to your home and got the thunder gun. If they were not afraid of me, I figured that they still just might have some fear of your gun. Although I did not know how to load it or fire it, I also took the powder horn and the bag with the other parts. I then thought to walk with the gun and fixings in plain sight over to my hogan. Sure enough, the three, as they turned away from watching what was being done to Frank to get back to me, saw me with my scary items. They did not come any closer.

"'Look at the old hag run from us and go into her hogan!' they had said. 'Go ahead and hide. We will come for you and your family later!'

"I knew from the confusion that was happening and all the treasure they were helping themselves to at the post that they would not come after me," Hanabah said. "I was so thankful that you two were gone. I would have given my life to stop them if they had tried to harm you."

I knew that this old, wiry woman with nerves like steel and determination beyond measure would have done some damage to the lot of cowards if that had come after her. They might have succeeded in burning her hogan and killing her, but I would bet she would have drawn blood in some way before she was finished. I was so thankful she was spared all of that possibility and that she was my mother.

"I watched from a crack in the logs that I made with my knife in the back of my hogan," Hanabah said. (Remember that all hogans face east. Her hogan was to the east of the post and up the canyon, so the door faced away from it.). "First, I saw them knocking down all the corrals and trying to herd the mixed group of horses, Jake, cows, sheep, and some goats down the canyon. All the animals were frightened, and then there were the first wisps of smoke coming up out of the post. Soon, the flames were shooting up over the building, and then there were the sounds of ammunition going off from the heat. This was the final straw for the milling confused animals. They scattered in all directions, and two of the drunken fools fell off their ponies in the chaos. I hoped they were hurt. Some came around to the back and broke open the warehouse, but what were they going to do with a room full of wool and hides? It was about this time that Frank must have come to. Several of the group dropped the items they had stolen from the post and ran over to him and began beating on him again. Oh, how I wished I could have been able to fire your thunder gun! But I knew that it was no use. They had either killed Frank with these last blows or would soon do so. I kept hidden and blocked my door as best as I could. I prayed I would live to tell the story."

Her choice of words struck me with awe. Over the last few months, May Fern and I had told her of our thoughts about God and his son Jesus Christ. We had explained to her about praying to God in the name of Jesus Christ. We had even instigated prayer at our meals, showing her what we had been taught by Frank and Mary as we had occasionally been invited to eat with them. I knew that she and also Jimmy were very spiritual from all they had said and taught us. I had just never heard either one of them use the word "prayer" before. Oh, as my testimony had grown and I had felt support of the spirit as never before, I was hoping that Hanabah would also learn. May Fern and I were doing all we could by example.

"Several tried to burn the wool and building, even throwing kerosene on it, but it just smoldered and did not ever really catch on fire," Hanabah continued. "In their drunken condition and with their arms full of loot, they just milled around in confusion, occasionally falling over and then staggering back to their feet. A couple of them tried to tie items to their pony. But again, with liquor controlling their movements, they had very little success. They were determined to make sure Frank was dead or, in some way, that he paid a price for his supposed wrongs. They tied ropes to his feet and drug him with several of the ponies down the canyon and out of my sight to where you found him. That was the last I saw of the group. Is it true, when you found him, my son, that they had scalped him?"

"Yes, my mother, they had."

Although I did not believe that I would ever forget the vivid picture in my mind of the gruesome sight of Frank's bloody, mutilated body, I did not expect anyone would ever ask me for any details. In fact, I had told May Fern when I first saw her again after finding Frank's body, but before we had retrieved it and put it into the box to convince Mary that she did not want to see him in that condition. She needed to remember him as he was as he kissed her goodbye on that fateful day.

* * *

The second step of our plan – after getting the post operational so the local families would have a place to trade, get mail, socialize, and get back to a somewhat normal life – was to do a survey. With Junior and Hanabah tending the limited store operation, May Fern and I spent the better part of a week riding out to each of the family hogans. We wanted to get the feeling of their spirits and get their reaction and suggestions about reopening the post. Although we had already committed to opening it and were moving forward, we wanted to make sure we were in sync with those who were potential customers. We did not want the evil undertow to prevail, which had been part of the cause of the tragedy. We felt that it was just good business to visit with our neighbors and get their ideas of what they wanted and needed.

May Fern, although with child, would not hear of staying home. She rode a pretty little paint pony, and I rode old Jake. I really believe you cannot kill or lose a mule if you bond with one. He had run up the canyon when spooked by the culprits when they broke the corrals down. Hanabah remembered seeing him running up past her hogan just before she went inside with the thunder gun. Anyway, we must have made a strange sight with May Fern on the little paint pony and me on big old Jake with my six-foot frame and tall Indian-style cowboy hat. May Fern had on a beautiful Navajo outfit with silver buttons and a silver comb holding up her beautiful long shiny black hair. I had also packed an oversized pony with a bedroll, food, and canteens of water so we could camp out if we needed. As I recall, we spent two nights out while trying to find all the hogans in our trading area.

The results of the survey were as we thought they might be. Almost 84 percent wanted the post to continue. They even wanted more items to trade for, especially a greater selection of airtights as more and more foods were now being packaged that way. A very strong suggestion came to do a better job of letting them know the condition and amounts of their accounts. A bookkeeping system with periodical written statements – what a novel idea! Why hadn't it been instigated by Frank? Perhaps he could have averted the attack with better communication such as this. But that was hindsight type of thinking.

All in all, except for two hogans, we were received with great courteousness. These were the family places of two of the perpetrators. In fact, they both were located not far apart and way to the northeast of the post. As we were riding along the trail to the homes, we were met by Hasteen Benally and one of his younger sons and his wife. They were blocking the trail with their ponies.

"We do not welcome you to our lands," he said before I could even greet them in the normal Navajo way. "Go back where you came from and do not ever come this way again. We are not your friends. We are your enemies. You have sent the *solados* (Navajo for "soldiers" or "lawmen") after two of our young men who your mother says killed the trader and burned the post. Hasteen Etsitty is my neighbor and brother-in-law. His son has never even returned home since that day, and he does not know where he is. He says it is your fault that his son is missing. He says he will kill you if he sees you and has the chance. I will not kill you, especially with your wife here with you and because she is a daughter of Hasteen Willeto. He also is part of our clan. But never come here again."

Before I could gain my senses and even begin a reply, they whirled their ponies, turned their backs to us, and quickly disappeared down the trail toward their home. As he was talking, I could feel more than see my wonderful bride easing her pony up alongside of Jake on my left. I knew she was getting ready for a fight if one should be started. For you see, I had placed over her saddle horn a special set of small saddlebags that looked just like a small set of saddlebags. But inside of each was a fully loaded Colt Single Action in .38-.40 caliber, ready to do some damage. I noted, as she fully came up alongside of me, that each of her hands was down in the appropriate bag. I was sure she was ready to draw, cock, and let fly. I have always fully appreciated teamwork. The words of Benjamin Franklin ring in my ears at times like these when he said, "Gentlemen, we either hang together, or we will surely hang separately!"

I should mention here about where this matching pair of Colts, and where the beautiful Colt .45 I was packing under my vest in a shoulder holster, had come from. A few days before we set out to take the survey, we were again cleaning up the old burned-out building. As evening was drawing nigh, May Fern and I were working carefully in the area where the pawn room had been. We were carefully sifting the ashes. We had directed the family and community people when first cleaning up the burned-out shell of the post to leave the pawn room alone, so no one had worked it. As we were sifting, we were finding a few pieces of turquoise from melted jewelry and, in fact, some almost-perfect pieces of jewelry. There was nowhere the number of pieces that Frank had in that room. The thieves had taken most of it when they pilfered the store. In addition, I discovered where the rugs, which now were just a stack of ashes with bits and pieces of rugs barely identifiable, had been stacked. The gang had stolen or burned thousands of dollars of very valuable items – not only valuable because of the market value, but because they were pieces of art that would never be seen again. Such foolishness and waste!

"Look, darling!" I said as I pushed the ashes and blanket remnants aside to reveal a metal trapdoor in the concrete floor.

The door had a latch but no lock. I turned the latch, and grabbing the D handle on the side away from the hinges, I pulled the heavy metal door open. The door had an opening about three feet wide by about four feet long.

"What do you suppose it was for?" May Fern asked.

"I can't imagine," I said. "I never knew it existed. I have been in this room many times and even helped Frank do inventory of the blankets one time. Now that I think about it. When we got down to the last blanket, he quickly started piling the ones we had counted back on this spot. He made sure that I did not see this trapdoor."

The sun had set, and the gentle evening darkness was falling. A small breeze began to blow and stir the ashes that were still present in great abundance. I could barely make out the first step of what was probably a stairway descending into the dark hole. It seems funny in this day and age that we could not just grab a flashlight and start looking around, but you have to know that in 1900, there were no such things as flashlights in our part of the country. We only had candles and kerosene lamps if we wanted to diminish the dark.

May Fern volunteered to go up to our house and bring one of our kerosene lamps and matches. She would also look for some candles that we had. I kept cleaning around the door opening so it would be easier if we found anything down there we needed to bring up and stack. I could not imagine what could be in such a place. In fact, I wondered if the spiders and other critters who liked such places really wanted me down there.

It did not take her long to return, and she brought Hanabah with her. Hanabah was as excited as we were, and it would be good to have an extra set of eyes to watch out for anyone who might see what we were doing. Remember that this room was at the back of the post, and the walls of the post were about ten feet high. The floor in the main part of the store had burned in the fire. The roof over all the building, including the pawn room and the living quarters, was destroyed in the fire. Where we were searching was not very visible to anyone unless they looked through the opening where the front door had been or through any of the several window openings. A lighted lantern within the spooky walls of the burned-out post might stir up curiosity, but generally, no one in the community traveled at night anyway. A lot of superstition prevailed about men who turned into wolves at night and that they could only be killed with a silver bullet.

May Fern had found a couple of fairly large candles and one of our lamps. Neither of these necessities would make a lot of light, but we had to have something. I lit a candle and used it to help guide me down the stairs. There were ten wooden steps that took me into a room about ten feet square. The room was very clean and tidy, and the cobwebs were scarce. To my amazement, shelves and racks on two sides of the room were filled with guns, pawn, and general survival items such as sacks of piñon pine nuts, flour, several cases of airtights, cold weather clothing for a man and a woman, ammunition, and several barrels of some types of liquids. There was a spigot coming from the wall, and when I turned it, water began flowing.

"What do you see? Are you okay? Can we come down?" May Fern asked.

"Just a minute, let me put the candle in a safe place so it won't start a fire," I said. "Light the lamp and hand it to me so I can help you see to come down the steps. You won't believe what is here."

In looking for a safe place for the candle, I found four kerosene lamps all filled and ready to light!

"Never mind the lamp," I said. "There are lamps already down here. I will light them with the candle, and then you will really be able to see what is here."

The lamps were of the modern type of that time with tubular woven wicks with a center ventilation system as well as glass chimneys. They smoked if you did not keep adjusting the trim of the wick, but with these four lamps and our candle, the room was really lit up.

May Fern and Hanabah safely descended the stairs. They were in awe as I was at the numerous items that had been squirreled away in this apparent "safe room." And to think that poor Mary did not even know about it. Could it be that Frank had truly been stealing from customers or pilfering from the profits of the post?

We all started looking through all of the items and were trying to make sense of it all.

"Look, here is one of my melted gold pieces. And look, here is another one of them," Hanabah said. "Maybe he used the gold that I traded to come up with this place. He did drive a very hard bargain, and I never did really know what my melted lumps were really worth. Could he have been cheating me by many times the value of the gold and then used it to build this safe shelter?"

"My mother, I do not know if we can call this a safe shelter, for it was not safe for him," I said. "But maybe if Mary and I had been at the post and could have seen the men coming with a fight on their minds, just maybe, Frank would have been able to get us into this place. And we could have hidden from them."

"No," said May Fern, "we cannot go there! We can think of many ways that day could have been different, but I say that it all happened as it was supposed to, and it could not have been changed. We are here now for a reason, and we just need to figure it out. This new treasure and this safe room will be the start of our new post and what we can do for all the people who will rely on our judgment and business practices. We have been given much, and so much is expected of us. Let's go home now and rest, for we have much to think about and do as tomorrow comes."

Oh, how I loved her! She had a way to look through situations and know exactly which trail to head down that would be the best for everyone.

When the new day dawned, we set about opening the trading post, feeding the animals, and creating a plan for rebuilding the buildings, corrals, and all the aspects of the property so we could operate. May Fern and I decided that the safe room would be the core around which we planned the new structure. Using that point as the center, we drew the plan for the new store part of the trading post. We chose to incorporate a feature that was not in any of the other posts. We designed a section for tools and other large items like sacks of flour and cases of airtights where customers could help themselves. In addition, we made the counters deeper so more merchandise could be placed on them as the patrons ordered the items they needed and the staff placed them for counting and billing.

We set aside the left front of the trading area for the post office. There would be a window for selling stamps, sending special packages, and just general post office business. This area would also have private boxes for the various families and ranches. The living quarters would be connected to both the post office and the store by one doorway. In turn, that doorway would lead into a hall with a doorway into the pawn room. The pawn room could also be entered from the back of the store from the receiving room. The receiving room was a separate room with double doors and a dock from which the wagons and later trucks would unload merchandise for the store. The dock was covered to protect against inclement weather. The two doors into the pawn room were specially made to be almost like vault doors. Once inside, they could be barred by lowering a piece of metal into armlike holders. Thus, once in the pawn room, time could be bought to open and hide in the safe room. I designed a fake wooden floor for the pawn room that hid the door in the floor very well. In addition, an old thick worn rug was glued to the fake wooden floor so that when the door in the floor was closed, the rug covered any possible clues as to its existence.

The old adobe walls were of no use, having been superheated by the fire. We advertised and put together a crew of stonemasons to build the walls with stone. They worked under the direction of Hasteen Moore, who had built our home up the canyon. He had done a fine job of that and did a wonderful job in rebuilding the trading post, living quarters, and an addition to the warehouse. For raising our family, we also enclosed a yard with an eight-foot rock fence with several shooting ports not only at the corners, but spaced along the walls. We also had well-disguised shooting ports at various locations in the trading post and the living quarters' outside walls.

The big old cottonwood trees at the rear of the post had been so badly scorched that we cut them down and replaced them with new plantings we dug from way up the canyon. We even staked out a small garden in the backyard where we wanted to raise our own vegetables and herbs. We had a lot of fun designing these buildings and planning how they would all function to create a wonderful enterprise.

Jimmy and May Fern's mother and brothers and sisters came over several times and camped as we were going through all of this planning and construction. Jimmy and Hanabah would, of course, get with us and help with the planning of the flow of funds needed to make it all happen. Jimmy and Hanabah had been very careful with moving any of the melted gold or silver for over a year. Finally, we arrived at the point where we needed to make a substantial payment to Mary and for the goods, the workers, and the materials. Jimmy also indicated that he had some expenses for his family that needed to be taken care of.

I had been going to the bank in Gallup about every two weeks while on the regular merchandise run and learning all I could about gold trading. Hanabah and I had taken the mold given to us by the banker and melted silver items left over from the fire and added some silver pieces she had retrieved from the treasure site. This bar of silver, we hoped, would be low-key enough to trade in Gallup at either the government assay office or bank. The assay office was part of a jewelry store run by an old-timer who claimed to have worked in the California goldfields in his younger days. I started at the assay office first. How is the old saying? "You get wisdom from having experience, but for the most part, bad experience is what gives you the best wisdom."

"What can I do for you, young man?" asked the old-timer.

"I have some silver I would like to sell," I said.

"Let me see it, and we will find out how good it is," he said.

He took the ingot from me and hefted it and then took a monocle and looked at it from various angles.

"Looks like you have some pretty good stuff here," the old-timer said. "I will need to take some of it and run some tests. If it is of the right value, I can make you an offer if you like."

I nodded in agreement, and he went to work, chipping away at the ingot, putting pieces in some beakers, adding liquids of some type. I wondered what it was all about but figured by taking it to an assayer, I should be able to get an honest answer. I was wrong.

I had never thought about my demeanor or how I was dressed. Where I lived my everyday life, I was clean, my clothes were clean, I dressed like everyone else, and looked like I belonged there in Navajo country. My haircut was the same as all of the other men. I was not into the current fashion of the white man's world. It must have shown, and with some pretty heavy bias on his part, he finally handed me back the bar.

"Son, this here material has a lot of impurities in it, but I will still buy it from you," the old-timer said. "I can only give you half of what a pure sterling silver material would be worth. However, if you have more where this came from, maybe I can make you a better deal."

The wholesale merchants I dealt with for the trading post merchandise told me that pure silver, or sterling silver as it was called, was worth about 62¢ per troy ounce. My calculation, with some help from my banker contact, was that the cast iron mold was designed for ten troy ounces of pure gold. This would mean that the mold would turn out 5.4 troy ounces of silver as silver only weighs about half of what gold weighs by volume. It was a lot to learn for a young man with only a reading education. One of my strong suits in life was that I could always figure out a place to get the information I needed.

Now again, my banker contact confirmed that pure silver was going for 62¢ per troy ounce and that pure gold was going for $20.67 per troy ounce. Two more valuable pieces of information were needed so I could maximize a return from the melted treasure pieces. First, I had to learn how gold and silver is measured and weighed; and second, I had to learn about the purity of silver and gold and how this purity affected the real value.

I soon learned that a troy ounce is the measure used only to express the mass and/or weight of precious metals such as gold, platinum, or silver. There are twelve troy ounces in the now-obsolete troy pound. A troy ounce is equal to 480 grains compared with the avoirdupois ounce, which is equal to only 437.5 grains. The avoirdupois ounce is what we use to measure all of the many items in commerce and life in general. There are sixteen of these ounces in the avoirdupois pound when it comes to purity of the gold and silver we were dealing with. I found these very important parameters that had to be dealt with. For gold, the purity of each unit is measured in karats.

Having prepared myself with the basic facts, I knew that if our silver and gold were pure, each ingot would be worth about $3.35 for silver and about $206.70 for gold on the retail market. There wasn't much of a decision as to what we should be melting down, but we had to learn where to market our treasure so it would not stir up any conflict.

"So what is this silver bar worth to you?" I asked.

"As I told you, I can only give you about half, and that would be just $1.70," the old-timer said.

At that young age, I had not learned to put my mind in gear before my mouth started moving.

"What would a bar the same size be worth if it was gold?" I queried.

"Gold, you say? Why, I haven't seen any gold of that quantity for years – not since I was in the Sacramento area during the great gold rush," he said.

He shifted his position on the hard wooden stool and put down his monocle.

"Now where would you come up with that much gold, sonny?" he asked.

I felt like he had me boxed in although in reality, I did not owe him any type of answer. It seemed for a moment that he was looking right through me and could see that I had knowledge of a huge treasure. Thankfully, I waited a moment to let my mind clear before I again opened my mouth.

"Oh, I was just curious if that should ever happen," I said. "I have heard of people who trade in gold, and I just wondered what they would be looking at in value."

"Well, if you ever come across any such quantity," he said, with his eyes still seemingly looking right through me. "I would be very happy to do an assay for you and help you convert it into currency."

Assay – what a fascinating word. "Assay" literally means to examine or analyze. This was what I must learn to do independent of some outside source or person. I determined that I would learn this process and set up a location where we could do our own work of determining the purity of the items in the treasure room. Then there were the "other" treasure rooms that Hasteen Navajo Jim Begay had told Hanabah about! In all the excitement of my life up to this point, I had almost forgotten about his description of the gold map plates showing the other sites. Oh, what a wonder life was to me at this point!

Once having made up my mind to learn about "assaying," I dove into learning in a very intense way. I looked in books, which in that day were almost nonexistent in the Gallup area about such scientific things. I then remembered what the old-timer had said about helping me if I should come up with some gold in sufficient quantity. Could I trust him? Would he teach me? Would he sell it for us at market price, less an appropriate commission, so we could maximize our return? And what was an appropriate commission?

These questions haunted me, but I could not come up with any other source for learning – and we needed this knowledge now! We needed to move on and pay our debts and invest in our plans for rebuilding the post. Even though Jimmy and Hanabah had gone to the treasure site and retrieved some items, they had not comprehended the large amount of money that was needed. In addition, they felt they had been followed; and so being very careful when the door opened, they quickly gathered a few handfuls of jewelry and then shut the water off so the door would soon close.

"My mother, I thank you and Jimmy for going to the treasure room, but what you brought will not be enough for what is needed," I said. "I feel that we need to go to the treasure room again and get enough items to melt down to make fifty of the gold bars from the mold. This number of bars, if they are pure gold or very close to it, will pay our debts, give us money to keep building, and provide Jimmy enough for his family."

"Buckshot, you have proven you are the man of our family," Hanabah said. "You have a wife carrying your child, and you have great responsibility to help the people of our trading area. I do not know how much treasure this will take, but can Jake pack it for us?"

"Yes, Jake can carry all we need very easily," I said with a smile on my face. "It will not even be the weight of one sack of flour from the trading post. I'm not sure where we can melt this treasure down into the bars. We will need a hot furnace like the blacksmiths use in town, and we need to have even more of the molds."

We worked on the necessary setup first. We took part of the stone warehouse and made it into what appeared to be a very well-equipped blacksmith shop, complete with a hand-driven bellows. Then with a fairly large cast iron melting pot, which I had to order, we were set up to produce bars. And by the way, as I was making a deposit for the post, my banker friend approached me and said that they did not want the other five molds they had received and wanted to know if I could use them!

Work was progressing on the trading post buildings, which included the store, post office, pawn room, and the new living quarters for May Fern and me and the baby we were expecting. We contacted Jimmy and May Fern's mother to come to the post so we could complete our plans for financing. Somehow, in the communication, someone overheard one of us, perhaps Jimmy, talk about making a "treasure run"; and this information made its way to where the two leaders of the first raid were still in hiding. As we put it together later, these two somehow knew what it meant; and they figured if they could get their hands on some riches, they could somehow still live a great life. Perhaps they even thought they could do all of us further damage – which they did. I have found in life that this is the way most evil ones think.

Jimmy set out with May Fern's mother and three of their children in one of the family wagons to travel to our Toahani Trading Post. We were a little over thirty miles from his home. While camped a little over halfway from his home to our post, Jimmy told me later that he felt they were being watched. He tried to discover them, but to no avail. The next morning, a sheep was missing. They were herding a small flock of five to present to us, but they only arrived with four. Like most Navajos, Jimmy and his family were experts at tracking. They found some sign that someone had taken the sheep, but probably only after smothering it and carrying it away, being careful to step on rocky ground where they would leave no trail.

"I am so sorry that you lost a sheep," I said. "It is of no matter. We thank you for the other ones and will make good use of them. May Fern and I want you and your family to stay in our home while you are here. Our new living quarters in the post are almost finished – at least finished enough that we can stay there. Is there anything we can do to help you?"

"Buckshot, my son, you are too kind to us. But we will take advantage of your hospitality," Jimmy said. "I will get the children to move the wagon up to your home and unload our things. We are so happy to be here with you and learn of all that you have done since we were last here. I can see much has changed."

I had tried and tried to get my mother to let me hire someone to herd our flock of sheep so she could stay near the post and help us or take it easy. Her age was catching up to her, in addition to the tough life she had led. She was more respected in the community now more than ever before, but the reputation she had carried with her for so many years was still evident. Whenever she came into view, you could especially see the children sort of cringe and stare with wonder. Her thin frame and pockmarked face was not the norm for a Navajo woman of her age of that time. In addition, although she wore clean clothes and was herself a very clean person, there was always something unorganized about her appearance. Even though May Fern had tried and tried to suggest and help Hanabah with various arrangements of her hair, it always seemed to have a windblown look. She walked now with a little limp and most of the time had a staff she had made herself to help her over the rough spots as she moved the flock through the day. I had learned to love this woman deeply. She had saved my very life and gave and taught me everything she possibly could.

My mother was an early riser. She would have the sheep going up the trail to the day's grazing area by daybreak. This made it so she was usually back at the post and had the sheep in the corral by just after noon. It was time for her to be returning. I expected to see her come down out of the canyon at any moment or perhaps down the ridge on either side of the canyon with the flock of sheep. As I was conversing with Jimmy and May Fern and the family, I noticed movement in the trees off to the north. I turned to see that it was one of her two favorite dogs working his way down through the trees and brush. He seemed to be limping. In addition, she and the dogs would be in the rear of the flock, pushing them toward home. I ran toward the hillside just as Hanabah emerged from the trees. She was bloody and walking very haltingly, using her staff to keep her steady. I yelled for help as I ran to catch her in my arms.

"My mother, my mother, what has happened to you?" I asked. "Here, sit down and let me hold you. Soon, I will have help for you, and we will get you taken care of."

She was bleeding from a bad wound on the back or her head; and she had bruises, scratches, and cuts on her arms and legs as though she had fallen down a hillside. She collapsed into my arms and just gave out. She knew that I would see that all would be well from here.

Jimmy's wagon came fast to where we were at. His son had immediately seen the need for a way to get her to her hogan or wherever it would take to help her. We gently loaded her into the wagon and made her as comfortable as possible. I don't know how she made it as far as she did, for she was now passed out and breathing erratically.

May Fern, even though heavy with child, and her mother had the hogan prepared, including a fire going in the stove by the time we carefully drove the wagon to the hogan door. We took her inside and laid her down on a several-layer thick sheepskin bed. Jimmy, who had a great knowledge of healing, took over and gave directions to the family so she could be ministered to in every possible fashion.

My first thoughts were that she fell over an embankment into some type of hole. I would never have believed what I was to find out really happened to her. My brother-in-law James offered to go and find the sheep and the other dog that we figured was probably still with the flock. Being very stressed, I said I would go with him as I knew my worried presence would not be what she needed. Along with our prayers, she was in the very best of hands.

Ever since the raid, I had gotten into the habit of taking a gun with me on any trip of any kind. In fact, I was determined that no one was ever going to ambush me and my family like they had done to poor old Frank. I vowed to never be more than fifty feet from a loaded gun of some type and made sure that May Fern was in the same mind-set. She and I had taken several walks up the canyon to a good shooting place and practiced. She was very good with the Colts in .38-.40. Her rifle shooting needed some help, but I figured it was mainly due to the stock being too long, and I was going to fix that.

I sprinted over to our house and got my hat and a holstered loaded .45 Colt Single Action with about thirty rounds of ammo in the belt. I also grabbed a Winchester in .30-.30 caliber for James and a buckskin bag of extra cartridges. I knew of his ability as a rifleman and knew he would feel comfortable with this weapon.

We followed Hanabah's track back for over a mile. She had come down a long tree-lined ridge keeping in trees. It was not the most direct way she could have come, so I started to become suspicious that my first assumption might just be wrong. I could see ahead where she had probably crossed a large open area in a saddle along the ridgeline. This would put James and me in the open where anyone observing us would learn our numbers, how we were armed, and in which direction we were going. These are all considerations when one is hunting, whether the game be animal or human. Most act and react in the same manner while either laying a trap for their hunters or wanting to steal from them. In my many big game hunts over the years, I have relied on such thinking and usually obtained the trophy I was after. This type of thinking was first instilled by my father and then expanded upon by my many treks with Hanabah, my years herding sheep, and conjuring up what-if scenarios with various animals I encountered in the beautiful mountain landscape of the plateau.

I knew that James could feel my anxiety and uneasiness as I carefully followed the back track of Hanabah. He too had learned the many lessons that are learned by spending time in the vast outdoors of these lands.

In a very low voice and with small motions, I told and pointed to him my next plan as we moved to find the sheep and tried to figure out what had happened to Hanabah.

"James, you go to the right and gain as much elevation as you can so you can always see me as I cross the large clearing," I said. "Watch for any movement above me and do as you think if we stir up anything. I do not think that my mother was wounded in such a way just from carelessness."

He nodded in agreement and slipped easily through the thick stand of juniper trees as effortless as the wind and as quiet as a ghost. Truly, an Indian who has learned as a young man the ways of the great outdoors is a marvel to watch and a very formidable enemy. In our situation, if we had enemies in front of us, they were probably Indian; and we needed to outmaneuver them. This could be done because they would be thinking an unarmed person or persons would come to find the sheep, and even then, they would probably be just children or, at most, teenagers. And they would expect these rescuers would just come sloppily walking along, not suspecting danger, and so could be easily heard and seen as they would walk across the large opening in the trees. Well, we had a different plan – I would be the bait, if this was the case, and James would deliver the sting!

I waited for a few minutes until I felt that James had probably reached the rocks to my left and carefully placed himself in position where he could watch me move across the opening. He would also be able to see as much as possible the ring of trees on the other side of the opening that I was heading for.

I was wearing a light brown flannel pullover shirt that May Fern had made for me. The cloth had the texture of light buckskin. She made it extra long so it easily covered the holstered .45 and gun belt.

I was about halfway across the clearing intently following Hanabah's tracks when two young Indian men stepped out from the upper tree line. I immediately recognized them as Tony and Larry, two of the thugs who had been part of the raiding party and who had threatened my mother, calling her "an old hag." They were the ones who threatened to abuse my wife. My very being jumped into high gear, but since I was suspecting a scenario like this, I was able to hold everything in check.

"Hey, old Buckshot, I see that you do not have your thunder gun or your mother to protect you," Tony said. "We will now see who runs our community, who steals from the people, and who keeps us from having all that is ours. You are a *ch'indi bilaganna* (devil white man) who thinks he is one of us just because he marries our most beautiful woman."

"You know, Tony, even though each of you have guns and knives and talk like you think you are men, you are nothing but women dressed up like men," I said. "You are thieves and murderers who have to sneak up on people and threaten old women."

They each leveled their Winchesters at me and kept walking toward me. They were just holding their rifles at hip level, and I knew that even if they fired, they would probably miss their first shots at that range. They were a good one hundred yards off; and I knew that, in turn, I could not do them any damage either with my Colt even if I could get it uncovered fast enough to draw and fire. We all had to get closer, so I kept taunting them. They were going to pay for their insults to my mother and wife and for killing Frank.

They kept walking toward me.

"Buckshot got his name from shooting a poor, helpless lion," Tony said. "Wait until you see that we are not helpless, and we know how to torture you until you will scream for mercy just like the old trader. Look, see what I have hanging around my neck? It is the hair I took from his head!"

My blood ran cold as I could see that he had taken Frank's scalp and stretched it out over a thin frame and hung it from his neck. It reminded me of such atrocities I read about in the Book of Mormon that the people did to one another as they completely lost the spirit and become as animals.

Inside, I was praying that James had his Winchester locked and loaded with the front bead centered in the buckhorn sight and lined up with Tony's chest. For James, the shot would be an easy one; and with quick action, even if I did not get off a shot, he could take them both out. At least that is what I was hoping the outcome would be.

"You are a woman to have to sneak up on Frank and hit him from behind," I said, further taunting them as they kept coming toward me. "You will not get that chance from me. I will face you straight on and show you what it is to try and take a real man. Even now, you hide behind your rifles because you are afraid to fight me like men. And even then, you are cowards because it takes two of you. Did it take two of you to hurt my mother? Did you have to sneak up on her because you knew that woman could beat both of you? Come on, you little girls. Let's see what you are made of."

To my amazement, Tony dropped his rifle and pulled out a big shiny skinning knife.

"You call us girls?" he yelled. "Wait until you are screaming like one as I remove your manhood and scalp you alive. I will skin you alive. Larry with his rifle will see to it that you do not run as your mother did."

I have read of many accounts of how when riflemen fire their first shot in battle, they always shoot high, even though they are taught to aim low. It seems that in the thick of battle, with all of the adrenaline pumping and the fear of what is to come, the riflemen miscalculate the distance and aim high – thinking the enemy is farther away than they are. At least this is one of the theories. I just think it is pure excitement and that instinct kicks in and the rifleman just puts the gun up to his shoulder and, on the command to fire, fails to use his sights as he points the rifle downrange and pulls the trigger. In his exuberance, he misses the shot because he is holding the gun angled upward. Oh well, so much for theories.

As Tony closed to about fifteen yards and I was uncovering the holster and pistol and drawing my Colt, James's first shot, true to form, was a little higher than his intended aim of the largest part of the body, Tony's chest area. The 150-grain soft point smacked Tony right in the side of his head, which came apart and sprayed bone, brains, and blood onto Larry. Tony, of course, only took one more step and crumpled into a lifeless heap.

I knew what James had in mind and knew that his second round was already headed for the chamber of that Winchester. It would soon be on its way toward Larry. The mushroomed slug that took Tony's head apart must have just missed Larry by inches as he was a couple of steps behind Tony. Not only the gore, but the sound of the damage and that slug passing in front of his face caused him to come to a complete halt.

The mind can think and evaluate at tremendous speed. Larry worked his overtime to try to come up with a worthwhile conclusion and plan of action. He must have felt uncomfortable with his Winchester as he dropped it, and it hit the ground at about the same time as Tony's body. Larry then proceeded to pull his knife from its sheath. The knife had barely cleared the sheath as my Colt cleared my holster, and I thumbed back the hammer. All of this took place in mere seconds.

My next recollection is seeing small parts of Larry flying through the air as a bullet from James's rifle hit him just above his left hip. His knife spun from his hand as he fell to the ground.

I could see that he was hit solid and that it would be fatal without any assistance from me. He let out a grunt as he hit the ground and momentarily lost his senses. He then attempted to sit up, but to no avail, and so he proceeded to curse at me. He followed Tony's lead and called me a *ch'indi bilaganna.* (It is unique that there are no cuss words in the Navajo language. The worst thing they can say about you is that you are a devil.) He muttered something about how he was going to cut my heart out. His blood was spilling out of him, and he started to go into shock.

As James trotted up to this scene of carnage, I heard him jack another cartridge into the Winchester.

"I will blow his head off as I did the other one," he announced and raised the rifle to do so.

"Let him be," I said, pushing the rifle aside. "He will die soon enough, and who are we to speed his journey to hell?" I then directed my words to Larry.

"You rotten coward, who can only fight when it is against helpless old women or when you are in a pack like wolves," I said. "You can see today that your kind is finished. We have made you hurt, and I would do even more to cause you pain if I did not know better. Tell them on the other side of your false bravery and stupidity and how you were fooled!"

His eyes rolled back into his head. His body twitched a couple of times, and he was gone.

I was standing there with my pistol cocked and ready to fire. I slowly lowered the hammer and put the gun back into the holster. I did not fully comprehend all that had happened, but I was elated that our side had won.

"James, you saved my life today," I said. "I thank you for your bravery and friendship. We will tell this story many times over the years."

We were too wound up from all the excitement to even think about the sheep. We just left the bodies where they had fallen and turned and headed back toward the post. I was now very worried about Hanabah, knowing what she had been up against and possibly what they had done to her.

I saw a dreaded scene as we cleared the last of the trees and looked out over the little valley. There, wrapped in a blanket in the shade of a small lonely cottonwood, I could see a body. Jimmy and his wife and children, including May Fern, were sitting a few feet away, talking in muted voices as those who are in mourning do. Other people from the community were by the trading post, sort of milling around. The sun had set, and the coming darkness was bringing a close to a terrible day and the final goodbye to a wonderful lady.

We buried my mother on the little hill next to Frank.

Jimmy told me that Hanabah had come back from her coma long enough to tell him that she had been ambushed by the two thieves. Her dogs saved her and gave her time to slip away and head toward home. She was delirious from the terrible blow to her head and probably had some internal injuries, but in spite of doing all he could, Jimmy and the family could not save her. She came to just before she died and requested that they take her outside of her hogan and let her be in the sun. They pretty well knew what she was really saying. She knew she was going to the other side, and she did not want to put any burden on the family. It is a custom that if anyone dies in the hogan, it has to be burned to the ground because it would be haunted by the spirit. She wanted to save her hogan and ease the family's mind, and after all, she lived and loved in the great outdoors amid the creations of our Father in Heaven.

"Tell Percy I love him," Hanabah whispered to May Fern soon after they made her comfortable in the shade of the tree. "Tell him I will be waiting for him. And I will be waiting there for you also . . . you are my daughter . . . take care of my grandson."

A part of me was gone. All who have lost a loved one know of this hollow feeling. She was a gem among us all. She had given us all so much. Her spirit would be part of us. How did she know that May Fern was carrying a son?

Chapter 7

I WAS VERY fortunate that there was so much going on. We were rebuilding the post and melting down the treasure pieces so we could keep moving.

Before I tell you of the details and the joy that my son brought to us with his birth on October 10, 1901, I must mention a circumstance that later set the stage for a strong reputation for our family. About two days after my mother died, two Indian agent representatives came to the post accompanied by two deputies from the McKinley County sheriff's office.

At that time, the tribe did not have a formal government. In fact, it was not until 1923 that the tribe formally had an established government. From the Long Walk period in the 1860s until 1823, the Navajo people where governed by the ambiguous rules and regulations of Indian agents. Complicating matters was a constant conflict with the local county government, and in our case, it was McKinley County. This is why, after the news of the shoot-out, representatives from both the Indian agents and sheriff's deputies showed up. It was always a mystery to me how news traveled so fast in those days. We had no telegraph, no phones, and no automobiles. The fastest mode of communication was horseback, and I never did see anyone travel at the speed it would have taken to get the news around as fast as it always did.

One of the agency representatives, a Mr. Boyden, took the lead and assumed a position of authority.

"Are you the trader for this post?" he asked in a demeaning tone. Before I could answer, he said, "I have been hearing that the old trader was a scoundrel and that there have been killings and all sorts of other illegal activities. Is this true?"

"If I may address your questions one at a time," I said, "yes, I am the new trader here in the community at the invitation and support of the majority of the people. And yes, there have been killings, and I am very happy that someone is here to investigate and get the true story of what has been going on."

"So there have been killings? Who was killed and when? And who killed them?" Mr. Boyden almost shouted, "Just like so many other bureaucrats I have met in my day. They all think they have some authority and set out to prove that they also have all the answers."

Feeling that there probably wasn't any dialogue that would satisfy our bureaucratic friends without a long drawn-out conference, I figured that the site of two decomposing, stinking bodies would be the fastest way to bring them into reality. It was August, and it was very hot.

"Gentlemen, I know that your time is very valuable, so let me show you the crime scene and let you judge for yourself what has been going on," I said. "I want you to be satisfied that we here at the Toahani Trading Post community are law abiding and that any problems you have heard about have been solved. Please follow me."

In those days of my youth, I was a very good runner and in great shape. The four men were mounted on some fair horses. I knew from experience that if taken over rough enough terrain, I could outmaneuver and outrun a horse. So I proceeded to lead them up the canyon past the hogan and up into the thick trees. In just a short distance, they were cussing at riding through the stand of juniper as the branches were hitting them in the face and tearing at their legs and clothing as they tried to urge their horses to keep up with me. I had invited James to go along with us. By this time, he and I were way ahead of the riders and enjoying a good laugh as we heard them struggling on their steeds to get to the ridgetop and follow us on up to the clearing. I would shout encouragement to them from time to time so they would stay on course and keep coming. Finally, we all arrived at the edge of the clearing.

"Mr. Boyden, here is the site of the last killings," I said. "Would you like me to explain the circumstances?"

Even at that young age, I could recognize an oversized ego. I knew that this fine bureaucrat wanted badly to show off his authority and superior abilities.

"Why no, son, I am perfectly capable of determining what has happened here," Mr. Boyden said. "Just show me the evidence."

From atop their horses, they could easily observe the scavenger birds working on the two bodies in the middle of the clearing about 150 yards away but had no idea exactly what they were looking at. James and I had no desire to partake of the stench and view the putrefying bodies.

"Right over there, you will find the latest victims of violence and the weapons that were involved," I said, pointing at the place where several birds were jockeying for position to get their fill. "James and I will wait right here so we can be of any help, should you need it."

"Fine," said Mr. Boyden. "I am sure we can figure out what happened and come to a conclusion as to who did what. You both wait right here, and let us be the judges of these circumstances."

In most cases, Navajos, even though they have a great sense of humor, do not let it show around strangers; but poor James had to turn away to hide his laughter as we watched them ride into that mess. Remember, this was in the middle of the summer and a little after noon. Winds were basically calm but were set for an evening push uphill. As the four riders approached the bodies, the horses, being more astute as to what was coming into view and that the smell was not a pleasant one, began to dance and get fidgety. The more they were pushed toward the bodies, the greater the activity of the horses. Being more experienced with such scenes, the two deputies began to circle wide to the left around the corpses to keep their horses in check while Mr. Boyden, in his exuberance, and his assistant rode right up to the mess.

Both their mounts went wild as the full stench hit their noses. The wind also picked up about that time, and even the deputies' horses circling the spot caught the terrible smell. All four horses went wild!

Mr. Boyden's assistant's horse started to crowhop buck. He threw that man right into one of the corpses. That poor man! I bet he is still trying to wash himself clean. Anyway, one of the deputies caught the horse and brought it over to where we were. After checking his runaway steed up at the far edge of the clearing, Mr. Boyden turned him and rode really wide of the bodies back to where we were waiting. The poor assistant was vigorously brushing, wiping, and even rolling on the ground as he tried to get the nasty goo off him. He even took his coat off and threw it away. He then came sheepishly toward us.

"I am sure you saw the two Winchesters there near the bodies and the knives Mr. Boyden," I said. "I can explain how that came to be if – " I started, but Mr. Boyden cut me off.

"Any fool can see that they shot each other in a fight and got what they deserved," he said in his finest authoritarian voice, trying to stay away from his smelly assistant. "I will note the place and what I saw in my report. If no one has any further questions, this case is closed, and we have to get back to the agency."

He whirled his horse back toward the trading post and yelled over his shoulder to his assistant.

"Leroy, I thought you were a better horseman than that!" he said. "You stay way behind me, damn you, until we can get to the first major water spot where you will strip and get clean! Don't you get anywhere near me!"

That was one time I did not try to lead out and beat the horses. In fact, James and I even took a different trail down into the canyon and then on back to the post. When we got back to the family, they were full of questions, mostly wondering why the visitors were in such a hurry to leave. They told us that the four horsemen didn't even slow down when they arrived back at the post. The four hit a lope toward Gallup, and in no time, they were out of sight. One of them was riding way behind the others and seemed to not want to catch up.

Our reputation grew from this incident. Everyone knew that you did not mess with the Buckshot clan. Not only did we have a thunder gun and Winchesters and

Colts, but we were willing and able to take out whoever would try to cause harm to any of us. And the various governments supported our actions. This was a good, strong position to be in. We could now concentrate on finishing the post buildings, developing our business, and taking advantage of working the treasure.

We concentrated on finishing the buildings while waiting for the baby to come. Junior was a real anchor and mainstay for all that was going on. I sent him into town with James several times with the teams and wagons to get supplies and trade in the wool, hides, sheep, rugs, and pine nuts – all cash-producing products. The cash produced by this exchange allowed us to keep the business going.

I can't remember whose idea it was, but in building the post back with the rock walls, we actually put rifle or shooting ports in all of the walls. It was a little late in the scheme of things, but we figured that it might be better to be prepared in case any such event may ever happen again. We even put ports in the rock wall that enclosed our yard just off our living quarters.

As I have stated, our son, James, was born on October 10, 1901. What a wonderful present! May Fern and I were so happy and had so much to look forward to. By the time James was born, we had fully finished the living quarters at the post and had all the comforts of the time.

With the passing of Hanabah, only Jimmy and I had been to the treasure site and opened the hidden door to go inside. He had taken May Fern with him a few years back but would not let her go in because he was afraid she might get trapped inside. We needed, almost desperately, to visit the site and take sufficient treasure from the room to melt down. We had to pay our debts to Mary, our construction workers, and Jimmy's families.

Jimmy and Winona and their three children stayed on, living at our rock home and helping us with running the post and herding our flock of sheep. We had finally found all of the sheep and worked with them to get them back into shape. Winona wanted to be with us when the baby was born, which she was. What a wonderful and memorable time! That Christmas was especially memorable with so much family around. It had been a tough year, but we had many blessings to count. We were so thankful for the Gospel and to remember the birth of our Savior.

Jimmy and I agreed that we needed to have an additional person who could go to the site and know all about how to open the massive door. In addition, we needed to be more careful than ever with all that had transpired. We determined that he and I and May Fern should be the new active committee. James was not considered because he was still a little too young, even though he had proven himself in a tight spot. His day would come. Winona did not want any part of the operation, especially going into a dark room, and she did not believe in melting the beautiful artwork of the ancients. I also had concerns about that, but circumstances dictated otherwise.

All we let James and the rest of the immediate family know was that we had a process of making income that was secret. Someday, as members of the family, they could earn the right to that knowledge. We did not, in any way, let on about the treasure site and all the ramifications of the gold map plates. In fact, that was to be one of the major areas we needed to investigate – the gold map plates showing where other sites were. Hanabah had seen one such site.

Since May Fern had just given birth and needed to nurse the baby, Jimmy and I decided to plan the trip. We chose a day and worked on a special pack for Jake. After recalculating our needs, we decided to try and bring back about one hundred pounds of just gold items. From Jimmy's experience, in order to get that much, we needed to bring larger articles, such as serving plates and cups. Therefore, we needed a larger volume pack for Jake, and it had to be one that was not easily broken. If he should be spooked, or we lost him to some circumstance, we wanted the treasure load to be intact when we did find him. We needed to think of contingencies like these.

Because of the potential of running into others who had raided the post, for they had not been pursued by either the McKinley County sheriff's office or the Indian agency, I prepared us with arms. I personally carried my favorite Colt .45, holstered under my long shirt and wearing a coat. Jimmy did not like guns but agreed to let me hang a similar holstered pistol over the horn of the packsaddle and cover it. In addition, I strapped two Winchesters in scabbards, one on each side, on to the packsaddle. And of course, I made sure all the weapons were fully loaded and that we had extra ammunition. Jake could carry way more than what our arms weighed, plus the gold.

Before I tell you of our trip, I should mention that we had done as planned and fully restored the safe room in the floor of the pawn room. Only Jimmy and I and May Fern even knew it existed. Just as Frank had done, we hid the special doorway with a Navajo rug, and then we stacked other rugs on top of that. This would be the place to hide the treasure items while we worked to melt them down out in the warehouse/blacksmith shop. With coordinated movements, at night, it was easy to take items from the pawn room out the back door and into the blacksmith shop. We could then heat up the forge unit with coal, of which we had an abundant supply from the many veins in the general area. In fact, later on, the tribe would develop these veins into working mines and bring in a lot of income. With our hand-turned bellows, we easily coaxed the forge to give us the heat to melt the gold items. Sometimes, we had to break them into pieces to get them to fit into the casting pot, but we could produce several bars each night.

Jimmy and I set out early one morning before daybreak. We did not want anyone to get curious as to why we would leave the comfort of the post to go searching for anything. It would be hard to come up with a cover story. Even though he was getting on in years, old Jake was willing to accompany us at a fairly brisk pace as we set out to follow the switchback trail up to the top of the plateau. The trail had frozen that night, so there was ice on several spots along the way. We could see that there was a skiff of snow up on top. We were dressed warm and had on extra clothes for the occasion. Man Fern and Winona had packed us some great food. We only planned on being gone one night. This was our first trip where we were to take out such a large quantity of items.

"Jimmy, I still do not feel comfortable with how they figure the purity of the gold," I said. "I know that if we take in some bars and they are tested and they are contaminated with other metals, they will not bring as much money. I also know that they can cheat us by telling us our gold is not pure. I really must learn how to make the test for us before we ever take them to sell. While we have the gold as a liquid, it should be a good time to test for other metals. In fact, I think that when melting, the other metals should go to the top of the pot because gold is the heaviest of all. What has been your experience in melting down some of the gold pieces?"

"First, Buckshot, let me tell you how thankful I am to be with you here today," Jimmy said. "I am so happy that you have married my favorite daughter, May Fern, and you two have produced such a handsome strong son. You have been good to me and my families, and I know you are a true blessing from him who made and rules everything."

As though catching his breath and gathering his thoughts, as was his way, he shifted his position on the rock he was sitting on and stared off across the expanse toward the Tohatchi Mountains. It was a crisp, clear January day and oh so quiet. Only Jake, chewing on some dry grass, produced any sound. An eagle circled lazily overhead. Way below in a draw, I watched as a coyote jumped across the small wash at the bottom of a canyon and continued his canter, looking first to the left and then to the right, trying to find food to attack.

"Buckshot, I do not know much about the metal things you talk about," Jimmy said. "I have only melted down small pieces over a small fire. Sometimes, it has taken a lot of blowing and fanning to get the fire hot enough to just get the pieces to turn into a lump. I only know that the traders I have traded with never complained to me about poor quality. I know that they were not fully honest with me as to the value, but I am uneducated in such things. It was a blessing to just find the treasure and have a way to help raise my families."

"You are fortunate to have just one beautiful wife," Jimmy continued. "When I was young and could see the many women who could not have a husband because there just were not enough men, I followed the council of the old ones and took three wives. To some, this might sound good, but it is really not all that good." He chuckled and then added, "Sometimes, they fight each other for my attention, or they get jealous if one gets something and the other does not get the same thing. I am just a poor man and cannot get three of everything to hand out. Yes, be happy with one good woman and do not ever wish more trouble on yourself."

We arrived at the spot where we would set up camp. We were on a hilltop surrounded by some large rocks and trees. This would keep the wind out, but we could see anyone approaching us from several places. We unpacked Jake and then split up to look in all the nearby draws and possible hiding places. We did not want anyone to see us open the treasure room.

"Did you see any fresh sign of anyone?" I asked.

"No, Buckshot," Jimmy said. "There are some old tracks where two people traveled toward Crown Point. I think they probably were coming from Gallup. They were both leading a pack animal. I think it was about a month or maybe longer that they went through. They did not go anywhere near the picture stone or the doorway. I did not see any sign at all, and I went very close to the doorway just to make sure. What should be our plan?"

"We still have over half the day left," I said. "I think we should open the room and determine what we want to take. It has been a long time since I was in there, and I do not remember all the items. Usually, when I have gone in, I am in such a hurry that I have never really counted all the items or put them in piles so I can know what we have. That is what I think we should do."

I was squatting and playing with a stick and drawing what I remembered seeing. I too felt that we must, sooner or later, get an inventory so we could plan ahead and have a feeling of what we really had. I had brought an accounting pad from the store with me and a pen and ink. As we were talking about this all-important trip, May Fern had reminded me that candles or a kerosene lantern would be very handy if we really wanted to take a full count. I did not want to take the lantern due to the kerosene possibly leaking, but I had her package up about a dozen large candles. They would give us good light, especially if we were not going to be in there very long.

"I agree," Jimmy said. "Let's take the candles and light as many as we need to get good light, and I will write down what the pieces are that you count. I am a little excited to both be in there together because if the door closes, I do not know if we can ever open it. But it must be done."

"Let's plan well," I said. "We must tie up Jake so he does not wander away. I think we need to tie him close to where the water comes from the hill. We can put the box next to the doorway so we can load it fast. Remember that as the water fills the hole on the back side of the door and it tips open, we only have a little while to run in and count and move pieces out before the water starts to drip out and the door begins to close back. I have never stayed long enough to see the door reopen as the hole fills back up, but I know this must be how it works. I wonder if they had a way to block the door open with another rock or log. What do you think?"

Oh, such excitement and anticipation! We knew what we would be seeing again; but this time, we were really going to be in charge and control the whole treasure, at least from an inventory standpoint. What would we really find as we moved pieces around? How much time would we have before the door started closing and the candles went out?

We did as we planned, and I moved the rock dam so the water flow would go down the ditch to the rocks behind the big door. Then we both went and sat on the rock in front of the big door with our candles, lucifers (matches), notebook, and pen and ink. The special pack for carrying the gold pieces in was at the door.

I did have a watch with me. In those days and on the reservation, we really did not have use for timepieces. We jut went by sort of a gut feeling. My guess was that it took about thirty minutes before you saw the big doorway rock begin to tilt back as the water filled the tank at its top. Then it took another thirty minutes for the doorway to fully open. Both of us were watching it happen very carefully. What a marvelous engineering feat! I wanted to learn all I could about how they set this balancing system up and how the large rock tilted on the two side ones. The contact points had to take a lot of pressure. What if they broke? I did not want to contemplate that. How many times could the doorway be opened before the system failed? *Tick tick tick* . . . we watched the system work. Finally, the large rock tilted away, and we had our opening!

There was a very light grinding sound as the rock tilted back, but it was muffled by the immense treasure cavity.

And then I saw it! We had all been so excited at the various times the door had opened that none of us had noticed that the hinge points were being lubricated with small streams of water! What masterful engineering! Water is a great lubricant if continually applied, and this was the case here. That discovery led me to the next one. To the side of the opening on the inside were two curiously shaped rocks. They were key stones for blocking the doorway open!

"Look, Jimmy, as the door tilts back, there is a hole in the side of the support rock on the right so this stone can be placed to block the door from closing," I said. "And look, as the door has balanced back, I see the hole for the other stone."

"Yes, I see. And look, even I can stand on this ledge and hold the door rock as it reaches the balance point," Jimmy said. "Quick, put the blocking stone in before all the water drains out, and it starts to close back down."

There it was for our discovery! The very large and heavy doorway stone tipped back to a balance point before the water cistern built into the back of it started to empty. At this point, the upper key stone could be inserted to keep the door in the open position. Then you had all the time you needed to inventory, examine, and choose the numerous treasure items in the treasure room. Then when you got ready to leave, you simply pushed ever so slightly up on the stone doorway rock just enough to take the pressure off the blocking stone. Then you removed the blocking stone and let the doorway stone begin its descent. Remember, as it descended, there was still water coming into the cavern and pouring into the cistern of the doorway stone. This slowed the descent; and in fact, as the water reaches a critical volume, it caused the door to move back open. The safety feature was the lower key stone that you put into place as soon as you could squeeze into the room. Should the doorway, in its slow descent closing, have the water volume stopped, it could only close to where the lower key stone stopped it. The doorway stone, at that blocked point, was still open enough for you to exit. Pure genius!

"Now that we have the blocking stones in place," I said, "I will go get our rifles and the special pack to put the gold pieces in that we left outside. You start placing and lighting the candles so we can begin looking for just the right-sized gold pieces for our purposes."

I moved the rifles in first and set them against the wall. Then I went back out and retrieved the special pack we had set up to carry the gold pieces in. The room was beginning to light up with the several candles that Jimmy had placed around and lit. Because the doorway was fairly large and the sun was shining almost directly into the treasure room, we had a great view of all it held.

I was in the middle of taking all this wonder in my view when a shadow jumped across the sunbeams shining in from the doorway. I know that my heart must have skipped a beat as my mind raced to comprehend what the shadow must represent. I quickly reached for one of the Winchesters, jacked a cartridge into the chamber, and whirled around, ready to shoot.

There, silhouetted in the doorway with that goofy look of his, was Jake. He had gotten loose somehow and decided he better find out what we were up to. Jimmy had seen the shadow also and watched my action to defend us.

He broke the tension with his infectious grin.

"Buckshot, I thought for sure you were going to shoot that old mule!" he said. "I really appreciate having you with me as a partner. You are the fastest man I have ever seen with a Winchester. I would have changed your name to Mule Shooter if you had dropped old Jake!"

I tried to see the humor in it all; but at that time, my adrenaline was so high. I just set the rifle down and yelled at old Jake to get out of there and go mind his own business.

We quickly went to work attempting to take an inventory. I was to record the items as Jimmy spotted and described them to me. We soon found out that for every item stacked along the walls, there were two to three more behind them. Also, the workmanship was so exquisite and ornate that we had a hard time staying focused. I wrote down about a hundred items and found that no two items were the same. They were all handmade and therefore uniquely different. I then shifted to counting items by large category configurations, but even that was hard as the pieces varied so much.

"Look, Buckshot, this looks like one of my *yea-bi-cha* sand paintings," Jimmy said. "I have never seen one in gold before. Besides, my paintings are all done on the floor and do not have shapes like this one. He would be just the weight we need if we could get him to melt down. And I wonder what stones these are as his eyes and in his crown."

We could have spent a whole week in there looking at all the pieces and studying the wonderful designs. But our time was getting short before the sun would go down, and we had found perfect pieces to put into the pack for our needs.

Then I saw it. On a sort of rock pedestal to the left of the doorway and about halfway back in the room under a large gold serving plate was the greatest find of all. Jimmy froze as he moved the plate to study it.

"Oh, Buckshot, here are the gold map plates that Hasteen Begay told Hanabah and I about!" Jimmy said.

In his excitement to get at them, he dropped the large serving plate on the floor. As I was still trying to write some type of inventory description and not seeing what he had done, I jumped, dropped my ledger, and reached for the Winchester . . .

In the midst of such treasure and knowing that many would kill to obtain it – and with Jake scaring the heck out of me – and now with the dropping of the heavy gold plate, my nerves were really frazzled. Jimmy had not even noticed how I had been so startled. He was so engrossed in the gold map plates that he could care less what was going on around him.

"Quick, come over here and tell me what you think these picture plates show," Jimmy said. "I have not ever traveled very far and have not seen anything like these. You have read some books and learned about faraway places. Where and what do you think these pictures show? Two of them look like when you are high on a mountain, like on top of the Tohatchi Mountains, and looking down at the valley floor.

There were ten metal sheets about ten inches square all made out of gold. They all had writings or drawings on them. And Jimmy was right – two of them looked like maps. You could plainly see river courses and lines that I would think were trails. There were markings of various types, sizes, and shapes throughout the plate surface. The writings appeared to be in Spanish although I did not know that language.

"These are so beautiful!" I said. "Whoever made these were very good artists. I'll bet when we get a chance to study them that they will be maps of the Navajo lands and all the great lands around them. And look! These plates with the writings must tell about the markers on the map plates. See, the triangle markers are given some words that I do not understand – and the same with the other shapes like the squares and circles. We should take them back with us and try and find someone who knows Spanish. They could tell us what the works mean, and we could then figure out their secrets."

"I remember now that when Hanabah and I were here many years ago, we found a plate like this, and we took it with us," Jimmy said. "She studied it and felt that it showed places to the north. She thought that Shiprock was one of the drawings on the metal, and then there was a trail going north from there into some mountains. Yes, I remember . . . that was the trip she was coming back from when she found you so sick and . . . I am so sorry, I did not mean to bring up sad times."

"Oh no, Jimmy, that is a long time back," I said. "It does not bring the pain anymore. But I do wonder what she did with that drawing. Do you remember if she took it with her?"

"I think that she just memorized it or maybe drew a copy on a piece of cloth with some charcoal," Jimmy said. "Yes, I remember. That is what she did because she said that she did not feel that taking such a picture would be good for us. Let me look over there in that part of the room, for I remember that is where we first found it."

He quickly walked across the room and started moving some of the cups and dishes and baskets. About this time, I gave a fast glance at our candles and could see that we did not have much time left before they would be going out. I also noticed that the one Jimmy had placed the farthest back in the room seemed to be flickering like the wind was blowing it.

"Yes, here it is, Buckshot, just like I remembered," he said. "See, near the bottom of the page is a perfect picture of Shiprock that I have seen several times as I have traveled north to ceremonies and to trade back when I was young. And look, now that we have had time give us some knowledge, would you think that this mark is the treasure room we are standing in now?"

I adjusted the plate so I could better see it with the sunlight coming through the doorway.

"Yes yes, I do believe you are right. And look, this must be the Tohatchi Mountains," I said, pointing at them. "And look, there is a small mark there at the bottom of the mountain by that canyon. We must go over there someday and try and find that place. I wonder how much treasure it has in it."

A strong gust of wind came through the doorway. I could feel it move through the room toward a crevice near the back of the room. The candle that had been flickering was blown out. We still had adequate light to see and shift the hundreds of items. Jimmy was so enthralled with all he was seeing that he had not noticed the candle go out. In fact, he was choosing pieces that he felt we should be loading up and taking outside the doorway. I was not too happy about that as I thought it was bad enough that Jake was wandering around out there. If someone should see him and then the gold pieces and then the doorway – well, then we'd be in some trouble. My mind shifted back to the candle. I had some of the lucifers in my shirt pocket, so I went back into the room to light the candle. I broke it loose from where it had melted to the rock ledge Jimmy had put it on, lit it, and held it up so I could see. There was a narrow crevice that could not be seen from the front of the room. The opening spanned from the floor clear to the ceiling. It was just wide enough that I could enter it by turning sideways. I couldn't see very far back in, but it did look like there might be another room.

This is how I found the other entrance to the treasure room. On that trip with Jimmy, I discovered the crevice but was not able to fully explore all it had to offer. On several later trips, with better lighting, more time, and better circumstances, I was able to fully explore what it held. I will only mention here that we found a large cache of obsidian-imbedded wood clubs, spears, and slings that had deteriorated. In a side hole near the floor, we found a body all wrapped up in a hand-woven netting. There were some beautiful pieces of ornate pottery. Some had corn in them, and several had more gold pieces. Again, not wanting to get off track with my story, I will only say that the fissure goes on through the rock formation for several hundred yards before it ends in a pile of rocks on the side of the next canyon over. These rocks can easily be moved, and the treasure room can be entered from there – or was it an escape route for those who originally built it all?

And what of the body? Was he placed there to guard this rear entrance, or was he one of their leaders who died during the course of construction, and he earned this final resting place? I have often wondered about his burial. In all of my years living with several Indian tribes, I have never fully understood all of the burial customs. Some seem to prefer tombs like the Savior was first relegated to; others just wrap the body in blankets, place the body in a deep wash, and cave the wash off to cover it. Some tribes place the bodies in crude wooden platforms in trees. Most of the folks that I have dealt with, and perhaps it is because of their Christian learning, place the body in the ground, with or without a box or coffin.

"Hey, my son, must I do all the work while you play?" Jimmy said in a half-fun, but half-serious tone.

"No no, I will help you, but I think that I have found another entrance to this room," I said. "I do not believe it is for us to explore this trip, but at another time, we need to bring more candles and even some kerosene lanterns and really look around. Here, let me help move some of these pieces outside so we can put them in the box. Do you think we should take any of the metal plates?"

"No, I do not think that we have any time in the near future to go exploring, and we do not want them around our houses so any of the family will get curious or maybe even a stranger would somehow get hold of them," Jimmy said. "Let's wait a while. When we come back, we'll do a better job and have more time. Then we can decide."

We loaded the special pack box with about one hundred pounds of gold pieces. I pushed up the doorway rock so Jimmy could remove the upper key stone. As designed, when I let go, the stone slowly came down as the water in the cistern spilled out. In the meantime, we had removed the lower key stone, and I had gone up the draw and changed the rock dam so the water no longer flowed in the ditch to the cistern in the back of the doorway rock. The engineering of all of this was a marvel to behold. Those Aztec designers and artisans put a lot of time and effort to make such a perfect hiding place for their marvelous treasure. They must have been so dedicated. Their hope for the futures was one of great intensity.

We watched the huge doorway shut tightly as the sun was just about to set behind the ridgetop. Jimmy – in his outdoor wisdom and, I am sure, with some premonition – suggested that we "cover our tracks."

"Buckshot, you take Jake and our load and go back over toward Hanabah's old place and find us a place to camp," Jimmy said. "Make sure to fill the canteen. Take a way that will be over mostly rock so no one can easily backtrack us. I will stay here and fill in the lines of the doorway rock and the ditch where the water flows to it with dirt and needles and other items so no one will know we have been here. I will cover Jake's tracks and ours by brushing over them with some tree branches. I do not want anyone to discover this place."

"Okay, I will take care of that and have a warm fire going," I said. "It is going to be cold up here tonight."

In the excitement and thrill of all we were doing and accomplishing, I had almost forgotten my years with Hanabah up on this multifaceted plateau with all of its beauty.

Her or, should I say, our old home was still about an hour away to the north and east. Jake followed me as I chose a path that was mostly on smooth rock outcrops so we would leave no trace. Jack, of course, was not shod and so did not leave the telltale scratches that a shod animal would have with the metal shoes scratching the rock. I, in turn, had on a traditional set of Navajo moccasins that had a hard-formed sole that would not leave tracks. I decided to play a trick on Jimmy and do everything I could to hide our tracks and see if he could still find us. I knew that that would be almost impossible, but it would be a fun challenge. Besides, if he did not come into camp in an hour or so, I could fire one of the guns or yell to get his attention. He wouldn't get lost.

"Were you trying to lose me, or do you just know how to hide your tracks?" Jimmy asked as he slipped so quietly into the flickering firelight of camp that I did not hear him until he spoke.

"Oh, you know that I have learned well," I said. "I figured that no matter how hard I tried, I could not lose you, even in the dark. I respect your old age, but I did think that maybe your eyesight might cause you some distraction."

"You did well, and I hope you always remember to be very careful when you come to this sacred, special site," Jimmy said. "There are many who would kill to know what we have. I noticed the clouds rolling in from the Southwest. I think by morning, we will see some snow up here on top. That will be good because it will really cover our tracks. I do not know why, but I feel uneasy with our load of so much gold. Old *Hasteen* Begay did mention one time that there was a special curse on the treasure, but it was tied to those who would steal it for bad purposes. I have always tried to have pure thoughts in my mind about what we are going to do with it. I hope you feel the same."

We awoke in the morning to find about three inches of snow on top of the tarp we had placed over us and the one we had placed over our special box and other equipment. We soon had a good warming fire going, and we broke out the food items we had brought along. I saw where old Jake had lain down under a big old piñon tree, but he was now up, scrounging for the grass clumps that stuck up through the snow. I had not paid much attention to our equipment as of yet as we were eating and getting warm. Our Winchesters were still under the equipment tarp as were the two holstered Colts. I had not felt we were in any danger, nor would I have ever guessed anyone would be up on top of this old mesa in a snowstorm.

"Why are you camping on these grounds?" a big rough-looking Navajo said in the familiar Navajo tongue from behind me.

He had a blanket-sheathed Winchester cradled in his left arm with his right hand in the blanket end dangerously close to the trigger. He wore only a flannel shirt and a type of breechcloth. His legs were bare down to the tops of his tall moccasins, which looked like Apache make. His jewelry configuration of several silver with turquoise rings and a turquoise-inlaid silver concho belt had given me the impression he was truly a Navajo. The disconcerting feature about him was the large scar that extended from his scalp above his left eye diagonally across his face, just missing the tip of his nose and ending with his upper lip. He left eye showed only a withered white eyeball.

As you know, the two languages are very close. The Apache form of speech is faster; but the words, to the untrained ear, are similar.

Again, in my youth, I had not fully learned to put my brain into gear before my mouth started speaking; so I dove right in, being taken aback by his audacity of questioning us about land that I had been raised on and him sneaking up on us with his Winchester.

"And what are you doing on my land?" I said.

He shifted so as to point the Winchester more directly at me and not between us as he had started out.

"Your land? You are not even a Navajo," he said. "What rights do you have here? I believe that all white men who come to our land should be killed. You have killed many of us with your Long Walk and disease and poor rations and stupid agency rules."

"Now I ask you again, why are you camping on my land?" he said in a fair English dialect.

"We are coming back from Gallup and heading back to our home," I said, trying to stall and throw him off.

"You are lying to me!" he yelled "You would not have gone so far to trade and come back with just one little box of things that I see you have covered. You have just one old mule to carry all you traded for? I do not think so. You uncover all your things, and I will take what I need."

I was in a predicament. If we uncovered our box, guns, and packsaddle, he would surely kill us for what it represented. Should I make a desperate leap for one of the guns?

Jimmy saved the moment. He was a good peacemaker or at least knew how to diffuse an explosive situation between a young hothead like me and a determined troublemaker who wanted whatever we had. Jimmy attempted to use logic and the truth to get this surly brute to back off his intent to take advantage of the situation. Jimmy had a plan of his own that just might work.

"Now, my friend, we welcome you to our camp," Jimmy said. "This young man is my son-in-law. He helps me in my old age. Would you like some of our food? It is not much as we are headed home and will be down off this mesa in just a few hours. You are welcome to the warmth of our fire. Here, let me hand you some of our bread and meat."

I kept still and did not move. I did not know how I could get my hands on one of our guns before he would kill me with that Winchester, but I kept pondering it.

Jimmy opened one of the sacks of food, and our guest saw the airtights.

"I want some of those," he said. "You open them for me."

"Sure," Jimmy said. "These are very good. I will open them for you."

He produced the opener, and in seconds, he had one and then the other open. There were no manners. He took first one and then the other container in his right hand and gulped the contents down. As he was doing so, he made two errors. First, he took his hand away from the operating end of that Winchester and moved to where Jimmy guided him, or should I say bribed him, to stand under a big old ponderosa pine with its branches loaded with snow. The snow that had been falling during the night was heavy and wet. Do you believe in miracles? Well, one happened.

Whoosh! The snow from the branches just above the culprit's head fell and startled him. He stumbled and fell back, dropping his Winchester. The Winchester was so buried in the snow, he could not readily find it. In those several moments as he was trying to regain dominance of the situation, Jimmy grabbed our camp axe and headed toward our visitor. I threw back the cover over our guns, yanked a Winchester from its scabbard, and jacked a shell into the chamber.

Now I had never heard Jimmy cuss before, but he fully explained the changed situation to our guest.

"You damned *ch'indi* coming into our camp and threatening us and demanding to know about our business," Jimmy said. "You are nothing but a *la' cha i*" (dog) coward, and with this axe, I would send you to hell where you belong!"

I had also never seen Jimmy fully lose it and have his temper surface in such a displayed way. It even made my blood run cold to see him standing over old scar face with that axe poised to split him open.

"Jimmy, back off," I said. "I have him covered with this Winchester."

I motioned for our snow-covered friend to roll over to his left, away from the pile of snow and to a clear spot under the tree where I could watch him.

"Put your hands on top of your head and sit very still, or I will shoot you right here," I said.

"Buckshot, I will find his gun, and then we can decide what to do with him," Jimmy said.

The demeanor of our guest changed rapidly at the mention of my name. He turned to face me.

"I did not know that I had come into the Camp of Buckshot," he blurted out. "I have heard that you do not leave anyone alive who comes to fight you. I have heard that the birds and coyotes eat out their eyes and drag their body parts away because everyone is afraid to bury them."

It is hard to describe my feelings at that time as he expounded on my reputation. Being young, I was swelled up with pride that many thought of me that way; but at the same time, reason and my understanding of the Gospel also made me ashamed. I wanted to be tough and protect my family; but I wanted my family and my friends to know of me as a just, honest, and generous person. I had a lot of work ahead of me to change my reputation.

We dug his gun out of the snow to find that the real reason he had it covered was that it was all rusty, and it is doubtful if it would have ever fired. Guns are wonderful tools if used for the right purposes, but ownership requires more than just shooting them. They are constructed of close tolerance parts that have to be lubricated and protected from the elements.

"Buckshot, I feel we should kill this man and just leave him here to rot," Jimmy said. "That is what he would have done with us if he had looked at all we have, but you and I are of a different kind, and we must not bend to his low ways."

"What is your name?" Jimmy asked.

"I am Hasteen Harry Benally," he said. "My mother is of the Bear clan of the Apaches, and my father is from Iyanbito. I was a good man until I lost my eye in a drunken fight at a squaw dance by Perea. No one would let me work for them, and I lost my wife and son. I am trying to find my way to Two Gray Hills where I have family. My pony is over there in the trees across the canyon."

We retrieved his pony and checked out his poor outfit. Then Jimmy and I tied his hands behind his back with some leather thongs we took from his saddle and made him sit back under the tree. We had a conference away from him where he could not hear us. I had my Winchester handy, and he knew I could easily hit him if he chose to jump up and run. He was very scared after what he supposed was our reputation and what Jimmy had said about doing him in and leaving him for the coyotes.

"I am not a man of hatred, even for my enemies, unless they are an immediate danger," Jimmy said. "We have taken his fangs away from him and brought him back into real life. He has been taught a very tough lesson and probably, right now, thinks his life is over. I feel we should keep his Winchester and his moccasins and his knife. We can put him on his pony and send him toward Tohatchi. From there, he can find his way north to Two Gray Hills. We will give him some food and fill his water gourd. Then we put fear into him about ever coming this way again or ever threatening our families. I am not sure how much he will learn from this, but letting him live will perhaps help your reputation. These are my feelings."

"You seem to read my mind," I said. "I too feel these same things. You tell him of not ever coming near our families. I will stand nearby with the Winchester and be the one he knows will enforce your instructions."

Well, we did just that, and then we packed up and headed for home. All in all, we had had a fully packed two days. We arrived back at the post to find all was well with our families.

"I am so happy to be here with you in our own home and with James," I said when I saw May Fern. "You are the most beautiful, wonderful woman a man could ever have for a wife. I love you so much and thank you for all you do to make our life so special."

"You know how much I love you also," she said. "What brought this flowing string of words on as this new day is dawning?"

"Honey, I had a situation up on the mesa where I was forced to see who I am and what I have accomplished so far in life," I said. "My reputation is not one I am very proud of. I was told by a man that I am a killer and a hard man to be around."

"First, you must consider the source of the comments," May Fern said. "Did they come from someone that really matters? Was he someone who has contributed to life? Does he have family and a goal in life like we do?"

"I get your point, and you are right," I said. "Maybe it is good that those who would try and make our lives miserable think that I am a hard man. That way, they stay out of our way, and we can concentrate on living a wonderful life. I want you to know that you are a queen, and I want you to have all that it takes to make you happy."

"And I am happy, with you here by my side as the sun breaks over the mountains and shines here into our bedroom and lets me caress your strong face, knowing you are mine and that you will take care of us," she said. "I love you."

Later that day, after we had completed our normal bookkeeping chores, checked inventories, and saw that the crew was finishing up the walls of the backyard and the trim on the post, we sat down to a late lunch. It was so special to sit across the table from such a beautiful person. James was in a homemade crib that Junior had built from a picture he saw in one of the catalogs we kept on hand. It was such a beautiful time in life as we contemplated life and made dreams of where we wanted to go.

We both wanted to have a real ranch like the one my father and mother had tried to put together. We felt that with the business and profits from the trading post over a few years – and a shot in the arm from the treasure – we could have just about any kind of a ranch we could dream of. We wanted to raise cattle and not sheep. We both had experienced about all we wanted of sheep and their unique habits and personalities.

Sheep smelled bad, spooked easy, and never seemed to go where you wanted them to. And then there were always the "bum lambs" that were discarded by their mothers that we had to take care of. We had watched and helped skin a dead lamb and then tie the hide on a lamb whose mother had abandoned him or maybe died. With the hide having the smell of the lamb she had given birth to, even though it was a weird-looking configuration, most ewe sheep would let the lamb so dressed up suckle and thus survive. There always seemed to be a number of lambs that we had to bottle-feed that were difficult to pull through. No, we did not want sheep. We knew cows also brought problems, but for some reason, they seemed to be "more our type" of animals.

"Oh, by the way, I almost forgot a crazy experience I had while you and Jimmy were up on the mesa," May Fern said. "A young man rode up to the post in a buggy and asked some funny questions. After listening to him and asking a few questions of my own, this is what I put together: Remember a few years back when Jimmy was attacked by those three men, and I hit one in the head with a rock? Well, it seems they learned their lesson, but the man I hit in the head had a son, and this is who I was talking to!"

"Well, what did he want or know?" I asked.

"This is the interesting part," she said. "I guess he thought that we would not know anything about the incident and definitely not know why they were after my father. He thought we were too far away from my father's land. And to think he was talking to the person who had hit his father in the head with a rock," she said with a devilish grin.

"Anyway, it turns out that the hit did some permanent damage to this young man's father," she continued. "He developed some clotting or something that made him limp. But all he could do was talk about 'that crazy old Navajo' they beat up and just about had him tell where some secret gold cache was. This is where the crazy questions came in. He wanted to know if we had any people in our community who occasionally traded using melted gold pieces. Can you imagine that?"

"So what did you tell him," I asked with a fun grin and chuckle.

"I told him that we did not have anyone now trading with gold," May Fern said. "I told him that I had heard of that same thing, but I also heard that it was no longer happening as far as I knew. I also warned him that asking such questions could get him hurt and that he should be looking to get rich in some other way."

This same type of scenario popped up from time to time over the next ten years or so we operated the post. Of course, we were operating in a very different way with the ingots; and even then, we learned how to go to Santa Fe and even Denver to convert them into cash. But first, I had to learn about assaying.

We had to learn how to measure the purity of the gold. That is, we had to assay our ingots. It turned out that the Aztecs used almost pure gold from either a high-quality source of ore, or they learned how to process the ore. They must have been very good at smelting the ore to remove all the nonmetallic impurities and then refining that mixture to remove any other precious metals such as silver.

As we became better acquainted, I found out from the Don, the local assayer in Gallup, that the oldest method of determining purity is called a fire assay. This is one of the most accurate methods used.

As I learned about this process, it worked right into our plans in that as we melted the pieces and they became molten in the blacksmith shop late at night, we simply sampled the molten mixture by taking a capillary tube sample. We measured the amount very accurately with a special set of scales. We then wrapped the cooled sample in assay lead foil, along with a quantity of pure silver. This wrapped ball was then placed in a cupel (a cupel is a special porous disposable crucible pot made of bone ash or clay). If there are any nonprecious metals, they are absorbed by the hot cupel. The gold and silver is then left as a button within the cupel. The cupel is removed form our crude furnace heated with the hand blower using coal for fuel. The button of gold and silver is brushed to remove any remaining bits of the cupel. The button is then hammered flat, rolled thin, and reheated in a porcelain crucible with a weak nitric acid solution. The acid removes the silver, which is then poured off, and the silver can then be recovered from the solution. The gold is then washed in distilled water we made ourselves with a type of still with condensation tubing. The washing removes any residual acid. The gold is then dried. The gold would then be at least 99.99 percent pure! The sample is then weighed again. The original weight of the impure sample is divided into the weight of the now pure sample. This, then, is the assay.

As I stated earlier, the Aztecs were very good at smelting and refining or had great pure ore. As we tackled variances in purity, we too learned how to refine the melted pieces, as needed, to give us the best purity possible.

But here again I get ahead of my story. I must mention that May Fern, the love of my life, came up with a dedicated method of learning that I recommend to all. I cannot remember who exactly came up with the idea, but it really does not matter.

We realized that we had not had the opportunity to get a formal education and that there was so much to learn about life in general and so many specific items, systems, and ideas to explore. In reading the Doctrine and Covenants, we came across the admonition, "And as all have not faith, seek ye diligently and teach one another words of wisdom; yea, seek ye out of the best books words of wisdom, seek learning even by study and also by faith; Organize yourselves; prepare every needful thing, and establish a house, even a house of prayer, a house of fasting, a house of faith, a house of learning, a house of glory, a house of order, a house of God" (D & C 109:7-8).

We began a special habit in those early days of our marriage. Each and every day, right after supper, we would sit down and read from the scriptures or other books for one-half to one hour. We would always insist that all who were in our home join us. Then we would have a discussion of what we had read. Sometimes, this discussion could go on for quite some time. We took turns choosing what to read and so made a game out of it. The value to our marriage, education, and friendships was incalculable. We followed the council of the Lord and were thus extremely blessed.

One evening, as we were reading from the scriptures, we happened upon the following passage:

> In the celestial glory there are three heavens or degrees; And in order to obtain the highest, a man must enter into this order of the priesthood [meaning the new and everlasting covenant of marriage – Temple Marriage where through the power of the priesthood a man and a woman are sealed for not only this time on earth, but for all eternity]; And if he does not, he cannot obtain it. He may enter into the other, but that is the end of his kingdom; he cannot have an increase. (D & C 131:1-4)

"My sweetheart, I could never live without you," I said. "I could not stand it if we did not become sealed for time and eternity. I think it is time we do what is necessary and go to the temple and be sealed."

"Buckshot, I feel the same," May Fern said. "What do we have to do?"

"I will contact the bishop this week when I go into town for supplies and start the process," I said. "It will be a special experience. I hear the St. George Temple is so beautiful."

"But how will we get there? How long will it take?" she asked.

"Be calm, my wonderful wife," I said with some patience and a grin. "In talking to other church members in Gallup, I find that they have traveled to the St. George Temple as have many from not only there, but from all over the Arizona territory to be sealed. In fact, the trail they take goes near Tuba City through a Hopi village called Moenkopi. From there, the trail goes north to a crossing of the mighty Colorado at a place called Lee's Ferry. Then the trail angles northwest across southern Utah to St. George. Understanding the eternal importance of eternal marriage, so many young couples who have wanted to start their marriages correctly by being sealed in the temple of the Lord have traveled this route to the St. George Temple that the trail is even called the Honeymoon Trail.

"It will take us about a week to travel to Tuba City and Moenkopi area and then about two more weeks to the temple," I said. "We should try to schedule our trip in the fall – perhaps October and November so it is cooler traveling over the hot desert country."

"What about James?" May Fern asked. "I am not sure that a trip of that long would be good or safe for him."

"We have a lot going on right now with building our business and working to learn how to best trade the gold we have been blessed with," I said. "It will take some time to put such a trip together. Let me work on it. I promise we will go as soon as possible, for I could not stand it if you were not sealed to me, and I knew we could not be together for all eternity. You are the best. I love you!"

It took quite some time for me to keep my promise and work to set up our trip to the St. George Temple. I made several trips to Santa Fe to exchange gold bars. We finally got ahead of our funding needs, at least temporarily, and went on a scheduled freight trip into Gallup with Junior.

When we arrived in Gallup, I had Junior take the teams, wagon, and trailer to the warehouses and start getting the supplies we needed. I walked to the bishop's home and arrived about the same time as he did for lunch. His gracious wife invited me to stay, and I enjoyed a very pleasant and delicious repast, along with an in-depth talk with the bishop about May Fern and I getting temple recommends. He discussed the requirements of living a chaste life, being honest in our dealings, treating our bodies like the temples they are, and paying a full tithing. We were doing all of these things. He even alluded to how well the post must be doing based on the amount of tithing, 10 percent of our income, we had paid.

"Buckshot, I strongly urge you to make time in your busy lives to make the trip to the temple," the bishop said. "It will be such a comfort to know that you and your spouse will not be separated in the eternities. I cannot fathom how others who do not take the time to learn of this and other eternal principles do not have this true concept to look forward to. 'Until death do you part' is about the scariest statement ever made if you truly love someone. Especially if you have children."

Chapter 8

I HAVE ALLUDED to our gold-ingot processing. First, I relied on Don to help us move several ingots, but he too soon became too inquisitive and was not giving us a fair price. He was taking too large of a commission. I did not trust our local bank or, I should say, bankers. I was afraid they would in some way let the word get out that we had a gold source. This would bring more pressure and perhaps danger that we did not need or want.

We came up with a plan that I would take a number of the molded ten-troy-ounce ingots in a special box to Santa Fe via the railroad to a gold-exchange place and try our luck there. I wanted so bad to take May Fern with me, but it was thought that I should go alone and to dress and act like a prosperous white man. I was to do everything I could to make sure no one would trace me back to Gallup or our home.

These first trips were quite adventuresome. I was so paranoid that someone would find me out or was following me that it is a wonder I accomplished the assignment. I took twenty-five bars in a special box that I insisted stay with me in the passenger car. That alone should have brought the curious to question who and what. Additionally, I purchased a short Colt and two derringers that I carried. Although no one could see them, I might have gotten into trouble with that scenario in the right or wrong circumstances.

"May I ask a few questions please?" I asked.

"Sure, what can I help you with?" the man behind the counter asked.

"Is this the largest exchange operation here in Santa Fe where someone can sell gold bullion?" I asked.

"We are the largest private exchange here in Santa Fe," he said. "You can go over to the government offices. They do a larger business, but they also take a lot longer to assay any bullion, and they have a ton of forms for you to fill out. So what can I specifically do to assist you?"

I pulled one of the bars out of a valise where I had several other bars.

"Here is a ten-ounce bar of gold that is very pure," I said. "I want to sell it. If the price is right, I have several others I would like to turn into cash."

"We must assay the bar, which includes weighing it and determining purity, before I can give you a price," he said. "Do you understand our procedure?"

"Yes, I do. How long will it take to get your price? And then how long will it take to receive my money?"

"If you will trust us by leaving it here and take a tour of our plaza and perhaps get some lunch, we should be done in about three hours," he said. "Would this be satisfactory?"

I was excited that they could perform an assay in such a short time. I was not comfortable in a strange town. Santa Fe was definitely unique with its old winding streets lined with adobe buildings that almost seemed windowless. The cobblestone streets contributed to a lot of noise as the wagons of merchants traveled along them. The plaza was lined with various types of business. In addition, the portico that covered the entire front of all of the buildings was filled with individuals trading their wares. They had beautiful woven blankets, exquisite hand-turned pottery of many colors and designs, jewelry of all types, and various shawls and silk scarves to mention a few of the items for sale.

I believe it is pretty evident with the explanations I have given about my great love for my wife that that I succumbed to purchasing presents for her on these trips. In fact, every time I returned home, it became quite a ritual for us to have a special time together in our living quarters where I would tease her with gifts. After all, isn't this what life is really about – pleasing your spouse with special gifts and acts of appreciation for the happiness they bring into your life? Many marriages could be saved and built into everlasting unions if selfishness would be eliminated and the desire to please magnified.

"Oh, Mr. Hutchinson, you are right on time as we agreed," he said. "Our assayer just handed me the report. You have some very pure gold here. It assays at 99 percent pure. As you may know, the market right now is at $20.55 per troy ounce. Our measurements show your bar weighs right at ten ounces. As is customary, we take a 10 percent commission. We are prepared to purchase your bar for $184.95."

He was a good salesman. He just stood there waiting for my reaction or answer in a matter-of-fact way, making the assumption that I felt comfortable with the offer. And I did as this was $50 more than I was able to get from Don in Gallup. Of course, I had extra expenses coming to Santa Fe; but with volume, which I hoped to have, and with trust, perhaps I could get an even better price. And maybe I could just ship the bars and not have the expense of a trip.

I too knew a little bit about trading and bargaining. Frank had taught me never to take the first offer. There is always more if you ask.

"Let's see," I said, "I did not catch your name."

"Oh, I am so sorry," he said. "I thought I had introduced myself. My name is Russell Jackson. I am the managing officer of this branch of our firm."

"Well, Mr. Jackson, I appreciate your candor about the price," I said. "But I believe the full price is more like $20.60 per ounce, and 10 percent commission is unacceptable."

And this is the way it started out. I used the pseudonym of Hutchinson because it sounded close to my real name, so perhaps I would not be caught off guard in some future exchange. I too knew how to look stone-faced with that look of confidence, and I knew that there were several other exchange outfits in town.

"Excuse me for a moment," he said, clearing his throat, which is always a good sign that a man feels uncomfortable with his beginning position. "Let me talk to my supervisor and see if there is any leeway in our price."

I won and got a better price. From then on, as they purchased more and more of the bars, they became very comfortable dealing with me. Over the next few years, I had an open account; and all I had to do was ship the bars via Wells Fargo, who insured the bars for full value. By return courier, the money was placed in a fictitious business account that I could draw from. I had the exchange send my money by bank draft without their name on it. That way, my bankers did not know or suspect that the money coming into my account was from the sale of gold. It took time to develop these relationships, but I played the role well, and we succeeded. The exchange company eventually even offered to pay for my fare to Denver where its home office was located. It was a calculated gamble, but I decided to go. I figured they would try to pressure me into telling them the source of my gold bars and how come the bars were so pure. But on the other side of the coin, perhaps I could get a better price. Every little bit helps, especially when you are dealing in volume.

By this time, we had the post and the entire inventory paid for, and we were making a good profit. We probably were offering the best prices on the reservation, and we had people coming form other communities to trade their commodities and purchase from us. We were building a good reputation of honesty and fairness. I still would get a jab every once in a while about my reputation as Buckshot. The story had been told and embellished so many times that I did not even try to bring it back into reality. All in all, we were making good progress.

* * *

After months of planning and arrangements, in the fall of 1906 – with James coming onto five years old – we felt we had everything in order for us to go to the temple of the Lord and be sealed for time and all eternity. We would take James with us to be sealed to us.

I had purchased a new heavy-duty double-sprung surrey. That is, it had springs from the undercarriage along the sides tied into the front – and rear-axel systems.

In addition, it had springs crossways on the front and rear axel. It had a heavy-duty canvas top with a bright yellow fringe hanging down about six inches all the way around. Isinglass curtain side covers were rolled up and attached by buckled straps in case of inclement weather. The silk fringe waved in the breeze as we traveled along. In addition, the four seats were covered with leather, and few even had a beautifully quilted brown leather dash. The wheels were yellow with black pinstripes. The hubs were of the new Sarven design, and I even had them mount a spare rear and front wheel on a special rack on the back of the surrey. No one in our part of the territory had ever seen a rig so beautiful and useful. I had Junior and a couple of the men who worked with us remove the last two seats and heighten the sideboards so the back half would carry a goodly amount of supplies. We would need them for such a long trip. I also had two barrel platforms, one on each side, made to carry two thirty-gallon water barrels. The extra weight of supplies and water were needed to "soften" the stiff springs.

In addition, I had been shopping for quite some time for a pair of matched buckskin mules about twelve years old with black manes and tails and about sixteen hands high. It was a blessing when I saw six mules of that color and size at the stockyards in Gallup about two months before our planned trip.

"Hey, mister," I called to the stockman moving the various animals to certain corrals for shipping or selling, "who owns those mules?"

"Mr. Hollister down Ramah way just brought them in," he said. "I believe he is shipping them to Albuquerque to a client there."

"Is he in town?"

"I think so," the stockman said. "I saw him about a half hour ago going toward Main Street in his buggy. I don't think you have much of a chance of buying them. I heard him talking to an auctioneer and saying he was really thrilled to get top dollar for them."

"And what did he say top dollar was?" I asked.

"Well, as you know, a good horse brings about $80. And a good mule will fetch about $90 to $95," he said. "Well, Mr. Hollister says that he has been offered $125 apiece for these buckskins. I don't know if he has collected the money for them, but he talked as though the sale had been made. Look for a red buggy with yellow wheels. Then look for a big man, about six feet four inches, wearing a Texas creased hat with a beaded hat band."

I headed for town and finally found Mr. Hollister at the Cattleman's Café talking to several other ranchers.

"Mr. Hollister, my name is Buckshot Higgins," I said. "I have the post at Toahani. Might I have a word with you about some of your animals?"

"So you are the famous Buckshot. We have heard of you down Ramah way. Not all of what I have heard is bad, but I have heard that you are not a man to trifle with."

"Well, as you know, you do not want to believe all you hear," I said with a grin to break the icy stare he and his companions were giving me.

Mr. Hollister was a big man with a very casual demeanor. I learned from getting acquainted with him over the next few years that he did not appear to ever be in a hurry for anything, especially when it came to making a deal. Whether it was a trade or a purchase, he was very thorough in analyzing the transaction from every angle. He was about twice my age and was very experienced in running a ranching operation.

"Well, son, I have also learned that if a man does have some type of reputation, at least part of it must be true," Mr. Hollister said. "Yes, I will talk with you about some of my livestock just as soon as I finish with these gentlemen. Why don't you go over to that table in the corner, and I will be with you in a short time."

Thus began a wonderful relationship that led me down several very important new trails in my life. He was a no-nonsense type of person with some very firm ideas about life, but he was fair and generous to those he respected as friends.

"Mr. Hollister, getting right to the point, I am interested in a couple of the mules you have at the stockyards," I said. "Are they for sale?"

"They are only for sale if you beat the prime price I have already been offered," he said, with a very stern look that I later found out was his trading face. I have been offered $125 apiece for those beautiful, well-broke mules. And as you saw, they are all perfectly matched in color."

"Are they broke to pull or pack or ride?" I asked.

"Buckshot, I have been raising mules for over thirty years on my ranch," Mr. Hollister said. "You can believe me when I tell you that one of my mules is well broke. I am not like others as I do not consider any animal to be well broke unless you can ride, pack, or put him into harness. To me, that would be only partial broke."

"Well, you are talking my language as I feel the same way," I said. "I figure if you own an animal, it should be for the reason of that animal doing what you want him to. Disposition and obedience are the two attributes I look at first. And then there is beauty as you have in those matched mules. In the interest of time, what I am really looking for is a fully broke, matched buckskin pair of lively molly mules about twelve years old and about fifteen hands. Can you produce such a team?"

"Why, yes, I can," he said with a bit of a smile. "But you will have to come to my outfit in Ramah to see them. I have a four-up team that meets those requirements. I use them for myself and family. They are prime and will cost you top dollar. Are you interested?"

He really did have my interest. I had wanted to go to Ramah for years but never felt I had the time or need to go. I had been curious to see what my father had been enticed to go look at when we left Utah. Let's see, I believe that the friend of my father's was a Mr. Philip Manning. I felt that I could use this information to slow down the bartering, and it just might keep the escalating price for a couple of mules from getting higher, if this makes sense.

"I have heard of a man that was a friend of my father by the name of Philip Manning who lived in Ramah," I said. "Do you know him?"

"Yes, I did," he said. "He passed away several years ago. In fact, I purchased his ranch as part of my layout. His old log home and corrals are still on the land. Another interesting thing is that he had a couple of mares that I used for a number of years in my breeding program. They threw some beautiful mule foals from my mammoth jack, Lynch."

"So what price range are we looking at for those mules at your place, provided they are what I am looking for?" I asked.

"I hate to quote you a price without you looking at them as you just might not like them," he said. "I tell you what – you come on down as soon as you can. My ranch is just outside of Ramah. We are about forty miles from Gallup. It is a full day's travel with a good team. We will put you up, and you can get a chance to see the country."

No doubt, he was smooth and offered just what was needed to possibly make a trade. The enticement was more than I could turn down. I set a date for the following Thursday for me to arrive. I would then have Friday to look around and get back on Saturday. I have always disliked traveling or doing any business on the Sabbath. To me, it is not what the intent of the Sabbath is all about.

This would be an ideal "practice trip" for May Fern, James, and me before we made our trip to the St. George Temple. I also figured that if I did things right, I could take my four-up team of horses we used to pull our freight wagons and work out a trade for a four-up set of mules. It was a bit of an overkill to pull the surrey with a four-up team, but I needed them with us to work out a full trade. What a fun trip this was going to be! I have always loved trading, especially with an experienced trader. There is much to learn as it is a real art.

"May Fern, my wonderfulness, are you and James just about ready?" I asked. "Here it is, nine thirty, and we were going to leave the post by nine to go to Gallup. Junior and I have had the team harnessed up for over a half hour."

"Yes, we will be right out. Do you have our food and water loaded in the surrey?" May Fern asked.

"Yes, that has also been taken care of," I said. "In addition, just to remind you, I have your special pair of saddlebags with the fully loaded .38-.40 Colts in them. In addition, I have put the new Remington 10-gauge double-barrel shotgun with several boxes of cartridges and a .30-.30 Winchester in the surrey. Under my vest, I will be carrying my special cut-down .45 Colt Single Action in a shoulder holster."

We were still very concerned with the possibility of being robbed. We tried not to show off our wealth, but there was always loose talk. We were told by Junior and others that some suspected we had a hidden cache of money, for we seemed to have all we wanted of everything. There were those who would gladly kill for just a chance at some poke.

It took the four-up team a mile or so to get used to the fact that they were not pulling the big old heavy freight wagon and trailer. In fact, even though it was a heavy-duty rig, this surrey was like pulling a feather for these two big old workhorse teams.

I had Junior construct a special seat for James so he could sit up high in the seat right behind us and be strapped in. We brought Sarah along to tend him. She was a special older lady in the community that had taken to James right after he was born. She had watched him for us off and on and did light housework for May Fern so she could tend to her post office duties and help me with the post books.

James was the apple of my eye. I had so much fun with him. We often hiked into the hills above the post just far enough to lose all sight of civilization as we knew i, and have lunch. I would tell him stories and teach him about tracking and all there was to learn in God's wonderful school of nature. He was a willing and great student. Of course, I did not tell him about the treasure site or the goings-on in the blacksmith shop at night. He would be old enough in due time. He was a handsome young man with his dark complexion, but with my blue eyes.

And oh, how I cherished my exquisitely beautiful wife. She was the center of any gathering at the post or when we traveled into Gallup. Her beauty and demeanor perpetuated by her quick wit and intelligence caught everyone's attention.

We had been invited and stayed the night with the bishop and his wife at their house in Gallup. What an enjoyable afternoon and evening! We spent a good portion of the time talking about our coming trip to the St. George Temple. We discussed the significance of the endowment and, of course, our being sealed as a family. As they both had attended sessions in the temple before moving to Gallup, they gave us insight as to the building and construction of the temple. Their description of the beauty of the temple gave a boost to our anticipation of what we were so looking forward to.

"Buckshot and May Fern, you are going to be so pleased and inspired as you see and enter into the ordinances of the temple," the bishop said. "The building itself is a symbol of great sacrifice of the saints in that area. It is said that for the six years of its construction, not less than one hundred saints were present each day except on Sunday volunteering their services. The site was marshy, so wagonloads of lava rock had to be hauled in and compacted using an old cannon barrel as a pile driver.

"All of these facts aside, the most rewarding aspect of your trip will be the spiritual feeling you will have as you engage in the services in the temple," he added. "Nowhere else on earth will you have such a feeling as in the temples and then to know that your family is sealed for time and all eternity."

"Thank you so much for your guidance and encouragement, bishop," I said. "We are excited and know we are doing the right thing."

We were up and on the road before daylight as we knew the forty-mile trip ahead of us to Mr. Hollister's ranch would take all day. I would put the team to a lope every so often, but they had not been bred to be stage animals; and so most of the time, they were at a walk. They stepped right out, and I kept them moving, but it still took us until just at sundown to make the trek.

"Hello, and welcome to our humble abode," said Randy Hollister as he came out of the front door of their ranch home.

"Thanks, Randy. We could use a stretch of our legs," I said. "You sure have a beautiful setting here among the pine trees. May I leave the surrey here in the yard?"

He strode over to the lead team to a spot where the surrey would be parallel to the house and facing toward the barn and corrals.

"This will be a good spot for your rig," he said. "I will help you unhitch and take the teams over to the corrals and feed them. They are sure some fine-looking animals." Then with a grin, he asked, "Are you sure you need this much horsepower to pull this fine surrey?"

A man of his experience knew full well that I had brought the extra team for a possible trade. This was the fun and subtle maneuvers of trading. It was like playing chess. You had to anticipate the other player's moves and be sizing up what might be offered against what you were offering.

As we entered the beautiful living room, after seeing to my teams and hanging the harnesses in the tack room of his barn, his wife had had everyone else refresh themselves and begin gathering around the large dinner table.

"Mr. Higgins, this is my wife, Gerry; our daughter, Susan; and my two sons, Tom and Ralph," Randy said. "Your wife and Sarah and James have been introduced and refreshed themselves. Over by the back door is a wash pan, towels, and soap if you would care to clean up before we eat."

After we had all sat down at the bounteous-filled table, Randy asked Ralph to offer a blessing on the food. You can never mistake a blessing on the food when given by a member of the church. The use of "thee" and "thou' throughout the prayer and the closing, "in the name of Jesus Christ," is distinctive.

"Randy, I perceive that you and your family must be members of the Church of Jesus Christ of Latter-day Saints," I said.

"Why, yes, we are," he replied. "My families were some of the early settlers here in the valley. They were sent here by President Brigham Young. What do you know about the Mormons?"

"We are also members of the church," I said. "In fact, we are preparing to go to the St. George Temple to be sealed in about a month or so."

"That is wonderful!" he exclaimed. "We are so happy for you. We took the same trip about ten years ago. It will be a special time and event for all of you."

That is how our friendship began. From there, it evolved into a true love of the families. We stayed the night. Then the next day, Randy, Gerry, May Fern, and I hitched up a team of buckskin mules to our surrey; and we took a tour of the community. After exploring the whole valley, we had lunch at the local café at noon.

"You know, Randy and Gerry, the main purpose of this trip was to look for some mules," I said. "I want a pair to pull May Fern and me on our trip to the temple. I am so impressed with the two we have been using all morning. But I wonder if you would humor me, and after lunch, we could go back to the ranch and trade this team out for the other matched team. And let me try them out for the afternoon as we go over to Inscription Rock as you had suggested."

"Why don't you men go do your mule thing," May Fern interjected. "I am so tired from yesterday's long trip and the ventures of today. I would just like to go back to the ranch and relax. Gerry, would that be okay with you?"

"Yes, of course. In fact," she replied, "I was thinking the same thing. We can go back and relax and talk in the cool of the house. I even have a great drink we call Brigham's Tea that I can serve you pretty cold from our cold-water spring cooling house."

I was relieved to have the women let Randy and me get about our business of trading without risking their ideas. Now don't get me wrong, but every once in a while, I have observed some women get involved in a trade with too much sentiment and ruin the whole transaction. Anyway, we would have a real opportunity to talk about a lot of men's subjects and get into a trading mood.

After dropping the women off and changing teams, we headed out to Inscription Rock. I was able to give this "other" team of mules a real workout without the women riding with us. Once we got out on the open road, I touched them with a long buggy whip I kept in its holder on the dash. They seemed to lurch forward from the trot they were already on. Their gait was smooth and very coordinated. With the double springing on the surrey, its heavy build, and the fine springing of the driver's seat, I was elated with the total performance and ride.

"Well, tell me, Buckshot," Randy said, "how do these beauties stack up to what you have in mind for a team to take you and May Fern to St. George?"

"Even though I have been trying, I cannot find fault with this team in any way," I said. "They are the size, disposition, color, and have the training. How old are the four mules we have been working? I have not taken the time to check their mouths."

"Even though they come from two different mares, they are all sired by one jack," Randy said. "In fact, with some real work and trading, the two mares are full sisters. The first pair are fourteen, and this pair are twelve. And like I told you, they are in a premium class all by themselves. Please let me take the reins and show you what they will really do."

Randy took the reins, and with a swift flick of the popper on the end of the buggy whip, he made those mules almost fly! Luckily, the road was in good shape, and it was a straightaway. I had never seen this kind of speed and performance before. I was really impressed. Later on, this speed would save our lives.

"Randy, I really need mules for my business," I said. "Our post freight has picked up, and I am looking to double my freight runs. I have even thought of maybe just purchasing a larger wagon set. If I did that, I might need a three-up team. What I would really like to do is trade my fine four-up team of horses for this four-up team of mules."

There, I had it all on the table. Randy had the team down to about half speed from the maximum run he had had them at. About this time, we were coming to a road on our right that required a sharp ninety-degree turn. Without saying a word, but with just using the reins, he had those mules execute the turn. The surrey, just like the cannons did when horse-drawn field artillery were placed in action, turned with the back wheels chattering around to finish the turn. What a maneuver and feeling of elation! Power and control – this is what I was looking for! Now could I work a trade that would not cost me too much?

"If you do not mind, I have turned into this ranch road to introduce you to my younger brother and his wife," Randy said. "They are also members, and you would enjoy meeting them. He does most of my training of the mules for me and can tell you further about these fine animals."

He was working me. I knew it, and he knew it. I was at his mercy due to the time constraint and distance from my home, but now that we knew each other as members, I was counting on him doing right by me if he had a market for the horses.

We all know that the Lord works in mysterious ways, and here I am not referring to the trade. After traveling about a half mile and up over a small saddle, we could look down on a beautiful little side valley with a large pond, barn, corrals, and good-looking log home made of large logs. The ranch dogs began to bark as we got closer.

"Kent is over at the corrals," Randy said. "We will go over and talk with him and then come back to the ranch house so you can meet Martha, his wife."

Hearing the name Martha after so many years sent a bit of a shiver through my system, but I wrote it off as just a coincidence. I met Kent and further discussed the characteristics of the teams and how he had worked them for sacking them out to ground driving them and to teaming each one with a broke mule until they got the idea of pulling equally. Kent really knew his stuff. I was greatly impressed with all he had put into them.

"Buckshot and his beautiful wife are members, and they are going to the St. George Temple in a month or so in this fine surrey," Randy told Kent as all three of us got into the surrey and headed for the house. "They are looking for a good team of mules to pull it. They also own the Toahani Trading Post and are looking for more teams."

"Well, he has sure come to the right place if he is looking for the best," Kent said with an air of pride.

We have shocks in life. As we pulled up to the house and I saw his wife come out of the door in her long dress wearing an apron tied at the waist and her hair done up in a bun, I was completely stunned! There was my mother to a tee. She looked and walked toward us just as though I had stepped back into time some fifteen years earlier! Could it be that I had found my sister?

I did not want to show my excitement, but I did want to learn as much about her as I could. At the same time, the Hollister brothers were trying to work me on a trade. It was a fun and exciting position to be in and one which required all my faculties to keep it all balanced.

"Would all of you like to come inside where I can give you something to drink and some refreshments?" Martha offered.

"Sure, Martha," said Randy. "Your idea of drinks and refreshments has always held my interests. Your buttermilk and fresh homemade bread with some of your homemade current jam is my favorite. How about you, Buckshot?"

"That sounds great to me. You know, my mother used to serve exactly that," I mused. I was turning over memories in my mind of my childhood.

"Oh, really," she said. "And where are you from, Mr. Higgins?"

"From up north," I said casually. "And where might you come from?"

"I was born in the Utah settlements," Martha said. "My parents died, and the Farnsworth family took me in when I was a baby. In fact, I do not even know my parents' names. I was raised here in Ramah where I met Kent, and the rest is sort of history."

My mind was churning as I evaluated the possibilities. By this time, we had entered into a very spacious living room and had been invited to sit around a very sturdy dining table. But about that time, Randy brought me back to reality while we were waiting on Martha's refreshments.

"Buckshot, Kent and I know who to sell those horses to here in the valley area," Randy said. "There is a lot of logging and haying going on. With your plans for a temple trip and all, how about a full trade of your four horses for my four mules you have seen today – and you give me $40 per head boot?"

That was the fastest trade I ever saw Randy propose in the years I knew him. Later, he told me that he felt very strongly that helping me in a fair way would be promoting a whole lot of good. Bargaining and positioning would not be a good thing to do.

From my standpoint, I could see that this was a good trade; but having no special feelings about it, I had to give a counteroffer to make me feel good.

"Randy, that sounds like a pretty fair offer even though I do not believe you have thoroughly looked at my horses," I said. "I do not want you to be hurt in any way, but I think that the trade should be more like $30 to boot for each animal."

Martha brought in a large tray with freshly sliced homemade bread, homemade butter, and a large dish of current jam. She then returned with a large pitcher of buttermilk and glasses for all of us. I must have looked like I was in a stupor, for I was not paying full attention.

"Did you hear me?" Randy asked.

"I got lost there for a moment. What did you say?"

"I will split the difference with you," he said. "I feel that we have a fair trade. I cannot wait to see those mules pulling that beauty of a surrey!"

"Yes, I feel the same about the trade. Thank you for your kind consideration in all of this. I was just reminiscing about how long it has been since I had such a delicious afternoon snack. I need to get some cows and have May Fern learn how to do this," I said with a grin.

"Good luck with that if she has not been raised around such a combination. It takes some learning to make," Randy interjected.

"While we still have some daylight left," he added, "what do you say all of us go back to my place now that our business is completed and hook up the four mules to the surrey and give them a try? With Kent driving, he can help convince the mules what they should be doing. We can travel a few miles and help you get used to their temperament. We would be real pushed to make it to Inscription Rock. We can save that for another day."

"And I can take some of this food with me to pack for you for your trip back tomorrow," said Martha.

The way she said it and the way she threw her head back was just like my mother. I was so torn as I watched. I had a flood of memories come over me. I wanted so bad to have May Fern meet her so I could tell her all I had seen and felt. If she was my sister, I wanted to hold her tight and tell her of how I had missed her and to tell her all that had happened to me over the last years. I wanted to know about her life and struggles and happiness and thoughts.

"That would be a great idea, Randy," I said. "Just let me get a couple more mouthfuls of this fare and wash it down with this fresh buttermilk. Yep, I'll bet it has been sixteen years or better since I have supped so well."

Martha seemed to be taken aback for just a moment by my comments. It was if she too was reaching back to some other time and trying to make sense of some feelings. Oh, could it be?

"Randy, will you drop me off here at your house and take the surrey to the corrals so we can hitch up the other team?" I asked. "I have something to tell May Fern. By the time Kent and Martha get here, I will come down to help you so we can take them out."

Forgetting my manners and being so excited, I just opened the door and burst right into the living room. Gerry and May Fern were visiting and looking over some of Gerry's sewing work.

"May Fern, may I talk to you for a moment?" I asked. "Randy's brother Kent and his wife, Martha, will be here shortly with a special treat. We have made a deal on the trade, and I need to speak with you."

My words were coming out fast and furious, which made May Fern suspect that I had done something wrong or extraordinary. She got the hint and came over to the door.

"Please excuse us for a moment, Gerry," she said. "I will be right back."

I walked May Fern out past the freshly whitewashed picket fence that enclosed the front yard. There were lilac bushes and giant hollyhock stems with their unique expanded blooms presenting a panorama of color to set off the beautiful log house.

"May Fern, I have found Martha!" I blurted out. "Or at least I feel I have. She looks just like I remember my mother. Her actions are even the same. From what she told me, her background of adoption could make it true. She will be here in a moment. Please get acquainted and let me know what you learn. Don't let on about my thoughts. I could be wrong, but my heart tells me different."

About that time, Kent and Martha showed up in their surrey pulled by a pair of black mules with a high prancing gait. What a beautiful sight – the working mules, I mean. Martha looked so special and happy with her loving husband.

"Yes, my darling, I will find out all I can and let you know," May Fern said. "And by the way, do I need to know about the trade?"

"I did the trade straight across with a $35 boot per animal," I said. "I am very pleased. We are going down to the corrals to adjust the harnesses to fit the mules and hitch all four to the surrey. Kent, who does the training, will show me what they can really do." I gave her a peck of a kiss so as not to embarrass her too much. She was always shy about that in front of others.

The test-drive was even more than I expected. "I truly believe that Kent, with a little more training time, could get these mules to talk, Randy. He has done a superb job."

"Don't talk too loud about his qualities – he will want more pay," Randy said with a grin from the backseat. "You have to give my eye for breeding some of the credit. Without great dispositions and confirmations, he would have a hard time training. As you know, you can't make a silk purse out of a pig's ear."

We all laughed and continued a long circuitous ride around the Ramah Valley, working and stretching out those marvelous animals.

We had the teams hitched as dawn began breaking over the eastern mountains. The surrey was fully loaded with great gifts of fresh baked bread, homemade butter, and several jugs of buttermilk. We had learned to always have several thirty-gallon barrels of pinto beans in the back of any traveling wagon or surrey. Down in the beans we put anything perishable such as the butter and jugs of buttermilk. The beans cushioned them and even acted as insulation to keep the temperature cool.

Randy and Gerry had fed us a scrumptious breakfast, and we had the privilege to kneel abound the table in the living room with them and have a family prayer for the day. May Fern and I were so blessed to make such fine new friends and share a common faith.

"I am so excited to learn what you found out from Martha yesterday," I said. "What did she tell you? What do you think about her? Could she really be my lost sister?"

"Slow down, slow down, my love," May Fern said. "Give me a chance to tell you."

The four-up team of buckskin mules with roached black manes were pulling our heavy-duty surrey at a fast pace on the road to the Zuni junction and then onto Gallup. The golden fringe hanging from the dark canvas top was blowing briskly in the cool morning air. I had lowered and buckled into the place the isinglass curtains so we were protected from the breeze. The dash was high enough to protect Man Fern and me above our laps. We had several heavy blankets covering our laps, and we were wearing coats and hats. Sarah and James were bundled up in the seat behind us. Gerry had heated up several stones and wrapped them in some pieces of canvas. These were used to pass back and forth and hold to help us keep warm. We only needed such extra warmth and protection for about an hour until the sun made its way up over the nearby mountains and warmed us with its radiant beams.

"Sweetheart, I think she is a wonderful person," May Fern said. "From what she told me about being adopted by the Farnsworth family, I really think she could be your sister. Her story is not complete, but again, I do not think she has been told much about when they took her in. I somehow feel that the reason they did not tell her much about the full circumstances is because it would be difficult to explain why they kept her. I know you say she looks and has the same mannerisms as your mother, but of course, I cannot judge that as I was never privileged to have known your mother."

"Did she say anything at all about any memories she had of her real family?" I asked.

"I was a little afraid to ask too many questions as Gerry was right there talking along with us," she said. "I did not want both of them to get suspicious, but she did say in a matter-of-fact way that she had an older brother, and she remembers him being sick."

"I feel so strong that she is my long-lost sister that I did not think I would ever see again," I said. "I want so bad to help her and her husband, Kent, to make up for the fact that she did not really know her real parents. Maybe we can come up with a way to establish a bank account for them so they do not know who is funding the account."

"My love, you are such a special person, but I wish you could be content with the fact that you are only one person and that you are not in charge or responsible for everything or everyone," May Fern said. "Only God knows what is best and how each person will be challenged so they can grow and become the best. I know that you always want to be anxiously engaged in a good cause, but even you have your limits. Let's wait for it all to shake out. I am sure an opportunity will come for you to bring happiness into her life."

We made it to Gallup in record time with those great mules stepping right out. In fact, we beat our time coming down by a full hour. We stayed overnight in the local hotel and attended church services. I told the bishop of my find as to my sister and asked him to keep it to himself. I did not want to do anything premature. We were invited to lunch with the Elders' Quorum president Brother and Sister Bounds and their family. We had a very pleasant visit and then drove back to the post. James was a real trooper during the whole trip. I had him sit with me up front from time to time and would let him hold the reins to the wheel team. He learned to talk to those mules.

We were now ready to put the finishing touches on our trip to the St. George, Utah, Temple over the Honeymoon Trail.

I arranged for Junior to have the use of two teams of horses and harnesses, for they were the best available at that time, from the livery stable in Gallup. They would be delivered during the first week that we were on our trip. Junior and James and another man I hired by the name of Albert could handle all the normal freighting. I would take care of special orders upon our return.

Junior approached me with a concerned look and said, "Buckshot, I know that you want me to watch over the post while you take your family on a long trip. I will do my best, but I am not sure I can handle all of the work that needs to be done."

"What is your concern, Junior?" I asked. "You know how the system all works, and you know the prices and how to order inventory. I have Hasteen Willeto coming over with some of his family as a backup as you need extra help. His son James, who killed Larry and Tony, will also be here with his bride. You will have nothing to fear from anyone."

I have found through life that there are certain people that reach a pinnacle in life and cannot seem to get past it. That is, they can be the foreman on a job but cannot see themselves being the manager or owner of the operation. I used to ask myself what is the mind-set difference between a top sergeant, the highest-ranking enlisted soldier, and a second lieutenant, the lowest-ranking officer. Where does one change their mind-set and choose to move upward and onward? I have watched many who accept the challenge and take the big step into management, but alas, I have seen many who appear to just be afraid of responsibility. Junior had always been so loyal and dependable. I knew that he could handle being the trader. Almost everyone liked him and appreciated his quick wit. I knew he would do well if given the chance. I knew he just needed a vote of confidence.

"Yes, you are right," Junior said. "I guess I just feel the pressure of it all. I do want to thank you for your trust and for the extra pay for doing it. I will take care of everything." He paused and shifted his eyes away from me and then came back with, "But I guess I feel uncomfortable to tell you that I have heard that it is not the post that will be in danger, but you and May Fern and James."

"What do you mean?" I shot back.

"Well, you know that the only two who really were punished for killing Frank were Tony and Larry," he said. "The others scattered like quail to different parts of the reservation. Most were treated like heroes as the story got told. They were rewarded for killing a bad trader. Now you and I know that is not the whole truth, but you are blamed for killing Tony and Larry. The word has gotten out that you are going across the reservation with only your wife and Sarah and James. Some say that you will be attacked and killed. I do not really know about this. It is just a rumor, but please be careful."

"I appreciate you telling me this," I said. "I will be careful, and you know we are well armed. We will watch out for any ambush and take care at night. I think I will take the dogs with me."

Just like every Navajo family, we had several dogs. Dogs were plentiful on the reservation. Someone was always wanting to trade me a "really great dog" for supplies, or they just had some extra pups. I do not think you could really identify any particular breed, but there were some good sheepdogs and some good guard dogs. I had two that were particularly fond of James and were with him every minute he was outside. They could travel right along with the mules and keep up. I could shoot some rabbits along the way to feed them to supplement the jerky we had with us. I had ordered in and received some Hamilton rifles in .22 caliber. They were perfect for small game such as rabbits. I think it was a model 19 that I took on that trip to help feed the dogs. So that is how we ended up taking Duke and Bullet with us.

We left the Toahani Trading Post on Monday October 1, 1906, in order to travel when it would be coolest and yet not get into bad storms. Even though we were to travel across northern Arizona Territory and up into southern Utah, there could be bitter-cold snowstorms. The temperatures in the summertime can be almost unbearable.

Our surrey with the four-up team of mules was a gem. The double springing of the rig let us ride in comparative ease. I sat up front and drove most of the time although May Fern, who was a very capable teamster, took over from time to time. After much deliberation, we decided to take Sarah with us to help take care of James and assist May Fern with some of the camp chores. She and James rode in the second seat.

The storage part in the back where the other two seats normally go held all of our foodstuffs and cooking items, along with our clothing and backup items. May Fern and Sarah were both partial to Dutch ovens for cooking. It was an art in knowing how to prepare food in them, but the advantages were that the food stayed warm and was free of ashes that happened when just frying pans were used. They really knew how to cook great meals. We had several barrels of beans and one of flour with eggs and baked goods packed in them. We had handpicked a variety of airtights and had them safely stored in wooden crates. We had our two thirty-gallon water barrels securely tied to the barrel shelves, one on each side of the surrey. The waterproof top and the isinglass curtains provided us with weatherproofing. Yes, we were very fortunate for our time, and we were on our way to be sealed for eternity.

Junior helped me design a double scabbard on the back of the front seat. The two scabbards provided holstering for two .30-.30 Winchesters. One could be pulled from one side of the surrey and the other from the opposite side. In reality, it was not very hard to pull them from inside the surrey. A heavy piece of canvas was sewn along the top of the back of the front seat so as to cover them from prying eyes. Behind the second seat, I constructed a similar scabbard for the double-barrel 10-gauge shotgun with twenty-inch barrels. This wonderful weapon had outside hammers and steel barrels. It was made by Remington Arms. On the dash in front of the front seat, Junior and I installed three U-shaped spring clips. Just below them on the floor were holders for the stocks for the two Winchesters and the shotgun. What this allowed us to do was have them standing upright in front of us so that we could show off our weaponry and be able to choose what to shoot in a very rapid scenario. In addition, I had my .45 Colt Single Action, and May Fern had her special saddlebags handy with her matched pair of .38-.40s. Those were the days of desperados and bandits of all types and limited law enforcement. I would take no chances with my family's well-being.

"I am so excited to be going on this trip," May Fern said. "I have never traveled in this direction across the reservation. How many nights before we get to Moenkopi where we hit what they call the Honeymoon Trail for those couples coming up from central Arizona Territory?"

"As you know, we can only make about thirty miles each day, and according to the agency map I sent for, we have about 180 miles to Moenkopi," I said. "It will take us about a week to get there. I understand there is a chapel there, and we will spend Sunday resting the animals and ourselves and attending church."

The team pulled well. In fact, I had to hold them back in many places because the road was so poor. The holes, rocks, and washes made it so we had to go slow or break something. Even though we had the best wheels designed with the newer metal hubs, the right twist on the spokes could break one – and there were just not that many blacksmith shops. Even then, they did not always have a wheelwright who knew how to repair a wheel.

"I did not want to alarm you before we set out, but Junior told me before we left that we might be followed or that some of the thugs who killed Frank may be looking for a chance to get us since we are alone," I said. "I know of your ability to spot danger and being able to shoot. I do not have any fear, but let's not let our guard down. We will not let anyone into our camp, and we will keep anyone we do not like at a distance. The dogs will warn us at night. The Lord will watch over us if we are vigilant. I love you."

The first night, we made it to the junction where you turn to go to Fort Defiance. We decided not to take the side trip. We dry camped by some huge rocks where others had camped. There was some pretty good feed out a ways. I took the mules on long ropes, one of the dogs, and a Winchester while May Fern and Sarah fixed supper. After a couple of hours of grazing, I brought the mules back to camp; we ate and then went to bed. This was pretty much our routine for the trip.

"How far is it to the next good water?" I asked.

"You have about ten more miles to the Hubbell Trading Post, or you can go to the Ganado Mission for water," the freighter said. "The trading post has all the things you will need. We are freighting from there for Mr. Hubbell."

"Thank you very much for the information," I said. "Can I get some grain for my mules?"

"Yes. Just look for the big old barn," he said. "They have plenty of feed there. And by the way, those are the finest-looking mules I have ever seen. Mr. Hubbell will probably want to buy them from you or trade you, so be careful," the freighter said as he spit a stream of tobacco juice down from his high seat on the wagon.

Sure enough, in about ten miles, we looked down the grade to the valley bottom and could see lots of cultivated land and some impressive buildings.

"We will have some great food tonight and maybe even a place indoors to sleep," May Fern said. "Where should we go first – the trading post or over in that direction to the mission?"

"I think we should go to the trading post first and get a feel of the community," I said. "Then if we need to, we can go to the mission. What a beautiful oasis in the grand scheme of things. Here, all day, we have been traveling in desert areas with very little green. And now we have hay fields. This is sort of like Ramah."

I turned the teams at the junction and followed the sign toward the post. A fairly large bearded man wearing glasses in his midfifties was sitting on a bench in front of the post talking to several Navajos as we drove up. I skirted the post to an open space with a log fence that I could tie the lead team to. After helping the women down from the surrey and taking James in my arms, we headed to the front door.

"Welcome, folks," said the bearded man. "We are always happy to have visitors. My name is John Hubbell, and this is my trading post. We have a great selection of goods if we can be of service to you. And by the way, those are some fine-looking mules and rig. You will have to tell me about them."

His demeanor was all friendship and helpfulness. He had the reputation of being the best trader on the reservation. It is all in the service given, and he understood that.

"Why, thank you very much, Mr. Hubbell," I said. "I am Buckshot Higgins, and this is my wife, May Fern. This is my son, James, and this is Sarah. I am the trader at the Toahani Trading Post just north of Gallup."

"This would be about your second day out, right?" he asked. "I sort of heard you were headed this way. Come on in, and let's talk. I would like you to meet my wife."

We went into the spacious store part of the post. It was everything a post should be. There was at least double the inventory we carried. Of course, they had a larger trading area and were farther from any center of trade like we had just thirty miles away in Gallup. The large stone building was constructed very well. I especially liked the stone floor. There were customers being waited on. I have been to the post many times, but I will never forget my first impression of how large and well laid out it was, not to mention the grand aura of friendliness and service.

"Lina, this is Buckshot and May Fern Higgins and their son, James, of the Toahani Trading Post," Mr. Hubbell said. "And this is their friend Sarah. They arrived in a very special surrey pulled by four of the finest mules I have ever seen. While you welcome the others, I will go out with Buckshot and arrange for putting up their animals and rig."

We went outside, and as we rounded the corner of the post building, there came into view one of the most prestigious barns I have ever seen in my life. I stopped as I took in its size and construction.

"Buckshot, we can put your mules in the barn here and feed them," Mr. Hubbell said. "I specially built this barn for my freighting stock. Most of my horses and mules are out on the road right now, so your animals are welcome to be stalled for the night. I will charge you a minimal fee of $1 per animal to include feed, water, and stabling. Is that okay?"

He then went on to tell me about how he came about building such a wonderful edifice. I was so interested in how he had laid out his buildings and corrals as we had just gone through the same type of experience and still had much to do. Perhaps I could learn something from him.

"I purchased this post from Mr. Leonard in the early '70s," Mr. Hubbell said. "It took me a few years to settle on a spot to build my permanent buildings. Here in '83, I began my stone buildings. I constructed the post buildings first. I made some mistakes in that they should have been larger, and I should have thought ahead for growth, but I suppose that happens to all of us. I wanted to build all of my buildings from stone. As a young man, I had been an interpreter for the army and saw the total destruction of many wood buildings when accidentally or purposely set on fire. In addition, we were still open to Indian attacks back then, and I wanted to have a defensible position. I started to build the post from just laid-up rocks but soon found an impressive sandstone outcrop about two miles away. I decided to use that as my building material. Next, I had to find some stonemasons. Or I should say, we learned together how to lay up the rock."

"John, you have done a wonderful job," I said. "We too have been going through such a building process since Frank, the previous trader, was killed by a renegade bunch. My thoughts have been as yours in that we have built of stone and have even put in rifle ports in our walls. Our post was originally of adobe, and the fire made the walls brittle, and we could not fully use them in rebuilding."

By this time, we were standing by the surrey and the mules. John turned and said, "I heard of the unfortunate events at your post a few years back. I also heard that you killed a couple of the guilty ones and were a formidable man to come up against. Is this true? I see under your vest that you are carrying a Colt."

This was an observant man. He had a great reputation of fairness, but firmness. I had even heard that he was a sheriff at one time and was engaged in politics at several levels. He had accomplished a lot to be admired.

"As you know, John, stories get exaggerated as they are retold," I said. "I consider myself to be a fair man as most men will not be intimidated or threatened or stand for anyone doing harm to my family. If this makes me a formidable man, then so be it."

With a ready grin and a demeanor that put me at ease, he said, "Buckshot, I am of the same ilk. I too have had to stand up to a group of ruffians and tell them how it is. Luckily, I have never had to kill anyone. And thankfully, I do not know how close I have come. I had to feel you out in this matter and determine your attitude. I needed to know whether to side with you or to find out if you perhaps were one who was not of good character. Now that I feel you are a just man and are not looking for a fight, I must give you a warning. Several days ago, some young men came to the store and were inquiring about you. Seems they knew you were coming this way alone. They indicated from their questions that they may try and waylay you. They were asking how the road lay from here to the Hopi villages. If you do not know, there are several places where you have to cross washes and go through passes where you could be attacked."

"I appreciate the warning, John," I said. "These men are probably part of the group that burned the post and killed Frank. They know they are guilty and have never knowingly returned to the community. They have apparently been living as outlaws, and I would not put it past them to try and do us harm. I hope my reputation and . . . here, let me show you something."

As we were standing right alongside the surrey, I lifted the canvas cover on the back of the front seat to expose the two Winchesters.

"As you can see, we are ready and able to defend ourselves against such cowards, and these are not the only weapons available," I said. "I would appreciate it if you could put the word out through your network of community members that we are ready to defend ourselves and will do so to the peril of anyone who tries to do us harm."

"Buckshot, you are man of my own feelings," John said. "I will do you one better. I will put out our message, but I will add to it that anyone who attempts to harm you or your family will have me to deal with personally."

What a great feeling to know that there are good people in life who are ready and able to defend that which is right and not shirk from defending right. There are too many fence-sitters in life or cowards who say they do not want to become involved and, thus, support evil. This is one of many reasons I love the Book of Mormon. In that great book, there are examples of both types of people. Part of living is to choose what to stand for and then exert every effort to stand on the side of right no matter the threat.

"Buckshot, let me tell you more about building my barn as we unhitch your mules and get them to the stalls," John said. "As I told you, I determined to build the barn out of stone and started to quarry the stone about six years ago. I wanted the barn to be very large so as to hold the necessary quantity of feed and offer full shelter to twenty animals. I also wanted a workshop and a blacksmith shop. The timber I needed for ceiling and roof I hauled from the Defiance Plateau about fifteen miles away. I then covered the poles that were laid over the beams at right angles with bark and earth. That made the building about as secure as you can make one. Your animals will be safe and well taken care of for tonight, and your surrey will be safe. I have a guard who is in charge of it all at night, and besides, the community is made up of great people who would not put up with any foolishness to the post."

John and Lina invited us to stay the night with them. They had a couple of extra rooms. In addition, they fed us a wonderful supper and sent us off in the morning with full stomachs. We left before daylight in order to get as many miles behind us as possible. We were headed toward the Hopi villages. We hoped to make it to Jeddito even though it was about forty miles away. If the roads were in good condition, the four-up team would get us there. We were hoping for a good campground with water and feed.

"I don't like the three men on ponies that I see over on the ridge, May Fern," I said.

"I agree," she said. "And I don't know if you have seen, but there are two more to the left."

"No, I had not seen them, but I have a plan," I said. "I am going to stop here and adjust the harnesses. So if we have to make a run for it, the mules can perform to the maximum. From the looks of the road ahead, it might be very trying. It looks like we have several washes to go through that might slow us down. That would be a good place for them to ambush us if they are so inclined. While I am taking care of the harnesses, you walk around the surrey and pull both Winchesters and the shotgun. Make sure they can see you do it. Place them in the clip holders on the dash. Then get your saddlebags and have them between us where you can get at your Colts. They may think they can do some damage, but I guarantee you we will give them a fight they will never forget."

I figured that with the Winchesters, shotgun, and pistols, we had at least thirty rounds we could fire before reloading, and we could do that on the run. We had plenty of extra ammunition if needed. The only vulnerable spot in our situation were the mules. If they shot our mules, we would be at their mercy as far as making it to the next safe place. My hope was they wanted the mules alive so they could sell them for the high prices they would bring more than they wanted us dead or wounded. It turned out I was apparently right.

I made sure James was buckled in good and that Sarah was aware of all that might happen. Her job was to take care of James no matter what happened. I knew that they were not interested in her personally and that for them, to kill a child would really put them in bad with all reasonable people.

"Well now, don't we look like we are a tough outfit with these guns standing up here?" I remarked? "I noticed that as soon as you put that first Winchester in place, both of the groups quickly faded out of sight. I hope my terrible reputation is imbedded in their minds. Even though Jimmy did the actual shooting, I think the story goes that I killed both Larry and Tony. For my family, I hope that is what they believe."

"My darling, if they only knew the real you and how fair you are and how you try so hard to help and not hinder people, I am sure they would attack," May Fern said. "They would know that you would give them every benefit of the doubt before killing them. But you know how much I love you and James, and I recall reading a poem some time back. It was just a few verses on a man's view of things. I think he intends to make it a full-blown poem or such. I memorized the point of it."

> And Man knows it! Knows, moreover, that the Woman that God gave him
> Must command but may not govern – shall enthrall but not enslave him.
> And She knows, because She warns him, and Her instincts never fail,
> That the Female of Her Species is more deadly than the Male.[4]

With that statement by May Fern, I knew we would prevail. I spoke to the mules and let them know that we needed to move out with all they had and to follow the road without an accident. It was quite a challenge.

[4] Kipling, *The Female of the Species*, lines 49-52.

One needs to remember that when driving a surrey, stagecoach, wagon, or buckboard, brakes are not much help. That is when you realize the very small footprint the rear tires have on the ground – let's say about three inches by two inches per tire and only two tires had brakes. The front wheels were turned by the wheel team, and there was no method back then for a braking system. When you are moving along at a rapid pace and want to stop quickly, you cannot do so. It is like trying to stop a boat going at full speed. You have to plan ahead. I have heard many an old-timer tell stories of near accidents in such predicaments. They say that the driver, if he is worth his salt and knows he has to stop before a wreck, simply pulls his pistol and shoots the wheel team of mules or horses. The two bodies then cause the vehicle to stop – very permanently. These stories and thoughts were going through my mind as we picked up speed. I did not know the road ahead. I did not know the intentions of our adversaries. The best judgment on my part and those of the mules to "stay the course" was our only bet. And prayer.

"Do you see that the road has a sharp turn ahead and then reverses course to hit the draw bottom parallel?" May Fern asked.

"Yes, I do, and I can feel the mules see it also," I said. "They can handle it as long as there is nothing in the road around that first bend like another wagon or a big old rock."

Well, there was something in the road. And if we had not been moving at such a fast pace and just trying to slowly maneuver the road like prudence would have you do or if we had had only one team so our momentum would have been slower, we would have been stopped.

"Here, take the reins and let them have their heads," I told May Fern. "They will know what to do when we straighten out at the bottom of the wash. Don't slow down."

As soon as she had taken the reins, I had my Colt drawn and leveled it at the two scoundrels sitting on their ponies, hidden by the bend. They really had nowhere to go. They had a very steep bank behind them, and we came whipping down the center and then on outside of the road in front of them. Their ponies spooked and reared. At the same time, taking a calculated chance that my mules were not gun-shy, I fired into the air to cause even more confusion. I knew that once we hit the bottom of the wash and headed up to where there must be a dug way to take us up out of it to the other side, we would naturally slow in the sandy bottom. And even if my mules were gun-shy, they would just be encouraged to pull faster and get us up out of the wash.

I put my Colt back in the holster, took the reins from May Fern, and said, "Keep an eye on them and any others you can see so we can stay ahead of the game they are playing."

Sarah began laughing, and then May Fern joined in as they looked back.

"My darling, you really gave them something to remember," May Fern said. "Their two ponies reared over, crashed into each other, and then stampeded over the embankment down into the draw. Both the men were thrown, and at least one of them was rolled over by one of the ponies. Whatever weapons they had are long gone, and they will be a while getting their ponies back. No, wait, the ponies are following us."

I should mention that not only did the speed and mass of the heavy four-up-team surrey and the pistol shot scare them; but apparently, one of the two dogs got some action, barking and snapping at one of the ponies. What a wonderful mess!

"Look, it is as I expected," I said. "We have a long pull up the dug way to get out on top, and the mules haven't even slowed down. We are so blessed to have them and their marvelous strength and stamina."

The dogs stayed up with us, but the ponies began lagging behind. We never saw the two riders again on that trip. I do not know whatever happened to the group of three. Again, a good armed and willing-to-fire front puts almost all cowards back in the shadows.

It is sad to say, but in my years on the reservation, I have found that many ponies are broke to ride in such a manner that they lose their spirit and perhaps any stamina they might have. First, most of the horse-type animals are ponies. That is, they are of small stature. Second, to break them to ride, they are put in a corral for up to three days with no water. Then they are allowed to drink their fill and then taken out into a large sand dune. With a full belly of water, they are saddled tight, and a big person gets on them and begins to whip them. They try a few feeble bucks, but it is so painful that they meekly submit, and that is the beginning of their servitude. Then when they are called on to really perform like our thieves needed, they are not trained nor do they have the inclination to do anything but survive.

May Fern hailed at the family in their wagon as we pulled up alongside of them on the wide road.

"Are you going to Jeddito (Jádító)?" she asked in Navajo. "Is there a good place to camp?"

"Yes," was the reply. "Just go up the wash from the trading post, and you will find some trees with good grass and water for your mules. Where are you from? We are from Ganado where one of our children attends school with Mrs. Alice Bierkemper as her teacher. We just dropped her off for the school year."

May Fern answered her question and thanked them.

"You know, Buckshot, my darling, it is becoming more and more evident to me that English is taking over. And even though we try to teach him both languages, he needs to become really good at English."

We went to the trading post to make sure it was all right to camp up the draw. George, the trader on duty, or at least that was the impression I got, was very helpful in suggesting a better grove of trees a little to the right of the main draw up a side canyon. He explained there was better water and more grass for the mules.

"We are very unique here at this trading post," George said. "Note from your agency map here that we are an island of Navajo Reservation land surrounded by the

Hopi Reservation. In fact, you came onto the Hopi Reservation about ten miles back. And then about three miles back, you came back onto this piece of Navajo Reservation. When you leave here, in about two miles, you will be on Hopi land. Keams Canyon is the headquarters of the Hopi Indian Agency. Please be careful because there is some internal fighting going on with the Hopis. We think it will end peacefully, but tempers are high right now."

"Thanks for the update on the map," I said. "But what do you mean that tempers are high? Are we in danger?"

"Well, no, not really," George said. "What has happened is that there are two factions of Hopis. For lack of better terms, they are referred to as Friendlies and Hostiles. The Friendlies are the progressive group and want to come down off the mesas and join in the world as we know it with the modern conveniences and trade and education. The Hostiles want to keep the old ways and stay up on the mesas and preserve their religion and all with no interference. In the last month or so, they had an agreement as to how to settle it. They had an old-fashioned tug-of-war. They cut a line in the rock of the mesa. This line, cut in the rock, may still be seen on the rocks back of the village of Oraibi. Also, close by, is the following inscription: 'Well, it have to be this way now, that when you pass me over this *line*, it will be *done*. September 8, 1906.'"

George added, "It is said that this inscription was cut into the rock by Silena, one of Youkioma's men. The line must have been drawn on the rocks by Youkioma before the day of the battle. Well, the Friendlies won, so they are now free to move down off the mesa of their tribal center at third mesa, or as it is called Old Oraibi. The Friendlies are going to establish a new town a little north of the mesa location. Believe me, it has been strained around here this year."

We camped in the grove as suggested. The weather was great, and we enjoyed the campfire. The mules were tethered on long ropes. The dogs were nearby. We had a good night's sleep.

"May Fern, we are right on schedule," I said. "The scare the hoodlums gave us probably helped us to make better time, but I do not want to go through that again."

"Great. Where will we go today?" she asked.

"See the agency map here? This is Jeddito," I said. "First, we will go a little north and west to Keams Canyon. By the way, John Hubbell told me that he has just purchased the trading post there. We should at least stop and see what it looks like and how they operate. You never know, we might even learn something to help us in our business. We shouldn't stay long, no matter what you see to buy," I said with a grin in a teasing way.

We did go to the post at Keams Canyon, but we found it pretty run-down. That was probably why John was purchasing it. He could see the potential if run right with good customer service and organization.

"That was a waste of my shopping time," May Fern joked. "I could have ordered anything they have there from my catalogs and got a better deal. I hope John polishes the inventory and gives those folks some better selection."

"Fine, my love, let's get out of here and go on to Shungopavi," I said. "We will have put in a good day, and it should be a good place to stay. One of the Hopis at the trading post says they raise lots of corn down in the canyon, and so they have good feed for the mules. He also said if we ask around, we can probably find a couple of rooms to stay in. I do know that there is no love lost between the Hopis and the Navajos, so we should not have to worry about any sneaks looking for us."

The roads were better than what we had generally seen on the Navajo Reservation. I attribute that to the fact that the Hopi people could concentrate on roads as they had more population per square mile on their comparative reservation – and the fact they had been living in their particular locality longer than the Navajos and were a more domestic people.

Sure enough, at Shungopavi, we were cordially welcomed and offered a couple of plain rooms in a building at the foot of the mesa for a very nominal fee. We also found some good food to eat fresh off the fires of a couple of families. The mules were put in a corral, and the surrey was parked next to the headman's home. He guaranteed me that no one would bother anything in it. It made me very nervous to have those guns in it, but they were covered. My packing them into our place of lodging did not seem to be a very good idea with feelings running high.

I love mornings and was up before dawn checking on all of our supplies, guns, and other baggage. All was in order, so I went down to the corrals to check on the mules and began to harness them. I had the dogs with me. Old Duke gave a low growl as I approached the corner of a building.

"I don't know who you are, friend, or what you want. But this Colt that I am now cocking can put an awful hole in you if you don't step out where I can see you," I said.

The cocking of a Colt makes a very distinctive sound that can cause a lot of trauma if you feel it is an action to be directed at you personally.

"Please do not shoot," the voice pleaded as a man slipped into the early-morning light. "I had a little too much to drink last night, and my wife would not let me come in. I have been sleeping here on this bed of cornstalks as it was the only soft place I knew of."

It appeared he was suffering from a hangover as he stooped and sort of shuffled along.

"I'll tell you what, my friend," I said. "To prove your lack of evil intent, grab one of those harnesses off that fence railing and take it over to the near corral and put it on that closest mule."

I calculated that with a cocked Colt in my hand down by my side, and with him having his hands full of the harness, I could get the best part of any fight even if there were others with him. I watched the dogs as they watched him. I knew that either one of the dogs would let me know if there were others present.

"Sure, but I have never harnessed such a team before," he said. "Does the collar go on first?"

"Yes, it does," I said. "Just make sure the opening is at the top and do not spread it too much as you will break down the straw fill. Now put the hames in the slots of the collar and let the rest of the harness fall into place."

Convinced that we were alone and that I was getting the job done of hitching up, I kept him working on the other mules in getting the harnesses on. The more I talked, the more he seemed to be catching on to the process. I put my Colt back into the shoulder holster and led the wheel team to their places.

"I have heard that feelings have been running high over the major decision about whether to come down off the mesas to live," I said. "How heated have the arguments been?"

"If you knew us Hopis, you would know that we really are a peaceful people," he said. "In fact, we have been so beat up over the years by the Navajos, white men, Catholics, and other tribes and never really retaliated, that it is a wonder we are still a people. So when we have a fight among ourselves, it really does not amount to much. We believe in everyone having a say and in their freedom to live as they wish."

"I am very happy to hear that the height of the argument has not come to blows and that you are peacefully working things out," I said. "I do have one question though. What did you mean about being beat up by the Catholics?"

"First, do I lead these other two mules and place them in front of the two you have hitched up?" he asked.

He brought them up, and I guided them into position so we could hitch them to the double tree that was chained to the end of the tongue. Placing the bridles on and arranging the four reins finished the job.

"Hop up here with me, and we will warm these mules up with a little run around town before I pick up my family," I said.

"Let me answer your question about the Catholics," he said. "Way back in 1629, a group of Spanish coerced our people into starting a mission among us. There were a number of priests and a contingent of soldiers to enforce our conversion. As you travel west by Old Oraibi, or what we call Third Mesa, you will see the ruins of the foundation of the mission over on a mesa. We have never let anyone live there or finish building the structure. After our people were forced to carry the stone and lay up the foundation, timber was needed to complete the structure for beams and the roof. The soldiers rounded up all of our men and took them far away to the San Francisco Peaks to get the timbers. They were gone for many months as it was a big job, and they had to drag the timbers back by manpower. While the men were gone, the priests took liberties. When the men got back and heard the stories, they were very mad. They did not let their anger show but instead asked if they could have a welcome-back celebration there on the mesa where the timbers had been brought by the foundation. When all of the arrangements were all made and the party started, a signal was given. The men and some of the women attacked the soldiers and priests and threw them over the edge of the mesa and killed them. No one ever lived there or went there again, and we have not let the Catholics come back onto our lands. Then in 1680, the Pueblo Revolt resulted in a further decreased Spanish influence. We have had contact with other religions, but the only one who respects us and can tell us of our ancestors and relation to God are the Mormons. Do you know about them?"

We talked further until I could see that the sun was just about to start the day. I excused myself and picked up my family, along with some hot tamale-type food that May Fern had for me to eat as we traveled. We enjoyed our view as we traveled along below the massive mesas with their inhabitants so far up in the clear air. It would be many years before I had the opportunity to visit them in earnest and get acquainted with this proud people.

As we passed Oraibi, I saw the mesa with the old foundation and told May Fern and Sarah the story I had just heard.

"Isn't it so true," said May Fern, "as we are told in the Doctrine and Covenants that 'we have learned by sad experience that it is the nature and disposition of almost all men, as soon as they get a little authority, as they suppose, they will immediately begin to exercise unrighteous dominion. Hence many are called, but few are chosen'" (Doctrine and Covenants 121:39-40).

"You are so astute, my love. We must always remember this ourselves as we continue to prosper and be blessed by the Lord," I said. "We need to be humble and let him guide us."

I estimate that we traveled about thirty miles that day, and we were close to being back on the Navajo Reservation. There were no marked towns on the map. We did see a cluster of hogans way in the distance, but that was the only sign of people or commerce. We found a wash that had some water trickling down its center. This would do for the mules. We had our own supply in the water barrels. We camped away from the road behind some rocks. I had purchased some dried corn for the mules. I fed them and staked them out while May Fern, Sarah, and James made a fire and prepared us a great supper. It was another wonderful day.

On Saturday, October 6, 1906, I checked over the rig before harnessing the mules. I found I needed to grease the wheels. May Fern and Sarah finished the camp chores by the time I had jacked up each wheel, pulled it, and applied a liberal amount of grease. It was necessary to grease each axel end and the boxings of each wheel. This was back before we had any type of bearings. The wheel jack was a very important part for each rig. We packed up and sent out for the Moenkopi area. I heard that the church had had quite an influence in the Moenkopi and Tuba City area. Church members had been some of the first settlers and developers of the area.

"I thought I saw a wagon going down into that next draw," said May Fern. "It was hard to tell that far away, but we should be on alert. I would hate it for us to come up on them on a steep grade or on a narrow point of road with a drop-off."

"I was adjusting the reins and so was not paying attention ahead of us," I said. "I think I will pull over on that flat piece at the head of what looks like a dug way going down into that big old wash. I believe we are going to be crossing one of the main washes that feed into what they call the Little Colorado River. Just in case our fellow travelers are not of the friendly type, would you please have Sarah pull your saddlebags up so we have them between us? My Colt will get us by. But if I have to keep the mules in check or move out in a hurry, I will have a hard time shooting, let alone hitting anything."

About fifteen minutes later, I could hear the jingling of harness bells commonly used on freight teams just for the purpose of notifying others that a large outfit was coming. There were commonsense rules of the road that dictated that the outfit coming uphill had the right of way. That is because a wagon coming downhill could back up in a controlled manner in contrast to the loaded wagon coming uphill. This pleasing sound had prevented many a wreck, but it also contributed to ambushes. In about ten more minutes, there came up out of the wash area a six-up team pulling a very large freight wagon followed by another one similarly hitched. Each had a single driver. Trailing behind was a drover with another four pulling horses. As soon as both wagons and the herd were up on top, they stopped. It was good to meet outfits, showing that commerce existed, although I did not know to what degree of success. The drivers set the wagon brakes with the large foot-operated handles and tied the reins around them in case the teams spooked. They climbed down from their high seats to palaver with us.

The driver of the lead team walked over to our surrey and held out his hand.

"Hi, I am Josiah Smith. And this runt is my little brother, Emmett," he said. It was an obvious joke as Emmett, who then held out his hand, was a good six inches taller than Josiah and fifty pounds of muscle heavier.

Josiah continued, "We have just come down from Salt Lake with this load of special freight for Mr. Hubbell. Do you know of him? How much farther do we have to go to get to his new post at Keams Canyon?"

"Why, yes, we know Mr. Hubbell," I said. "In fact, we stayed with him and his gracious wife, Lina Rubi, at their home post by the Ganado Mission. We also stopped at his new post in Keams Canyon. That is about fifty-five miles still. The roads are not too bad. There is quite a bit of up-and-down hilly country through the Hopi lands as you pass by the mesas."

"Sounds like we might make that in three or so days," he said. "We are loaded pretty heavy. Our teams are good except for two that have been galled with a bad collar. Luckily, we have extra to change out."

May Fern, a very good judge of people and feeling comfortable with them, asked, "Might you like some bread and cheese and some airtight fruit? I can have it prepared in just a few minutes, and we can sit in the shade of our surrey."

Emmett jumped right in with his answer. "Yes, ma'am, I would sure like that. Josiah's cooking is not the best, and he never seems to prepare enough."

"Enough? Why, would you believe," he began with a big grin, "we started out with three wagons, and Emmett here ate all there was in that other wagon. And the driver starved to death, so we had to abandon it!"

We all got a good laugh at that and settled down on a ground cloth in the shade for a visit. Sarah got the bread and cheese out from the bean barrels, and May Fern found the fruit in the airtights and got them opened. We had a fun feast and learned some information about the area that would help us later on when we returned through there.

"We are members of the Mormon faith and were raised in southern Utah before our family spent some time in the Moenkopi area," Josiah said. "We never went east though as on this trip."

"We too are members of the church," I said. "We are from a little trading post by the name of Toahani north and a little east of Gallup. My wife and son are on our way to the St. George Temple to be sealed."

"Congratulations, congratulations, we are so thrilled for you!" Josiah said. "I too have been married in the temple. My wife and I were married in the Salt Lake Temple. We now live in Salt Lake. Emmett here is working on being married in the temple if his betrothed doesn't change her mind while we are on this trip," he said with another grin and poking at Emmett.

"Thank you. We are hoping to make it to Moenkopi by tonight," I said. "Do you know where we can go to church tomorrow?"

"Yes, you can go to Brother Mai-yaro's home," he said. "He and others hold Sunday meetings with the sacrament and some teaching. You will not find any Navajo members there as the two tribes are still not talking with each other."

"What do you mean?" I asked. "Aren't they members of the church?

"Yes, they are, but there have been some differences they cannot seem to get over," Josiah said. "I blame the Navajos more than the Hopis, but I suppose there have been transgressions on both sides."

"What is the history of it all?" I asked.

"As you know, the key to this whole area and even farther to the south in the territory is the crossing of the Colorado River at Lee's Ferry," Josiah said. "The ferry was put in by John D. Lee in about 1871, providing direct access rather than the tenuous journey of hundreds of miles up or down that mighty river in order to cross it. The ferry is about sixty miles north of Tuba City. The area then became a commercial route to and from Salt Lake City and provided a roadway to the St. George Temple."

"I had heard that there was a settlement at Moenkopi or Tuba City," I said. "Is this true?"

"Well, yes and no," he replied. "Let me give you a fast overview."

Josiah continued, "First, there was a trading post in Tuba City founded in about 1870 by Charles Algert, who hired a manager by the name of Samual Preston to run the post. Mr. Preston would later become a partner with the Babbitt brothers. About four years ago, in 1902, the five Babbitt brothers bought out Mr. Algert. Mr. Preston is responsible for building the big beautiful hogan-shaped portion of the post after becoming a partner. It's constructed of locally-quarried blue limestone, with logs hauled in from the San Francisco Peaks near Flagstaff. The Babbitts sort of fell into becoming traders by acquiring ownership of the Red Lake Trading Post in the early '90s after the owner was shot by a jealous lover. As the owner's major creditor, the Babbitt brothers assumed the operation. But that is another story."

"It was the first Mormon settlers in about 1873 who came up with the name of Tuba," he added. "The name is an alteration of the name of a Hopi leader among the Hopi farmers. His name was Tuuvi, which became construed to Tuba. The Hopis and Navajos had been fighting for probably centuries. The Hopis saw an opportunity to have some help when the Mormon settlers sent to this part of the Arizona Territory by President Brigham Young showed interest in establishing a settlement. The Hopis agreed to let the original fourteen families a place in the area called White Sands a ways from the Hopi village of Moenkopi for their community on one condition. That condition was that the Mormon settlers protect the Hopi and their lands from the depredations of the Navajos and Paiutes. Upon completion of the arrangement, Tuuvi and his wife traveled to Salt Lake City where they met with President Brigham Young. They became converted to the church and helped with the conversion of many other Hopis. Then other families began to arrive as they heard of the good land and the springwaters."

"Then there is a Mormon settlement there?" I asked.

"No, not quite," he said as he helped himself to another piece of cheese and bread.

"This arrangement was satisfactory for a while, but things changed," he said. "First, you ought to know that the Navajo name for Tuba City is Tsnaneesdizi, which means 'many springs' or 'tangled water' from the many 'eyes' or spring openings from the underground aquifer. With the increased number of settlers moving into the Tuba area, the chief told the Mormons that his people wanted to live in peace, but that the settlers must stop building farms next to every available source."

Josiah continued, "The settlers, wanting even more water to raise even more crops, tried to dam some of the watercourses. In 1877, one of the earthen dams gave way and destroyed some of the Hopi fields. This was one of several incidents that strained relations between the Mormons and natives. The settlers became numerous enough that Erastus Snow in 1878 mapped out the town of Tuba City. The community was patterned after the many other Mormon settlements with wide streets lined by Lombardy poplars, gardens, orchards, and irrigation systems, along with a location for a church. In fact, a cemetery had already been started, and a number of graves had been filled. But tensions continued to grow with competition for land and water for the three groups of Navajos, Hopis, and Mormon settlers. In 1892, there was a shooting that reverberated throughout the whole area."

"A shooting? I am a little familiar with what that can do to a community," I said. "Were all three groups involved?"

"No, but it did cause feelings within all three groups to where there was not longer full unity," he said.

"Ma'am," said Emmett, "may I please have another one of those peach airtights and more bread and cheese? This is almighty good compared to the salt pork and dough-stick biscuits that Josiah fed me this morning."

"Do you men ever fix eggs with the salt pork?" May Fern asked.

"Why no," Emmett answered. "The only times we have eggs is when we are near a settlement, and we can purchase them fresh. We have tried to carry them in wool fleeces, but they still break."

"Here, let me get you some more to eat," May Fern said. "Come over here and let me show you how to carry eggs that almost always stay unbroken – that is, unless you have a wild driver." She nodded over my way and gave me one of her special loving grins.

"While Emmett is learning how to carry even more food, let me finish my tale and about the shooting," Josiah said.

"Lot Smith of Mormon Battalion fame and noted for his bravery and audacity in the Utah War was one of the settlers at Tuba City," Josiah said. "He was a man of aggressive inclinations. One day, some Navajo sheep broke through a fence he had put around a pasture area that used to be common pasture. He attempted to get the sheep out, but to no avail. He went home and got a pistol and came back in time to see the Navajo owners taking the sheep out of the pasture. To teach them a lesson, I suppose, he fired at the sheep, killing several of them and wounding others. He then shot at a Navajo woman and her daughter to scare them. Now the hornets' nest was opened. Then the husband showed up armed and shot several of Smith's cattle. Smith, really riled up by now, shot at the Navajo. The brother of the Navajo got into the ruckus and fired at Smith, hitting him and mortally wounding him. Smith was able to return to his home and died about six hours later. This happened on June 21, 1892."

"In my neck of the woods, this could cause an all-out war!" I said.

"Well, Buckshot, it almost did," Josiah said. "But cool heads prevailed. The settlers buried Brother Smith in the cemetery with much mourning. The Navajos pulled back, and the Hopis just sort of looked on, preparing for what might happen. Several families moved out and went farther south. It seems everyone was especially careful about being neighborly, and so life went on, but there was still the competition for water and land. The federal government was looking into the situation, but nothing really ever came of the shooting. It did cause a land takeover that has brought an era to a close. By 1900, there were 150 settlers living in the community. Agriculture was the settlers' primary commerce. They planted some extensive orchards."

Josiah added, "Finally, as the federal government – in reality, the Bureau of Indian Affairs operated by its Indian agents – became responsible for operating schools, dispensing justice, distributing supplies, administering allotments, and leasing contracts. By 1900, the Indian agent had, in effect, become the tribal government. Mormon settlement occupation was short-lived, however, after the Tuba City area was added to the Navajo Reservation. The government pressured the Mormons to sell their homes, farms, orchards, and other improvements for a total of $48,000. And in 1904, they left for good. They reestablished themselves in places like Snowflake and Woodruff, Arizona, and Farmington and Gallup, New Mexico. That is why there is no church as you would think in the area. Just look up Brother Mai-yaro's home there in Moenkopi and enjoy the services."

As he motioned for Emmett to get going, Josiah laughingly said, "Well, we have got to get back to work. And with the way I see your wife loading up Emmett, you will need to get to the trading post to survive."

What a delightful break from our trek! It had not taken that long to learn and make new friends and take a break.

"My love, that was a fun visit," May Fern said. "Do you think that James will grow up to eat like that Emmett? I swear, he can't be filled! I wonder if he has a tapeworm," she added laughingly.

"It could be," I said. "Did you show him how he can pack more food for the return trip?"

"Yes, I did. He was very surprised how we carry eggs and cheese and bread and fruit in the bean barrels," she said. "I really think that he was more interested in how much we had in beans. He made the comment that he could sure eat a lot of those beans if they had any. I made sure to give him some in a flour sack."

We adjusted the harnesses, checked the surrey out, and were on our way. The promise of getting to an old established post before dark had me "open up" the team and let them trot right out. In fact, Kent had taught them to lope at a pleasant speed. Once all four picked up the rhythm, it was smooth going. They were such a great team that they could sense the road conditions and knew when to slow down for curves or rough spots or rocks in the road. What a pleasant day we had! The weather was slightly cloudy. The breeze we created with our speed was refreshing. The ride in that double-sprung surrey was smooth. My family was at my side, and we were on an eternal mission. Life was good.

We came to the community of Moenkopi with its quaint houses, fields, gardens, and animals. What a pleasant scene in the bottomland of that canyon! The mules had done their part, and we were in place a couple of hours before sundown.

"Hello, can you tell me where a person by the name of Mai-yaro has his home?" I asked.

"Yes, I can," he replied in perfect English although he was dressed traditionally as a Hopi. "Just go to the corner and instead of staying on the road to Tuba, make a left turn and go down to the bottom of the grade. You will find his place there. He is probably in his corn patch picking squash. I saw him earlier."

I tipped my hat and thanked him.

"Oh, by the way, if you need feed and a place for your mules tonight, he can help you with that also," he added.

I always remember those last thoughts that he left us with. In those days, the three things we wanted were a warm, protected place to sleep, a place or setup to prepare our food for the evening and next morning, and water and feed for our animals. Now I chuckle at how we look for a motel and restaurant and fuel for our auto. It's basically the same, but what a world of difference in convenience!

"Buckshot, now that we know where he lives, do you think we should go on to the post and pick up some additional supplies before they close?" May Fern asked. "Tomorrow is the Sabbath, and we won't want to shop then."

"Look, here is the road he lives on. And as you can see, it is only a short distance down to the end," I said. "Let's go there first and get acquainted. I can't believe the post will be closing for the day with this much daylight left. This will only take a minute to get lined out for tonight."

There was a big wide-open pasture at the end of the road in front of the houses that stretched clear down to the cottonwoods along the streambed. The leaves had all turned yellow, and the sun bouncing off them made a pure gold vista. The pasture still had plenty of grass in it, and I could see water rippling in the streambed. What a beautiful, peaceful place!

I had slowed the mules down to a walk as we came up in front of what I supposed was Brother Mai-yaro's home. I looked over to the west down below his fenced yard and saw a man and woman working in a large garden of dried cornstalks interspersed with squash plants. The squash were of several different varieties. They had an old wagon being pulled by an old horse that they were placing the cornstalks they were cutting into. They had several squash on top of the load. As I was admiring their harvest, a shot rang out; and up through the field from the streambed came three young men mounted on ponies, trampling the squash and intent on putting fear into the old couple.

"Here, May Fern, take the lines and do not let the mules move," I said.

I jumped down form the surrey, reached behind the front seat, and removed one of the Winchesters. I did not know the cause of this disturbance, but my blood ran hot as I could see the lopsidedness of the issue. It took one movement to jack a cartridge in and throw it up to my shoulder and fire. The first round took the leader's horse down instantly. The second round was ready to go when I saw the two others look my way and change their course toward me. The second shot took out the next horse, and the third shot took out the last rider's horse. The three, not used to such an uncouth method of dismounting, were in various stages of trying to get up and make sense of it all. Whatever weapons they had were gone in the melee and lying somewhere among the corn and squash.

"Walk toward me with your hands in the air!" I yelled. "The next shots will be to kill you if you still want to fight or if you run."

May Fern had fully sensed our situation and went into action. She handed the reins over the seat to Sarah and gave her instructions while I was shooting to keep the mules and surrey in place. She then took the Winchester from her side of the surrey and jacked a cartridge into the chamber.

We could tell the young men were Navajo from their dress, so she yelled in Navajo my instructions just in case any one of them had any doubts as to what was going on.

Then in an unusual stance for her nature, she yelled, "You cowards who would attack old people and destroy their work! Just give us one excuse to send you to the dark side. Now get over here!"

Her voice carried a threatening tone that caught their full attention, and they stumbled as fast as they could to get out of the garden and get to the grassy area. One of them started to complain about losing his favorite horse and that his arm was hurting. From his slurry speech and staggering, I knew that our old acquaintance whiskey was mixed into the affair.

The old man and the woman had run to the other side of their wagon as the three mounted men had come toward them, yelling and firing the shot. They now came quickly toward us.

"You have done us a special favor today," the man said. "I hope it does not come back on you. These men and a few other Navajos have been threatening us and the other families for several years. We have not had the courage to do anything, and the agency is too far away in Keams Canyon to care. By the time they send someone, the men are sober and away in the hills."

"Damn you, now you lie facedown in the dirt of the road and do not move, or I will shoot you," I instructed, emphasizing my directions with the muzzle end of my Winchester.

The four shots, three from a loud rifle, had gotten the attention of a number of people. I could see them sticking their heads out of windows or around corners of buildings. As they could see that we were in control and that no more harm would come from the renegades, they excitedly came to our grouping.

"What should we do with them?" someone asked.

"Shoot them!" I heard someone say.

Then another piped in, "No, if we do, we will have all the Navajos down on us. And they might even go get their friends the Paiutes and really do battle."

"But we must do something," another one said. "This is the first time they have been slowed down from scaring us and breaking or stealing our property. Maybe we should beat them or cut them."

I could hear the crowd's mentality start to build, but I – or I should say, May Fern and I – were in charge, and I had a lot to think about. I did not want retaliation against us or the Hopis. I did want justice, but that was probably out of the question due to distances. Knowing the Navajos, if we could show them that we were fair in what we had done and that three horses, bruises, and damaged egos were all that were lost, I felt they would do their own punishing. The Indian thought was that loss of face or embarrassment was the greatest punishment short of death.

Taking charge before the crowd could take over, I stood between them, and the three subdued men spread-eagled on the ground.

"How many of you can bring me empty airtights?" I asked.

Blank stares indicated, at first, that they thought I was crazy; but then one and then the other put it together and said, "I can."

In a few minutes, we had about fifty airtights.

"Now get me some wire or strong cords," I said. "Put a few stones in each airtight and mash the top shut. Then put a hole in it so we can tie them together. Now some of you men take rope and tie these men's hands behind their backs. Put long hobbles on them so they can walk fast but not run."

The Hopis are a fun-loving people. They could see the fun that could come out of this and knew also that their neighboring Navajos had been suffering from the actions of these "wild ones." What fun it would be to see them embarrassed and to know that they were not invincible.

Staying in charge so that we did not have a crowd mentality build, I gave further instructions. I wanted someone to get some paint and draw a chicken on their chests and backs.

"Now once these three are hooked up with enough rattling airtights," I said, "I want chicken feathers put in their hair. Do not hurt them any further. Just dress them as chickens. Take all their clothes away from them except what they need to cover their manhood. And take away their shoes. Now I need the men who know how to drive a team to get three teams and hook onto the dead horses. Pull them up to the community circle by the trading post. We must hurry as we are losing daylight. Put the horses in a pile along with the clothing and any weapons you find. Get kerosene and pour it all over the pile. I will herd the men ahead of my surrey up to the pile. Now let's get going."

Everyone was anxious to see the finale. I had already heard that some of the Navajos were stirred up and worried that their young men had been hurt or, worse, shot. With everyone doing what had to be done, we had it all together with about a half hour to dark.

I knew that I was in a very dangerous spot and that I had put my family in a bad spot, but to be a coward in life is also to go down a dangerous trail.

I found a large rock to stand on a little off to the side of the fire. I had May Fern standing off to my side with the two Winchesters ready to go hidden under a blanket. I had my Colt in the holster under my vest. I was praying that we would not have any more gunfire.

The three ne'er-do-wells had been embarrassed greatly, having to walk that distance with the airtights banging and clanging and people making fun of them. They could not run but had to keep going as I had the lead mules pushing them along. If they stopped, they knew the mules would walk on them. I had the Winchester in the clip on the dash. I made sure they had seen it was still handy.

About fifty Navajos were standing to my left, and about fifty Hopis were standing to my right. The three bravados stood in front of me with their heads hung low. I knew the speech I had to give must be short, to the point, and extremely convincing. I was praying that the audience, especially the Navajo part of it, were folks of common sense and a sense of justice.

"My friends, and I call you friends because we are all in this life together," I said, "we are here to see that this famous community continues to live in peace and have prosperity. These three men have tried to hurt members of the community. Not only did they try to scare them, but they were destroying the harvest that the two old people had worked hard to produce. The young men let whiskey do their thinking and govern their actions. This is not the way to live in peace and raise families and have plenty to eat and have celebrations. My name is Buckshot Higgins, and I come from far away on the other side of the Navajo Reservation. I am a trader, and I have with me here my beautiful Navajo wife and our son. I show them to you so you can see that I know what life is about and that families are the most important part of life."

I had everyone's full attention as I continued, "I bring these men before you as a community to let you bring justice. I am a very good shot as you can see from the dead horses. I could have shot these men just as well, but taking lives or putting fear into anyone is not justice. Now I ask, who do these men belong to? Is their family here? I do not wish you or these men any harm, but I will not tolerate their cowardly actions. This is why I have dressed them like chickens and hung empty airtights filled with rocks to make noise so people will know they are coming. This is the way that cowards should be dressed. To end this, I have ordered the horses I shot and the clothes of the men who did this cowardly thing to be burned. Is there anyone who wishes to stand up here with me and say anything about what has happened?"

My heart was beating so fast that I thought that everyone there could probably hear it. May Fern told me later that several men in the crowd made moves like they wanted to take me on but slowly calmed down when they realized that this was the right thing.

Slowly, an old Navajo walked over to the rock and reached his hand up to have me help him step up to where I was. He nodded to the men with the torches, indicating for them to light the pile on fire. I knew that as soon as the fire got going, folks were not going to stay because of the stench of the burning horseflesh. I hoped he was a fast talker.

In Navajo, he spoke to the crowd and basically told them that I was right, that the event was over, and for the families of the men to take them home and punish them and make sure that they did not ever do anything to stir up trouble again. He said further that with his power, he would see that great harm would come to anyone who would hurt me or my family or any of the Hopis. He closed by saying that we were all fortunate that this had ended with no one dead or crippled.

"And now all go home and remember that we are to live in peace and not make fights," he said. "Do what is right."

He stepped down, and the crowd melted into the dusk as the kerosene-fueled flames flickered high and bright, and the black pungent smoke rose into the night air.

Later, James would tell of the action and how he was a witness to right over cowardice. He would tell of how life is so fragile, how we only live once, and how we need to be vigilant so that peace and happiness can be pursued.

Sarah was our anchor. She kept James safe amid the turmoil. She kept the mules in check until they were needed to herd the culprits to the town plaza. Even then, as I had taught her to handle our weapons, she was sitting in the surrey with James with the 10 gauge on her lap hidden under a blanket. She was quite a storyteller and made sure all who would listen was told of the action. She was a good and faithful friend.

Later, as I was walking to the surrey to retrieve my family and put everything in order, the elderly man and woman who had been in the cornfield came up to me.

"Thank you so very much for probably saving our lives," the man said. "I am Brother Mai-yaro, who I believe you have been looking for. You came just at the right moment. I am so thankful to the Lord for sending you and your family!"

I reached out and took his hand and then put my arms around him and his wife. I introduced my wife and son and Sarah.

"We too are happy we could be of service in some small way," I said. "We came to you in hopes we could attend a church meeting tomorrow on the Sabbath. Will there be a meeting here in Moenkopi?"

"Yes yes, we always have a meeting," Brother Mai-yaro said. "It will be held at my home. I have a special large room that is usually filled with members. We are trying to repair the old church building over by the cemetery for future use. We are working hard to get our Navajo brothers and sisters to come and join us, but there have been too many such events as you saw today that seem to keep us apart."

"I see that you and your family need a place to stay," he continued. "We have the Jacobs' place right next to us. They were members who were bought out several years ago. My wife and I have kept the home and buildings clean and in repair, hoping someone would want them and settle there. Let me take you over there. You will find a comfortable place to stay. The barn and sheds will serve for your rig and mules. I have several families bringing food for you and feed for your mules. Please let us be of service to you and your family."

"We thank you so very much," I said. "Please show us where we should be. We have had a long day and are very tired."

I awoke the next morning with the sun shining through a window. I could not believe that I had slept so late. I am always up before dawn, taking care of chores and planning for the day. Then I remembered the events that had happened. My emotions had been taken to the top. This can be very draining.

"My love, I have some hot food here for you, now that I see you are awake," May Fern said. "Several of the families have been here for some time feeding us and waiting for you to wake. Please get dressed and come into the front room where the food is ready to eat."

I felt embarrassed to be waited on but knew that sometimes, we have to be the recipient so that others can give service. The breakfast was fantastic, with a wide variety of meat and vegetables and breads. There was a quiet murmur of talk that was prevailed over with joy, friendship, and a thankfulness to be alive and well.

"Brother and Sister Higgins, I would like to invite you and your wife to bear your testimonies today as part of our sacrament service," Brother Mai-yaro said. "Will you do us this pleasure?"

"Of course. We would consider it an honor," I said.

We so enjoyed our new friendships and the pleasant conversation. Then the families left to prepare for church services. I had a few moments to converse with my beautiful mate and make sure she was okay with all that had happened.

"I love you so much, May Fern," I said. "You do not know how thrilled I was when you backed me up yesterday. I knew that we would prevail as we were acting in the right. Your total support was something I will never forget."

I hugged her close to me and savored the moment as she whispered in my ear, "You are my hero. You were so magnificent and quick. Your leadership in all that happened was so pleasing, and I was so proud. It was the very least I could do to give you all my support and backing. I love you so much."

Tears of happiness flowed.

"Mommy, why are you and Daddy crying?" James asked.

I left the explanation to May Fern. I have never been good at explaining feelings. The real miracle of the event came as the sacrament service was about to begin.

"Brother Higgins, coming down the road is a group of Navajos being led by Brother Yazzie," Brother Mai-yaro said. "He was the one who spoke last evening. He too is a member of the church here and a very important Navajo leader. One of the young men whose horse you shot yesterday is his grandson. I know from the rumors this morning that there are two Navajo groups who have been talking all night. One group wants to fight and do us all harm for the embarrassment we put their young men through. The other group, led by Brother Yazzie, has been prevailing in convincing everyone that they got what they deserved for acting so foolishly and were very fortunate that they were not killed."

There were about twenty-five Navajos coming toward us. I was praying in my heart that they were truly coming to attend church and not for any other reason. It was just natural for families to want revenge if someone does any of their members wrong.

In my opinion, this is what separates the good from the bad. The good look at the facts in relation to revealed commandments of how we are to live with one another. The bad, in turn, go off feelings, completely disregarding what is right or wrong and thus perpetuate wrong actions.

"Brother Higgins," said Brother Yazzie, "I am here to attend sacrament services with my family. We have not been here for a long time. What happened yesterday made me think of what I have been taught and know to be true. We are all brothers, and we must act as such if we are to be successful in this life. Fighting with one another is not the right way. My grandson and his friends did wrong. You were right in stopping them. I thank you from the bottom of my heart that you chose to shoot their horses and not them."

Even though it delayed the beginning of the meeting, Brother Yazzie then motioned for his grandson, who was hiding in the crowd of Navajos following him, to come and meet with me and May Fern.

Brother Yazzie introduced his grandson, Ned, and said, "My grandson has something to say to you and Brother Mai-yaro. He is not good at English because he has not been going to school as he knows he should. He will tell you of his feelings in Navajo."

"I am not good with words, and I am hurting from the whiskey and fall, but my grandfather has made me see that I have done wrong," Ned said in Navajo. "I knew better, but someone gave me whiskey to drink, and it made me crazy. I have promised him I will not drink again. It is an evil thing. I thank you that I am still alive today. I know that you could have killed me, and today would be a different feeling for all. You are a wise man, and I owe you my life. I will always be your friend. I hope you and your families can forgive me."

Was not this what the Gospel teaches us in the simplest form? We are here to be tried. We are not perfect and make mistakes. Repentance and then forgiveness are the great gifts the Savior Jesus Christ has given us. For Ned to have learned and accepted would be a treasure of life that would guide him to do great things.

May Fern, James, Sarah, and I then attended a wonderful sacrament meeting. This was a memorable day for us.

It seemed the food would not stop throughout the day. Hopi families and Navajo families alike brought food and visited far into the evening. The community had been somewhat brought back together. There were those who still wanted to fight and support evil, but fortunately, they were in the minority. Adversity does not always create failure. Many times, such scenes bring about an awakening to where people realize they are on the wrong trail. For Ned and hopefully for his friends, this event would be a learning and turning point in their lives.

Chapter 9

WE AROSE EARLY, as usual, and packed up our gear. The people of Moenkopi were there to greet us with all types of food for breakfast and food to take with us on our trip. I double-checked our surrey and the weapons. I had help wrangling the mules and getting them harnessed. It was all a fun time for the community and almost like a competition to see who could be of the most service to us. The women loved May Fern and James to death. James received several hand-carved toys, and May Fern received a beautiful handmade shawl. Just as we got into the surrey and were ready to start out, about five of the brothers came up to me and presented me with a beautiful knife and scabbard. The handle was of a silver design inlaid with turquoise. I have kept it to this day. It was as if they thought I might not accept it if they gave me time to think about it.

We said our goodbyes with moist eyes. What a wonderful mixture of feelings!

"Darling, do you suppose the trading post in Tuba is open this early?" May Fern asked. "We need several things, including some more airtights. Emmett ate quite a number of them."

"I almost hate to go up there with the dead horses in their front yard, but I did it, and it would be better if I face the trader than have him think less of me. Please understand that we might be in for a chewing out, or there may be those hostile to my actions at the post."

Sarah, who was generally very quiet, added, "That type will not be up this early. The lazy ones who are up to no good always sleep in."

We got a chuckle out of that and proceeded up the road where we had herded the culprits the night before. I made a circle around the still-smoldering fire so I had the mules and surrey pointed out of town toward the road we would be traveling on.

I was not taking any chances in case we needed to leave in a hurry. I had Sarah and James stay in the surrey. Sure enough, the post was open, and I was about knocked over by a couple of men coming out with the obvious assignment of cleaning up the fire mess. They didn't seem to be too happy about the chore but had some tools to do so. Then I saw a team of horses hooked up to a slip being driven by a man walking behind it. A slip in those days was a type of scoop used to excavate dirt and move it to another place. This would be the logical way to move what was left of the bodies.

"Good morning, friend," the trader greeted May Fern and me.

"I am Samual Preston, the manager of the post, and I believe you are Mr. and Mrs. Higgins. You sure made a grand entrance to our communities yesterday."

Oh boy, here it comes now, I thought.

He did not look like he was upset, but that was not a very good description of our actions. I held tightly to May Fern's hand and prepared myself to exit if necessary.

"We have never had anyone here with the guts to do what you did," Mr. Preston said. "None of us had ever thought of just shooting their horses. You sure put a stop to their shenanigans and tomfoolery. On behalf of the post and most of the community, I want to shake your hands and thank you. We have been putting up with this type of sparring for a long time. We knew that sooner or later, someone was going to get real hurt or maybe even killed. As I am responsible for this considerable inventory and property, I personally have let the word out that I would shoot to kill the first person who threatened me or the post. This is a tough way to live. What you did took the steam out of them, and really no harm was done except to their egos. Thanks again!"

"Well, thank you," I said. "We didn't come here looking for trouble. We are peaceful, but I will not tolerate an unfair fight, especially when it is against older folks or the weak. May we look around and purchase a few items for our trip?"

"That is exactly why we are open," he laughed. "Is it true you have a post of your own?"

"Yes, we have a small post over by Gallup," I said. "Please stop by if you get over that way."

With the help of an assistant, May Fern soon had a pile of goods on the counter. The assistant was boxing them up as requested.

I stepped up to the counter to pay for the items.

"What is the total so I can pay?" I asked.

The Navajo assistant looked over to Mr. Preston who had stepped toward his office. The assistant appeared to know something about the transaction but was not sure of quite what to say. He had the total on an itemized pad, as was the custom, and was pushing it toward me to show me the total.

"There is no charge," Mr. Preston interrupted. "We want you to come back and visit. And besides, if what they tell me is right, we owe you for three rounds of ammunition."

On Monday, October 8, 1906, we only had about ten miles to travel west from Moenkopi to the true Honeymoon Trail that came from the southern Mormon settlements such as Taylor, Snowflake, Woodruff, Joseph City, and even farther south. At this junction, we would go north to Lee's Ferry at the mighty Colorado River and then northwesterly to Pipe Springs and on to St. George and the temple where we would be sealed as a family

"My darling, I hope that the rest of our trip to the temple is uneventful," May Fern said. "Not that I am fearful or would shirk from any experiences, but I would request peace as we prepare to enter the Lord's house. I want my mind to be open and pure to learn and receive all that I can."

"I too wish for that, my love," I said. "But as we have learned, the evil one does all he can to discourage those who want to take the right path in life. He has made the terrible decision to leave our Father's presence and go against all the council of what is good and right. He and his minions do all they can to interrupt and disrupt all actions for good. We must stay strong and plow through whatever comes our way. I love you so much and am here by your side and James's to make our travel through life the best possible."

The road to the junction was straight and in very good shape. The mules pulled at their best-synchronized pace. It seemed like just minutes, and we turned onto our road north. Looking ahead up the road about a mile or so, I could see a small wagon train of four wagons coming toward us. They were moving fairly slow as one of the pulling teams were oxen. They are great for heavy loads and plod on, but I am so grateful that I never had to use them to move with. We could go about four times faster with the gait my mules had been trained by Kent to do. And if need be, we could really shoot forward and put any team in the dust.

"Hey, friend!" the lead teamster hollered. "Where have you come from this morning? Anything about the road we should know?"

I eased the mules and surrey over to the side of the road and answered, "We stayed at Moenkopi last night. We have only been on this road for a few miles, and it was all good. What about you, folks, where do you hail from? Has your trip been good?"

"We are coming from Utah," the lead teamster said. "St. George to be exact. We have had a good trip. Only scare was with a road agent who tried to hold us up and the crossing of the Colorado. We are headed back home in the southern part of the territory."

By this time, the other horse-drawn wagons were up with us. The ox team was still lumbering along, trying to catch up.

"How do you like those mules?" he asked. "They sure are purty."

I really did not want to get into a conversation about the benefits of mules, and besides, his poor-looking team was probably all he could afford. They looked like they were beyond their prime and not getting enough to eat.

There were four couples – three in their twenties and an older couple driving the oxen. As the wagons stopped, the couples came over by our surrey to visit. We found that they had taken the Honeymoon Trail and been to the temple to be sealed. It was such a thrill to listen to them tell of their wonderful experience. Not one complained of the hardship of the trip, even though you could tell they were struggling in life to make it. Their outfits were worn and repaired in many places. There is a wonderful aspect of the Gospel that until you give it a try and fully embrace it, you cannot understand the happiness it brings regardless of physical conditions about you.

May Fern, always the generous one, piped in, "We have a case of mixed airtights that are too heavy for our surrey. Would you take them off our hands?" She and Sarah were already uncovering the boxes and slipping one of them to the edge.

What a ruse to use, but it worked, and they were very happy to help us out. I hope it made their day a little lighter and brighter.

It took us until noon on Thursday, the eleventh, to reach the Back Bone leading down to the ferry. This was a big old rock ridge that all had to traverse going to or from the ferry on the south side of the Colorado River. It was all rock, and so the iron tires of the wagons left their skid marks from the wheels being locked so they would not turn as they descended this slope. We again were very fortunate with two teams. I left the wheel team hooked to the wagon, and May Fern drove them. Her job was to make them sit back in the breechings of their harnesses to hold the wagon to a slow descent. I, in turn, took the lead team and hooked them to the rear of the wagon. When I purchased the harnesses from Mary, all four of them were wheel team harnesses. They all had breeching to help in holding a rig back if needed. I hooked a chain from the back axel to the neck yoke in front of the team. I then drove them, also holding them back to act as a brake for the wagon. Due to the comparative lightness of the rig and the fact we had four big old mules to hold it back, we went down with comparative ease. James and Sarah walked as a safety precaution. I kept razzing May Fern about her being the only one in danger and that if she did not treat me nice, I could very easily send her and the mules on a fast trip down to the river.

"Oh, my love, you so underestimate me," she said. "You know full well I could jump at the very notion of danger, and you know what I would do to you if I thought you were any part of any mischief," she added with her most endearing smile.

The ferry operator was always on the lookout for business and could see us coming down the hump several hours before we reached the bottom. They were there with the old wooden ferry attached to a cable to keep from losing it in the current. Not too far downstream from the crossing was the mighty Grand Canyon. If the ferry ever got away, the load would be dashed to pieces in the great and awful rapids of the fierce Grand Canyon.

"Welcome to Lee's Ferry and our headquarters, Lonely Dell. I am Jim Emett, the operator. We can take your outfit over in one trip. I will need you to unhitch the mules and just leave them in harness. We will need to remove the tongue of the surrey so we can push it all the way forward. I suggest that you and your wife stand holding the bridles of two mules each to keep them calm."

"Great, Jim, we can handle all that," I said. "We are the Higgins family, and we are on our way from Gallup to St. George. Please take good care of this load as we would like to return this way in a couple of weeks and be repeat customers," I added with a smile.

"I will take very good care of you and your family as I too wish to spend more time on earth," Jim said. "I take it you are members of the Mormon faith. Is this right?"

"Thanks, and yes, we are members of the church," I said.

"For members, because the church owns this facility, the fees are $2 for the surrey, $1 for each animal, or a total of $6 for your crossing," he said. "Is that satisfactory?"

"Yes, very fair considering the alternative of going hundreds of miles south or north where we could cross," I replied. "Do I pay you now or when we arrive on the other side, and is there any feed I can purchase for my team?"

"You can pay me after we get you across, and yes, we have both some hay and grain you can purchase for your mules," Jim said.

As we arrived across and hitched up our rig, we chose to go to the little store and feedlot for some supplies and feed for the mules. May Fern and Sarah went to the store while James and I saw to feeding the mules and looking at this small spot of civilization.

"I can sure tell why Mrs. Lee named this spot Lonely Dell," said May Fern. "I cannot imagine living here and trying to raise a family. The storekeeper says that they go days between seeing anyone and that flash floods down the nearby Paria River frequently take out their crops and flood their buildings."

"I have fed the mules and straightened our load," I said. "We have a few hours of daylight, and so I think we should head out toward Badger Creek. We can make it all the way there if we push."

Even the mules could sense that we were on an important errand. We started early each day and pushed late as long as we had light enough to see by. With the way that May Fern and Sarah had things organized, we could set up camp, eat, and be in bed in no time. In the mornings, I would wrangle the mules, check the wheels and axels, hitch up, and be ready by the time they were packed up and handed me my breakfast. James was a great provider of wood for our fires.

From Badger Creek, we pushed on to a place they called Jacobs Pools where there was plenty of freshwater and a good natural feed selection for the mules. I was able to tether them on long ropes, and they got their fill during the evening and part of the next morning.

"May Fern, this is the junction where we can go north to a little Mormon community called Kanab, or we turn here to the left and go on to Pipe Springs," I said. "Tomorrow being the Sabbath, we need to have a good camp. My suggestion is that we stay right here in this vicinity over the Sabbath. I can search around and find a good campsite. It is about six miles to Kanab, but it means backtracking on Monday as we continue our journey to St. George. What do you think?"

"I enjoy so much associating with the saints, and we have not really had a lot of time to do this over the years," May Fern said. "We still have several hours of daylight, and with only six miles or so to go, I say we push on. I would like to spend the Sabbath going to a formal ward and learn all we can about the saints in this area and their history."

"You are such fun! Always willing to learn and experience new places and make new friends," I said. "I will put these mules on a fast pace, and we will go and find a place to stay in Kanab for the night."

We arrived in Kanab way before dark. As we drove into the valley, we marveled at the beauty of the farms and ranches nestled in this mountain redoubt. What a beautiful place to have developed orchards, fields, and pastures! We drove to the center of town to make inquiry as to where to camp. A couple was just getting into their wagon with supplies in front of the mercantile.

"Excuse me, but could you tell us where we could camp for the night?" I asked. "Is there a place with water and feed for our mules? Where we can find wood for our fire?"

"Well, it all depends on what you have in mind for a camp," the main said. "First, let me ask you, what brings you to our community?"

"We are traveling through to St. George from over by Gallup," I replied. "We would like to lay over here in your tranquil valley being tomorrow is Sunday."

"Might I inquire what your business is in St. George?" he asked.

"Yes, you may, but it is sort of personal," I replied.

"May I guess that it has to do with the Mormon temple there?" he asked.

Not knowing what we might be up against, I hesitated to jump right in with an answer. I knew that there were those who were not of our faith and who might want to try and discourage or deter us in some way. I also did not want the appearance of an argument or mystery but felt that our personal business was just that, personal. Not only were there prejudices against members of the church, but with two Navajo women sitting with me in the surrey, who knows what other negative feelings I might be exposing ourselves to?

"Yes, that might be a fair guess," I answered while watching his demeanor very carefully.

"We too are members of the church," he said. "We were married in the temple in '92. We go there quite often to renew the special feelings that are there."

"George," his wife spoke up, "we can have them use the spare bedroom if one of them is willing to sleep on the screen porch. Their boy can stay with William, and their mules can be put in the corral. We are always here to help and have room for those strengthening their family ties."

"We are the Stevens family. George and Emily. If this sounds okay to you folks, just follow us," George said. "We live just on the other end of town. You will see the church as we travel along."

Without another thought spoken, just like an everyday occurrence, these wonderful people were opening up their home and all they had to help us. The Gospel, when it is lived fully, generates so much love and support.

We followed them past the church and then on to a very comely log home with well-constructed outbuildings. The outbuildings consisted of a barn, granary, wagon and equipment shed, and a blacksmith building. Corrals butted up against the barn so that hay in the loft could be dropped into mangers in an overhung type of stable. This open stable was on the protected side of the barn, away from the prevailing winds. George had so constructed the corrals so that he could easily separate the various animals easily with a common gate system as was extensively used.

We unloaded our luggage and arranged for May Fern and Sarah to share the bedroom. I chose to stay on the screened porch. William, who was eight years old, shared his bedroom with James. Their twin daughters, Miranda and Megan, had their own bedroom.

The Stevens were so kind and generous to us. We had a very simple but filling supper and then were treated to a very hearty breakfast the next morning before attending church. What a very spiritual uplift! We heard several very-inspirational talks and, of course, partook of the sacrament. One talk I will always remember was from a young man by the last name of Stewart. He had been called to serve a mission back east in New York. The power and depth of his testimony was superb. James and I went for a walk in the afternoon down by the stream running through the lower pasture.

"Dad, do you suppose that I will go on a mission when I am older like Brother Stewart?" James asked.

"I would be very pleased if you would plan on doing that," I replied. "You would be the first Higgins to go on a mission for the church."

"Where will I go?" James asked.

"James," I said, with an intense desire to instill an appreciation of spiritual attributes, "that will be up to the Lord. You will be called by your bishop who will submit your papers to the brethren in Salt Lake. The Quorum of the Twelve, with prayer, will receive the answer as to where you best will serve. Then your bishop will be notified, and he will give you the paper with the call."

"How will I learn what I need to know to teach others about the Gospel?" he asked.

"Your mother and I will help you to learn about the Gospel in our readings as a family," I said. "You will attend church where you will be taught even more. You will have the chance to serve in priesthood callings in the Aaronic Priesthood. And of course, you will pray and study on your own and learn. The Lord loves you and will not ever let you down. He knows of your desire and will make sure you are ready so you can be a great missionary."

That talk along that stream bank was one of the most memorable talks we ever had. It was the beginning of James's spiritual growth.

"Look, I think old Duke and Bullet have something treed," I said.

"But, Dad, we don't have a gun with us," James said.

"There are times in life when we don't have to shoot or even want to shoot," I said. "Whatever they have treed on this Sunday afternoon is not important for us to take. I hope in the years to come that life will be this peaceful every day for you."

James and I walked back to the ranch where he had to tell May Fern that the dogs had treed something really big, maybe even a mountain lion. She got a chuckle out of that but encouraged his fantasies and exploration of the great world around him. We were providing a great childhood for him, but the most important part would be the sealing in the temple coming up in a few days.

"Buckshot and May Fern, when will you be coming back through this way from St. George?" George asked as we were sitting in their spacious living room.

She and I had already talked about our return trip. We figured we would be sealed on the morning of the seventeenth. This would give us the afternoon to do some shopping and get set up to start the return trip the next day. Now that we knew the road and what to expect in grades, washes, dug ways, and passes, our return trip would be much faster.

Always wanting to be generous and kind, May Fern had suggested that we bring something for the homes of those who had been so gracious to us in putting us up. She wanted to be able to present them a gift from St. George that would be unique and useful.

"Providing it is okay with you, we would like to arrive back here in Kanab on Friday the nineteenth," I said. "I believe that my mules, barring any accident or washout, can make the full trip in two days. They are broke in really well to working with each other and can move us right along."

"That would work out very well, and we will look forward to you staying with us over the weekend and attending church," George said. "It will be fun to have two newlyweds among us," he grinned.

"Oh, this will be so perfect as the ward has an outing planned on Saturday to the lakes just north of town," Emily said excitingly. "It is such a beautiful place. There will be lots of food and games and music and just fun visiting. By the time you have partied with the townsfolk, you will want to move here."

We all laughed, and May Fern said surprisingly, "If I did not have all my extensive family waiting back home to be converted, I believe I could convince Buckshot to do just that."

Our conversation drifted into our personal lives and backgrounds. I was encouraged to tell the story of how I got my moniker. Their son, William, was enthralled as I stretched out the part of shooting the mountain lion during his attempt to attack Hanabah and me on that fateful day.

I learned that George and Emily had both come south from the Provo area with their families many years back. She and her family settled in Utah's Dixie to try and help establish cotton farming. George's family had spent some time at the Pipe Springs ranch. They had met at church meetings and were married not long afterward.

"George, how did Pipe Springs come to get its name?" I asked. "What is going on at the place now?"

"The place got its name from William, the brother of Jacob Hamblin, the famous Indian apostle, using his pipe as a target for his rifle. He shot and hit the pipe at fifty paces and, thus, the name. That occurred in 1858. The wonderful springs had been used by Indians and travelers for hundreds of years. A few years later in 1863, a Dr. James Whitmore built a dugout at the springs to live in while he established a ranching operation. A herder by the name of McIntyre was hired as a herder. The old dugout is still there just north of the fort."

"In January of 1866, Indians ran off all of the ranch livestock," George continued. "The eleven-year-old son of Dr. Whitmore, James, was living with the two men in the dugout. The two men decided to go look for the livestock and left James alone in the dugout area. The next day, the Indians returned to the ranch. And James went into the dugout for safety, not knowing what was to become of him. The Indians prowled around the ranch but would not go into the dugout due to their superstition of not going into the home of anyone who had recently died. After the Indians left, James realized that his father and herder were probably not going to return. He then walked the seventy miles to St. George and alerted the militia. Two groups of militia were finally put together, and they went to the area to try to find the missing men. Through a series of trackings and taking some Indians as prisoners, they learned the fate of the men and discovered their bodies. As it was winter, they packed a wagon with snow and transported the bodies to St. George for burial."

George continued, "Due to the Indian troubles, the place was vacant until after the Fort Defiance treaty was agreed to in 1870. On a scouting trip on September 12, 1870, President Brigham Young camped at the springs along with Jacob Hamblin and the Western explorer John Wesley Powell. President Young was very impressed with the area and so ordered a fort be built. In addition, a ranching operation was established to manage the southern Utah Tithing Herd of cattle owned by the church. The church members paid a tenth of their increase to the church as tithing, and this was sometimes paid with cattle. The church needed a location to keep the cattle that were donated in the southern part of the state. A brother by the name of Winsor was put in charge of constructing the fort. The fort was built out of local stone and timber hauled from the nearby forests. The fort was completed in the early part of 1872 and was known as Winsor Castle."

"By 1879," George added, "it is said that the tithing herd was at 2,269 head of cattle and 162 horses. Butter, cheese, and beef were the products the ranch produced and sold to travelers. Many folks passed by the ranch on their way from the Arizona Territory to St. George to be married in the temple just like you and May Fern. The fort was an important stop on the Honeymoon Trail. My parents and I and my brothers and sister lived and worked at the fort for a time. In 1888, the church divested itself of the property. It was purchased by a rancher by the name of Saunders. He is not a member of the church but did sort of keep the operation going. You can't get very many items there now. People usually just stop for water and to water their animals."

"George, that is quite a tale," I said. "Thank you so much for filling us in. I can't wait to see the layout and look for the old dugout. Do you know whatever happened to James, the son of Dr. McIntyre?"

"No, I do not know what happened to him," George said. "I need to ask around the next time I am in St. George."

"We had better get some sleep as I want to be hitched up and on the road by daylight," I said. "We have a couple of hard days ahead of us. We want to thank you so much for your hospitality and generosity. We hope you will come over our way sometime, and we can show you around."

We said our "good nights" and retired. As with all ranchers and farmers I have known, the Stevens were up way before dawn, and a scrumptious breakfast was prepared. George helped me wrangle and hitch up the mules. Sarah and James packed the luggage, and the dogs had a snack of milk and leftovers from the night before. We were on our way before daylight.

We made it to Pipe Springs before noon. Just as George stated, there wasn't much choice as to goods to be had; but the watering of the mules was taken care of, and May Fern did get us a head of cheese, which she put in one of the bean barrels.

We moved on up through the beautiful forests and then out into the plains of the red rock canyons and sagebrush. We made a dry camp up from the trail where we could see any travelers coming or going. As was our intent and plan, we had all the items of the time for a comfortable camp.

We were up very early to make the last push in to St. George, or at least that was the intent of all of our efforts. Just as we were finishing a breakfast of eggs, bread, and salt pork, I noted a movement down by the road. It was just daylight, but I could see clearly. I had the mules already wrangled, but not hitched to the surrey, so I knew it was not one of them. The two dogs were lying by the fire with forlorn looks, waiting for more scraps. Looking from a different angle, I saw a lone rider sniffing the air and pushing his horse up through the piñon trees, trying to pick up the exact spot of our fire.

In those days, one always suspected the worst until proven different. I motioned to May Fern to get the shotgun while I pulled one of the Winchesters from a scabbard. I already had my shoulder holster with my Colt under my vest. I ordered the dogs to stay in camp and had James and Sarah hold them to make sure.

I hiked down the hill far enough to be out of sight of camp, but where I figured I could intercept our visitor. I knew that if any trouble happened, the double-barrel 10 gauge in May Fern's hands would finish it. With the thickness of the trees around our camp, the choice of the shotgun was best.

As he came in under a ledge I was sitting on, I could see that he was a typical mountain man about five feet six inches tall with broad shoulders, large hands, and $12 shoes. His horse was of fair size and stature but had been run as it was all lathered up around the front shoulders and withers. His saddle was a well-worn McClellan with large army saddlebags. The army bridle with the large U.S. stamped disks had seen better days. A rolled-up blanket with protrusions was tied behind the saddle over the saddlebags. He had a heavy head of hair stuffed under a crude animal-skin cap. There was a bundle of hawk feathers attached to the cap, which fell back down toward his neckline. He had on an old stained leather shirt with a badly worn fringe down the arms. His pants were of a dark-colored denim cloth with burn holes, and they were grease stained. A Colt was in a holster on his right side, and an old saddle carbine of some sort was in a scabbard with the stock protruding forward under his right-leg stirrup strap. He was unshaven with a full black beard offset with beady black eyes. These I got a good look at as he stared right up at me.

"Well, neighbor, did you think that you could sneak up on old Webbsfoot without him knowing it?" he asked.

"No, I was just sitting here waiting for the sun to come up. What are you doing so far off the trail heading to my camp?" I queried.

"Your camp? Why, I didn't even know that anyone was camped hereabouts," he said.

I knew with this statement he was up to no good. He was trying to size up my situation to see if he could take advantage of it. Besides, no man traveled in that country at such a high rate of speed so as to lather up his horse and travel without a pack animal. This gentleman was running from something – probably the law.

"I do not have the time to palaver with you on this beautiful day," I said. "There is plenty of country out there for you to explore. Just turn your steed downhill, go back to the road, and keep moving. I want no part of your company or any requests."

"Now that is downright unfriendly," he said. "You know that Winchester is only good for one shot at a time, and I am a pretty fair rider. I could easily circle back and take anything I want."

At this point, I knew I was being threatened, and I was positive that ramped-up action would be all this highwayman would understand. I moved the Winchester that was cradled in my left arm to where it was aiming directly at him, and I cocked back the hammer. Unbeknownst to me, May Fern, ever vigilant, had slipped up on us to my left.

"Mister, this is my husband you are talking to, and I do not like your tone or threat," she said as she came around the tree. "You have exactly one second to hit a lope straight down this hill to the road and then stay on it for as far as we can see you. If you hesitate or try to double back this double barrel," she said, aiming directly at him, "that Winchester will take you right out of that saddle and do your horse in also. Now move!"

Old Webbsfoot must have had a determined woman order him around before, or he was well acquainted with the damage a 10 gauge could do – or he just had a lot of common sense in regard to his life. No more was needed. He did exactly as May Fern directed. We watched as he encouraged his steed at a very fast lope down that hill and onto the road. We watched him continue on the road toward Pipe Springs for a mile or more before we lost sight of him as he went around a bend in the road.

We quickly hitched up and headed for St. George. We never saw any more of our visitor. We did learn later that a man of his description had robbed a store in one of the local communities.

We arrived in St. George just as the sun was going down. What a beautiful sight as the sun set behind the mesa just to the west of the town! It took another forty-five minutes or so for dark to set in. By that time, we had found the home of Richard Stevens. They had been told by George that we were coming, and they were waiting for us with all the amenities. They even made arrangements for us all to take a refreshing bath and prepare for our special day. There was a common corral for folks traveling through for us to put our mules in and where they would have plenty of feed and water. We parked the surrey with all of our equipment and goods behind the Stevens' home, unharnessed the mules, and then had a young man take them to the corrals with instructions to have them back morning after next before daylight.

"Sarah, you have been such a wonderful help to us on this trip," I said. "We hope you have learned much about why we have come here. Even though we cannot take you into this special holy place, we want you to think and ask yourself what you feel about it. We need you to come with us and bring James. At the right time, they will ask you to let them take him to us so he can be ours forever. We want you also to be able to have these blessings and hope you will let us teach you about them."

"You have already taught me much," she said. "This trip has been such a wonderful experience for me. Sometimes, it has been too exciting," she laughed as she addressed May Fern. "But you and Buckshot have proven your friendship and protected me. I do feel something special is about to happen. I will be watching and listening."

The most important day of our family's life dawned bright, cool, and vibrant. The sun seemed to recognize the special event. As we looked down the block to that wonderful edifice, the sunbeams seemed to reverberate off the main tower and glisten from the rock walls. The white was pure and stark against the background of the mesa rock.

We were met at the door of the temple by President David Cannon. He had been the temple president since about '93. He was such a wonderful soul. He saw that our every need was met and fully explained all that we were about to do. What a wonderful sacred experience that can only be appreciated by fully participating in the event! We are so eternally grateful that we had that opportunity to be married for not only the time here in this life, but for all eternity. When James joined us in a special ceremony to be sealed, he was wide-eyed and in awe. As we held hands and listened to the words by the proper authority, we felt a profound, special spirit that testified to us we were at the right place doing the right thing.

It was hard to leave that special atmosphere, but we knew we could come back and renew the feeling.

We went into the town proper and enjoyed shopping for presents to take back with us to those who had been so gracious on this special trip. There was a generous selection of goods at the several markets. The commerce between St. George and Salt Lake was well organized; and of course, with the rail system connecting Salt Lake, the Crossroads of the West, with both coasts of our nation, all types of goods were readily available.

"Wouldn't it be a wonderful experience to live in this town where James could go to school, and we would belong to a ward nearby and where we could go to the temple often?" May Fern asked. "I so love this quaint valley surrounded by the lava-rock hills and mesas and how the streets are laid out in blocks and are so wide! I hear that President Young even had a winter home here. I wonder if President Joseph F. Smith travels here often."

"Yes, I too long for a permanent place we can raise our family where they can have all these advantages," I said. "With our special blessing of the treasure room and what it could lead to, we need to find a place near it that has as many desirable churches and education opportunities as possible. My mind keeps wandering to Ramah. That is where my family was headed. It is an LDS community. There is a school there, and we would not be far from your family. We owe them so much, and we have so much to share with them. My mind keeps prodding me about the real possibility that Martha is my sister."

"You are right, my darling. We have to balance all of or opportunities with the many responsibilities we have and will have. I love you so much for your willingness and desire for the best for all concerned. You know I am with you and James in all that has to be done. I will never let you down. I am so happy and proud to be your eternal companion."

Chapter 10

WE LEFT THE Stevens' with mixed emotion. They had been so kind to us and welcomed us into the brotherhood and sisterhood of eternal families. We left them a memento of our gratitude and were on the road with the mules in perfect swing by daylight.

"I have an inclination to check out our spot and see if our visitor, Mr. Webbsfoot, circled back around to that spot," I said as we approached the turnoff to the camping spot we had used on the way to St. George.

"We have made great time from St. George, and it will only take the mules a few minutes to take us there. I too am curious to see if my instructions were followed," May Fern chuckled.

I carefully drove the team and surrey up through the trees to our camping spot. I got out and circled the area, looking for tracks. Sure enough, there were the tracks of his horse and his tracks where he had dismounted and snooped around our campsite. There was no doubt as his horse was missing the shoe on the left hind foot and his $12 Durango boots left a distinct print.

"I do not want to camp here tonight as he may still be in the area, and he knows this layout," I said. "We made really great time coming back since we knew the road, and I knew where I could push the mules. Let's go on just a little ways farther and see if we can find a more open and defensible camp spot."

We went back to the road and traveled several more miles. May Fern saw a rock formation on the south side of the road that looked intriguing. I left her and James and Sarah with the surrey. I grabbed a Winchester and hiked over to the rocks. There, to my pleasure, was a formation of rocks that offered good protection on three sides and had enough elevation that we would be in control of the surrounding countryside. The surrey could be pulled, with some difficulty, into the opening on the fourth side. By placing the surrey across the opening, we could keep the mules within our natural compound tied to picket stakes.

"I have found a great place to dry camp," I announced. "We have enough water for us and the mules, realizing that we will be at Pipe Springs no later than noon tomorrow. Let's get camp set up, and then I will make another reconnoiter of the greater area to make sure we are safe."

The night went well with another great Dutch oven meal by May Fern and Sarah, with James furnishing the wood. There was a tranquility and special feeling as we sat around the campfire and looked up at the stars. The Lord created such a marvelous universe. Man cannot begin to comprehend it all during his short lifetime.

As we followed the road up into the forest, we were anticipating a short stop at Pipe Springs to water the mules, refresh ourselves, and fill our water barrels. It was such a pleasant sight as the building came into view. As we got close, we noted that there was not anyone out and about.

"Do you think there is anything wrong?" May Fern asked.

"As usual, I think we should be prepared," I replied. "You take the reins and be ready to drive away as fast as you can. I will take a Winchester and check things out."

"What about water?"

"We are not that hard up for water compared with our lives if this is a bad situation," I answered.

About that time, the main door opened with one of the occupants stepping outside with a rifle in hand.

"Is your party alone?" he hollered at me as we were still a hundred or so yards away. "Have you been bothered by any highwaymen?"

This statement really brought me to my senses. I decided it would be in our best interest if we fully prepared for a battle. I walked around to the other side of the surrey while May Fern kept the reins. I pulled out the other Winchester from behind the front seat and placed it in the rack on the dashboard. I then stepped back further and pulled out the shotgun from its scabbard behind the second seat. I also put it in the rack. I had checked them early that morning and knew they were loaded.

"No, we have not seen anyone all morning!" I yelled back to the person at the door. "We camped about fifteen miles back. What seems to be the trouble?"

"In the last couple of days, some of our stock has been run off. And then last evening, someone shot a rifle at the door. We have been holed up ever since."

This did not bode well for us, but we were ready to defend ourselves. I felt we could take care of any situation pretty well, but I would take no chances with my family. For all I knew, the person at the door might be a bad person. I did not want to get any closer to them, but I did want the mules to have water in case we had to make a run for Kanab.

"I am sorry for your troubles!" I said, again raising my voice. "We will just water our mules over there by the trees and be on our way. We are fully ready to defend ourselves. If we see anything, we will try and let you know."

Two more men came out of the door and moved around the building toward the corrals in the rear. They were not armed and seemed to be intent on checking their horses. I eased our team around to where they could get to the small stream of water flowing from the ranch. I kept watch while May Fern and Sarah uncoupled the lead team and watered them. At the same time, I drove the wheel team to where they could get water. I had James take two canteens and go just above where the lead team was being watered and fill them. I did not know the complete source of the stream water, but I felt we needed all we could get before moving on. This all only took a few minutes, and while doing so, we were watching for any surprises.

We hitched the lead team back in place and were on the road traveling as fast as would allow through the winding forest road. We did not see anyone other than a couple of wagons heading toward St. George. We had a short conversation with them and told them of our experience. They assured us they would be ready for any trouble and let us know that the road, at least to the junction, was open and clear.

Such was the happenings in those days, but I suppose that life has not really changed much. There have always been those who want something for nothing and would even take lives to get what they want. I have always found that being vigilant is the best policy and then to have the means at hand to back up my actions.

What a wonderful sight to once again view the community of Kanab and all the farms, orchards, and ranches! We saw numerous people all appearing busy with their families or commerce. We went through town and soon arrived at the Stevens' home.

"Buckshot, May Fern, James, Sarah, it is so good to see you! And right on time," George said. "Your mules really are an efficient way to travel! How was the trip and experience? Did your marriage go as scheduled? Were you able to stay at Richard's home?"

The questions came almost too fast, but they were easily answered. We unloaded our luggage and soon had the mules put away. We washed up and sat as invited around their table to partake of a wonderful meal.

"As you may recall," said Emily, "we have a fun trip to the lakes planned for tomorrow. We should leave at about nine in the morning. I have fixed a lunch for all of us as our guests. We are only going about six miles to this beautiful location."

We were so blessed to have such wonderful friends. We were looking forward to reacquainting ourselves with friends we had made at church the previous week.

There were four wagonloads of folks along with us in our surrey who started out that morning. The drive up to the lakes was so pleasant in the crisp fall air. Nature's magnificent beauty was all around us. There was laughing and singing and jokes and stories. We arrived at the lakes about noon. I have never seen such a spread of food of every kind. I wondered where it had all come from as the wagons had seemed to be filled completely just by people. They spread out tablecloths in the shade of the massive box elder trees in front of what is called the Dripping Cave. The water is so cold and clear. It drips in crystal drops from the roof of the cave into the placid lake.

Several brought musical instruments that included two fiddles, a guitar, a harmonica, and a new instrument to me called a banjo. It was a delightful time. Then we took a hike around the lakes.

May Fern and I found a rock to sit on and watch as Sarah took James down to the edge of the lake to throw rocks and play along the shore.

"My darling, isn't it wonderful how water sets a place off and brings a feeling of tranquility?" May Fern said. "Do you suppose when we buy our ranch, we can have a large pond or lake on it? And wouldn't it be grand if we had a stream running through it?"

"May Fern, you are reading my mind again. In addition, I have dreamt of having a waterwheel that I could hook up to several gearing systems. I would like one that would saw lumber from logs and another that would grind wheat into flour and yet another that would run the hammer for a blacksmith operation."

"Waterpower. What was it that *Hasteen* Begay told my father and Hanabah?" she asked. "Oh yes, I remember. He told them to – "

"Never forget the power of water."

"And of course, we know what a little stream of water can do to a rock that is balanced just right," she said. "I have such a feeling nagging at me to learn so much more from all that we have been given. Promise me that you will always keep looking and pushing to search for additional knowledge."

I never forgot that request on that beautiful fall day overlooking that lake with the exquisite love of my life sitting beside me and holding hands with me. The warmth of the sun seemed to penetrate our very souls and to give us such a prompting of energy as to almost open a hidden vista of life.

"Let's expand our walk," I said.

"Sarah and James!" I called. They were just below us. "Come! We are going to walk the shores of the lakes. There are a lot more rocks for you to throw into the water," I said with a chuckle.

We took our stroll along the shore of the lower pond and watched with enjoyment the seemingly unending thrill that James was having exploring, throwing rocks into the water, and just feeling the fun of life.

Then May Fern and I saw it, almost at the same time. There, carved in a rock wall about eight feet above the water level of the lower of the three lakes, was an Aztec treasure sign. There was one just like it at the treasure cave. It was a circle with an arrow pointing down. The one back home pointed to the diversion site of the watercourse. This sign was definitely a sign having to do with waterpower.

"Oh, Buckshot, what have we found?" May Fern asked. "Should we tell the others?"

"I do not think so," I replied. "It is too early to really know the secret of what it means. We would not want to ruin our great friendships by getting their hopes up and, because we did not know how to make it work, to have them think less of us. Let us wait and see how it all shakes out. Maybe we are supposed to come back here and explore – or maybe even live. I really have so many mixed emotions at this moment."

Later, after we arrived back at the Stevens' home in Kanab and as George and I were taking care of the mules and horses for the night, I asked, "George, have you ever noticed that funny carving on the rock above the lower lake?"

"Yes, most of the folks and I have wondered about it. There are a lot more of these carvings at the head of a canyon nearby. In fact, if you travel the hills and valleys throughout this area, you will find many ruins of a civilization. There appear to be homes and circular openings in the ground and even agricultural sites. Are you interested, or do you know something about these carvings?"

"Yes, I am very interested in such carvings," I said, not wanting to ever lie to anyone. "I too think there have been some very significant historical happenings wherever you see such signs. I would like to come back sometime and explore with you to see what we can find regarding them."

"Buckshot, you know you and your family are welcome anytime," George said with a very somber and sincere demeanor. "And in fact, Emily and I would like it very much if you would move here and become our neighbors. We feel a kinship in just the short time we have known you."

There is more to that interaction for another time. There is much there to be discovered as shown on the gold plate maps in the treasure room Hanabah and Jimmy and I have been blessed with.

We enjoyed a delightful Sabbath day as continued guests of the Stevens. We ate, attended church, and spent the Sabbath afternoon over at the home of Thelma Johnson. She was a relative of the Stevens. She had a way of getting the most from a group of people. We talked about life in general, the Gospel, and her experiences in Salt Lake as a child where her family lived close to Brigham Young.

As we were visiting, we saw a group of four wagons traveling south through town. Their wagons looked like used army wagons as they were painted a light blue.

"It is too bad they do not know about keeping the Sabbath," Thelma said. "I remember my parents telling me a number of times as they crossed the plains to Salt Lake that President Young insisted that they not travel on Sunday in order to keep the Sabbath day holy."

She quoted the fourth of the Ten Commandments to remember the Sabbath day and keep it holy:

> For six days you shall labour and do all your work.
>
> But the seventh day is a Sabbath to the Lord your God; you shall not do any work – you, your son or your daughter, your male or female slave, your livestock, or the alien resident in your towns.

> For in six days the Lord made heaven and earth, the sea, and all that is in them, but rested the seventh day; therefore the Lord blessed the Sabbath day and consecrated it. (Exodus 20:9-11)

"My parents told me of a number of times wagons and travelers would pass us on the road on the Sabbath as we were in camp resting as we knew we should and that our leaders instructed us to do," she said. "Invariably, within a day or two on the trail, we would come upon the group who had not observed the Sabbath. And they were broken-down in some way and delayed. They said it was a marvelous testimony to them concerning the commandments."

We left the Stevens' and Kanab with gratitude that we had experienced so much and became acquainted with such special friends. About that time in our life, May Fern and I decided to make it a practice to never say goodbye but from then on, to just say, "We are looking forward to seeing you again, and we hope it is soon." It lessened the stress of parting and created a greater hope for the future.

As we were getting ready to pull away from their home, May Fern presented them with some gifts that we had purchased in St. George to show our appreciation. With that, we bid them the promise of seeing them again.

We camped at Jacobs Lakes and then the next day, pushed on to Lee's Ferry. We arrived there early in the day and set up camp at a spot we were directed to. We had shade, and there was a cool fall breeze blowing. We could hear the majesty of the mighty Colorado River nearby and see its power.

"Hi, Jim," I greeted our host and the Lee's Ferry operator. "We are happy to be back and looking forward to you taking us back across the river."

"Sorry that I was not here yesterday, but Sister Emmett and I took a trip to the post at Tuba for supplies," he said. "It is closer to go there than to St. George, and I think they have a better supply of the latest items. Their merchandise comes by train to Flagstaff and then freighted to the post. They can order from either the West Coast or from back East."

"We understand about getting away for a few days," I said. "How was the trip to Tuba? Is the road in good shape?"

"It was a decent trip except for a washout by Navajo Springs," he said. "We and several other wagons pooled our labor and lay in a rock crossing. The other wagons were broke down anyway. Their animals had been pushed too hard and needed rest. Besides, they broke a hound on one of the wagons and were working to make another one – a real tough position to be in way out there with no decent wood to build one from."

"The wagons were not light blue in color by any chance, were they?" I asked.

"Why yes, they were. Do you know them?"

"Yes, in sort of an interesting way."

"Oh, and by the way, you folks wouldn't know about an incident at Moenkopi a while back where some horses were shot, would you?" he asked with a grin. "There were some exciting events according to what we heard. Because it happened on Hopi land, there was a representative from the Hopi Agency at Keams Canyon investigating it. You might be careful on your way back through. Some folks just might confuse you with one of the participants. The general feeling that I got was that it was the best thing that has happened there in a long time."

The next morning, we were packed and hitched up early but had to wait while Brother Emmett and others repaired a part of the ferry before we could load on board. It was such a thrill to be pulled and maneuvered over a massive waterway. To think that some of the water we were viewing had come thousands of miles and had hundreds of miles yet to go. Man's futile efforts to change, alter, eliminate, or even enhance the creator's handiwork are so evident on such an occasion. When we were almost across, a log hit the ferry and gave us quite a jolt. Even the mules became wide-eyed and looked around to see what our future might hold.

After landing on the other side, we hitched the teams back up and completely checked our outfit. In particular, I went over the harnesses. They had to be in good repair to withstand the strain of pulling our surrey up over the Back Bone. Again, I had May Fern do the driving of the teams while Sarah, James, and I walked behind to block the wheels when these magnificent creatures became winded from pulling up such a defile. I was so pleased with the comparative ease that we went up over this unique stubborn obstacle made of virtual solid rock and with no other choice of route in order to pull up out of that massive canyon of the mighty Colorado. What an adventure!

"Dad, is that really the cabin we camped by way down there?" James asked as we took a break to let the mules rest before completing our ascension.

"Yes, James." I pointed to direct his sight to an eagle floating lazily way above us out over the canyon. "Can you imagine his view of the cabin? He can see even better than we can."

"Dad, do you think we will ever be able to fly that high and see even more of the country? It would be such a thrill to see more of the earth and to travel through the air."

"I think there are a lot of wonderful experiences awaiting us," I said. "You know, in just my lifetime, I have seen so many new inventions. I think before long, these mules will not be necessary for us to travel. Already the telegraph lets us know the news almost instantly. Yes, I think someday, we will find a way to fly."

After reaching the top and giving the mules a good break and some grain and water, we pushed on to Navajo Springs. Sure enough, there was the rock dug way that Brother Emmett had helped build to get around the washout. Not very far up the road was the group of light blue wagons. They were still working on repairs and recruiting their animals.

We camped for the night. Several of their party came over to visit. They were pleasant folks on their way to California, seeking land to start a ranch. We got into quite a conversation about mules versus horses versus oxen. Then we discussed the various options after deciding on what type of animal to use for traveling or farming. This led to a wide-open discussion of the scriptures and to the creator and why we are here on earth.

"Now that you have let me explain to you why mules are the best all-around animal for work and travel, let me give you a little history that might be interesting." I opened my Bible to the Old Testament and began to read in 1 Kings. "And king David said, Call me Zadok the priest, and Nathan the prophet, and Benaiah the son of Jehoiada. And they came before the king. The king also said unto them, Take with you the servants of your lord, and cause Solomon my son to ride upon mine own mule, and bring him down to Gihon" (1 Kings 1:32-33).

"Here we have the man that history records as having great wisdom for riding on a mule, for do they not refer to the Wisdom of Solomon?" I smiled and chuckled as I said, "Now wouldn't you like to be known for wisdom and have mules in your stable of animals?"

They got the point, and we all laughed at our present situation in life. I then got very serious with them, and we had an in-depth conversation about why we are here on earth and how we can best get along if we help one another.

"Buckshot, my darling, here are a couple of pots of cobbler that our guests might enjoy," May Fern said.

They were so impressed with this trail delight that May Fern and Sarah had concocted from our campfire. Yes, camping can be very pleasant, and there is so much that can be done if you are organized and have the right equipment and knowledge.

We left early the next morning about daybreak. I noted that our newfound friends were not even up. They had apparently been able to make a fix on the broken hound on the one wagon but were still trying to recruit their animals. I wonder sometimes how people figure on succeeding without doing all they can to fully use each wonderful day the Lord provides.

We made it to Willow Springs for the night and then arrived at Moenkopi on Friday late in the afternoon. We were tired and in need of a bath and could almost taste the exquisite Hopi fare. We went directly to Brother and Sister Mai-yaro's home.

"Well, welcome to the newlyweds!" Brother Mai-yaro said as he first hugged May Fern. He wrapped one arm around me and scooped up James with the other. "Was the trip good? What did you think of the house of the Lord and your ceremony?"

While we were being greeted with such enthusiasm by Brother Mai-yaro, Sister Mai-yaro saw to it that Sarah was duly welcomed and made to feel she was an important part of it all. I mention this as this was the real beginning of Sarah's conversion. As she realized the true love among members, no matter their background, it opened her eyes. With the reading we did each day from good books, and mostly it was from the scriptures and our daily prayers both morning and evening, she garnered that special feeling and a true desire to learn more.

May Fern, being very comfortable with these sincere special friends answered, "Oh, thank you so much for recognizing how special our sealing is to us. And yes, we had a great trip and made many new friends! We had a small scare or two along the way, but the Lord was with us. Our sealing session was so deep with the spirit embracing the event. It was such a special time and gives us such peace each day. We want to thank you for helping us along the way."

Both Brother and Sister Mai-yaro had tears streaming down their faces as May Fern poured her heart out to them; and that, of course, triggered our tears. Only those who have experienced such unique internal feelings can truly know.

"We have been expecting you," Sister Mai-yaro said. "I watched as you drove into the community and saw the runners from several of the families hurry around to tell of your arrival. The food and visitors will soon start. I know you are tired, and I ask you if you would like to have some privacy with some bathing and cleaning before the party begins?"

"Oh yes!" May Fern exclaimed. "May we do that so we can be on our best behavior?"

We all laughed at such a description of the results of cleaning up.

"Sarah, we have arranged for you to go over to the neighbor's house to bathe so you will not be held back waiting," Sister Mai-yaro added. "You remember them. It is the Tohchi family, who are also members. Sister Tohchi will be here in a few minutes to take you to her place."

Brother Mai-yaro and I and several young boys, who seemed to come out of nowhere, took care of parking the surrey, unhitching the mules, and taking care of them as before.

The Mai-yaros had a very large unique tub in the lower corner of their home that they filled with hot and then cold water so that it was just right. There was a window to look out of as you took your bath that provided a vista of the field where they had been harvesting on the day of the event. You could see down across the field to the trees along the wash and the red rock cliffs beyond. As the day was drawing to a close, May Fern and I reveled in the comfort of our bath, the view, and of our love for each other.

James was next, and then as May Fern put it, we were clean with fresh clothes that she and Sarah had washed several days back at Lee's Ferry. We were on our "best behavior" to meet the many others who soon swarmed the Mai-yaros' home with food, friendship, and joy.

As the evening progressed with talking and laughing, for the Hopi people have a great sense of humor, the subject of Hopi beliefs came up. Always being interested in such matters, I pushed several of the men to tell me more.

They explained to me that the Hopis have a tradition or, as they put it, a theory. The Hopi word for a "theory" is *tutavo.* The members of the church said that it was easy for them to understand the message of the missionaries who brought them the Book of Mormon and explained to them the Gospel because of this theory.

"The Hopi theory is about a white brother or Savior that is called Bahana," Brother Tohchi explained. "All the villages know this story. He was with us from the beginning and had great wisdom and power. He then left us with a promise he would return with many benefits for us, his people. This is why we were so anxious to allow the Spanish priests to enter our communities and establish their missions until we discovered their evil intents and practices. But you have told us you already know of that part of our story. I have been privileged to do much travel as a trader for our people. I have found that all the villages to the east that live in stacked houses that are called pueblos have such a belief. It is the same belief that I am told the Aztec people way south in Mexico had. All are waiting for the true Bahana to return and bring total peace and happiness."

Brother Tohchi continued, "I have talked to some people who say they are descendants of other tribes from way south by Mexico City that the Spaniards conquered. They told me that they know of a similar tale. Their Lord was called something like Quetzalcoatl, and he brought them knowledge of crafts and arts and a calendar and of a great civilization. He did not require human sacrifice that later wicked men introduced for their own gain, much like we have seen. We believe that Bahana will return. And of course, we members of the church know that our Savior, Jesus Christ, as testified to in the Book of Mormon, is he. We are so grateful for the record of our ancestors here in this land that the Book of Mormon tells us of. We know he loves us, and so we have this record just like the people far across the ocean have their record as recorded in the Bible."

Such were the testimonies of the evening as we heard several more along the same line. One has to always look for the thread that goes through life with the truth. As Lehi explains in the Book of Mormon, once you find the rod of iron, you must hold tight to it in order to gain the full reward.

"I thank you all for such a wonderful evening and such a grand welcome and your friendship," I said. "You have been so gracious to me, May Fern, and James – who, by the way, was fast asleep in the corner of the large living room – and Sarah. We will look forward to more visits tomorrow. We will come to some of your homes as you have invited and become better friends. Good night."

* * *

I will admit to sleeping in on that Saturday morning. I awoke with a jolt as the sun crept up to where it pierced the room we were sleeping in and pushed across my face. I instinctively reached to my right for May Fern. To my surprise, she was not there. I quickly got dressed and went out into the living room area with a feeling that I was missing something on that wonderful day.

"Good morning, my wonderful Buckshot," said May Fern from her chair at the table. She, James, Sarah, and the Mai-yaros had food and drinks and so were greatly enjoying one another's company.

"Good morning to all of you," I said. "I apologize for my sleeping in."

"I had just told everyone that it was not your normal schedule, but that I thought you had finally relaxed and felt you were in a safe, comfortable place," May Fern said. "This allowed your body to rest and to do some catching up on sleep."

"Well, now that I analyze it, you are so right. I want to thank Brother and Sister Mai-yaro for such an atmosphere. I do feel so rested and ready for a wonderful day. What do you suggest?"

"Well, first, you must choose from this fruit and other food so you are strong," said Sister Mai-yaro in true Hopi thought.

"Brother Yazzie wants to talk to you as soon as you can get to his land," said Brother Mai-yaro. "It is about an hour away. He says he wants you and May Fern to come alone and to spend most of the day with him. We will take care of James and, of course, Sarah. You will probably want to take your rig. I will tell you how to get there. Please be cautious as there are still some feelings among some of the Navajos. I do not know how they can think their young men have the right to scare people in the community, but they do."

"Make sure you are back before sundown," said Sister Mai-yaro. "The members of the church, both Hopi and Navajo, want to have a party this evening in your honor and to celebrate your sealing."

The directions Brother Mai-yaro soon gave us had us well on our way in a northeast direction toward a hilltop where we could see several hogans and "shade structures." The roadway was rough as it went over exposed rock and down through several draws. We had bypassed the trading post. I had wanted to stop and thank Mr. Preston again for his generosity and perhaps purchase some items for our return trip.

"My dear, do you see the large group of people off to the left?" May Fern asked. "I cannot tell what they are doing, but I feel they bear watching."

"Yes, I see them but am not too concerned," I said. "We have open ground between here. And the hogans, I think, belong to Brother Yazzie. If they are up to no good, they would be very foolish to charge us over open ground with the firepower we have. Not that I ever want to be in a fight, but we must be ever vigilant and know our options."

As we approached the three hogans with a large "shade" near the center, the group to our left began to walk toward the same spot. In a few minutes, as we pulled up to the hogans, we were greeted by Brother Yazzie and his family. There were about fifteen sons, daughters, and relatives. They welcomed us very cordially, especially Ned, Brother Yazzie's grandson, whose horse I had shot out from under him.

"Buckshot and your woman, it is so good to see you today," Ned said in Navajo as he walked up and gave us a big hug. "I hope you have been well."

Sometimes, just a few words convey more than a whole speech. We each gave him a hug as the group watched. There was total approval and even some expressions of approval to see happiness instead of anger or regret.

"It is so good to see you again," Brother Yazzie said to us. "Please come over to the shade house and let me talk to you for a while. We have company coming soon, and I want you to know about the feelings here and how they have come about."

A shade house is just that – a cursory structure made in a square of a rectangle. A few poles are placed on top, and then fresh-cut branches are placed to create shade. Arrangements had been made to have some logs and rocks set up for seats.

"Buckshot and May Fern, a lot of discussion has gone on since you left," Brother Yazzie said. "I have had a hard time convincing those Navajos living around here that are either relatives of those other two young men or do not have good feelings for the white man or Hopis to stay calm. A number of the young men stirred up by their women and bad ones have wanted to start a total fight. Some have wanted to attack the Hopis and the trading post."

Brother Yazzie continued, "A very good man here by the name of *Hasteen* Begay, whom I spent time with on the Long Walk, teamed up with me to get the people to see reason. He is not a member of the church but is a very honest and fair man. We think we have finally won over the Navajo community to stay peaceful and, more importantly, to get them to see what really happened. Ned has been very helpful to tell what happened in the meetings we have held. He told of the whiskey and bad decisions. And he told all who would listen of your accuracy and how you could have easily killed him and his companions."

"I see a large group coming this way," May Fern said. "Are we in danger?"

"No no, I would not have invited you if there were any bad feelings that could cause you danger," Brother Yazzie assured us. "The large group coming our way is led by Hasteen Begay. Some of them are armed, just like some of my family have weapons, but they are just in case the bad ones should show up and want to do anyone harm. We are your friends and would defend you with our lives. You, of course, know of such stories that are told in the Book of Mormon where once the truth is known, it must be defended."

"Brother Yazzie, I believe that I understand all you are telling us," I said. "What do you wish that we do?"

"I ask you to meet these people and to listen to them as they tell you their feelings," Brother Yazzie said.

"We will do as you say and wait for you to tell us what else we can do to help keep the peace and make your community a good place to live," I said. "But I do have a question to ask while we wait for them to get here. Did you know my mother, Hanabah, and her clansman Jimmy Willeto on the Long Walk?"

He took a few seconds to begin to recall the events of many years before.

"Yes, I remember Jimmy and the young woman with the pockmarked face and body," he said. "Is she the one?"

What a coincidence! Could it be that we were tied even closer? What kind of an effect could we have on these people? What more was there to learn?

"Yes, my mother had the pox when she was young," I said. "She saved my life and raised me so I could be introduced to the Gospel."

"She was a special woman," Brother Yazzie said. "I wanted to be with her, and I wanted to take her with me here to my land. I lost her when we became sick. When I could travel, they told me she was one of those who died, and I was very sad for a long time. How is she now? Where does she live? Tell me of her. My heart still longs to talk with her."

With a heavy heart, I told him of her and about her death, but also of her goodness and wonderful example of a life fully lived helping others.

Hasteen Begay's group arrived. Brother Yazzie motioned for them to go and sit near a ceremonial fire area while we continued to talk. I could see pain in his eyes and in his heart as he leaned forward from his seat and digested the story of his onetime love.

"Hanabah did good to save you and bring you up so you could come and help my family," Brother Yazzie said. "I know she has something to do with all of this. She was so special and so good. I should have told her of my feelings before I got sick and lost her."

May Fern and I let him gather his thoughts. We opened a canteen, took a drink, and offered him some. He took the canteen and stared at it for a few moments before drinking. Lost loves can cause a heavy burden for many years. Regret is one of the worst aspects of life. The worst type of regret is not usually for what one does, but for what one did not take the opportunity to do – to tell someone you love them or that you are thankful for them – before they disappear from your life.

"Hasteen Begay, I wish you to meet Buckshot and May Fern," Brother Yazzie said. "I have told them of you. They are here to listen to your thoughts and council. Please have everyone come in and sit down."

I will not tell you all that was said because it took several hours for Hasteen Begay and others to speak their piece. May Fern and I sat and listened and nodded in agreement to most of what was said. There was good council as to staying peaceful, and we were thanked several times for staying calm and not killing anyone at the time of the event. We made good friends. I attribute much of our success and goodwill to the beauty of my May Fern – not only her external beauty, but for her wisdom and demeanor as the speeches carried on.

Finally, an end came, and Brother Yazzie said that we should tell our feelings. I felt that May Fern could make the best and most complete impact on it all. In the Navajo culture, usually, the women do not get to speak and expose points of view. The few that have the talent and wisdom are very well-thought-of and accepted.

"My friends, my husband and I are honored to be here today as your guests," she said. "The words spoken by your leaders are true. The only way to peace and growth in your community is to respect each other. It does not matter what happened yesterday. It only matters what we are going to do today and tomorrow and into the future. We can choose to do good, or we can choose evil. We can choose to take the path of love and harmony for our families, or we can choose hate and continual fighting. We are your friends, and we are so happy that you have chosen respect and harmony. We will help in any way we can."

Her words hit the mark. As she went to sit down, she was swarmed by the group, wanting to shake her hand and thank her. And of course, I received a portion of her goodness by being her husband. It was a tremendous experience. Food was brought out, and a feast started as we all talked and laughed and enjoyed the day.

I was able to get Brother Yazzie off to the side for a few minutes and talk to him further about my mother.

"Brother Yazzie, my mother and her clansman Hasteen Willeto had a friend on the Long Walk by the name of Navajo Jim Begay. Do you know of him?"

"Yes, I knew of him," he said. "He seemed to me a little different and talked of things that did not make much sense. He talked of rock pictures that would lead to lost gold. He told me of some of these pictures, and I have seen the ones he talked about north of here, not far from Lee's Ferry. They are on the other side of the Colorado in some very rugged canyons. They are where there are a lot of ruins of the ancient ones. I remember Hanabah spending time talking with him before he died. Hasteen Begay also knew him. They were related. His son has been to the pictures. That is his son sitting over there with his wife. I will take you and have you meet them."

After our introduction, I spoke to them and asked, "Have you seen the rock pictures that show a man and a circle and happy mountain sheep?"

"Yes, I have. Are they important to you?"

"My mother, Hanabah, was a friend of your father's on the Long Walk," I said. "She told me of them, and I have always wanted to see some of them."

"As you are a good man to us, if you ever want to come back, I will take you to where they are," he said. "It will take about six days, and we will have to ride on horses or mules to get to them."

That was how the door opened to an additional set of clues. By the time I had figured out the gold map plates and discovered the locations, I was able to get back to Tuba and have them take me to the location. I was able to immediately see the hidden treasure room doorway with all the other knowledge I had. Time would allow me to open it and view this additional unique treasure.

We headed back to Tuba City late in the afternoon, feeling we had accomplished some good and that most of the ill feelings that some had against us were gone. Brother Yazzie did tell me, though, that there were still some in the area who were of the old thinking that hated anyone who got the best of them.

"If they get a chance, they will kill or harm you," he said. "Be very careful on your way back home, for they have friends, and the word can get out that you are traveling back. There are a lot of places where you can be ambushed."

As we had to go by the trading post on this other road back to Moenkopi, we decided to stop in and do some shopping.

"Mr. Preston, it is good to see you again," I said.

"Well, hello Mr. and Mrs. Higgins. Likewise, it is good to see you. How have you been?"

"We have been doing well," I replied. "We have been to St. George, Utah. Our mules and rig did great. By the way, we just had a meeting over at Yazzie's where Hasteen Begay brought a group of people to discuss the event of three weeks ago. My impression is that it is pretty well diffused and maybe even made the community a better place."

"I have to agree with you," he said. "However, whenever some damn fool introduces whiskey and the Navajos get talking about the whites or Hopis, there is going to be an altercation. Until we get some type of law enforcement, we will always have the possibility of something happening."

"Good. I hope it stays calm, and your business grows," I chuckled.

"Thanks for the wish, and I return it right back to your operation," Mr. Preston said. "Oh, I almost forgot. A representative from the Hopi Agency headquarters at Keams Canyon showed up about ten days ago and began an investigation of 'the event.' Everyone kept pretty quiet as we knew he would not really do anything of substance. He did get a description of you and your outfit and says he will issue a subpoena for your arrest since the shooting took place on the Hopi Reservation. My advice to you is to just keep going and do not get involved with their bureaucratic setup. They will drive you nuts trying to put the blame on someone and ignoring the good that came out of it. Nevertheless, as you go through Keams Canyon, you can stop at the agency if you wish."

We did some shopping, and again, Mr. Preston would not let us pay for any of the goods. He noted, as before, that he thought they still owed us for three cartridges.

We arrived at the Mai-yaros' home about sundown to find many people there with food and drink of all types. As the evening progressed, some Navajos even showed up, and a good time was had by all. We became part of the fabric of the community, and they showed their friendship in every way possible. Games were played, and we even engaged in singing although we did not have a clue as to the words. James was in a trance as he watched all the revelry. He was presented with several presents as were we. That was a great time in our lives.

* * *

"Brother Buckshot, that was a special meeting," Brother Mai-yaro said. "That is the most people we have ever had at one of our church meetings. You noted that we had to redo the sacrament because we ran out the first time. They all enjoyed your talk and those of May Fern and James about your temple experiences. Please move here and help us build the church and make this a great community," he added in an almost-pleading way.

"I thank you for your compliment, and believe me, we love your village here," I said. "It is so beautiful and tranquil. You are all good people, and we would have a wonderful life. We have family of our own back in our part of the country that we must work to convert and to help build the church there. We will be back to go to the temple, and we will stay with you again. You must come and stay with us and learn of the good people in our community."

What a refreshing Sabbath among the Hopis and Navajos there in the Tuba City and Moenkopi communities. They have a special spirit about them that provided strength to us.

We left the next morning to continue our journey home. We gave the Mai-yaros presents that we purchased in St. George as a token of our appreciation for staying with them.

The first night, we dry camped and then traveled onto Second Mesa. The word was out and probably very embellished about "the event." The Hopis were so thankful we had protected the Mai-yaros and caused some sense to come into the community. Here again, we were treated with fanfare, food, singing, and revelry well into the night. They also recommended that we not stop at the agency and in Keams Canyon but to just keep going.

The rest of our trip back to the post and our home was uneventful except for a localized storm near Ganado. I was so thankful that we had the roll-down curtains on the surrey. They kept us dry and somewhat warm. We were able to find shelter at the school for the night. Charles and Alice Bierkemper were very kind to us. They had just completed the new church building and had a wonderful reputation of helping all those nearby with medicines and schoolings. We continued on with several more camps. We arrived at our post late in the afternoon on the third of November after having been gone for thirty-three days. We were tired, a little homesick, but elated that we were a forever family.

I believe you can imagine the reception we received as we pulled into the yard of the trading post. Junior, especially, was elated to see us. I figured that it was because he could now relax and not have the responsibility of running the operation, but he did seem to be sincere in welcoming us back. May Fern's parents, Jimmy and Winona, welcomed us with hugs – their hearts abound with love. And James, he would not quit talking to anyone who would listen about all of our exploits and his parts in directing the outcome.

"Buckshot, my son, we need to talk about our situation and our future," Jimmy said. "I am getting old, and my days are numbered. Many of my children are wanting to stretch their wings and go on with their own lives. Perhaps I could have done a better job, but with stories and embellishments, they feel it is time for them to be shown the secret of where I get my income. It has gotten to a point where they are demanding a meeting even with you and May Fern present to let them know what their legacy really is. I have run out of money and need more to keep my debts paid and take care of my family. What I am saying is that we must go to the treasure room and get more, melt it down, and sell it."

We had anticipated such a request.

"Yes, I agree with all you have said," I replied. "May Fern and I have been thinking this over and want to face this great responsibility. First, I would ask you to call a meeting of all your older children and let May Fern do the speaking of a plan. This will get everyone on a single plan and take some pressure from you. Second, you and I need to plan a 'business trip' where we go to the treasure room and bring back what is needed to melt and sell. And third, we need to bring the gold map plates with us and make copies of them. Then May Fern and I will go to schools or the library in Gallup and get map books and begin looking at where other treasure has been hidden. From that information, we can plan a larger system of getting more money for your family."

"May Fern and you are very wise, and I can see that this is a good plan. How soon can we have the meeting, and how soon can you and I go to the treasure room?"

"Hasteen Willeto," I started. This is what I called him in respect for his leadership in the family and when I needed him to really listen to me with something a little complicated. "Let us have the family meeting on Monday afternoon up in the old stone house after we get everyone settled down, and I check out the operations of the trading post. We have been gone a long time. We can set a date, but it will be very soon."

"That is a good plan," he said. "I will tell all my children. I say that I believe that all went well while you were gone. We had the normal problems, but we all worked hard so they would not be a burden on you. We had a couple of sheep and three cows die that had been traded for, but that happens. We have some large orders to fill and so need the mules to pull the full freight wagon with trailer into town and fill them. The horses, of course, need to be taken back and paid for. Junior and I have kept the money, hides, rugs, piñon nuts, and pawn items safe. I have had my son James sleep in the pawn room at night to guard it all. Winona and I have stayed, as you directed, in your home attached to the post. I believe you will find all is well."

"I thank you so much, my father," I said. "That is another thing I did not mention. I have funds left over from our trip because so many fed us and took care of us. Then we have the money you have received from trading. And we will sell all the hides, wool, blankets, and nuts as we make our freight run. This will provide the much-needed money for your family. May Fern and I have calculated that we owe you more than $2,000 just for running the trading post. And then there are wages for your children who have herded and fed and cleaned and stocked the shelves and all of the other work around the post and land."

I could see a huge relief come over him at this explanation. He was in dire need for his family, and he had earned more than what was needed. We just needed to get the money or goods to them. We would always take care of them, for they were family, and we had plans for their conversion and eternal happiness.

"As we have talked before, have you come up with any ideas of what we can tell the family about the treasure without getting them directly involved?" I asked. "I do not want them to think we are doing anything bad."

"I have been giving this much thought," he replied. "Maybe we can tell them that we have a gold mine. This is partially true, or maybe even the real truth. The only complication is they will want to know where, and then as always happens, one of them will tell someone they trust who will tell someone else – and then we will have the evil ones back. The only other thing I have thought of is that we have them think I am part owner of the trading post and maybe a ranch somewhere – and that these businesses are doing very well. With their lack of experience and not really having the books to look at, this might work. Again, though, I do not want to let the rumor get out that we are doing so good that those in the community get jealous, like what happened with Frank, and we have that scenario all over again. What are your thoughts?"

"Those are good ideas," I said. "May Fern and I have not come up with anything that would work other than maybe having the family think I inherited some land and money from my real family and that we are sharing it with you because we are family. What do you think about that idea?"

"Yes, that is the best idea of all," he replied. "For you did inherit the rich source from your second mother, Hanabah. This way, we do not lie, but there is no reason to tell all that we know. Even May Fern can hold her head up high and know that she too received such a blessing from me. She inherited the knowledge from my difficult time during the Long Walk."

So that is how we presented it all to the family and assured them that we would share all we had, provided their needs were good needs. We explained to them that preparing for families and raising them right to be honest and true and to be educated were the goals. We would help them finance any good venture they wanted to engage in, provided it was well thought out and added to the betterment of the community and the family as a whole. They all seemed to be very happy with our explanation and offer to be very generous with them. James was already courting a young woman, and they were planning to marry. He wanted to take over his father's place and expand the herd of sheep.

On Tuesday, Jimmy, my son James, Junior, and my brother-in-law James loaded the wagons with our trade goods, hitched up the mules, and tied the rental horses to the back of our wagon train. We headed into Gallup to do our business. We had to do the regular trading and then fill a large number of orders. We had two wagons to bring back. They were in pieces within crates that would fit into the "trailer wagon." As planned, I would go to the library for map books and perhaps to the local schools to see what I could find so Jimmy and May Fern and I could figure out the gold map plates.

"I have some banking business and other errands to do while you take care of the business for the post," I said as we drove along. "You do not need me for any of those transactions once I tell the wholesaler that you are my agents and will take care of the trades and purchases. Also, take the horses back to the stables, turn them in, and pay the fee with the funds you get from the trades."

In reality, I also had to go to the bank and check out the trading post account to make sure all of our bills were paid and to double-check the balance. Then I needed to check the fictitious business account where I had all the funds from the sale of our gold ingots transferred into. I had never given the exchange a way to contact me other than through the bank where they would send the checks. To my surprise and relief, I had a letter from them in a plain envelope. After checking my balance and transferring funds to the post account, I took the letter over to a corner of the lobby of the bank and read the note. It was from Mr. Jackson. He reiterated the invitation by the exchange to travel to Denver, all expenses paid, to become better acquainted and perhaps negotiate a better price as our volume of gold had impressed them.

I had never taken the time to go to the local library in Gallup. I had been to a bookstore located on the corner of west Coal Street and south Third Street several times. They had ordered books for May Fern and me for our family reading sessions.

"Ma'am," I asked, "can you direct me to where I can find some maps of northwest New Mexico and northeast Arizona territories?"

"The best we have is Rand McNally's new eleven-by-fourteen-inch map on Arizona or New Mexico," the librarian said. "You will find it over by that wall. There are several other older maps rolled up, but they are pretty well-worn."

I found the book and noted that it was copyrighted in 1895. It had a scale of 69.16 miles equaled one degree. I had no idea what that meant, but I looked at it; and I could see some wonderful drainages and locations of towns I had been to, such as Tuba, St. George, and, of course, Gallup. The major drainages of the various river tributaries were plainly marked. The area where the treasure room is did not have any detail, so one would have to know the country in order to really find it. Then I pawed through some of the old rolled-up maps. As she had said, they were pretty shopworn, but they were every bit as good as the Rand McNally book maps. They had all the major drainages on them and could be a great help in pinpointing what the gold map pages depicted.

"May I bother you again?" I asked. "This rolled-up map is old and badly worn. There are even some stains on it that look like someone spilled their coffee on it. How long do you keep such maps before you get rid of them?"

"Well, sir, I do not make that decision," she said. "We have a director who determines when we should get rid of an item. Usually, it is when we have funds to purchase newer books or maps. Oh, here she comes now. You might ask her."

"Ma'am, I was just discussing this map with your assistant," I said. "If I was to donate a fair amount to your library so you can purchase newer versions, might I have this copy?"

That was how I acquired the old Henry & Robbins map that I have framed on my wall in my office. From what I can discern, it was drawn by two old land surveyors in the early eighteen hundreds. They did a fantastic job. They crisscrossed the land in enough detail to really pinpoint all the mountain peaks and bends in the drainages.

Their great work fit so closely to the gold map plates. Of course, over the years, floods and such changes occurred; but it is not too hard when looking at them side by side to figure out where specific sites are located. Armed with the map and knowledge of rock symbols and how the treasure room doors are constructed, it is fairly easy to find the sites. I caution those who would like to get into this business that there are false sites and even sites purposely constructed to harm those who would be greedy. The gold map plates show all of this in great and magnificent detail.

Chapter 11

"MY SON, BUCKSHOT, you have been such a blessing to Winona and me," Jimmy said. "Your generosity and knowledge of business has given us all we need to raise our family. We are now okay and even have funds to carry us along for quite some time."

"You are so very welcome as it is really your treasure that allowed me and your wonderful daughter to move forward and have all that we have," I said. "And if you were not the great spiritual leader and healer and hard worker you are, we would be lacking in our lives. Truly, we are a great team. My heart is filled with love for you and Winona. I will keep on the trail you have put us on and will not fail you."

We had this conversation and several similar ones before Jimmy's passing. He was a great man. He was converted to the Gospel and was scheduled to be baptized. He became very sick with a fast-growing tumor on his abdomen. He succumbed before we could get him the help he needed. In his last talk with his wives and children, he instructed them all to be baptized into the one and only true church. They all did so. But again, I get ahead of my story.

"I am happy that you say you are getting too old to hike up the mesa to the treasure room site and need to ride," I laughed as we were saddling up three of the mules. "That is because I can also ride and not feel I am getting old too. I sure miss old Jake to carry our pieces of treasure. But his time came. Kate here will do the job with this new packsaddle with the stitched panniers. We can now bring out large pieces and cut them up in the blacksmith shop rather than trying to break them up in the treasure cave room. I have studied the old map I now have and feel comfortable I can figure out where the gold map plates show if they are here in the southwestern United States. I do not want to ever lose them or take them from the treasure room.

I am afraid someone will see them or steal them before we can find the many other locations."

"What have we for weapons today?" Jimmy asked. "I know you are carrying your Colt in your shoulder holster, but I need a rifle or shotgun if I need to help if we get in trouble."

"I have put your regular Winchester, fully loaded, in a scabbard on the left side of your saddle with the butt pointed backward," I said. "This way, you can quickly dismount, fall back toward the rear of your mule, and pull the rifle. Just work the lever one time, and you will be set to fire." Then chuckling, I said, "Make sure you don't shoot the mule."

May Fern and Winona packed us a fantastic food package that we put into the panniers. We also had plenty of room with a top pack for bedrolls and a shelter tent. We had never had it so good on any of our trips to the treasure cave room. There had been several storms leaving snow up on the mesa. This was both a blessing and a disadvantage. Someone could easily track us but, then again, we could see anyone's tracks if there was someone up there.

"Jimmy, let's go by way of the old hogan of Hanabah's," I said. "I want to do some remembering and see if anyone has disturbed our home. This will take us to the treasure site the back way. We will be able to look down on it, so make sure no one is in the area."

We headed out before daylight to make it hard for anyone to follow us. Every time we reached a saddle between draws or canyons, we stopped just on the other side, and I slipped back to look over our trail. I remember this trick of the wily old bucks when I tried to follow them. It would be best to catch anyone following us sooner rather than later. By the time we had reached the flat top of the mesa and were into the snow, it was full daylight, and a wind was trying to chill us. We had warm clothes with gloves and hats with tie-downs over our ears. My feet did get cold, but I knew we soon could build a fire in the old hogan.

"Isn't it funny how when you go back to a place where you lived for so long that the lay of the land seems to change?" I questioned. "I know where we are because that is my tower rock I used to climb to watch the sheep, but I do not remember that rockslide over there, or at least I do not remember it being in that direction."

"I too have had my mind play tricks on me when it comes to remembering," Jimmy said. "In fact, as I have gotten old, I really find it hard to remember things. I hope that we both remember where we are going and where it is at," he said with a bit of a grin.

I was like a kid at Christmas. I knew just around the bend in the trail by the big old pine trees in the rock cove, I would see the old hogan that Hanabah had so laboriously built over the years. Why, even old Jake had helped pull logs to stack up for the base frame.

It was not there – at least at the height it had been. There was just a snow-covered pile not over four feet high! I jumped down from my mule and kicked back the snow to find a mixture of charcoal and dirt. The hogan had burned to the ground, and the mud roof had fallen in on top of it. What a shock and hurt to my memory of so many happy days growing up!

"Look, Buckshot, the old corral has been pulled down and scattered," Jimmy said. "This did not happen by accident. Someone set out to do damage. I cannot believe it would have been anyone who knew about the treasure, but you never know. They could have followed us at times but never really discovered where the exact site is. They could have stumbled onto Hanabah's home and took their frustration out on it."

"You know, I had planned on going to the treasure site today and camp," I said. "I now think it would be wise to camp near here and let me scout out around the country to make sure no one is anywhere around. Over by the spring is a wonderful place to camp. We will have shelter from any storm, and it is very easy to defend. Let's make sure our fire is an Indian fire and not the big fire of a white man. The meadow below the old corral will be a good place for the mules. I sure wish I had brought one of the dogs. I can watch my mule Carol though. Her ears will point to any movement or smell."

We unpacked our pack mule and the items we had tied behind our saddles and in our saddlebags. We had tarps for ground clothes and to construct a lean-to shelter. Jimmy was a master craftsman when it came to camping. Now that he had so many conveniences he had not been used to, he was having a great time. I knew he would get a great meal going and have our bedrolls all laid out for a good night's sleep, so I took off while I had plenty of daylight to make a wide circle around our position to make sure no one else was up on the mesa. I rode Carol since she could see, hear, and smell more than I could; and with me sitting up on her, I had a better view of the countryside. With the snow cover, she would be able to walk almost without sound.

"You know, Carol, I appreciate your company," I said. "Let's ease around to the left and get a look at our back trail one more time. I do not trust that we have not been followed. The treasure we guard is almost beyond measure, and we cannot afford to lose it to someone."

A unique attribute of a mule is that they can work both ears independent of the other. It is fun to be riding one of these gallant steeds when you think there are animals or humans in the vicinity. The mule will be looking, smelling, and listening for any signs. The ears will be working independent, turning one way and then the other; and then all of a sudden, both ears point in one direction, and the head soon follows toward that direction. The reward comes from looking in the direction the mule is directing his attention. Most of the time, with a little variance of time and if you can see through the trees or other parts of the terrain, there will be an animal or human.

We rode to where I had an extensive view of our back trail. I could not see any movement, and Carol's ears or other senses weren't picking up anything. I crossed our tracks, and again, there were no other tracks. We kept circling to the left in a counterclockwise direction out to the end of the mesa and then began to return back, going way south of where Jimmy was camped and very near to the rock pictures and the treasure cave room.

As we dropped down off the south side of the mesa in order to catch a better trail so we could bypass a set of cliffs, I noticed that Carol's senses seemed to be directed toward a side canyon. I eased her up the trail and tensed up, ready for some type of action. There, in a bend in the trail back into the canyon, was a campsite. No, it had not been used for several days, but the fire was still giving off smoke from under the snow. Many times, people do no fully put out their campfires due to poor practices; or sometimes, the wood they are burning contains a lot of pitch. This pitchy wood will burn for a long time, especially coupled with the knot of a tree branch.

"Carol, I do not see any fresh tracks," I said. "This snow has been around for about three days. There is nothing in the camp to indicate what the person was doing. Maybe they were just caught in the storm and stopped to build a fire. Oh, look there is a piece of deer hide. I bet he was hunting and got himself some deer meat."

Just in case, I dropped farther off the mesa in the direction I felt our camper would have gone if he was headed home – downhill and drifting to the west. This would be toward the nearest families that I knew of. About a mile down off the trail, sure enough, I found the drag marks of someone pulling a deer. It looked about two days old. About the time I was down off my mule examining the tracks, Carol gave a snort. I looked up, and there was a young Navajo boy about fourteen years old watching us from about fifty yards away.

I squatted down in front of Carol, holding the reins in my left hand. I was trying to show him that I meant him no harm by being in a relaxed mood. I held up my right hand to give him a friendly gesture. He did not move but just stared straight ahead at me and Carol.

We were a good four miles from the treasure cave site. I did not believe that he was a threat to our goal of pulling more gold pieces, but I wished to talk to him and find out why he was out in the mountains like this. We were below snow line, and so he could be just hunting. The important thing was if he knew me and if he was wondering why I was out here like this. The tension seemed to build, even though we were not in an adversarial situation.

Then I saw the reason he was there. There behind him and downhill through the branches of the scrubby juniper trees, I caught a glimpse of sheep. He was herding the family sheep and had pushed up toward the mesa, hoping for better feed.

"What are you doing so far from home with your herd?" I asked him in Navajo.

"I was hoping to find the parts of the deer that my cousin said he left behind because they were too heavy," he said. "We are poor and hungry and do not want to kill any of our herd. My cousin said the deer was sick, so that is how he got it."

My thoughts went back to my younger days and how it felt to be hungry and struggling to make life work. I had a couple of airtights in my saddlebags. I slowly got up and took them out. I tossed them across the little wash to him.

"Here, this may be good for you," I said. "I am hunting here and up on the mesa. Do not come up here while I am hunting with my partner as we may mistake your for a deer. We will be up there for a few days. Do you know where the Toahani Trading Post is?"

"Yes, my mother took me there one time before my father died," he said. "We made a good trade. We do not have a wagon to go there anymore. When my father died, we had to sell our wagon."

"I know how to help you and your mother. Does she make blankets or have you gotten any nuts this year to trade?"

"Yes, she makes blankets, but now she does not have any string to start one," he said. "We have eaten all of our nuts we gathered for we are poor."

"How far do you live from the trading post at Toahani?" I asked.

"From our hogan, it is a good day's walk."

"I am Hasteen Buckshot, the trader. If you will bring your mother to my post in two days, I will help you with the things she needs to make blankets, and I will help you to earn food and other things. Can you do that?"

By this time, he had opened one of the airtights with a rock and was reveling in the juice it produced. I had a warm, long-lost feeling swell up inside me as I remembered Hanabah and me struggling to make ends meet and the help that Frank and Mary had given us. Was this my turn to pass along the challenge and opportunity to the next generation?

* * *

I rode on up the hill to the mesa and circled around to the west where I could capture the faint smell of wood smoke mixed with coffee. We rode up to camp with the confidence that there was no one up on the mesa looking to do us harm and that we could go about our business tomorrow.

We arrived at the rock site early in the morning after a great breakfast and with all our gear packed up. We wanted to open the cave, choose a full load for the panniers, and make it back to the post by nightfall.

"I have started the water to flow," Jimmy said as I came upon him in front of the doorway. "It will not take long from here. I want to take the maps off the pedestal and bring them out here into the light so I can study them. Will you gather the pieces you think we need and put them into the panniers? I will then help to lift them onto the packsaddle."

"I know this place so well, and I know what I want to load up," I said. "There are plates that have always been too thick and heavy. Now we can take them. They will melt down into many ingots. I also want to take the gold axe. It has always been one of my favorites but again too heavy for our special box we had on Jake."

The pedestal had not only the gold map plates, but a very curious type of symbol arrangements all hanging from a metal ring that appeared to be made of gold. When the symbols were rotated on the ring, they formed a puzzle that made a complete picture of an apparent water system – much like the one we had there that opened the treasure room.

I compare my old Henry & Robbins map to each of the gold map plates. I was so thrilled to find that of the eight plates, five of them fit to drainages on the map of the great Southwest. I drew on the map how they lay and where the sites were the map plates indicated. The anticipation of going there was almost beyond my ability to contain as I thought of the vast riches the sites must contain.

Because of shadows caused by the door, I had never noticed before the magnificent gold head with its exquisite headdress with beautiful red and green stones inset into the crown just above the pedestal. The full-sized head appeared to me watching over the pedestal and maps and maybe even the whole treasure itself. I could imagine the architects of this all putting such an eternal guard to keep this entire vast quantity safe.

It had started snowing just as Jimmy had forecast several days before. He claimed his left elbow and right knee were hurting. This, he said, was always a sign that a major storm was coming. This was another reason he said we should go to the treasure cave site. Our activity would be covered by snow.

"There, that looks good or at least it will look good when the snow melts in the spring," I said. "The mud in the cracks of the joints of the doorway system are all filled. As it keeps snowing, our tracks will soon be gone. Do you think that when the snow melts, someone can tell we have been here?"

"No, Buckshot. I have a short log I will drag over the area where we have been in front of the opening down to the meadow where the mules have been tied. If anyone reading the sign sees it, they will just think we had three mules and were on some kind of camp or hunt."

"This has to be the biggest load we have ever taken," I said. "I am so happy that we have a stout mule and a great saddle with panniers that can hold up to the weight. As you know, May Fern and I want to buy a ranch down by Ramah, and we need all the cash we can to purchase it. The ownership will fit right into our plan for the family story. In addition, if we can successfully raise cattle there and add more profit to our endeavors, we can all benefit."

"Now that you have brought it up," he said, "I have been wanting to talk to you about our plan. Winona and I are finding it difficult to have you and May Fern live so far from us. With my poor wagons and large family, it will be almost impossible for us to visit. We need and want you and May Fern close by, let alone my special grandson, James. With our aging years, we want to enjoy your company. Do you have to buy a ranch so far away?"

We continued on down the mountain toward the post with our valuable load. The snow was now coming down at a pretty good rate. The flakes were small, so we knew that it would be a good storm. Most of the people had a saying that "big flakes mean a small storm, and little flakes mean a big storm."

"We have considered this also," I said. "We love you and your family so much, and we are partners in this grand adventure. We do not want to leave you either, but after carefully looking for other land, we cannot find any place with all the features that the Hollister Ranch has. There is water with a stream running through it and an irrigation system for raising hay. The buildings are all in good repair, and it is already stocked with some good cattle and mules. And there is another reason that I have not told you about. When I was found by Hanabah, another family had just taken my little sister from where my parents lay dead. I think that I have found her, and she lives on a ranch nearby to the Hollister Ranch. She looks and acts just like my mother, and she is of the right age. She is married. I have not approached her yet, but it all fits together. I would like to be near her and help her also."

I do not know to this day why this explanation should or would have any real bearing on our relationship, but from that point on, Jimmy was very cold to me and May Fern. He was almost surly in all our meetings and associations. It was like he felt that after all we had gone through, I was trading it for a stranger – or that I loved this stranger more than them because she was white or some other strange reasoning.

* * *

May Fern and I had several long talks about Jimmy's reaction to our desire to purchase the Hollister Ranch in Ramah. She thought at first that he was just having a bad day or that some other problem was bothering him. Being the peacemaker in Jimmy's family, she tried several times to draw him out and determine what his thinking might be, but he was just ornery in his stance and would not even talk to her about it. Next, May Fern tried to talk to her mother, Winona; but she was also very stoic about the matter and would not open up.

Finally, after a year went by and it was time to go on another trip for more gold, Jimmy said he was too old for such a trip. This really disappointed me because I thought we had a great relationship based on trust and full communication. Not wanting a confrontation that might just ruin what little respect and relationship we had left, I went by myself. I pondered about taking James, but being only about six years old, he was just too young. I did not think I could trust anyone else with all that was at stake. May Fern wanted to go, but I felt the camping and everything else was too much and that she needed to be at the post as we had prospered very well. She was the official post mistress besides running the trading, ordering, animals, etc.

"My darling, I have brought another large load of gold from the room," I said, setting my bag down. "As last time, it will take several months for me working at night to melt it down into ingots and ship it off to the exchange. I have really been giving a lot of thought to our plans, and this is what I think we need to do. I do not want to have any regrets because we waited to move forward. I know we are still young, but in my opinion, that is the time to be 'actively engaged in a good cause.' I feel we should take another load from the treasure room in the next month or so and then go to Ramah and purchase the Hollister Ranch. I see the competition taking a bite out of our trading post business as Gallup becomes more and more a shipping center. We cannot compete with their prices because of our freight costs here to the post, and the fact that we cannot purchase as much at one time as the larger operations. As the community becomes more mobile or moves closer to Gallup, I feel our business will continue to go down. And one other thing, I want to look into purchasing one of the new automobiles."

I let all that sink in before I dared add more. Knowing her quick mind, I knew she was already up with me; but if she too had not been thinking along these lines, I just might be in trouble.

"Buckshot, I too have been thinking about the ranch and our future," May Fern said. "I agree with you about the future of the trading post. The posts the farthest out will have the longest life because the communities have to go there to trade. The first posts to go will be the closest ones to major commercial centers as they grow. A ranch can be our future, but I feel we need to slow down about moving there. With the apparent rift with my parents and all that is at stake with the treasure, I feel we need to stay put and concentrate on perfecting our business in every way possible to keep it profitable. I have been thinking of helping the women make even better rugs with better quality dyes and warp. I hear that up at Two Gray Hills, this has worked, and they are getting a great deal more for their products. What if we purchase the ranch on terms and let someone else run it for us – such as Kent and Martha?"

Oh, how I loved this woman! She was ever the true helpmate in every way. She was always looking for ways to make it work, rather than so many partnerships I have seen where one of them is always trying to find fault with any idea presented.

"Yes yes, I can see that might work in the grand scheme of things," I said. "We can build for the future and not upset anything or at least not upset it any worse than we have now. We can continue to work with your parents. It is tough to say, but they will leave us someday, and we will then be in a position to make a major change. It would be great to have the ranch all set up to move to. As to the automobile, I think we should wait until we are just a little more settled. It seems that they are just toys as of yet. Maybe when they can haul freight for the post, or we can use one to find those several places on the maps of more treasure sites."

And so our plans proceeded. We purchased the ranch from Randy and Gerry. They moved to Albuquerque to be near her folks. We arranged for Kent and Martha to manage the ranch for us. We made occasional trips there and fell in love with that special valley and the wonderful people of such stout pioneer stock.

Chapter 12

"MY DARLING HUSBAND, we need to make a change in our living quarters," May Fern said. "You will have to divide the rooms differently or add another one on for your office."

Caught unawares as I was concentrating on some inventory figures, I replied, "Sure, whatever you want. I will have Junior talk to Mr. Moore and see what they suggest is best."

I never really gave her request much thought as I trusted her judgment explicitly and was on automatic.

"Junior, please talk to Mr. Moore and see what you two can come up with for an extra room in the house."

"Do you want it next to the bathroom, and are you going to move your office?" Junior asked.

This stopped me cold.

"What are you talking about?" I asked. "I don't really know. May Fern just wants an extra room."

Then . . . *bam*! It finally hit me, and I turned and ran from the store into our living quarters. May Fern and I were on track to be parents again. What joy and anticipation! We wanted a large family. We had so much to share. Not just the wealth, but what we knew to be true about the Gospel – that God lives and is watching over us to help us learn and become the best we can become. One of our favorite scriptures had always been as follows: "And we will prove them herewith, to see if they will do all things whatsoever the Lord their God shall command them; And they who keep their first estate shall be added upon; and they who keep not their first estate shall not have glory in the same kingdom with those who keep their first estate; and they who keep their second estate shall have glory added upon their heads for ever and ever" (Abraham 3:25-26).

We knew we were here on earth for a purpose. We were here to see if we would do right. And oh, such a great reward for doing good!

We had our eternal foundation established by being members of the true church and by being sealed for time and all eternity. Our new addition would be born "under the covenant," and so would grow our eternal family. What a great feeling! We needed to now concentrate on enduring to the end.

"May Fern, sweetheart, have you told your mother and father yet of our great news?"

"No. I wanted you to be first although the way you went about realizing what I was trying to tell you, half of the community knew about it before it sunk into your head," she said laughingly.

"Well, then let's do this. Let's go over to their home and tell them and take James. We will let him stay with them while you and I travel to Denver and further our business. Besides, it is about time that I plan another trip to the treasure room cave. I only wish I could get your father to go with me this time."

* * *

Our trip to Denver was our honeymoon that we had never been able to have. I made it as special in every way that I could. We traveled first-class on the train from Gallup to Albuquerque. There, we were treated to a stay at the Alvarado Hotel. Completed in 1902 at a cost of $200,000, it was considered the finest railroad hotel of its time. We also saw and rode in our first automobile. We spent a day of shopping and just frivolous fun. As we were walking along the main street, we saw the Galles Motor Company showroom with several shiny autos just begging to be driven.

"Come on, you beautiful creature," I said. "You know how bad I want to purchase one of these. You have got to go with me for a ride."

"I do not believe that you will ever grow up," she said laughingly. "But just this once, I will let you seduce me into doing such a crazy thing."

Oh, how I loved her sense of humor and teasing!

"Good morning, folks," the salesman said. "Welcome to the Galles Motor Company. My name is Charles. And what might your names be?"

I introduced us and inquired about going for a ride in one of those marvelous machines. He referred to the experience as a test-drive. It was an open-top type, and the wind seemed to rush at us. He told us that just recently, the new speed limit there in Albuquerque had been raised to ten miles per hour, up from their first speed limit in 1908 of eight miles per hour, just two years earlier.

The next day, we continued our trip north from Albuquerque to Denver. We enjoyed all the luxuries of the day in the riding, sleeping, and dining cars. It was such a thrill just to sit by her side, look out the window, and see the excitement as her whole being opened to the grandeur of this part of the world she had never seen before. Of course, I was not that much of a "world traveler" myself at that point and was impressed also. I especially remember the mountain scenery as we traveled to and from Denver in the Trinidad area.

Later, as I became acquainted with the Aztec history of Pecos, New Mexico, just north of Santa Fe and the Eternal Flame site mandated by Montezuma, I had wished we had paid more attention to that historical gem. Eventually, I was able to spend some time there and see the awe-inspiring kiva and all that had been so painstakingly constructed.

Denver – with its magnificent size, activity, buildings, traffic of both teams pulling wagons, the fancy surreys and buggies, and the automobiles – was indeed awe inspiring. Up until that time, we had only really heard about automobiles. In fact, in the Navajo language, a new word had been added. The word was *chidi*, and it meant "automobile." The reasonable explanation was that as they saw their first auto crossing their lands, it was from a distance. All they saw was that it was not pulled by animals, and it made a funny sound of *chidi chidi chidi* – yes, it was more than likely a first-production Model T Ford that was assembled at the Ford Piquette Avenue Plant in Detroit. They began production on October 1, 1908. Over the next nineteen years, Ford would build fifteen million automobiles with the Model T engine that made that very descriptive sound of *chidi chidi chidi*. The tires were called *chidi bi ke*, which literally meant "car his foot"; and gasoline, which we began handling at the post in large metal barrels, was called *chidi-bi-toh*, which directly interpreted was "car his water."

The exchange arranged for us to stay at the eight-story Brown Palace Hotel. This was the finest of accommodations for the time. We learned from the ever-courteous staff that this wonderful edifice had been constructed in 1892 by a Mr. Henry Brown for over $2 million. May Fern pointed out the beautiful walls in the lobby made of beautifully streaked imported Mexican onyx. The ceiling of the lobby was like nothing we had ever seen before or imagined. The intriguing stained glass creation was almost beyond description. The colors reflected a unique lighting that radiated warm and vibrating elegance. Our rooms were very luxurious with a grand view of the city and all of its hustle and bustle. Our days of business, shopping, and sightseeing were some of our most memorable times; and we came away with an even-better pricing and accommodation for shipping, assaying, and converting our gold bars into bank drafts.

"Now, Mr. and Mrs. Hutchinson, we are so thankful for you as customers with our exchange. And I hope you feel our employees are taking the very best care of you," said Mr. Kelly, the exchange manager. "Has your stay here in Denver and at the Brown been to your satisfaction?"

"Yes, it has, Mr. Kelly," I said. "May Fern and I wish to thank you so very much for this wonderful trip and for all of the amenities. And by the way, Russ has been very helpful at your Santa Fe office. And now that we can ship directly to your facility here in Denver, to whom should I be addressing my communications?"

"Mr. Edgar, whom you met yesterday, will be your account manager," he replied. "Of course, if you ever have any concerns or questions regarding shipments or payments or whatever, please telegraph me directly. I assure you we will help you in every way possible and guarantee you of the best pricing and service."

"Well, thank you very much, Mr. Kelly. We look forward to a long and prosperous business relationship."

We could tell that Mr. Kelly was in a quandary, trying to figure out how to ask where we were getting all of the gold bars. He was afraid of offending us and possibly losing the account and so did not quite know how to approach the subject. It would be several more years before he mustered up the courage to ask.

May Fern, as the lady she was and accepting of the business protocol of the day, had been quietly at my side through all the negotiations as my radiant, effervescent, beautiful companion. I could see the eyes of all the associates flitting back and forth between the business at hand and her elegant being. I do not exaggerate one bit when I say she was truly a queen among women who could not be ignored. I had attempted to assist her shopping, but having studied all the latest catalogs we regularly received at the store, she sensed what the current fashions were. She very capably chose and purchased what was needed so that she was dressed in the finest and latest fashion of the day. Her articulate communication ability coupled with her beauty impressed all.

A pleasant change of agenda occurred when she ascertained we were about finished with our business and would be saying goodbye.

"Mr. Kelly, I also want to thank you and your fine firm for all you have done for us on this memorable trip," she said. "I have enjoyed this experience so much. You and your people have been so gracious to me and my husband. As my husband's partner in all of these matters, I have been so impressed with the professionalism here. I too look forward to a long and continued accommodating business relationship. Thank you."

There were four other people in the room besides Mr. Kelly and us. One was a woman who was his personal stenographer and was taking appropriate notes. The other three were officers of the firm. You have to understand, even though my beautiful wife was dressed in the latest fashion and had her hair done up in the trim of the day, there was still no doubt that she was an Indian. In those days, there were still some negative prejudices, and I think a lot of it had to do with the fact that women were not accepted for their full potential in the business world – and definitely not an Indian woman. I also think the feeling prevailed that an Indian woman could not possibly have the capability of not only comprehending business matters, but that she would not have the verbal ability to express any polite form of expounding such.

Mr. Kelly's mouth literally dropped open as she spoke. He acted like a love-struck teenager as she addressed him. The other three men reacted in similar fashion. You could see they were infatuated with her beauty, demeanor, and astuteness. The lady stenographer dropped her pencil noisily on the hardwood floor in the middle of it all, but rather than reach to pick it up, she sat looking straight forward at May Fern as though in a trance.

We had accomplished the goals of our trip. First and foremost, it was a wonderful all-expense-paid honeymoon trip by the exchange. Secondly, we got the prices we knew we deserved for our gold bars and all we had to do to refine and smelt them. We could now just ship them to Denver instead of travel with them. And finally, we were facilitating it all with a pseudonym so we could enjoy our privacy and structure our finances so we could help others in an anonymous way.

With Albuquerque becoming the larger business center of New Mexico at this time, we choose to do all of our banking there. The bankers at Gallup had become a little too nosey for my liking. Now that we had sufficient funds in investments, accounts, and our gold bars, which we were now storing in the safe room at the post, rapidity of getting funds was no longer a priority. Life was good.

* * *

A few short months of anticipation later, after our wonderful trip to Denver, May Fern went into labor. She was at home at the post, and we had a very capable midwife at her side. Jimmy and Winona and some of the family were even staying in the rock house and hogan up the canyon. They had come several weeks early to be there for the birth. Jimmy and I were finally planning another trip to the treasure room after the birth, and this time, we were to take lanterns and really explore the fissure we had not had time to fully look at during prior visits.

Her labor did not proceed normally. The midwife and Winona, assisted by Jimmy and another knowledgeable woman, did all they could; but both May Fern and the baby died. We buried them in a handmade coffin on the hill next to my mother. They were dressed as mother and daughter, with May Fern holding little Martha on her chest.

I had lost my parents, all three of them, but I was not prepared for this blow. Death is so final. Death is so complete. Nothing that man is capable of doing can reverse it. Anger, despair, wealth, physical strength, nor pleading can undo the terrible darkness. Only through faith and knowledge of the plan of salvation instigated and opened by our Savior is there any peace. I truly do not know how anyone who has not taken the time and opportunity to gain a testimony of the Gospel and the great plan can stand to go through the loss of a loved one.

Even to this day, I cannot stand to dwell for very long on this happening in my life. For you who have suffered such a loss, I need not say any more. For you who have not, I cannot find the words to describe the pain, devastation, and loss. I pray that you are not tested in the same manner. Needless to say, I just seemed to melt in all ways and could not gather my senses for several months after. Jimmy and Winona and their family were my strength as were so many in the community. They all loved her so much.

There always seems to be good that comes from bad. Jimmy came to me shortly after and opened his heart to me.

"My son, with a very heavy heart, I come to you knowing that your heart is heavy also, And I do not want to add to your burden. But I must confess to you that I have been wrong for these several years. It has taken the loss of one I loved so dear to break the hold of evil on my heart and feelings. When you told me about your sister as we were coming down off the mesa, an evil entered my mind and heart. I was told that you were not true to our friendship and family ties and that you would drift to support others in spite of all we had achieved and had gone through. I was without love and filled with a hate that I regret more than you will ever know. Now that I cannot put my arms around my lovely, special daughter ever again and tell her how much I love her, I fully know my terrible sin. I do not want this to happen to us. I know you have been true in all ways. I love you for loving my daughter and grandson – and the granddaughter that neither one of us will get to hold. Please forgive me and tell me what I have to do to earn your respect and love once more."

This was the beginning of Jimmy's conversion as I have told you about earlier and how it affected his family on into eternity.

This was also one of the greatest lessons I experienced about regret. Never fail to tell someone you love them. You do not get to choose the last time you will be able to be with them.

It took me several years to numb the pain of my loss, but even those years had their moments of joy. Jimmy and his family, James, and I had wonderful times together – but some trying times as well. By now, I know that happiness doesn't mean anything until you've known sadness.

My prayer is that you will seek the good and endure to the end. What they say is true: "Life isn't about how to survive the storm, but how to dance in the rain."

LaVergne, TN USA
22 January 2010
170908LV00005B/84/P

9 781436 387316